This special signed edition is limited to 200 numbered copies.

This is copy _____

BLACK & WHITE

BLACK & WHITE

A NOVEL BY

LEWIS SHINER

SUBTERRANEAN PRESS 2008

Portions of this book have been previously published, in somewhat
different form, as follows: "Renewal" in *Southwest Review*, "Wonderland"
in *Black Clock*, and "Ceremony" in *Subterranean*.

Interior design by Lewis Shiner
Set in Bembo

First edition

Limited edition ISBN
978-1-59606-172-9

Trade hardcover ISBN
978-1-59606-171-2

Subterranean Press
PO Box 190106
Burton, MI 48519

www.subterraneanpress.com
www.lewisshiner.com

For Orlita

MICHAEL

2004

Monday, October 18

H E L O O K E D A T the angry red 5:05 on his travel alarm and knew he would not get back to sleep.

He swung his legs off the foldout bed and walked five steps to the tiny kitchenette. He was still dressed in last night's jeans and gray T-shirt, his mouth stale from recycled hotel air. He brushed his teeth and washed his face in the sink, combing wet fingers through his hair.

Go, he thought.

His suitcase was packed, as it had been for most of the last month. The only hanging space—as well as the only bathroom and the only exit—was in the bedroom where his mother slept in a tranquilized haze. The rest of his belongings lined up next to the suitcase: a small drawing board, a FedEx box, and two plastic Harris-Teeter grocery sacks.

He put on his glasses and shoes and added the clock and shaving kit to the suitcase. He was able to roll the suitcase with his right hand and carry everything else in his left.

He stopped by the door to the hall. His mother's snoring suspended momentarily as he took his jacket off a hanger and slipped into it. She was in the farther of the twin beds, near the window. The other would have held his father, except that his father was across the street in the Durham VA Medical Center, dying of lung cancer.

M I C H A E L W A S 35, too old, he thought, to spend this much time with his parents, no matter what the circumstances. From the lobby he called a cab and picked, more or less at random, another faceless suite hotel out of the phone book. The new one was just off I-40 at the eastern edge of Durham, where the city proper blended into Research Triangle Park. During the tech boom RTP had been the Silicon Valley of the East Coast, pumping millions into the North Carolina economy. When the bubble burst with the new century, it left behind inflated housing costs, thousands of overqualified, unemployed tech workers, and an abundance of empty hotel rooms.

I

The dispatcher told him it would be half an hour. Michael left his belongings with the desk clerk, a heavyset woman with meticulous cornrows. "If my cab comes, tell him to wait for me," Michael said. "I'll be back in a few minutes."

"All right now, hon."

He crossed the street to the hospital and took the elevator to the sixth floor. The charge nurse was at the station and managed a tired smile. "He had a good night," she said. "Some coughing, but he slept."

"That's something, I guess."

"He'll be sleeping more and more," she said. "It's like they make the transition kind of gradual, a little less hold on this world every day."

Michael stood in the hallway and watched his father sleep. He had faint wisps of white hair that had grown back since the initial chemo fallout, and his skin had turned a nicotine-stain yellow from jaundice. His thin forearms protruded from red VA pajamas, the left hooked to a morphine infusion pump. An oxygen cannula ran under his nose. As Michael watched, his father coughed wetly, cleared his throat, and shifted his head, all without seeming to regain consciousness.

After he turned 30, Michael had gone through a period of seeing his father's face in his own when he looked in the mirror, especially first thing in the morning, when he was still puffy with sleep. That was a different face than his father had now. Now his father's face was crumpled like a used towel. When his eyes were open they were bloodshot, restless, and haunted.

It had all happened with terrifying speed. One day his father had seemed all right; the next he had coughed up a huge mouthful of blood. In retrospect he'd been tired and had lost some weight, but there'd been nothing to prepare him for what the doctors found. It was "everywhere," his mother told Michael on the phone, nearly hysterical. This had been back in Dallas. Michael had flown up from Austin to do what he could. Tests had revealed small cell lung cancer, already in both lungs and metastasized to the lymph nodes, too far gone for surgery and not within what the doctors called "one radiation port." He'd had a round of chemotherapy and then, inexplicably, insisted on coming to the VA hospital in Durham for what everyone understood would be his final weeks.

Logic was clearly not the issue. There was a huge VA hospital in San Antonio, and one of the world's finest cancer centers, M.D. Anderson, in Houston. But North Carolina was where he and Michael's mother had met and married, where he'd begun his career in the construction business, where Michael had been born. And it was apparently where he had determined to die.

"Take care of him," Michael said to the charge nurse, and went back to the Brookwood Inn.

•

HIS CAB DRIVER had a heavy accent and was playing a cassette with jangly guitars and hand drums. "What part of Africa are you from?" Michael asked.

"Benin," the driver called over his shoulder. "You know it?"

"I know the name," Michael said.

The driver seemed as grateful for someone to talk to as he was for the fare. In the two months he'd been in the US, the dream that had brought him eight thousand miles had already begun to fade. He worked 24-hour days, dozing in the cab between infrequent jobs. "Too many cabbies, not enough work," he said.

It was Saturday morning and the sun was not yet up. They were heading east on the Durham Freeway, the road Michael's father had helped to build. As they crested a hill, the lights of downtown Durham spread to the horizon on Michael's left. The city seemed frozen in time, low to the ground, built of old-fashioned brick and granite and concrete. Liggett & Myers and the American Tobacco Company, sometime rulers of the city's economy, had long since moved to New York. The red brick shells of their office complexes and warehouses had been reborn as condos and mini-malls. American Tobacco's signature water tower and smokestack, complete with newly repainted Lucky Strike logo, now overlooked the last stages of a major renovation project.

Michael's father had smoked Lucky Strike for over 50 years.

Next door was the swank new Durham Bulls Athletic Park, whose brick-work seamlessly matched its surroundings. Next to that was an auto dealership, and after that, absences. The parking garage that took the place of the train station that had given Durham its name. The vacant lots and abandoned buildings that used to be the most prosperous black neighborhood in the South.

It was called Hayti for the Caribbean island, but pronounced with a long final "i": HATE-eye. Over 500 black businesses had fallen to the bulldozer when the Durham Freeway went through the middle of it. All that was left was St. Joseph's African Methodist Episcopal Church, coming up now on the right. The original building dated to 1891; the modern brick extension that grew out of the south side was the Hayti Heritage Center. Further south along Fayetteville Street were the sprawling Victorian homes that had once belonged to the first families of Hayti, and beyond that the campus of North Carolina Central University, formerly North Carolina College for Negroes.

These few facts Michael had learned in the last week from a black jani-tor at the hospital, a man Michael's age with wild hair and a long, pointed beard. He called Michael "young brother," and asked where he was from. He'd started talking about Durham's history before Michael could tell him about his father's part in it; by the time he'd finished, Michael no longer wanted to mention it.

The sun was lightening the sky in the southeast, and suddenly Michael saw something at the top of the St. Joseph's steeple that he'd missed in the dozen or more times he'd driven past it in the last month.

"Turn around, can you?" he said to the driver.

"Sir?" Michael could see the driver staring at him in the rearview mirror. He realized how unhinged he must look—over six feet tall, not overweight, exactly, but soft and pale, thinning brown hair, bloodshot eyes, slept-in clothes, possessions in plastic bags.

"Take the next exit, turn around, and come back to that church."

"You don't want to go to the hotel?"

"Yes, in a minute. I need to stop at the church first."

The driver shrugged, exited, and turned under the freeway. Run-down houses were visible from the access road, partly obscured by oaks and syca-mores in a riot of autumnal orange and yellow. They crossed the freeway again and pulled into the asphalt parking lot.

"Stop here for a second," Michael said. Along the south retaining wall someone had painted names and primitive likenesses of famous Hayti resi-dents: Moore, Merrick, and Shepard, who'd founded North Carolina Mutual Life, along with other names that Michael didn't know. Steps led up to the brick and steel of the Heritage Center, and above it all towered the steeple.

Michael reached for the car door.

"You are getting out here?" the driver asked nervously.

"Just for a second."

From where he stood, resting his hands on the open door, he could see the thing at the top of the steeple clearly. It was made of black wrought iron, an intricate design of intersecting curves, heart shaped, on an axis like a weather vane.

Michael reached into the cab and dug a sketchbook out of one of the plas-tic bags. "Keep the meter running," he told the driver. He got the thing down in a couple of minutes. Roger could tell him exactly what it was, but Michael didn't need him to know it had no business on top of a church.

He got in the cab. "You know what that is?" he asked the driver.

"It's a church, sir."

"The thing on top of the steeple. Where the cross should be."

"I never saw that before."

"It's called a *vévé*," Michael said. "It's the symbol of a voodoo god."

MICHAEL WAS THE ARTIST on a comic book named *Luna,* and issues 17 through 20 had been set in New Orleans. The writer, Roger Fornbee, had sent the title character there to battle the Haitian snake *lwa,* Damballah. Roger had made a point of saying vodou instead of voodoo, and he'd shipped Michael stacks of books for research. His scripts, detailed as always, called for *vévés* woven into the background texture of the panels. The heart shape belonged to Erzulie, a sort of vodou love goddess, though potentially a rather prickly and dangerous one.

When he used his credit card to check in at the hotel it occurred to him that he was leaving an obvious trail. His parents could find him with little effort, if they wanted to. Whether they would bother was another question.

He carried his things up to his room and used his cell phone to call Roger. In LA it was barely past 3 AM, meaning Roger would be in full caffeine and nicotine stride, sending out long, rambling emails, flipping through reference books with page crumpling intensity, and, if up against the tail end of a deadline, possibly even writing.

His wife of some years, whom Roger had known since they were kids, kept normal hours, sent their two daughters off to grade school, cooked, cleaned house, and answered most of Roger's fan mail in his name. She never traveled and Michael had never met her, never even talked to her on the phone, as Roger always used his "mobile," as he called it.

"It's me," Michael said.

"So it is," Roger said, in what he'd once explained was not a "British accent" but a North London public school accent. "What's the latest on the old man?"

"Well, in our last episode, you may remember, they had to discontinue the chemo because the cancer had moved into his spinal column and they needed to irradiate that. Now they've had to knock off the radiation because his lungs are losing function."

"Christ. Poor bastard."

"Stubborn bastard. This is probably it. I don't think he's got more than a couple of weeks left at most, and he still won't talk to me."

"Maybe you're wrong. Maybe there's not some vital secret he's keeping from you."

"No. Yesterday he let something slip. We were talking about hospitals and I mentioned being born in Watts Hospital, which used to be here in Durham, right? And he looked at me and said, 'Watts?' in that tone he has, like I've just said something too stupid to be believed. Then he recovered and said, 'Oh yeah, Watts, right.'"

"C'mon, Michael, with all he's been through..."

"So I went to Durham Regional, where they still have the old files from Watts, and there's no record of my birth."

"There's any number of..."

"You weren't there. You didn't see the look on his face." Michael felt his throat closing, realized how close he was to tears.

"Michael. They've got social workers there at the hospital. You might want to talk to one of them. Things with your father were screwed up enough before this, and trying to put all that in order under this kind of pressure is more than you can ask of yourself."

"This isn't me, it's him."

"Listen to yourself, mate. You need to back off a bit."

"That's what I just did. I moved out of the Brookwood and got my own place."

"What did they say about that?"

"They don't know."

"Wow. Are you—"

The connection was suddenly gone, a not infrequent experience with Roger. It was typical of the US in the 21st century, Roger said, that they'd all been willing to trade the quality and dependability of land lines for convenience and free long distance.

Michael dialed again. Once, after a similar interruption, he'd waited to see if Roger would call back, and he never did. That was Roger: People only truly existed for him when they impinged on one of his senses.

"Look," Michael said when Roger picked up again, "I just called to let you know. I've got the computer and I'll be checking email and everything."

"And drawing? Will you be drawing any pages? Number 25 is due in—"

"A week and a half," Michael said. "I know."

To ease his conscience, he spent a couple of hours working at the kitchen table in his suite.

Most commercial comics involved an assembly line process. One artist did penciled breakdowns based on either a script or a plot outline from the writer. The pencils might be rough or detailed, depending on the artist, the editor, and the deadline. If the writer had only provided a plot, copies of the pencils went back to the writer for dialogue. Then a letterer put in the word balloons, captions, and borders, and an embellisher "finished" the pencil art in black ink. Finally yet another artistic team scanned the black and white art into a computer, added color, and made the separations for printing.

Michael had made his reputation partly through speed. He'd sketched in ink as far back as high school art class, and he did his own lettering. He blocked out his pages in non-reproducing blue pencil, only going to graphite in a few places where he needed to be sure of detail—the niceties of a facial expression, the exact gesture of a hand. He did the lettering to relax, two or three pages at a time, and then went back to inking.

The process gave his art a spontaneity and energy that fans responded to. His editors happily paid him for all three jobs and still saved money on FedEx charges and missed deadlines.

He'd hooked up with Roger in 2000 with a Batman graphic novel called *Sand Castles.* Roger lagged substantially behind the first wave of British writers like Alan Moore and Grant Morrison, who'd conquered US comics in the late 1980s, and he'd spent a few years proving he could be as weird, surreal, and violent as any of them. Michael had been drawing superheroes at Marvel and waiting for his chance to break out. *Sand Castles* had been the turning point for both of them. Later, when Roger finished his proposal for *Luna*—AKA *The Adventures of Luna Goodwin*—he offered it to Michael first.

Luna's title character was a magician who was first coming into her powers, late twenties, smart and cynical. And attractive, of course. The comics audience was overwhelmingly male, and adolescent in taste if not always in age. Luna worked in Hollywood as a script consultant, where her—which was to say, Roger's—extensive knowledge of the occult was much in demand. She'd changed her name to Louann and was more or less in denial of her abilities and history.

That history included a Wiccan mother who lived in a tiny Northern California town full of eccentrics just like her. The town was named Lunaville—Looneyville to Louann—and provided comic relief when the main plots got too intense.

Louann had grown up without a father, and her mother claimed not to know which of several possible candidates was the one. When Michael's own father got his diagnosis, Roger suddenly decided it was time to address the paternity issue.

Roger delivered the news in one of his typical phone calls, with Michael along only for the ride. He wouldn't do it if Michael objected, he said, though his investment was obvious from the way the ideas came tumbling out. He was putting off the follow-up he'd planned to the vodou story. Instead, Louann would go to New Mexico, where the Native American shaman she believed was her father was dying of cancer. Louann would try to learn his secrets before it was too late.

Michael had gone along, as he always did. Roger had been idolized by so many for so long that he no longer seemed to understand the concept of refusal.

The first script had arrived via email within a week. For the sake of form it came through Helen Silberman, their editor at DC's Vertigo line of mature audience comics. The few electronic comments she'd left in the margins were not enough to provoke Roger's notorious sensitivity to interference.

As always, Michael was impressed with Roger's ability to make the story visual. It was set in Chaco Canyon, New Mexico, among the Anasazi ruins and the alien landscape of the Four Corners. There were ghosts of Anasazi warriors, Native American gods, and the giant talking moth that Roger used to symbolize Death. There were high tech hospital scenes and a little gunplay. In other words, a typical Roger Fornbee story, something that Michael knew how to draw.

On the road, Michael used a hardwood laminate drawing board that was only slightly larger than the 13 × 20 inch sheets of Bristol board that Vertigo provided him, preprinted with borders and DC logos in non-repro blue. He spent hours at a time with the board in his lap, turning it from side to side, letting the blacks on the page find their own natural weight and balance, the TV or radio on in the background, his mind wandering as he worked.

Today, though, was lettering, which meant the board lay flat on the table, T-square against the metal sides, Ames lettering guide sliding across it to pencil the guidelines. He wasn't aware of the words as he copied them from the script, only the zen of the letterforms: no hitch in the S or the C, the O just outside the lines, the bars of the E, F, and T tilted fractionally upward.

When he looked at the clock it was 10 AM. He called a nearby car rental agency and had them deliver the cheapest thing they had, which happened to be a silver Toyota Echo, tiny, light, with its trunk sticking up in the air. He dropped off the driver, got a North Carolina map, and merged onto I-40 East.

MICHAEL HAD TWO names on his list. The first belonged to Greg Vaughan, his only living relative in North Carolina. Vaughan was some kind of distant cousin on his mother's side, still living on the Bynum family farm in rural Johnston County. Despite the area being prime tobacco country, his grandfather had grown little there but government subsidies.

At least that was the way Michael's father told it. Michael himself had only seen his grandfather on two occasions, when the old man came to Dallas for Christmas while Michael was still in high school. Wilmer Bynum had been in his seventies then, unkempt, surly, and recently widowed. The tension between him and Michael's father had been like an electromagnetic field that left everyone's hair standing on end.

Michael's mother had shown no inclination to go out to the farm since they'd come back to Durham. "Your father needs me here," she'd said. Over the years she seemed to have taken on the same attitude that Michael's father had toward her family, as if she too now found them crude, embarrassing, and best ignored. She hadn't even gone to her father's funeral two years before.

Shortly after he passed through Raleigh's concrete sprawl, Michael exited the Interstate onto the US 70 bypass and crossed the Johnston County line. The trees grew more sparsely than in Durham, and closer to the ground: live oaks and scrub brush between spindly pines. He passed through a couple of small towns and finally stopped at the first likely looking business he came to in West Smithfield, an antiques store in a freestanding white building.

A woman in her sixties wandered among the shelves of colored glass bowls, aluminum pots, dolls, cookbooks, and broken lampshades. "Can I help you?" she asked.

"I'm looking for the old Bynum farm. I know it's somewhere around here, but I don't know the way. I was hoping you might."

She straightened up and gave him a thorough looking over. "What's your interest, if I may ask?"

"I'm Wilmer Bynum's grandson."

"Which grandson would that be?" She didn't sound so much hostile as cautious. "I don't see a lot of family resemblance."

"I'm Michael Cooper, and I'm his only grandson that I know of." He put out his hand and left it there until she reluctantly took it. "They tell me I take after my father, Robert Cooper. He married Ruth Bynum in 1962."

"I was at the wedding. Most of the county was." She squinted at him. "You hoping to find Wilmer there?"

"Is that a trick question? He died two years ago. And yes, I guess I am hoping to find something of him there. And if not him, maybe Greg Vaughan."

She nodded. "I'm Martha Wingate. I've got a son Tom your age. Sorry to be suspicious. Hasn't been anybody asking after Wilmer in some time, but I guess old habits die hard."

"What was it people were asking about?"

She looked down at the green Depression glass pitcher in her hands. "Wilmer was pretty important around here. People always wanted to consult him on things."

"What sort of things?"

"You name it. Crop rotation, politics, domestic disputes."

People wanting to discuss crop rotation, Michael thought, would already know where to find Wilmer Bynum. He saw nothing to gain by contradicting her. "So how would I get to the farm?"

Mrs. Wingate drew him a map, complete with landmarks, on the back of a photocopied flyer for a flea market. Michael admired her strong, clear lines. "This is perfect," he said. "Thanks."

"You see old Wilmer hanging around, you tell him hey for me."

"You think that's likely?"

"Wilmer never did concede anyone dominion over him. Not the state of

North Carolina, not the federal government, not even God Himself. It's hard to imagine Death fared much better."

As the map promised, the mailbox still said "Bynum." Michael could see the house from the road. Once it had been a standard Victorian style farmhouse, complete with wraparound porch and gabled second story, until someone with more ambition than skill had begun building on.

As Michael inched the car up the long, rutted dirt driveway, he made out at least three separate additions, two angling out from the ground floor and a third sprawling across the other two. The lower walls had been finished with wooden siding at least vaguely similar to that on the rest of the house, while the upper was done in decorative exterior plywood. In places the once-white paint had blistered away, exposing gray wood underneath; in others the paint looked fresh. All the windows were intact, and the roof didn't show any obvious sag or damage.

The fields were in a similar holding pattern, mowed and free of trash, yet not growing anything useful. The place seemed habitable at the same time that it looked like no one had lived there in years.

It was a bright, cool October day. Michael rolled his window down and inhaled the vivid odors of dust, weeds, and distant water.

The driveway intersected another dirt road at the house. Michael turned left and finally saw his first sign of life, a vegetable garden behind a tractor shed, surrounded by chicken wire to keep out the deer and rabbits. A few late tomatoes made splotches of yellow and orange against the green.

When he looked back at the road in front of him, a huge German Shepherd was charging straight at the car.

Michael hit the brakes, afraid the dog would go under his wheels. It began to dance around the car, barking furiously, and lunging at Michael even as he quickly rolled his window up again. Michael hadn't paid for the damage waiver on the car, so he hit the horn. The dog jumped backward, barking with a deeper and more threatening tone, the black hair standing up along its spine.

He took the window down an inch and said, with as much authority as he could manage, "Hey! Chill out!" The dog quieted for a second and looked at him almost wistfully before going ballistic again. "Okay," Michael said, "fine. I can take a hint." He put the car in reverse, and as he looked over his shoulder he saw a man walking toward the rear of the car.

He wore jeans, a T-shirt, a red plaid flannel shirt, and a John Deere cap pulled low over his eyes. He had a short beard and dark blond hair hanging to his shoulders. "Henry!" the man shouted, and the dog turned to look at him as if to say, I'm doing my job here, what's your problem?

"Heel," the man said, and snapped his fingers twice. The dog looked at Michael to let him know this wasn't his idea, then trotted over to the man's side and stood with his right shoulder by the man's knee. The man snapped his fingers once, pointed downward, and said, "Sit," and the dog obeyed.

Michael rolled his window the rest of the way down again. "You Greg Vaughan?"

"Last time I checked." The man hunkered down to stroke the golden fur of the dog's chest.

"I'm Michael Cooper. I'm Wilmer Bynum's grandson."

Vaughan, to Michael's surprise, stood up without making a move toward the car. "I know who you are."

"You do?"

"You and your father and Ruth came back to Durham a month ago."

Vaughan's accent was a more pronounced version of the one Michael's mother had, like a cross between Deep South and Boston. "That's right," Michael said.

"You didn't call, didn't write, didn't let me know. I had to find out about it from my neighbors."

"That was my father's doing. If I get out of the car, is Henry going to take my arm off?"

"Not unless I tell him to."

Michael hadn't been much at sports, and he'd gotten roughed up in junior high. By high school he'd grown up and filled out and he found he didn't have to do a lot to get smaller kids to back down. It was more like stubbornness than courage, and the habit had stayed with him.

He got out of the car, squatted by the dog, and offered the back of his left hand. Henry looked at it, seemed to shrug, and gave it a non-committal lick. Michael stood up and offered the other one to Vaughan, who took it with reasonable grace.

"I don't know what went on between my father and the Bynum side of the family," Michael said. "That was him and not me. Can we talk?"

Vaughan took a moment to consider. He was older than Michael had first thought, in his early to mid-fifties. The sun had creased his face like a note that had been folded and refolded and kept in a dirty pocket. "All right," Vaughan said at last, and as he turned away Michael noticed for the first time a trailer in a field beyond the tractor shed, a small green single-wide on a cinder-block foundation, with a built-on screen porch. A battered half-ton pickup was parked next to it.

They walked together toward the trailer. Vaughan's silence was amiable enough and Michael relaxed enough to note the warmth of the sun on his skin, the uncomplicated joy of the dog orbiting around them, the crunch of their shoes in the dry soil.

Vaughan opened the screen door and gestured for Michael to go in first. The interior surprised him; it was as spotless and tightly organized as the galley of a submarine. The living room held a foldout sofa, recliner, TV, VCR, and two painted metal TV trays. The white walls were devoid of pictures, mirrors, or knickknack shelves. Michael looked through into a small kitchen with gleaming counters.

"Coffee?" Vaughan offered. He gestured to the couch and Michael sat. "There's still half a pot from this morning if you don't mind reheated."

"That's fine."

"I expect there's a beer in the fridge if you wanted something stronger."

"Coffee would be great. I'm not much of a drinker."

Vaughan nodded his approval. He stood at the stove with the air of a Japanese *sumi-e* painter in front of a sheet of rice paper. He took a box of wooden matches out of an overhead cabinet and struck one. As it flared, his face responded with something between fascination and hunger. Michael found the rawness of it uncomfortable. Slowly Vaughan reached for the knob that turned on the right front burner, and slowly brought the match to the gas. He didn't react at all to the whoosh as the gas caught, just watched the flames for another second or two and then shook out the match an instant before it would have burned his fingers.

He set an old-fashioned aluminum coffee pot on the burner and put the matches away. Reaching into the same cabinet with both hands, he took out two oversized ceramic cups, turned them right side up, and set them on the counter with perfect economy of motion. "Cream or sugar?"

"Black is good for me."

Vaughan took out a plastic canister of sugar, opened the top with the same crisp precision, and put three spoons of sugar into one of the cups.

"Did you ever tend bar?" Michael asked.

"No, why?"

"The way you move, I don't know."

"I went into the Army out of high school. Did two hitches in Vietnam, right through to the end, and got out in '74. After that some carpentry, handyman for an apartment complex, security guard for a while. Been farming the last twenty years."

Steam began to waft from the pot. Vaughan cut off the gas and poured two cups, handing the one without sugar to Michael.

Vaughan didn't ask, so Michael didn't offer his own history. He tasted the coffee instead. It was strong and acidic, but far from the worst he'd ever had. Finally he said, "My father came back here to die, you know."

"Yes. Cancer." Vaughan pronounced the word the way Michael's mother did: first syllable like "cane," no "r" in the second.

"That's right. End stage lung cancer. I don't think he has more than a few days left. I came up here with him thinking he would talk to me, that maybe we could..." His own rising emotions cut him off.

Vaughan nodded with something like sympathy. "I never knew who my daddy was. My momma died when I was nine and Mr. Bynum took me in to raise. She may have only been a seventeenth cousin or some such, but that was good enough for him. I was family. That was the kind of man he was."

"Look, I'm sorry I never knew what kind of man he was. That's part of the reason I'm here."

Vaughan took a long drink and set the cup on a coaster on a TV tray. "So what do you want to know?"

"Did you know my mother before she was married?"

"Only to speak to. She was already gone off to college when I came here."

"Do you know what started the trouble between Grandpa and my father?"

"I don't think Mr. Bynum ever knew. Try as he might to be philosophical about it, you could see that it really hurt him. He loved your mama, and he couldn't understand why your father had to move so far away, and why he got shut out."

"What's the story on the house?"

"What do you mean?"

"Is nobody living there? What's with all the weird additions?"

"Nobody's lived there since Mr. Bynum died. He was a very old-fashioned kind of man, the kind of man that changed the world to fit him instead of the other way around. Liked to do things himself, with his own two hands. He needed a new roof, he'd round up some of the neighbors and put one on. He got to feeling cramped, he'd take out a wall and add on some floor space. Maybe not the best carpenter in the world, but he got the job done."

"Who owns the place now?"

"Well, it got carved up pretty good when Mr. Bynum died. At one point he owned fifteen hundred acres. He was a very big man in these parts. But he had to sell off a parcel here and a parcel there, and then a lot got sold for taxes after he passed. Your mother and her two sisters got parcels. This here piece you're sitting on, including the house and on out to the highway, is mine now. Mr. Bynum left it to me."

"The house didn't go to any of the sisters?"

"They had no interest in working the land. They'd all gone off—your mother to Texas, Esther to California, Naomi to Minnesota. They all sold off their parcels, the way he knew they would. I was the only one stayed around to take care of him all those last years. None of the sisters even came for the funeral. 'I have nourished and brought up children, and they have rebelled against me,' the Lord said to Isaiah. 'They are gone away backward.'"

"I thought Aunt Esther was in Virginia." Naomi, he knew, had been dead for several years.

"She moved to Richmond a few years ago. So I hear."

"You haven't seen her."

Vaughan shook his head, a movement so small it was almost a tic.

"So if the house is yours now..."

"Why don't I live in it? It's a reasonable question. The answer is it's too big for me. I'd rattle around in there like a BB in a boxcar."

"Can I see the inside?"

It was like he'd asked to borrow Vaughan's last fifty dollars. After a pained silence, Vaughan said, "Mr. Bynum never did like having people inside his house."

"I heard people used to come around all the time, looking for advice."

"Mr. Bynum liked to chat with folks on the front porch, sometimes in the parlor in the winter, but he was a very private man for all of that."

"I'm not folks. I'm family. I'd like to see the inside."

They played Mexican standoff for a few seconds more. Michael felt he had the edge: *My father is dying while we're sitting here.*

Apparently he got it across. Vaughan finally stood up, took one last drink of coffee, and said, "All right. Come on."

He took a set of keys off a hook by the front door and then held the door open for Michael. As they walked toward the main house, Henry the German Shepherd trotted up and fell into place next to Vaughan.

Michael attempted to make nice. "What do you grow here?"

"This used to be cotton country. Back before the War, of course." He smiled as if he were joking and Michael realized with a chill that it was the Civil War he was talking about. "After the War it was tobacco. Up until the 1950s we would ship the cotton and tobacco both over to Durham to get milled or processed. All that's gone now. Tobacco companies moved up to New York, and then the government scared people off cigarettes. Mills are all gone too. People want that Egyptian cotton or Indian cotton or NAFTA cotton. These days I mostly grow produce, sell what I can't eat over to the Farmer's Market in Raleigh. My needs are pretty simple."

"There's worse ways to be."

"You can write that on my tombstone. I seen some of the world when I was in the service, and I lived in Durham for a while, but the older I get the less I want to do with any of it."

They climbed six steps to the porch. There was a wooden swing and painted wicker furniture, all of it clean and in good repair. Michael held the screen door while Vaughan unlocked a deadbolt as well as the lock on the knob. Vaughan went in first, then snapped his fingers again for Henry to follow. Michael brought up the rear.

The house was dark, even after Vaughan flipped a wall switch and two table lamps came on in the parlor. Heavy drapes covered all the windows; it felt like they were holding back time as much as daylight. A yellow pine floor, dark with age, showed around the edges of carpets whose floral patterns had worn away under decades of feet. The furniture was faux Victorian, with intricately curved lines, wooden legs, and threadbare tufted upholstery. Doilies covered the end tables, and the candy dish on the marble-topped coffee table held wrapped Starlite mints of questionable age.

Feigning casualness, Michael approached a wall of framed photographs. Score, he thought. There must have been 30 or 40 of them, in all shapes and sizes.

The biggest frame held a matte with four oval cutouts, each holding a black and white photo. Three showed women in their late teens; the fourth, on the far right, was a poor match for the others. Its subject was a girl of no more than six or seven, with dark circles under haunted eyes. To her left was Ruth, Michael's mother, pretty and self-conscious; he vaguely recognized the other two high school girls as his aunts.

He turned to Vaughan. "There were *four* sisters?"

Vaughan stayed where he was, leaning against the wall by the door. "You're talking about the little one? Orpha died not long after that picture. She was seven. She had TB. They kept treating it and it kept coming back. This was 1953. Your mama never told you?"

That put the sisters' photos in order, oldest to youngest. "No. She only called her sisters when my father wasn't around. It wasn't something we ever talked about. I mean, that was all I knew when I was a kid. My father's parents died before I started school. I guess I was an adolescent before I figured out that other families included aunts and uncles and grandparents."

He found the three surviving sisters in another photo, gathered around their father. Ruth nestled in one shoulder and the other two leaned in, but Wilmer wasn't actually holding them. Ruth must have been in her early teens, and Naomi, the oldest, well into her twenties. Wilmer was not much taller than his daughters, his hair cut close to the scalp and receding from a face with sharp features, narrow eyes, and a smart-ass grin.

One of Michael's few recollections of Wilmer Bynum was his open leering at women on the few occasions that the family was out in public. Michael immediately saw more photos that confirmed the memory: Wilmer with his arm around one woman or another, all taken at outdoor gatherings at the farm. The women's smiles were embarrassed, as if only the presence of the camera kept them from objecting.

Here was Wilmer again at his own wedding, barely out of his teens, by the look of him. Michael had to struggle to come up with the name of Wilmer's wife: Regina. She was stiff and somber in the photo, wearing a high-necked, long-sleeved wedding dress that looked more to the next life than to any pleasure in this one.

The wall held a dozen more family shots: Wilmer on a tractor, looking as if he didn't quite belong there; Regina on the porch in a new Sunday bonnet, old beyond her years; the girls playing with a puppy on the lawn.

Then came the celebrity shots. The first featured Wilmer with US Representative Randy Fogg, drinking iced tea on the porch and laughing. The picture must have been 30 years old; Fogg was still reasonably thin and his hair still black, and Wilmer looked no more than middle aged. The photo was signed, "To the real man of the people—Always at your service—Randy Fogg." Michael would have recognized him without the signature. Fogg was a gift to editorial cartoonists, with popping eyes and big jowls that earned him the nickname Congressman Frog, after the character in the *Pogo* comic strip. His racist politics, friendship with the gun and tobacco lobbies, and fist pounding harangues against "Commonism" had made him a legend as far away as Texas.

In the next picture Wilmer stood shaking hands with Richard Nixon, again with the farmhouse in the background. This one was signed also, with just Nixon's name. Michael figured the date for late seventies or early eighties, well after Nixon's resignation, but it was clear that neither Vaughan nor Mrs. Wingate had been kidding about Wilmer Bynum's importance.

One large photo showed a barbeque at the house, complete with checkered tablecloths, big pots of food, and an enormous, partly dismembered pig, its flesh cooked white, stretched out next to a blackened pit in the ground. The words "pig picking" came into Michael's head. The voice was his father's, and it held a sneer. Randy Fogg was in this photo too, along with other important-looking men in suits, none of whom Michael recognized. Signs in the background urged Fogg's reelection.

All fascinating, Michael thought, but none of it was what he'd come for. He wanted to see Ruth pregnant, or Ruth with a newborn Michael in her arms, preferably standing in front of a hospital with its name clearly visible.

Double French doors led to what appeared to be a den. Michael glanced at Vaughan. "Okay if I go in?"

"Suit yourself," Vaughan said, meaning "no." He was clearly uneasy and anxious to get Michael out.

Michael went in anyway. There was a big-screen television, a leather couch, and a matching recliner. More photos lined these walls, all of them showing Wilmer with Duke football and basketball players.

Vaughan had followed as far as the French doors. "So he did leave the farm," Michael said to him.

"Mr. Bynum loved the Blue Devils. He had season tickets until it got to be too much of a hardship for him to make the trip. I drove him the last few years, but even that was too much in the end. He got the dish so he could watch all the games here."

All the players Wilmer posed with, Michael noted, were white. He doubted it was coincidence.

"What's this?" Michael pointed to a display cabinet next to the TV. Inside hung what seemed a random assortment of objects: headline-sized lead type from a printing press; a rubber roller; a ball peen hammer; a brace and bit; and what Michael thought might be a shoemaker's awl, a wood-handled punch with an eye in the middle of the blade.

"Like I said, Mr. Bynum liked working with his hands. He used to collect old tools. There's a bunch of old rusted whipsaw blades and tillers and post hole diggers and the like out in the shed."

"And the piano?" Michael asked. "I can't feature him as a musician." A black baby grand sat at the far end of the room, topped with the largest doily Michael had ever seen. A single framed photo of Regina as a young woman sat on top.

"Mrs. Bynum played. The piano used to be in the parlor. She would play hymns and old Stephen Foster songs and the like. Christmas carols every Christmas. Mr. Bynum moved it in here as a kind of memorial to her."

Michael trailed one finger over the keyboard cover. It was waxed and buffed to a high polish and completely dust free. Startled, he went to the TV and touched the screen. No dust there either. He tried the top of the glass cabinet. Clean.

He looked at Vaughan. "You keep it like this all the time?"

Vaughan seemed even more uncomfortable. "It's a way for me to show my respect."

This, Michael thought, is getting creepy. He took a cursory look through the rest of the ground floor. The huge, dark dining room had a doily and candles in the center of the massive oak table. The kitchen was spotless and the empty refrigerator was plugged in and running cold. Vaughan, leaning against the door of a broom closet, said, "Is there something particular you're looking for?"

Michael blushed and closed the refrigerator. For future reference he noted the back door, with its six narrow windowpanes and a deadbolt that opened from the inside without a key.

In the formal study Michael was surprised to find a late model Dell desktop connected to an Ethernet cable. "Wilmer was on the Internet?"

"Through the dish. It was hard for him to see people in the later years. He used email to keep in touch with his friends."

The computer still seemed functional. Michael pictured Vaughan coming over late at night for cable sports and Internet porn, and found the thought more lonely and depressing than anything else. He sat in Wilmer's solid oak desk chair, ignoring Vaughan's look of alarm, and said, "When did you go to Vietnam?"

"My eighteenth birthday was July twenty-third of 1969. This was before the lottery, so with my not being in college or anything, the chances of my getting drafted were pretty good. I tried to make the best of it, went to downtown Raleigh and signed up, hoping I'd get some choice about what they did with me. I didn't. They shipped me out for Fort Ord in California at the end of August, and thirteen weeks later I was on a C-141 headed for DaNang." The dog decided they would be there for a while and lay down at Vaughan's feet with a heavy sigh.

It was the opening Michael had been aiming for. "So you just missed my being born."

Vaughan looked at him like he'd started talking in Russian. "August of '69, I'm talking about. You weren't born until July of 1970."

Michael felt like the room had tilted sideways and he was rolling away from Vaughan on the wheels of the chair. "My birthday," he said carefully, "is September thirteenth, 1969."

"That's not possible. Aunt Ruth came to see me off when I left, and she wasn't even pregnant. She was two months gone when they moved to Dallas, and she didn't tell anybody about it till she got there. You were born there the next summer."

That, Michael thought, would certainly explain the missing hospital records. "Why would they lie? Why say I was born here?"

"Some kind of tax dodge, maybe? Why don't you ask your parents?"

"Because I don't know that they would tell me the truth. You're sure about all this?"

"In July of 1970 I was deep in country, blowing up gook tunnels in the central highlands. Every night I would try to imagine I was in North Carolina, and I would memorize every detail of every letter I got from home. It was in July that Mr. Bynum wrote to tell me that Aunt Ruth had had her a baby boy, named Michael."

"I need to go," Michael said. The desire was suddenly overwhelming.

"Sure, I understand," Vaughan said, already moving toward the door. Once outside he locked the deadbolt and hesitated. "I really do know what it's like to have all those questions and not be able to get answers." Though his arms were folded across his chest, Michael sensed he was reaching out to the best of his ability.

"Thanks," Michael said. "I appreciate it."

They walked in silence to the car, where Michael knelt again, ran his hand by Henry for permission, and then scratched the dog's thick chest fur. Henry licked his chops and squirmed with pleasure.

"You like dogs?" Vaughan asked approvingly.

Michael stood up. He considered himself more of a cat person, but in truth he could watch any animal for hours. "Sure. What's not to like?"

"They're God's creatures," Vaughan said, with a smile completely free of irony or condescension. "Give me a dog over a man any day."

MICHAEL DROVE as far as I-40, then pulled off into the weeds beside the access road.

Until he was 12 and began spending as much time as he could at his friend Jimmy's house, Michael had assumed his parents were the same as anyone else's: his father's long working hours and unpredictable moods, his mother's exaggerated, artificial cheerfulness. The times his father would stare at him with a kind of mournful longing were as bad as his fits of frustration and tightly contained anger. Michael hid from both extremes, as he hid from his mother's intermittent and clumsy attempts to hug him or pet him, as if he were a lapdog or stuffed animal. He spent many hours in the walk-in closet in his bedroom with a reading lamp and his sketchbook and comics. It wasn't enough that his parents never came into his room without permission. He needed to be where there were no windows.

He couldn't remember his father ever throwing a ball with him, but on weekends when he was very young the two of them might visit a construction site. Michael would sit in a silent grader or crane, pretending to work the controls while his father explained the job to him: the tilt wall forms, the crushed gravel for the roadbeds, the grids of reinforcing rods.

It seemed to be more about his father wanting an audience, a witness to what he did, than any expectation that Michael would find a calling there. When Michael showed no interest in drafting, his father let it go; when Michael wanted to draw superheroes and dinosaurs, his father showed him the one thing he could offer, which was the mechanics of perspective—one point, two point, and finally three. Even then Michael felt his father's lack of emotional investment, as if Michael were a pet whose real owner was expected back any minute.

The affection Michael's mother displayed for her husband seemed far more real than the shows she made for Michael. Michael's father put up with it, barring the occasional outburst that drove his mother back and often left her in tears. Michael had grown up thinking him cruel, but by high school he saw all the ways she brought the anger on herself, doing the kinds of things Michael had long ago learned to avoid, like asking him too many questions when he was watching TV, or following him from room to room.

His friend Jimmy's parents were divorced, and Jimmy lived with his mother, brother and sister, and stepfather. They'd converted their garage into a game room with a ping-pong table and stacks of worn records—Bill Cosby and Lenny Bruce, the Beatles and the Electric Prunes. When people in Jimmy's family hugged each other, Michael felt envious. He couldn't understand why his own parents stayed together, why his mother wanted to be with someone who didn't want her, why his father would continue to punish her. It was a question he'd never answered, and it was among the reasons he was 35 and still single.

He took out his phone and called information. They gave him the number for RHD Memorial Hospital, only a few blocks from his parents' first house in Dallas. The hospital put him through the same procedure that Durham Regional had—birth date, names of both parents, including mother's maiden name—and the results were the same: no record of his birth.

That left the other name on his list.

His father had worked closely with two men all the years he'd been in Durham: Leon Coleman and his nephew Tommy. Information had a listing for Tommy only.

Michael keyed the number into his phone and then, suddenly nervous, hesitated before pushing the call button. He sat there in his rented car, traffic rushing by him in both directions, and suddenly he felt the past falling away from him. Catch it, he thought, catch it now.

The voice that answered was deep and wary. " 'Lo?"

"Is this Tommy Coleman?"

"Who's calling, please?"

"My name is Michael Cooper. My father is Robert Cooper. He used to work with Mr. Coleman in the sixties."

"Robert Cooper, you said?"

"That's right."

"What's this in regard to?"

The man's reluctance hit Michael physically, draining his resolve. "Look, Mr.

Coleman, I'm not trying to make trouble for anybody. My father is dying, and I need to talk to somebody about him."

"He's sick?"

"He's got cancer, Mr. Coleman. He's at the va Hospital in Durham."

Now Coleman seemed genuinely alarmed. "Here? Here in Durham? I thought y'all was in Texas."

"He came back here to die."

"I'm very sorry to hear that." In more ways than one, it sounded like. "How did you know my name?"

"My father always talked about you and Leon. He said you two were his right and left hands."

"Yeah, that'd be the Captain all right. My uncle Leon passed last year."

"I'm sorry. Mr. Coleman, can I come talk to you?"

"To my place? You mean now?"

"Yes, sir. That's what I would like."

"What do you want to talk about?"

"About my father. Maybe you were working with him when I was born. I would like to know about that."

"I don't really know anything. I just worked for him, that's all."

"Mr. Coleman, what is it you're so afraid of?"

After a long half minute, Michael said, "Mr. Coleman? Are you still there?"

"Yeah, I'm here." Michael heard surrender in his voice. "There's no getting away from it, is there?"

COLEMAN'S APARTMENT COMPLEX was near the western end of the Durham Freeway, where it merged into I-85. The complex formed a long figure 8, the two-story brick buildings facing into roughly landscaped courtyards. Michael saw the Durham Freeway at the top of a rise beyond Coleman's building, lightly masked by pine trees. The fine weather had brought the neighbors outside. They were mostly in their twenties, mostly black and Latino, sitting on steps or on the hoods of cars. Michael smelled grilling ribs.

The second-floor apartments opened onto a walkway. There was no bell. Michael knocked on the glass outer door and the inner door opened on a man in his sixties, handsome, a little overweight, running to gray, in need of a shave. He wore a white T-shirt, khaki pants, and fuzzy slippers.

"Mr. Coleman?"

Coleman opened the glass door without saying anything, as if recovering from a shock. Michael walked past him into a wide room with an oak floor, well lit by a long window that faced the walkway. An entertainment center to Michael's right held a TV and stereo; to the left was a couch and coffee table. The room took an L-shaped turn into a dining area, where a newspaper fought for space on the table with dirty dishes and a coffee cup. Coleman began to collect and fold sections of the paper.

Michael gripped the back of one of the sturdy oak chairs. "Mr. Coleman, I—"

"You can call me Tommy," he said. "Sit down."

Michael sat.

"The Captain always called me Tommy. You look ungodly like he looked, the last time I saw him. You drink coffee?"

"I'm fine, thanks."

Coleman finished clearing the table and sat with his hands around the coffee cup. "You came here with your daddy?"

"A month ago. He insisted on coming here, and I think there's something he's not telling us. Some kind of secret that he's been keeping."

Coleman didn't answer. His hands stopped turning the cup and his eyes lost their expression.

"Something happened," Michael said. "Something about Hayti. Didn't it?"

"What makes you think it was about Hayti?"

"The way he talked about it. Like he was afraid of something. Afraid and guilty."

"How much do you know about it?"

"I know it was a black neighborhood and they put a freeway through it."

"They didn't just put a freeway through it. They wrecked it. *We* wrecked it. Tore it down to the ground."

"Why?"

"They called it urban renewal in those days. Black people used to say urban renewal wasn't nothing but 'Negro removal.' White people said Hayti was run down, and they were going to fix it all up for us colored folks. So they had a referendum, and us colored folks voted for it just like the whites did, and then they started to tear everything down. Long before they really had to, just to show they could, I guess. That would have been 1963 that they had the vote, and the Captain and me and Leon, we was part of it from the first."

"And you all worked for Mason and Antree."

"Truth of the matter is, there was two companies. There was Mason and Antree, Architects and Engineers, which the Captain worked for. Then Mr. Antree had his own company, One Tree Construction, which was the name on me and Leon's paychecks. One Tree and Antree, don't you see, though I always thought it was a odd name for a construction business. He needed to keep his name off it so it wasn't so obvious that the two companies was really just one big one.

"Anyways, Mr. Antree was the Engineering side of Mason and Antree, and he would sometimes have your daddy supervise us. That was the way of it back then. Even in Durham, which was fifty percent colored, it went easier if there was a white man there watching while the colored men worked.

"We liked your father well enough. He didn't try to act like he knew what he was doing when he didn't, like when we was doing demolition work. Now, when it came to pouring concrete, the Captain knew about that. The man had almost a religious feeling about concrete."

"I know."

"I expect you do. For five long years, we didn't pour any concrete in Hayti. All we did was knock things down. There was other work that was construction, but when it came to Hayti it was the wrecking ball and the bulldozer. Homes, businesses, schools. Like a war zone. Wasn't until 1967 that we started building there, and then it was the expressway to take the white folks out of Durham altogether and get them over to RTP."

"And that was barely started when my father left."

"I think it broke his heart, all that destruction. People would be standing there on the streets while we knocked down the drugstore they'd gone to for candy when they was kids, or knocked down the splo house they used to go to on Saturday nights."

"Splo house? What's that?"

"Splo is what we used to call that moonshine liquor. Short for explosion, I guess, which is what it did inside you. A splo house might have a still in the basement and then upstairs they'd sell what they manufactured."

"Do you remember when I was born?"

"What do you mean?" Michael's question sent Coleman back in his chair, his right hand raised across his chest to hold his left shoulder.

"I mean, when I was born, my father must have told you. Didn't they hand out cigars or something in those days?"

"Maybe he gave one to Mr. Antree, but not to us."

"You do remember when it happened, right?"

"We were the hired help, we didn't—"

"You were his right and left hands. He wouldn't have told you when his son was born?"

Coleman withdrew. He didn't move physically, but he was no longer available. He was staring at the table in front of him, his eyes not focused on it.

"You have to help me," Michael said. "All my life I've known something was wrong, but I couldn't put that feeling into words until we came here. I feel like I don't even know who I am anymore."

"Sometimes it's better to leave the past alone," Coleman said.

"Just answer one question. Was I born in Durham?"

Slowly, reluctantly, Coleman nodded.

"When?"

"That last fall, before the Captain left town."

"Then what is the big secret that everyone is keeping from me? Is it something to do with why we left Durham?"

"You should talk to your father."

"He won't talk to me. He's afraid to tell me himself, but he wants me to find out. That's why we're here. He wants whatever this is to come out before he dies. It's eating him up as surely as the cancer."

"It's eating at us all."

It took Michael a long second to realize what Coleman had said. When he did he had the sense to shut up and sit back in his chair and wait.

Coleman got up slowly, shuffled to the kitchen, and took a long time to refill his coffee cup. He poured in milk from the refrigerator and stirred in a packet of sweetener. "You sure you don't want no coffee."

Michael shook his head.

Coleman sat down again. "I've been waiting thirty-five years to talk about that night. There was four people there: Mitch Antree, your father, and me and Uncle Leon. Leon and me, we never once talked about it since that day, though there hasn't been a lot of days I don't think about it. Every time the phone rings and it's a voice I don't know, there's a part of me wants to run and hide. Like when you called today.

"Maybe they put me in prison for my part in it. Don't know that I care anymore. Been in a kind of prison all these years anyhow. However long I may have left, I don't want to spend it living like that."

Michael nodded and kept his silence, afraid Coleman would change his mind.

Coleman sat and looked at his coffee for a bit, and then he said, "It was September, September of 1969. Thirty-five years ago last month. It was the fourth, I remember, the month had just started. It was a Thursday. I got the call at two in the morning."

"So Thursday was the day before, or it was 2 AM Thursday morning?"

"Two AM Thursday. The phone was in Uncle Leon's room. He had a house in Walltown then, Old North Durham. Him and his wife was separated, and I was sleeping on his couch, trying to get the money together to get a place of my own. Well, the phone commenced to ringing. Uncle Leon could sleep through the Rapture, and after I got tired of yelling at him to wake up, I answered the damn thing myself. Well, it was Mr. Antree, and he said we was to meet him at a particular part of the job site, which was the overpass at Fayetteville Road, there where St. Joseph's church is. You know what I'm talking about?"

"I was there this morning."

"Every time I drive by there, I still get a chill." He drank from his coffee cup as if he needed the warmth. "Anyway, I asked Mr. Antree what he wanted us for, and he said we were going to pour some concrete. Now he had just woke me up, remember, so I didn't have all my best manners in place, if you understand what I'm saying. I asked him if he knew what time it was and so forth, and his voice got cold like I never heard it before, and he said, real quiet, 'Tommy, you get your uncle and get down to the site like I told you and I don't want to hear anything more out of you tonight but "yes, sir." You got that?' and I said, 'Yes, sir,' and that was that.

"Now, Mr. Antree, he was what we used to call at the time a jive-ass white man, tried to act like he was black, and talk and dress that way too. The way he was talking that night was not his way, and for some reason that made me very afraid.

"I woke Leon up and we got into our work clothes and I made us a thermos of coffee and we drove out to the site.

"Now we was scheduled later that day to pour a retaining wall for that overpass. The form was already put together, the steel was tied inside the form, it had all been ready for a day or two. We had a generator there, and Leon cranked it up and turned the lights on. There wasn't nobody else there yet, just the two of us standing around drinking coffee and not saying anything. Leon was shivering like I was, even though summer was barely gone and it was not cold at all.

"For some reason Leon decides he's going to move this fourteen-foot aluminum ladder that's leaning against the plywood form. Only the ladder ain't moving, and the lights that are shining down into the form, they're at an angle so you can't see the top of the ladder. Leon, maybe it's his nerves or something, he don't want to let it go, so he climbs up the ladder to see what it is wrong, and two seconds later he's down the ladder again and his face is gray. 'I need you to climb that ladder and tell me what you see.'

"'You know I don't like being up on no ladders,' I told him, but he was looking at me the same way that Mr. Antree was talking to me on the phone, and the next thing I know I'm sure as hell climbing that ladder. And I looked at what I saw, and I came down again."

"'What'd you see?' Leon asks me, and I say, 'There's a man in there.'"

"'What kind of a man?'

"'A dead man. All pushed down into the steel. He got one hand caught on the last rung of the ladder, which is why the ladder don't move.'

"'You know who that man is?'

"And I said, yes, I knew who it was, because it was Barrett Howard. You know who Barrett Howard was?"

It took Michael a second to realize Coleman was talking to him and not to his dead uncle. "No. No, I don't."

"Nobody remembers him now, but he was a thorn in the side of the white man all through the sixties. He was always the one talking about how the black man needed to arm himself for self-defense. When they had that referendum on Hayti, he was the one saying it was all a boondoggle, that the white man would tear Hayti down and pave it over and never build the things they said. In the late sixties he got more militant, like the Panthers and all that, and the talk was he was going to start the Revolution right here in Durham.

"Only he didn't. He disappeared instead. And the word got around that he had taken the white man's money and gone down to Mexico. Flat took the heart out of the Movement around here. And I knew that it wasn't true, and I never said a word."

"Go back to that night," Michael said. "What happened after you found the body?"

"Well, Leon, he got in the truck and just sat there, staring. I couldn't sit down. I remember the night was so still and clear it was like you could see every star that ever was. You don't get nights like that no more. I was praying for clouds because I didn't want God to see what we was about to do.

"I kept jumping every time I heard a car, and then finally I hear a cement mixer coming. Mr. Antree is behind the wheel, and the Captain, your daddy, is in the passenger seat. The two of them look about the same as Leon did when he came down that ladder.

"The mixer is turning, got a full load, and Mr. Antree backs it up toward the form. He's so nervous he keeps backing into this cinderblock, and it's too big for the mixer to back over, until finally he gets out the cab and throws the cinderblock off to one side. Throws it so hard it cracks, and that sound, that breaking sound, makes everybody freeze for a minute. Then Mr. Antree gets in the cab again and backs it up to the form, and he gets out and says, 'Let's go to work.'

"So Leon gets the vibrator out of our truck and fires it up—you know what that is? It's like a chainsaw without the chain, this big vibrating paddle you use to get all the air bubbles out of the mud. Mr. Antree is trying to swing that chute out from the back of the mixer, and I'm waiting for somebody to say something, anything, I don't care what, so we don't have to go through with this thing. The thing is, Mr. Antree don't know what he's doing, and if I don't help him he's going to pour that mud all over hisself, so that 400-year-old habit takes hold of me and I drag the end of the chute over the top of the form and give the signal. Mr. Antree opens it up and now it's too late to say anything because the concrete is going in the form.

"Leon goes up the ladder with the vibrator, and I hear the sound of that blade hitting something soft like flesh, and I know Leon has pushed the dead man's arm down inside the form. All this time the concrete is coming down with that thick, wet plopping sound, and you can smell it, you can smell the lime and the dirt in it, and the smell is making me sick to my stomach on top of all that coffee, and there's the diesel smell from the truck and the racket from the vibrator and the generator. When I die, where I'm going, I'm going to hear those sounds and smell those smells for eternity, and serve me right.

"I guess it wasn't but twenty minutes or so, longest twenty minutes of my life, and during that time the Captain never got out of the cab of that cement mixer. When we was done, Mr. Antree got in the driver seat and drove away, didn't say a word, not even a thank you. Leon rinsed down the vibrator and I put the ladder in the back of the truck, and when we got in he started the motor and he looked at me and he said, "Tommy, you ever say one word to me or anybody about this ever again, as long as I live, you are no blood of mine. You understand?'

"I nodded and that was the end of it. We went home and we both of us pretended to sleep. I heard him in there the rest of the night, that old metal bedstead creaking every time he tried to find a comfortable spot. I could have told him not to bother, because there ain't any." He looked up and met Michael's eyes for the first time since he started the story. "There ain't any."

They were silent a long time. "I'd take that cup of coffee now," Michael said at last.

"I imagine so." Coleman got up and poured it. "Anything in it?"

"Just like it is is fine," Michael said. "Who do you think killed that man—Barrett Howard, is it?" Coleman put the cup in front of him and nodded. "Was it Antree?"

"I don't think he had it in him. He liked his jazz, and he liked his wine, and he liked the ladies. Ladies of color, from what I heard. He was not a violent man. I never saw him angry. Everything was 'cool,' you know what I'm saying? I think he admired Barrett Howard. Used to quote things he said in the *Carolina Times*. That was the black paper back then, published out of Hayti, and Howard would write for it sometimes. Mr. Antree wanted real bad for black people to like him, so he would say a lot of things he thought we might want to hear."

"If it wasn't Antree, who was it?"

"I expect somebody wanted it done, and they got somebody else to do it for them, same way they got Antree to cover it up. Same way Antree got us to pour the concrete. Maybe it was the Durham Select Committee, the same bunch of old white men that got the idea to do RTP, same ones that decided

who got the contracts to 'rebuild' Hayti. Same ones that always has run everything and always will."

"And what about my father? How much do you think he knew?"

"You want the truth? I think he knew everything. I think they all did. I
think whatever they intentions was, no matter how good, they ended up doing
what they was told to do, and nobody heard another word out of their mouths
but 'yes, sir.' "

Michael drank some of the coffee. "So," he said. "What happens now?"

"You're asking me?"

"It's your story. You have to make the decision."

"About calling the cops, you mean."

"Yeah."

"If this goes to the cops," Coleman said, "it could come back to your
daddy."

"Maybe that's what he wants."

"He's dying. How could he want that?"

"The same way you do." Michael pushed back his chair. "Why don't we ask
him?"

MICHAEL DROVE. Belatedly he asked after Coleman's health, and Coleman
said, "I'm all right. I got the cholesterol, I got some blood pressure, but I quit
smoking years ago, don't drink too much. I should have a few good years left."

"Are you working? I didn't know if I would find you home on a Monday
or not."

"Been working nights on highway repair crews, supervising. I'm off tonight.
It's good work, just not steady, is all. The construction business, it's mostly
Mexicans now. They'll work all the hours you want, don't ask no overtime. You
can't compete with that."

Coleman didn't ask any questions of his own. It was a short drive to the VA
from Coleman's apartment, most of it in silence.

The sixth-floor rooms were semi-private. Michael's father shared his with
a black man in his forties, a veteran of the first Gulf War, who was suffering
from an undiagnosed lung ailment. When Michael and Coleman walked in,
the roommate was watching CNN and Michael's father was sleeping. Michael's
mother was sitting against the wall, crocheting Christmas ornaments for a
charity in Dallas.

"Where have you been?" she asked when she saw Michael. "Where are your
things? I didn't know what happened to you."

"I moved out," Michael said. "We can talk about it later."

She looked past him to Coleman.

"I don't know if you remember me, Mrs. Cooper," Coleman said. "I'm Tommy Coleman. I used to work with your husband."

Michael's mother blinked at him, looking puzzled, then smiled brightly and took his hand. "Of course I remember you," she said. "How kind of you to come."

"I'm very sorry to hear of his condition," Coleman said.

Michael said, "Look, we need to talk to Dad alone for a few minutes."

"Alone? What do you mean, alone?"

"It's just some personal business of my own, Mrs. Cooper," Coleman said, with the perfect touch of embarrassment.

Ruth looked at Michael, then at Coleman again. On the TV, a commentator noted that Russian President Vladimir Putin had endorsed George W. Bush in the upcoming election. Blushing, she gathered her things and stood up. "I'll be down the hall if you need me."

"Thank you," Coleman said.

The commotion woke Michael's father. Lately he'd been having trouble remembering where he was when he first woke up, and the sight of Coleman seemed to frighten him. As Ruth left the room, he struggled up onto one elbow.

"Relax, Dad," Michael said, moving in to put a hand on his shoulder. "It's Tommy Coleman, come to see you."

"How you doing, Captain?" Tommy said. Tommy himself did not appear to be doing well. He couldn't seem to find a place for his hands.

"Tommy and I have been talking," Michael said. "He told me about the body in the concrete."

Michael's father stared at him blankly.

"Barrett Howard," Michael went on. "Buried in the overpass by St. Joseph's church."

Michael's father closed his eyes, his face registering relief, confusion, fear. "So it's true," he whispered.

"What do you mean, 'true'?" Michael said. "You were there."

Michael's father nodded, and didn't say anything more.

"Dad, we need to call the police. You knew that, didn't you? This is what this whole exercise has been about, isn't it?"

"Not all of it," his father said. "I would have skipped the cancer part if I could."

"Do you want to talk to me now? Do you want to tell me what happened?"

"No," he said. "Go ahead. Make your call."

Michael looked at Coleman. "All right? Is this what you want?"

"Do it," Coleman said.

Michael called 911 from the bedside phone. "I don't know if this is exactly an emergency," he told the operator. "I need to report a murder, a thirty-year-old murder."

He ended up with a homicide detective named Frank Bishop. Bishop's manner was kind and unhurried. He let Michael work through a summary of the situation, then said, "First off, I need to get statements from you, Mr. Coleman, and your father. The best thing would be if you and Mr. Coleman can come down to the station, but if that's a problem I can meet you there at the hospital."

"No," Michael said. "We'll come to you."

DURHAM POLICE HEADQUARTERS was five stories of late 1950s modernism, vertical stripes of glass between concrete panels. It sat on the western edge of downtown, a block from the Durham Freeway. As he drove up, Michael's eyes went to the North Carolina Mutual Life Insurance building on his right. NC Mutual was the most successful of Durham's black businesses, and the first to "jump ship" from Hayti, as Michael's custodian friend had put it—initially to Parrish Street downtown, the "Black Wall Street," and then, in the 1960s, to this new freestanding building of its own, almost identical to the police headquarters across the street.

He and Coleman had driven mostly in silence, Coleman apparently as lost in his own thoughts as Michael. They parked in the police visitors' lot as the sun buried itself in clouds at the horizon. The day was cooling and Michael wished he'd brought a jacket. He'd never liked fall. The gaudy colors and lessening daylight seemed like a fatal disease in nature, something from which there could be no recovery.

Inside the glass front doors they found a high-ceilinged reception area with a white terrazzo floor and a tall, semicircular desk on the right. The desk officer, young, with sunglasses on top of his head, called Sgt. Bishop, who arrived five long minutes later. He had sandy-colored receding hair, aviator-style glasses, a blue oxford shirt and striped tie. He was in his late thirties, stood over six feet tall, and conveyed a sense of mass and hardness that Michael associated with serious body builders. He took them to the second floor in a chrome elevator and left Michael in an anteroom. "I need to take your statements separately," Bishop said. "Sorry to make you wait."

"It's okay," Michael said. In fact he was jealous and did not want Coleman alone with Bishop, for fear of missing something important.

Michael sat and leafed through a copy of *People*. There were two officers in black uniforms behind a desk, and more file cabinets than comfortably fit. A sign over the door where Coleman and Bishop had disappeared said CRIMINAL INVESTIGATIONS DIVISION.

Michael wondered what kind of criminal investigation his father was capable of participating in. Would they even charge him when he was already under a death sentence?

Part of him wanted to see his father taken away in handcuffs, dragging his oxygen bottle behind him. He found a depth of anger and frustration in himself that he had not expected. Lies and omissions—from the details of his birth to the existence of Orpha to the dead man in the overpass—left his entire childhood open to question. What else had they not told him? What sinister meanings lay behind those peculiar, haunted looks his father would sometimes give him, or the sobs he would hear his mother make inside her locked bedroom?

When Coleman returned he looked wrung out. Bishop nodded to Michael, and one of the uniformed cops buzzed them through into a hallway. They turned right and then left into a stark, fluorescent-lit office with windows that looked out onto Chapel Hill Street. A cassette recorder the size of a fat hardcover book sat on a plastic veneered desk, and there was a black PC monitor on a credenza against the wall behind it. Michael sat in a metal armchair facing the desk. Mounted on the wall to his right was a corkboard that held the only personal items in the room, including a photo of a team of officers in black Kevlar body armor and a citation to Bishop from his fellow members of the Special Enforcement Team. Bishop turned on the recorder and listed Michael's name, the date, and the location.

"I don't know anything about this except what Tommy told me," Michael said.

"That's okay," Bishop said. He seemed easygoing and friendly despite—or maybe because of—the intimidating physique. "We basically just need a record of your saying that."

"So what happens after that? What happens to my father if he's involved in this?"

"I'll need to talk to him. I understand that you and your parents both have your permanent addresses in Texas these days?"

"That's right. My parents in Dallas, me in Austin." The realization suddenly struck him that his father would never see Dallas again. The thought hit him hard and he had to push it away. He gave Bishop the number at the Brookwood, his father's room number at the VA, and their addresses in Texas.

"You a Longhorns fan?"

"I don't really follow sports that much. What about the body in the overpass? Are you guys going to look for it?"

"We'll make that decision after I talk to your father, but yeah, most likely."

"Can I be there when you talk to him?"

"Sorry."

"No, of course I can't," Michael said. "Dumb question."

"Why don't we get going?" Bishop said, and turned on the tape recorder. He led Michael patiently through the story, starting with his father's illness, the decision to come to Durham, his calling Coleman that afternoon, Coleman's story as Michael remembered it, his father's reaction. Michael found himself talking more freely than he'd intended to, at one point suggesting to Bishop that there might be a ritualistic aspect to the location of the body.

"What kind of ritual?" Bishop asked.

Michael told him about the *vévé* on the St. Joseph's steeple that overlooked the burial site, and Bishop made notes on a legal pad in addition to the recording.

When they finished, Michael said, "Listen, you've got access to all kinds of databases, right? Can you check something for me?"

"What do you want to know?"

"I was supposedly born in Durham, but I can't find any record of it."

"I can take a look. I need your social and your mother's maiden name and social."

Michael gave him the info and watched Bishop work through a series of brightly colored interfaces. After ten minutes, Bishop shrugged. "I'm not finding anything, but we didn't have computers in 1969. What you're looking for could be on microfiche, or it could be on paper in some warehouse."

Or, Michael thought, it might not exist at all.

IT WAS SEVEN O'CLOCK and fully dark by the time they came out. Coleman seemed badly shaken. "I should never have talked about this. Bad things going to come of it."

"You had to do it. You'll sleep better now."

It was like he'd predicted Coleman would find a million dollars under his pillow. "You think?" Coleman asked.

"You want to get some dinner?" They were back at the rented Echo, and Michael was looking across the roof of the car at Coleman. "I haven't eaten all day."

"I appreciate the offer," Coleman said, "but I need to forget what I just did. If you don't mind, there's a place down the street here that I go to sometimes. You could drop me off. I can get a ride home from there."

"If that's what you want." Coleman's second thoughts stung Michael like an accusation. He got in and started the car, feeling guilty and rejected.

Coleman directed him to a hole-in-the-wall bar on Holloway Street east of downtown. Two young black men, in sports logo wear from head to foot, loitered on the sidewalk. It was the kind of place that Michael, as a white man, would have been terrified to walk into alone, and he wondered if that was one of its attractions for Coleman. The gulf of race seemed at that moment hopelessly vast.

"I feel weird about going off and leaving you here," Michael said. He took out his wallet, ignoring Coleman's suspicious look, and took out one of his business cards. "That's got my cell phone number. Let me know if you need a ride or anything." He remembered that it had a 512 area code and said, "Call collect."

"I'll be all right," Coleman said. He put the card in his jacket pocket. He didn't invite Michael to join him, just got out of the car, held up one hand, and waited for Michael to drive away.

HE ATE DINNER at Torero's downtown, the closest thing he'd found to authentic Tex-Mex in the area, then drove to his hotel. After nearly a month on a foldout couch in claustrophobic proximity to his parents, he felt something like joy at the thought of a place of his own, antiseptic and rented by the week though it was.

He turned on the TV for background noise and settled on the bed with his drawing board. He had occasional nightmares about working in an office, answering telephones, trying to remember something vital he'd forgotten to do. He always woke with a renewed sense of gratitude for his chosen profession. Even now, with so much of his personal history in dispute, he was able to lose himself in his work. When his cell phone rang an hour later, it came as a shock.

"How could you?" said his mother, with no preamble.

"Hi, Mom."

"The police just left. Your father won't tell me what it was about. It was about that black man, Tommy, that you brought here, wasn't it?"

"What did he say?"

"Who?"

"My father. When you asked him."

"He said, 'Ancient history.' When I asked if this was something you'd done, he said, 'Not really.' That's when I knew it was your fault. Tell me what you did."

"I found out why he wanted to come back to Durham. He was involved in a murder in 1969."

"What are you talking about? That's simply not possible."

"He helped bury a dead body in concrete. Somebody named Barrett Howard, a black activist."

His mother didn't answer, a silence of held breath.

"Mom, what do you know about it?"

"What everybody knows. This Howard was a troublemaker, and he raised a lot of money for some radical cause and used it to run off to Mexico."

"Apparently he didn't get that far. While we're at it, here's another question for you. Who was Orpha?"

"Orpha?"

"Your sister Orpha, who you never told me about."

"You certainly did know about her. She died before you were born."

"And when was that?"

"That Orpha died? I don't remember exactly, but—"

"No, when was I born?"

"You don't remember your own birthday?"

"I'm asking you."

"September nineteenth, 1969." There was no hesitation in her voice.

"And I was born here in Durham?"

"Yes, here in Durham. At Watts Hospital, which was only a few blocks from our house."

"Greg Vaughan says I was born in Dallas in July of 1970."

"Greg? When were you talking to him?"

"I went out to the farm today. That's when I learned about Orpha."

"You've had a busy day."

"The lies have to stop, Mother. It's all coming out now anyway. Please, tell me what you know."

After another short silence, the phone beeped to tell him she'd hung up.

Tuesday, October 19

MICHAEL WORKED until 5 AM, until he was nodding off at the board, then put his tools away and collapsed into a restless sleep. The phone woke him after what seemed only a few minutes, though the clock said 9:22.

It was Tommy Coleman. "I just talked to that policeman," he said. "They want me down to the overpass at 11. They going to see can they find that body."

MICHAEL PARKED on the access road north of the freeway. The temperature had dropped overnight and had only made it up into the forties. The sky was cloudy and the wind danced around him, snapping the legs of his jeans and stinging his eyes.

From where he stood, at the top of the grassy bank, he could clearly see the *vévé* on top of St. Joseph's. Twenty feet below, the police had blocked one of the two westbound lanes of the freeway with orange cones, backing traffic up over the horizon.

Michael climbed down the slope and made his way through a crowd of on-lookers. A WRAL news truck had parked in the breakdown lane and cranked up its broadcast mast. Shout it from the housetops, Michael thought. Get everybody who knows anything about this out of the woodwork.

A handful of uniformed cops milled around, eyeing the civilians and the passing traffic suspiciously. Sgt. Bishop, in khaki pants and a corduroy sport coat, stood with Coleman in a cluster of official-looking people directly beneath the overpass. They both had their hands in their pockets. Somebody, probably Coleman, had marked the outside corners of a search area in red chalk on the surface of the embankment.

They were watching a middle-aged man in jeans, navy windbreaker, and billed cap. He was setting up a device that resembled a lawnmower; four solid rubber wheels supported a yellow box the size of a small, flat suitcase. On top of the handlebars was a smaller yellow box with a color LED screen.

Coleman saw Michael and waved. Bishop's expression was neutral. A cop stopped Michael at the line of yellow crime scene tape that they'd strung from more of the orange traffic cones.

"I'm here to see Sgt. Bishop," Michael said.

The cop looked at Bishop, who gave a grudging nod and beckoned Michael over.

Michael shook hands with both men and said, "What's that thing?"

"Ground penetrating radar," Bishop said. "Known as GPR in the trade. They use it to find pockets—'voids' is the term they use, I believe—in concrete."

"Like bodies?" Michael asked.

"That's the idea. We got lucky. Nobody in the Triangle has one of these rigs. I remembered that these folks tried to sell us a system a few years ago to find buried dope or what have you. I managed to talk them into driving down from Roanoke."

"Who are all these people?"

"It always turns into a circus when it's this public," Bishop said. He gestured to the slim young woman next to him. She had light brown skin, golden cornrows, and a black leather jacket over her skirt and sweater. "This is Leticia Townsend. She's an Assistant District Attorney. Leticia, Michael Cooper."

"Hi," Michael said. "Are you going to press charges against my father?"

Townsend looked in confusion to Bishop, who said, "She's here to keep an eye on the chain of evidence. Makes things go smoother if we do end up in court."

Michael nodded and Bishop went on. "That woman is from the Medical Examiner's office. The guy next to her is a structural engineer from NC DoT. He's supposed to let us know how much we can tear up if we have to."

Michael nodded. "So what did my father tell you?"

"You know I can't answer that."

"You're here. He must have said something."

"I get the idea you two have had some problems. I had a hard time with my old man, too. Really, the only way to deal with it is to talk to him."

"I've tried that."

"You should keep trying. He doesn't have a lot of time left and he really cares about you."

"People have told me before that he cares. I can't tell you what it makes me feel like. Cheated, I guess. He won't show it to me, no matter what I do."

"Detective?" the man in the cap said. "I think we're ready."

THE UNIFORMED COPS moved everyone away from the embankment, including Michael and Coleman. Bishop, the woman from the ME's office, and the ADA huddled with the machine operator for a minute or so, handed him a piece of chalk, then left him to his business.

The man muscled his machine up the steep incline and then let it roll down again, keeping a slow, even speed. Around the middle of the designated area, he stopped and thumbed a button on a keypad at the bottom of the screen. The image—nothing but wavy lines as far as Michael could see—shifted forward and back, and the man made his first chalk mark on the concrete.

It took him five minutes to go over the area Coleman had marked, and when he finished he connected the dots he'd made. They formed a shape like a rounded arrowhead, pointing up and away from the road. Then he came back to talk to Bishop.

"The instrument shows a good-sized void there, down in among the steel. Closest point is maybe twelve inches below the surface, furthest point less than three feet."

"You think it's a body?" Bishop asked.

The man shrugged. "I'll send you a full report, with a lot of fancy charts and graphs you can take to court. But between you and me, if there's a body in that concrete, that's where it's at."

Bishop made a call on his cell phone. Townsend, the ADA, was on hers as well. Civilians were holding digital cameras and cell phones over their heads and shooting anything that came in their viewfinders. The TV news reporter spoke into a microphone with hushed urgency, awash in the glow of portable lights. Michael's entire body hummed. He had unleashed a juggernaut, and he was sure that answers would be exposed in its wake.

Bishop closed his phone and turned to the Department of Transportation engineer. "Marvin?"

The engineer shrugged. Michael saw that the stretch of concrete in question carried no load, simply followed the upward slope of the hillside between a set of load-bearing Ts and the point the overpass began its reach across the freeway. "Break out the jackhammers," the man said.

There were three of them, and six men to take turns. All wore hard hats, though Michael was at a loss as to why. Insurance reasons, most likely. Once they began drilling, the noise in the confined space was unbearable and the crowd quickly moved away.

Coleman was the only one who hadn't caught the excitement. Michael put a hand on his massive shoulder as they walked out onto the grassy slope. "You're a hero, you know."

Coleman looked at the ground. "Hope you still feel that way in a week or a month. Hope *I* feel that way." His gaze shifted to the dust billowing out from the overpass. "It's cold. I'm going home."

THE WORK CREW made good progress, stopping every few minutes to clean chunks of concrete out of the hole. The crime scene unit, in earplugs and clear plastic goggles, sorted through the rubble and periodically looked at the hole itself. A separate worker with a cutting torch stepped in twice to burn through sections of rebar.

Still they were unable to finish by nightfall. As they began to pack their gear, an unmarked Crown Victoria, lights flashing from its grille, crunched to a stop on the access road above. A beefy white man in a cheap suit and a flattop haircut got out, frowned at the muddy slope, and picked his way carefully down. Once under the highway he paused for a quick, unhappy look at the wreckage in progress, then headed straight for Bishop.

Michael circled around behind them. They both faced the embankment and didn't see him.

The big man was saying, "—thought about what you're going to do when you get him out?"

"I've got some ideas."

"Was that six men you had balling those jacks?"

"We need to get the body to a secure location."

"Well, now, that's well and good, but don't go hog wild over this."

"I'm thinking," Bishop said, "that when it gets out that it's Barrett Howard under there, the media is going to be all over us."

"I give a crap about the media. Whoever did this is no threat to my city tonight. Maybe we need to do a better job of keeping the press out of this."

As badly as Michael wanted to butt in, he willed himself to be invisible, turned slightly away, and pretended to look at something on the ground.

"Dave," Bishop said, "you can't block traffic and start tearing up part of the freeway without anybody noticing. And we're not going to dress up like DoT workers if we want this to hold up in court."

"I've got just as much interest as you do in closing unsolved cases," the big man said, "but not at the expense of this year's murders."

"We can't ignore the fact that this is going to be big. The papers—"

"I give a crap about the papers," the man said, walking away. "I'm not saying don't investigate. I'm saying keep this under control. I already can't afford the overtime I need to keep these goddamn kids from shooting my citizens."

When he was gone, Michael eased up to Bishop. "Who was that?"

"That," Bishop said, "was Sgt. Goetz, head of the Homocide squad. I hope you weren't eavesdropping."

"I heard a little. What's his problem?"

"His problem is he's a good cop in a tough job." Bishop's tone was patient and pleasant, as if giving driving directions. "Over in Raleigh, on the radio, they play a recorded gunshot every time they say the word 'Durham.' There are people over there who have never set foot in Durham because they're afraid to. Yes, the crime rate is higher here—we've got a gang problem as bad as LA's. We've got a lot more people living below the poverty line, and the whole idea of social services is out of fashion at the moment. We've got a recession, and we've got institutionalized racism that makes it harder for black people to get what few jobs there are. Which leads to people giving up. I wouldn't want Goetz's job."

"So does that mean you're going to back off the investigation?"

"It means I'm going to make time to do it, even if I don't get to sleep much for a while."

Wednesday, October 20

FOR ALL HIS EXHAUSTION, Michael had another bad night. He worked late, then lay awake with his head spinning when he finally crawled into bed.

When he got to the crime scene at ten next morning, the workmen had the chunk of concrete loose. They'd cut a rough bowl shape out of the retaining wall and attached two massive ring bolts to the top side. A police cruiser, parked on the shoulder upstream from the overpass, had its lights flashing. The news team was back, set up east of the cruiser.

Bishop was talking with one of workmen, a beefy white kid with a light brown beard. "—rule of thumb is a hundred and fifty pounds per cubic foot," the kid was saying, "so you're looking at probably six to eight tons of concrete there. You wouldn't want to drop that on your foot."

"I hate to shut down the freeway to bring in a crane in the middle of the day," Bishop said, "but after what happened last night, I want that body out of here and under lock and key. Do you guys know where the impound lot in Raleigh is? Behind the surplus property agency there on Chapel Hill Road?"

"Yeah," the bearded guy said. "My brother-in-law buys his cars there."

"Call me when you've got it loaded, and I'll meet the driver there." Bishop turned and saw Michael. "Hey."

"What happened last night?" Michael asked.

Bishop began walking Michael away from the site. "Somebody tried to blow up the body."

"What?"

"Around two A M. We don't know if it was kids pulling a prank or something more serious. A woman walked up to the officer watching the site and told him she was having car trouble and needed help. He started to go with her and then thought better of it. When he turned around there was a pickup stopped under the underpass and there was a guy with a bundle of dynamite and a cigarette lighter, about to light the fuse. The guy saw him and jumped in the truck and drove away."

"What about the woman?"

"She ran across the freeway. There was a car waiting on the shoulder there and it took off as soon as she got in."

"So at least two cars, three people, and some high explosives. That's no prank."

"No," Bishop said, "I suppose not. The T V stations had Barrett Howard's name. From what I hear, he always had a way of getting people riled up. Even thirty-five years dead."

"What happens to the body now?"

Bishop stopped walking. "Look, Michael. I know you want to help. There's nothing you can do right now. Hang loose and let us do our job. I'll call you if something comes up."

Michael hesitated, saw he wasn't going to get any further. "Okay," he said. He climbed up the slope and then, on impulse, turned left across the overpass toward St. Joseph's and the Hayti Heritage Center.

Inside the front door he found a gallery space and an exhibit titled "Common Cause: Collecting African American Art." The small selection they had came from an impressive roster of artists: Jacob Lawrence, a painter Michael had always loved; Elizabeth Catlett, whose sculptures he admired particularly; and drawings by John Biggers, whose "Starry Crown" Michael had grown up with at the Dallas Museum of Art.

Biggers was a particular favorite. He'd been born in North Carolina and had ended up in Texas, painting murals that tied the shotgun houses of Houston's Third Ward to the Yoruba *shogun* house in Africa. That had led him to the symbolism of the triangular roof over the square frame, the triangle representing the heavens and the square the earth. The shotgun house originated in Haiti and had come to the US through New Orleans, just like the vodou that inspired the *vévé* on the steeple over Michael's head.

Roger had told him that vodou—that all magic—operated that way. It found the connections between things, whether in history or looks or wordplay, and expressed that connection in symbols. A change in the symbols was supposed to effect a change in the world. What was the connection between John Biggers and Michael Cooper, also an artist, also born in North Carolina, who also ended up in Texas?

Michael sometimes thought his own inability to believe in God made it that much harder for him to disbelieve in hoodoo, bad luck, or the devil. He was a spiritual Belgium, occupied by one transient ideological army after another. All the invaders left behind was a vague sense that things were not what they seemed, a sense that his cynicism could never overcome.

Idle curiosity took Michael through a walkway into the church itself. He found himself at the top of a steeply raked bank of seats that faced a proscenium stage. The room was dark and peaceful. He took a moment to soak it in, then crossed the gallery again to the information desk.

The man behind the counter was in his late thirties, skin the color of dark khaki, wearing a knit cap in red, gold, and green. He was close to Michael's size and, like Michael, didn't look particularly fit. He was reading *The Collected Poems of Langston Hughes,* rather conspicuously, Michael thought.

"Hey," Michael said. "Can I ask you some questions?"

"Sure," the man said. "If I know the answers, I'll tell you."

"I was wondering about the symbol on top of the steeple. You'd usually expect to see a cross there."

"As I understand it, that's an African symbol. This is an *African* Methodist Episcopal church, after all."

"Can you tell me what it means?"

"I'm not much of an expert."

"Can you tell me how it got there? Whose idea it was?"

"Sorry. There's a picture of it on one of our brochures. You could take that to the library down the street..."

"Well, what about the history of Hayti? Do you have any books about it?"

"There are a couple of books, one by a woman who used to work here, Dorothy Jones. And there's a book of photos that a professor over at NCCU put together. They should have those at the library too."

"You don't have anything at all here?"

"Well, there are a lot of papers and some audio recordings. I'm afraid it's all in a bit of a mess."

"Is there somebody in charge of that stuff?"

The man hesitated, his eyes shifting to Michael's right. A woman's voice said, "That's okay, Charles, I'll talk to him."

Michael turned around. She was about 40 and a foot shorter than he was, with lustrous straight black hair that curved to points under her chin. She had a crooked smile and, he couldn't help noticing, a beautifully formed body. Her skin was the color of dark stained teak, and she had a cocky, bantering look that Michael liked.

"Denise Franklin," she said, sticking out her hand. "Can I help?"

Her grip was firm. "Michael Cooper," he said. "I'm trying to learn something about Hayti."

"Can I ask what your interest is?"

"My father worked for Mason and Antree. He helped knock Hayti down."

"I see. Why don't you come down to my office. Charles, you want to join us? Get Lateesha to cover the desk."

Her office was one floor down, an anonymous cube with windows at ground level of the parking lot. Cheap steel shelves were piled with black videotape storage cases, audio cassettes, stacks of photocopies. Michael picked up a stack of magazines from one of the metal chairs and added it to another pile on the floor.

"I'm sorry for the mess," Franklin said. "My predecessor spent nine years trying to get this organized, but she died last year. I just stepped in a few months ago and I am ... overwhelmed."

Michael heard an accent come and go. "You're not from around here," he said. "New York?"

"Queens. I came down here after college because of RTP. I'm a programmer. I was, anyway, until my job moved to India without me."

"How did you get into this line of work?"

"Answered an ad. I didn't mean to stay, but this job has a way of getting to you."

"Ms. Jones used to say the same thing," Charles said.

"Something about Hayti?" Michael asked. "Or..."

"It's the people. Urban renewal, that's just government jargon. We've got hour after hour of oral history in these files, and I've gotten to know some of the people that used to live here, and I've looked at every photo and piece of film I can find, and at some point it starts to become real to you. I can drive up there to Pettigrew Street and if the light is right, I swear I can see the ghosts of the Biltmore Hotel and the Donut Shop."

She reigned herself in. "What about you? You don't sound like you're from 'around here' either."

"I grew up in Texas. My parents left Durham at the end of '69."

"You must have heard all the clichés about Durham from them."

"They weren't exactly the Chamber of Commerce. Try me."

"W.E.B. DuBois—who is a pretty big hero of mine—said, 'Of all the southern cities that I have visited I found here the sanest attitude of the white people toward the black.' He called Durham 'the city of Negro enterprise.' That was all because of Hayti."

"That was also a long time ago," Charles said.

Franklin nodded. "When they were through wrecking it, four thousand families and five hundred businesses were gone. It broke the back of the black middle class. Most of the families never found anything like what they'd had here—they went from owning their own homes in a nice neighborhood to renting an apartment in the projects, or living in a back room in somebody else's place. Most of the businesses simply went under."

"And the city did it just to get some government money?"

"There *was* government money, to the tune of twenty-five million dollars for Durham alone. And there was talk that some of the principals involved, like Mitch Antree, used what they knew to buy houses cheap and then sell them to the city for big profits, based on their own crooked appraisals. Then they'd collect another check for knocking them down."

"Mitch Antree did that?"

"He had an expensive lifestyle. Fast cars, sharp clothes, rent for his girl-friends' apartments."

"Wow. You don't know what happened to him, do you?"

"I seem to remember reading somewhere that he died. Some kind of ac-cident, maybe?"

"That's okay. Go on."

"Well, the real question is, why was the government handing out money for projects like this in the first place?"

"It was the sixties, right?" Michael said. "There was a lot of money around, and everybody was all about the bright new future."

"Urban renewal focused almost exclusively on black neighborhoods. Nothing was ever rebuilt, only destroyed, in city after city. *Brown v. Board of Education* was May of 1954, and three months later Congress passed the Housing Act of 1954, which was where it started. But it was 1959, the same year Prince Edward County up in Virginia shut down its schools rather than integrate, that Congress put up 650 million bucks for urban renewal."

"You say that like urban renewal was calculated revenge for integration."

Franklin let his question hang for a good two or three seconds before she said, "Would you like a cup of coffee, Mr. Cooper?"

"No, but I would like it if you would call me Michael."

"All right ... Michael." There was that smile again. Was she flirting? Michael hoped so.

Charles cleared his throat. "Was there anything else?"

"A couple of things," Michael said to Franklin. "I was asking Charles about the symbol on top of the steeple. Maybe you know something?"

"The weathervane?" Franklin said. "Dr. Aaron Moore brought that back with him from the island of Haiti a hundred years ago. That's one version of the story. Another is that he brought the workmen from Haiti, and they made it here."

"So there's a connection between Haiti the country and Hayti the neighborhood? Beyond the name?"

"Oh, absolutely. Dr. Moore was the one who named it, supposedly. You'll find neighborhoods named Hayti all across the South. Because of Toussaint L'Overture, of course, and the first independent black nation in the hemisphere, and the only successful revolution in history by slaves of African descent. Did you know Britain sent more troops to protect their slave trade in Haiti than they sent to fight the American Revolution? It was only after the Haitians beat them and the French both that they finally started to pass laws against slavery."

"Did you know that your 'weathervane' is a *vévé*?" Michael asked. "A voodoo symbol?"

"I've heard that theory," Franklin said.

"It's not a theory, it's true. It represents Erzulie, a sort of love goddess."

"How do you know that?" Charles asked. The question carried a larger freight of hostility and suspicion than seemed appropriate, and Franklin looked at Charles curiously.

"I'm an artist," Michael said. "I've used those symbols in my work. Were there a lot of Haitians here when they were building the church?"

"Nobody knows for sure," Franklin said. "There was probably a small community—artisans, wives, families."

Michael leaned forward. "So was there—is there—voodoo in Hayti?"

Charles snorted. "Sure, all us colored folk practices that hoodoo."

"Did I do something to piss you off?" Michael said. "If so, I apologize."

Charles declined to back down. "Look, we get people coming in here every few months—newspaper people, students—all busted up about poor Hayti. They shed a few tears and then they're gone again."

"I'm not claiming to be here for anybody's benefit but my own. I've got a personal interest. If you don't want to help me with that, that's your call."

He and Charles stared at each other for a while. As much as Michael disliked confrontations, Charles's sniping was getting on his nerves.

Franklin said, "I'm worried that we may have left Lateesha up there on her own for too long. Charles, would you go relieve her?"

Charles got up, turned his glare on Franklin briefly, then slouched out.

"So how does this all tie together?" Franklin asked. "Voodoo and your father and Hayti?"

Michael went over the high points: his father's cancer, the missing birth records, the body in the concrete. Franklin nodded. "I saw that in the paper this morning. I was devastated."

"They haven't confirmed that it's Howard, yet."

"But from what you say—"

"Yeah," Michael said. "It's him."

Franklin got up to stand by the window, though Michael doubted she was seeing anything. Eventually she said, "If I'd lived through this, maybe I'd be tougher. Sometimes the frustration just overwhelms you." She turned around. "How much difference would it have made if people hadn't believed that Howard sold out? Worse yet, if they knew he was murdered? Would it have changed history? At the very least there would have been riots. They might have burned Durham to the ground."

"Would that have been a good thing?"

"I don't know," Franklin said. "We're supposed to take consolation in the fact that the evils of urban renewal ended up in a new interest in historic preservation. And the betrayal of black people by politicians started an upsurge of black people running for office. To me that's like saying I should be grateful for slavery because otherwise I'd still be in Africa and might not have a car. It's too little, too late, at too high a price. And that goes for this ATC business too."

"What business is that?"

"The old American Tobacco Company factory downtown. Now known as the American Tobacco Campus, part of the American Tobacco Historic District. I'm sure you've seen it—that's the chimney and the water tower with the Lucky Strike logo on them. This outfit called the Black Star Corporation is reopening it as a multi-use complex. Shops, offices, concerts, high-end apartments. You may remember that the Black Star Line was Marcus Garvey's steamship company, which was supposed to take us back to Africa. Anyway, it's a consortium of black businesspeople, and two of the board members used to have stores in Hayti. They're straining for a historical connection, trying to make this out to be a rebirth of the 'spirit of Hayti,' trying to recruit black-owned restaurants and so forth."

She gestured at the chaos on her desk. "They want photos, quotes, and artwork for the grand opening—basically they're using me as an unpaid employee. I understand they made a donation to the Center, but they're getting more than their money's worth."

"That kind of publicity has to be a good thing in the long run."

She sighed. "It is, and I shouldn't be so cynical about it. I wish it wasn't keeping me from my other work."

Michael saw the hint. "As am I. I really appreciate your taking the time to talk with me, though."

"That's okay. I enjoyed it."

She sounded like she meant it. He stood up and said, "Do you have a card or something?"

She produced one from the chaos and held it out to him. Michael's mouth was dry. "Does it have your home number on there?" he asked.

The smile stretched one side of her mouth as she held his eyes, then slowly took the card and wrote a number on the bottom of it. "That's my cell. That's your best bet."

"Do you ... is there..."

"You're not very good at this, are you?" she asked.

"No," Michael said. "I'm trying to ask if you're involved with anybody."

"That's a complicated question. We can talk about it sometime, if you want."

He took the card and put it in his jacket pocket. "Thanks."

Denise held out her hand again, gave his a small squeeze. "Good luck," she said.

CHARLES DIDN'T LOOK UP from his book as Michael left. For his part, Michael had no desire to get into another pissing contest. Instead he sat on the steps in the cold wind and got out the pocket-sized sketchbook he always carried. He drew Denise Franklin's face while it was still fresh in his mind, spending a while getting the mouth right.

He'd never dated a black woman. White flight had shaped the Dallas neighborhoods of his youth, and Thomas Jefferson High School had been as affluent and Anglo-Saxon as its North Dallas surroundings. He'd seen his first real diversity at Pratt Institute in Brooklyn. At that point his sense of adventure was completely exhausted by the process of getting safely back and forth between campus and his apartment near the Navy Yard.

And in there somewhere was the knowledge that his parents would never have approved of an interracial romance. If he'd come home with a black woman there would have been awkward discussions later about "cultural differences" and "fighting uphill battles."

Charles's bitterness notwithstanding, Michael could still see the remnants of what had moved DuBois about Durham. At the big Harris Teeter on MLK Boulevard, virtually all the employees were black. Michael had taken his parents' rental there two or three times a week, usually late at night. As he got to be on a first name basis with them—Shawn in produce, who worked nights so he could spend his days on the golf course, and whose brother was in Iraq, Dwayne in the bakery, whose new Expedition had electrical problems no one could seem to fix, Charlene at checkout, in her fifties and playing a series of boyfriends off against each other—he felt his constant awareness of color, for the first time in his life, begin to fade.

What had it been like in 1961, with Hayti proud, strong, and confident? What had his father been part of?

He put the sketchbook away and walked to the edge of the overpass. True to his word, Bishop had shut down the northbound lanes of the freeway and cars had backed up on the access road. A flatbed truck had parked under the overpass and a crane was maneuvering into position behind it. Meanwhile, workmen had run a steel cable through the ring bolts and were connecting the loop of cable to the crane's massive steel hook.

Michael stayed to watch, remembering when those machines had held the promise of magic and transformation for him, unable to say exactly when his feelings had changed. Certainly by high school and his one summer working for his father, when it was all noise and dirt and the constant threat of injury to his hands.

At the hotel, he ran a few laps around the two story parking deck and adjacent lots, up to the roof and down again. He showered and worked and ate, and at nine that night, when he couldn't stand it any longer, he dialed Denise's cell phone number.

"We can't take your call right now," her voice said. "Please leave a message."

He hung up before the beep. There was, apparently, a "we" there. The situation was probably not that complicated at all.

•

Thursday, October 21

AN EIGHT-FOOT HIGH chain link fence topped with razor wire surrounded the impound lot and the dozens of cars for sale inside, from abandoned wrecks to drug dealers' souped-up rides. The long rectangular warehouse of the NC State Surplus Property Agency, filled with dead computers and gray metal desks, ran the length of the lot to Michael's left, half outside the fence and half in. Extending from the back of the building were several metal sheds, like mini-warehouse units, each with its own rolling door.

A uniformed cop in a wooden booth by the gate copied the name and number from Michael's driver's license onto a yellow legal pad. "Do you know if Sgt. Bishop is here?" Michael asked.

"Try that second shed over there," the cop said.

"Thanks."

The metal door was open a foot or so, enough to let a swirl of dust motes out into the morning sun, along with the sound of hammers and chisels. Michael tapped on the door, then gently lifted it to chest height and crouched to look in.

The bowl-shaped lump of concrete, ten feet across and four feet high, rested on a gray canvas tarp and filled the space nearly from one corrugated wall to the other. Three high-watt utility lights were clipped to the channels at the top of the walls. Perched on wooden stools and wielding hammers and cold chisels were four college-age kids. They all wore sweat clothes or coveralls and had dust masks over their noses and mouths. Bishop stood next to one of them, listening while the woman pointed and talked.

They had already made considerable progress. A pile of rubble had accumulated by the door, and the four stools clustered by a hollow they'd dug into the smooth surface.

Bishop turned as Michael stepped inside. The clinking stopped and Bishop said, "Found us on your own, did you?"

Michael didn't answer. The kids had straightened up, and now Michael saw what looked like a body trying to crawl out of the concrete.

Except for two funerals, Michael had never seen a dead body before. This one was a shock, like something from a horror movie. Only the head, left shoulder, and left forearm were exposed. The skin of the face had dried and wrinkled to an oily brown color, now dotted with cement dust. The nose and cheeks had collapsed, the eyes sunken shut, tufts of hair disappeared, the lips pulled back in a kind of buck-toothed rabbit mouth.

The shoulder and arm were literally skin and bones, the skin having shrunk as the flesh melted away underneath.

"Wow," Michael said.

"You shouldn't be here, Michael," Bishop said.

"Is it Howard?"

After a second Bishop said, "Yeah, it's Howard. One of the retired cops from the department identified him about an hour ago."

"Who are all these people?"

Bishop seemed unable to resist answering the question. "Grad students from the UNC Anthropology Department. It was the Medical Examiner's idea. It saves the city some money and gives them something different for their résumés." He made quick introductions, and Michael and the students nodded at each other.

"Isn't Duke closer?" Michael asked.

The woman Bishop had been talking to was named Jennifer. She was big-boned, with long brown hair in a ponytail and nice eyes. She said, "Duke has cultural and biological, but they don't do archeology."

"He's mummified, right?" Michael asked her.

"That's what it looks like," she agreed.

"The cement would have sucked all the moisture out of him," Michael said. "I worked at my father's precast plant one summer, and my hands always looked like that at the end of the day."

After a moment's consideration, Bishop said, "As long as you're here, let me show you something." He beckoned Michael over and pointed to the left arm extending from the block. The skin was several shades of deep brown, with a texture like unevenly stained hardwood. A faint sweet smell came from the skin, like burned sugar, not entirely unpleasant.

"You mentioned knowing that voodoo symbol on St. Joseph's," Bishop said. "Do you recognize this?" He pointed, not quite touching the back of Howard's wrist. "There's some kind of tattoo there."

It was like an optical illusion, there and not there at the same time. Michael stared, blinked, and finally saw it, fine purplish-black lines barely distinguishable from the skin. An inch above where a watch might be, and not much larger than the size of a watch face, was a cross with arms of equal length, emanating from a circle at the center. There was another, smaller circle at the end of each arm of the cross.

"I don't know what it is," Michael said, "but I know who would. The writer I work with, Roger Fornbee. He knows everything about symbols and folklore and that kind of thing. I can ask him."

"I don't want too many people to see this," Bishop said.

"Roger can keep a secret," Michael said. "He's all about secrets."

"Okay," Bishop said. "Just make sure he keeps a lid on it."

Michael dug out his sketchbook and drew the entire wrist. Since he was there, Michael sketched the face as well.

"I'm due in court in half an hour," Bishop said. "Let me walk you out."

They walked together to the gate. "You had a chance to talk to your old man again?" Bishop asked.

"I'm thinking on it."

Bishop nodded. "Call me on the cell if you find out anything about that symbol."

"I will."

He got in an unmarked gray Crown Victoria, identical to a handful of others for sale on the lot, and drove away. Michael got in his own car and headed for Durham on I-40, intending to fax the drawing to Roger from his hotel. Instead he found himself taking the Durham Freeway cutoff toward the Hayti Heritage Center.

Don't do this, he thought, but he did it anyway.

To his disappointment, Charles was at the desk again. "Is Ms. Franklin in?" Michael asked.

Charles picked up the phone and punched a two-digit extension. "Your voodoo friend is here again," he said. Charles didn't answer her either, just hung up and said, "I'll walk you down."

Self-consciousness attacked Michael on his way down the stairs. Was his pulse racing? Would he give away his nervousness by not being able to catch his breath?

When they got to Denise's office, it was clear she was nervous too. She didn't seem to want to look at him. "Come in," she said. "Sit down."

"That's okay," Michael said. "I won't take much of your time." He got out his sketchbook and held it closed in his left hand. "They found something at the crime scene. It's a tattoo on the dead man's hand."

"Is that a drawing of it?" Denise nodded to the sketchbook.

Michael saw that Charles was lurking by the doorway. "This has to be in absolute confidence," he said. "If this gets out, the cops won't trust me again."

"I won't talk about it," Denise said.

She looked at Charles, who said, "Yeah, okay, whatever."

Michael laid the sketch on the desktop. Denise looked up at him. "You drew this? It's really powerful."

He felt his face heat up. "Thanks," he said. "Have you ever seen that symbol before?"

"No, sorry," she said. "It looks like it could be African, maybe. How about you, Charles? It looks like it's ringing a few bells for you."

Charles did look nervous. "No, I ... at first, I thought it was something else."

"What did you think it was?" Michael asked.

"I don't know, a gang thing, maybe. There was a lot of gang stuff going on when I was in high school."

"You were in a gang?" Michael said.

"No, no, I ... my sister dated a guy in the Bloods for a while, they would be around the house. They used to give me a hard time."

Denise came to his rescue. "You might take this to Dr. Donald Harriman at UNC. He teaches a course on African Myth and Religion. He's helped us here from time to time."

Michael was still watching Charles. Charles's face lit with a flash of the same buried rage Michael had seen the day before. "You don't like that idea?" Michael asked him.

"Dr. Harriman is a busy man," Charles said. "He doesn't have time for wild goose chases. I'm sure the police have their own sources for this kind of thing."

"You're probably right," Michael said. "I should go." He reached for the sketchbook, but Denise stopped his hand.

"Hang on. Charles, will you give us a second?"

Charles walked out. Denise suddenly seemed to realize where her hand was and took it away. "Can I look?" she said, pointing at the sketchbook. Before he could stop her, she had flipped to the drawing of her own face, the sketchbook still lying on the desk between them. Michael felt himself blush again.

"You didn't happen to call my cell phone last night, did you?" she asked. "I heard it ring around nine, but there was no message."

"Yes."

"I've got a teenage son. His father is still ... a part of things. That's what I meant by complicated. We don't live together, but sometimes we do things together, for Rachid's sake. Last night he was over for dinner."

"Are you divorced?"

"Legally separated. We never went through the divorce. It's been ten years."

"Wow."

"His father has lived with other women. I've had some relationships, nothing very serious. They tended to happen when Rachid was with his father or at school or at camp or something."

"How old is Rachid?"

"He'll be sixteen in December."

"Isn't it about time you had a life of your own?"

"People always tell me that. I have a life. I have my work, I read a lot of history, I go to art museums. Having a life doesn't mean I have to have a man in it."

Though gentle, the rebuke was clear. "It's none of my business," Michael said, hoping she might contradict him.

Instead she looked down at the drawing. "Do you really think I look like that?"

"Like what?"

"Beautiful," she said, and looked up at him.

They were standing on opposite sides of the desk. She was leaning forward, and Michael saw that if he leaned forward also it would be possible to kiss her. "Yes," he said. The notion, crazy as it was, lodged in his brain. He caught himself looking at her full lips.

She turned away. "I don't know what's eating Charles," she said. "He's hinted at this troubled youth business before, not that I see why that matters. You put two people through the same set of circumstances and one is going to be fine and the other is going to be angry all the time. I love to travel because I spent my whole life in one apartment in Queens, whereas Rachid's father hates to travel because he never traveled as a kid. Am I talking too much?"

"You already know I'm no good at this," Michael said. "Do you want to have dinner with me or not?"

"Yes," she said, and that seemed, finally, to calm her. She sat down and said, "I worry that you'll get frustrated with me. Trying to deal with my schedule."

"What's your next opening?"

"Saturday night. Is that possible?"

"It's fine."

"Call me tomorrow and we'll figure out the details. All right?"

"All right," he said, and gathered up his sketchbook.

"You're a wonderful artist," she said. "Is that what you do for a living?"

"Would it freak you out if I told you I draw comics?"

"No. And Rachid would probably go out of his mind."

"I'd like to meet him."

"Maybe. For now, you need to take it very easy, Michael. Any minute I might come to my senses and start asking what the hell I'm doing."

"Okay," Michael said. "I wouldn't want that to happen."

"Did you want Dr. Harriman's number?"

"Yes, please."

When she gave it to him their hands did a brief pas de deux—him accepting the paper, transferring it to his left hand, then taking hers again for a quick squeeze. "Thanks," he said.

"Talk to you soon."

Not even the sullen look on Charles's face could shake Michael's good mood as he all but danced out the door.

•

AT THE HOTEL OFFICE, he copied the symbol onto a blank sheet of paper, scrawled some question marks underneath, signed it, and fed it into the office's fax machine. He dialed Roger's fax number from memory.

Roger called half an hour later.

"It's called the Four Moments of the Sun," Roger said. "Technically it's a cosmogram, a picture of the way the universe works. The horizontal line divides the land of the living, above, from the land of the dead. The vertical line shows the link between the living and the dead. The four smaller circles represent the position of the sun at dawn, noon, sunset, and midnight. You'll note that at midnight, the sun is in the underworld. It's about the cycle of life, y'see—as the sun moves freely from the land of the living to the land of the dead, so our spirits die and are then reborn."

"Where's it come from?"

"It's from the Kongo culture, that's Kongo with a 'K,' from West Africa. You'll find variants in Cuba and Brazil. And in Haiti."

"Haiti."

"Sure. Those *vévés* that you did in number 17, a lot of them were descendents of cosmograms like this one. The ones based on cross shapes belong to Legba, god of the crossroads, where the world meets the realm of the *lwa*. Same deal, basically. So where did you find this?"

Michael found himself suddenly reluctant to get Roger fully engaged. "It's connected with this Hayti business, you know, that neighborhood my father knocked down."

"Connected how?"

"It was at the Hayti Heritage Center." That was more or less true. "It gave me a spooky feeling."

"Is there something you're not telling me?"

"I don't know, Roger. I'm trying to work on *Luna* and figure out my own history and deal with my father dying and I'm not even sure what's happening here myself."

"All right, then. Keep in mind that I can fly out there. You only have to say the word."

"Not necessary. I promise I'll let you know if that changes."

"All right. You did say you were working?"

He reassured Roger and then called Bishop. He heard the keyboard rattle in the background as Bishop took notes. At the end Michael said, "I didn't tell him what it was about."

"That's good, Michael. You've been a big help."

Michael had hoped for more. "Any time," he said.

He was too restless to work and haunted by the symbol on the dead man's wrist. Rather than risk a brushoff over the phone, he decided to confront Harriman in person. He used the Web on the slow dial-up connection in his room to locate Harriman in the African and Afro-American Studies Department at UNC, then called the department and got his office hours. By the time Michael ate lunch and drove to Chapel Hill, Harriman would be in.

HARRIMAN'S OFFICE WAS in the Battle Building, facing the Franklin Street campus drag. Michael parked in a lot behind the retail strip. There seemed to be an excess of beautiful girls crowding the sidewalks, full of laughter and dramatic gestures. Some had broken out their fall clothes, and he loved the way the ribbed sweaters clung to their bodies, the exaggerated topographical relief of the widening and converging lines.

He took the stairs to the second floor and found Harriman's office easily enough. The door was open an inch or so, and he heard voices inside. He took out his sketchbook and sat on the floor in the hallway, working up some minor background characters for the *Luna* script.

Fifteen minutes later a kid with a backpack came out, and Michael got up and stuck his head in the door. "Dr. Harriman?"

Harriman was what Roger would call portly, not fat so much as big all over. He looked to be in his fifties, with short, receding wiry hair, aviator-style bifocals, and a massive jaw. His skin was medium brown and his suit had an understated elegance that said money to Michael. His look was not friendly.

"I'm sorry," Harriman said, "did you have an appointment?"

"No, sir," Michael said. "I'm not a student."

"Does that absolve you from the basic social niceties?"

"No, sir. I have a very quick question and I wondered if I might—"

"Impose? Take advantage? Intrude?"

"Something like that, yes, sir."

"All right. I suppose we should reward your honesty, if not your methods. Come in."

The office was dimly lit. Harriman had softened the academic sterility with an antique-looking rug over the industrial carpeting, a standing lamp, and three well-ordered oak bookcases. Red lights glowed on a rack-mounted stereo in the far corner.

A whiteboard to Michael's left, between the door and Harriman's desk, was clean enough to glisten. "May I?" Michael asked.

Harriman nodded, and Michael used a red marker to draw the symbol from the tattoo. "Have you ever seen this before?" he asked.

"Possibly." His expression was difficult to read. "Where did you find this?"

Michael had an answer ready. "I'm an artist, and I wanted to use it in one of my drawings. I remember seeing it in something I read, but now I can't remember where."

"What kind of artist?"

If you ever have to lie, Michael's mother had told him, make it as small as possible and surround it with the truth. "I draw comics."

"What, like Superman?"

"I did a Batman graphic novel, called *Sand Castles*."

"You're Michael Cooper?"

Michael nodded, startled.

"Indeed," Harriman said. "I enjoy Roger Fornbee's work. I thought *Sand Castles* had elements of a genuine postcolonial cultural critique."

"I'm sure it did. Roger reads a lot."

"And you were thinking of using this symbol in what way?"

"I was looking for something kind of mysterious and exotic that somebody might use, I don't know, on a piece of jewelry. Or a tattoo, maybe." Again, no discernible reaction. "I didn't want to use it if it had a meaning that was inappropriate, or offensive. The way a swastika would be, you know?"

"Why didn't you ask your associate, Mr. Fornbee?"

"It's for somebody else. He's a bit jealous when I have work overdue for him and I take on a side project."

"And how did you come by my name?"

"Denise Franklin at the Hayti Heritage Center mentioned you."

"Ah. The redoubtable Ms. Franklin. So you want to understand the semiotics of this symbol."

"I don't know. Is that what I want?"

"Semiotics studies the relationship between a sign and what it conveys. Let me see if I can find this one."

Harriman rolled his chair backward and plucked a book from one of the shelves. Then he rolled forward, set the spine of the book on the desk, and opened it a third of the way in. He turned the pages as if he had white gloves on and the book was a crumbling antique, which it clearly was not.

"Ah," he said. He handed the open book to Michael. "Does that look like what you remember?"

It was almost the same drawing, except that the central circle was flattened into an oval along the horizon line, and counterclockwise arrows pointed from one solar disk to the next. The caption read, "*Yowa*: the Kongo sign of cosmos and the continuity of human life." Holding his place with one finger, Michael checked the title: *Flash of the Spirit* by Robert Farris Thompson.

He handed Harriman the book. "That looks like it. Maybe I saw it in this book. I do a lot of research—it's hard to keep track."

"A luxury those of us in the academy don't have. We must keep track of everything." He glanced again at the text. "Yes, I remember now. This is a very fundamental symbol. It shows up throughout the Diaspora."

"Diaspora?"

"A polite word for the spread of African peoples across the Atlantic. On slave ships."

It was all Michael could do not to look away from Harriman's stare. "So," Michael said. "If I had this symbol on, say, a T-shirt, what would it say about me?"

"It might say any number of things. The cross at the center is not Christian; it signifies the intersection of the earthly and divine realms. Like the crossroads where the Devil tuned Robert Johnson's guitar. It's a profoundly dangerous place." Michael got the stare again, and then, finally, Harriman looked down at the book. "It's known as the Sign of the Four Moments of the Sun. According to Thompson, God is above, the dead below, water in between." Harriman closed the book. "It could be as simple as saying that the wearer is knowledgeable about life and death and the order of things in the universe. Does that help?"

It was an invitation to go, and Michael was happy to take it. Things were starting to feel like he was out in the ocean and the bottom was not where he'd thought it was. He stood up. "Yes, actually, yes, it helps a lot. Thanks."

Harriman offered his hand and Michael took it. The gesture was slow, nearly ominous.

As he turned to go, Harriman said, "A word of caution."

"Yes?"

"Symbols are powerful things. You might be better off making something up."

"Is that more semiotics?"

"Call it common sense."

IT WAS A RELIEF to be outside in the cool air. Nice that Harriman knew *Sand Castles,* but otherwise Michael hadn't learned much. It left him restless, needing more.

He drove north out of Chapel Hill and through the booming, gentrified southwest corner of Durham, past Duke and the VA hospital and east into downtown. He parked behind the seventies-style precast building that housed the main library, with its thrusting columns and architectural optimism.

A thin, older woman with a wild thatch of white hair showed him to the index for the *Durham Herald-Sun* and gave him quick instructions on using the microfilm reader. It took only a minute to find what he wanted in the index and locate the reel of film in a gray file drawer. The story was on the front page of the local news section for Thursday, September 5, 1974. Mitchell Edward Antree of Durham, 49, was pronounced dead early the previous morning at the site of a one-car accident near downtown.

Michael printed out the story, including the jump page, and took it over to a table to read the whole thing.

There was a photo, from the mid-sixties, to judge by the clothes. Antree was handsome, with short black hair, black framed glasses, and a boyish smile. His shirt was a dark solid color, and his narrow tie seemed to sparkle.

It was ironic, the story noted, that Antree died on the East-West Freeway when his One Tree Construction firm had been one of the major contractors involved in that stretch of the road. The East-West Freeway, Michael remembered, was the original name for the Durham Freeway. Even the state highway number, 147, had come later.

"Antree apparently lost control of his car," the article said, "and crashed into the concrete columns supporting the Fayetteville Street overpass."

Michael felt dizzy. He read the line again and then looked up, suddenly convinced he was being watched. Nothing had changed. Two children chased each other through the nonfiction stacks. An overweight high school girl in the chair across from him chewed on one fingernail as she read an encyclopedia.

"The accident took place Wednesday between 2 AM and 3 AM, according to Durham Police. Investigators speculate that Antree might have fallen asleep at the wheel, as there were no indications of skidding or an attempt to apply the brakes. The car, a late model Corvette, was traveling well in excess of the speed limit, police say.

"The car's fiberglass body 'basically disintegrated' on impact, said a department spokesman. 'Nobody walks away from a crash like that.'"

Michael didn't think Antree had fallen asleep. Not on the anniversary of putting Barrett Howard into that very overpass.

There was one final revelation. Antree, whom Michael had always pictured as a clichéd sixties swinging bachelor, had left behind a widow named Frances.

Michael went to the index and found a single entry for Frances, on the line before the ones for Mitch. It turned out to be the wedding page for Sunday, July 27, 1980. The former Frances Antree had married career Army officer Major Richard Stanley and moved to Fayetteville, North Carolina, home of Fort Bragg.

The library's Fayetteville phone book had no listing for Frances Stanley. On impulse, he checked the Durham directory and there she was, on Emerald Pond Lane. Emerald Pond was a retirement complex that his parents had looked at when they still had some hope of his father's recovery.

Michael's hands trembled as he walked out the front of the building, dialing the number as he went. A woman answered on the second ring.

"Mrs. Stanley?"

"Who's calling, please?"

"My name is Michael Cooper. My father, Robert Cooper, used to work with Mitch Antree."

"Oh dear."

"*Is* this Mrs. Stanley?"

"Yes, it is. I didn't mean to be rude, dear, it's just that you gave me a bit of a shock. The past never quite stays put away, does it?"

"I'm in Durham, Mrs. Stanley, and I'd like to come talk to you."

"This is a very busy day for me, believe it or not. We've got a book club this afternoon and two birthdays tonight."

"I understand. Would you be available tomorrow?"

"Well, yes, I suppose so. Can you tell me what this is about?"

"I promise to let you know as soon as I figure it out myself. Is ten in the morning all right?"

Friday, October 22

EMERALD POND WAS ONLY a few years old, and the landscaping around the small artificial lake meant to be its namesake had yet to finish growing in. The entrance road wound past a series of duplex cottages before arriving at the massive main building. Michael parked in the visitors' lot and went in the front double doors.

To his right was a crafts room and a large dining area that looked out on the pond. There were offices and a hallway to the left. All the residents Michael saw were white and upper middle class, the men mostly in short-sleeved dress shirts and slacks, the women in jogging suits, frequently with embroidery or appliqué.

He took the elevator to the third floor and found Frances Stanley's apartment easily. In addition to a nameplate, her door had red tissue chrysanthemums and an origami crane. Michael looked around and saw decorations on most of the other doors as well: flags, bells, ribbons, plastic or ceramic animals. They weren't just relieving the monotony, he realized, but providing a series of intricate landmarks to help jog failing memories.

Frances Stanley was out of breath when she let Michael in. "Time got away from me," she said. "I meant to get the place straightened up before you came." She was about five-six, thin in the face and arms, with a small paunch. She'd dyed her hair an unnatural shade of orange and had on quite a bit of makeup; still Michael found it easy to conjure a 40-year-younger image of her, freckled and somewhat delicate, with a sparkle in her eyes.

The apartment was scrupulously clean, and a small canister vacuum cleaner stood on end in the doorway to the kitchen. "I'll just put that away," she said.

The Japanese theme that started on the door continued with a glass-framed red and gold kimono that took up most of one wall, and a black enameled folding screen inlaid with an elaborate maple dragon. Soapstone figurines sat on the low tables at either end of her black futon. If there was a TV, it was shut up in one of the low wooden cabinets. The overall effect was spaciousness, peace, and elegance.

Mrs. Stanley reappeared in the kitchen doorway. "Would you like some tea? I have a weakness for hot tea in warm weather."

"No, thank you," Michael said. "You go ahead, though."

She pointed him to the futon and settled herself in a chair with wooden arms and black fabric cushions, holding a white porcelain cup with no handle. "How is your father?" she asked.

Michael told her about the cancer.

"I didn't know him well," she said. "I don't think I saw him in person more than half a dozen times. Please give him my best wishes."

"I'll do that," Michael said. He wasn't sure where to begin. "Your apartment is beautiful. I wish my parents had your taste."

"My second husband and I spent many happy years in Okinawa. He was with the 1st Battalion, 1st Special Forces Group."

"He sounds very different from Mitch Antree."

"He was. Night and day."

Michael noted the past tense. "When did he die?"

"Two years ago. His heart simply gave out. He was a good deal older than me. So I'm twice a widow. I think it's remarkable the different lives one can lead in a single lifetime. My life with Richard was so unlike my life with Mitch, it was like I became another person. And a much happier one. Everything about Richard was there in front of you, in plain sight."

"You're saying Mitch had secrets."

She laughed with what seemed genuine amusement. "Oh my. He was like one of those unsinkable ships, where every compartment is sealed off from every other, watertight and impenetrable."

"Something finally sank him."

"Yes, I never believed the accident explanation. They told me he'd been drinking. I didn't want to accept it at first, because he'd quit. He'd been sober for two years. Everyone smiled at me in this very condescending way when I would say that. People don't change, is what they wanted me to believe. I don't think that was the case. I think he was fighting, and he was winning, and he had a setback, and it was just bad luck that killed him. I would rather believe in bad luck than believe that people can never change. Wouldn't you?"

"Yes, ma'am, I would. Did anything specific happen that you knew about? Problems with his job or anything like that?"

"Not that I know of. I didn't find a stack of unpaid bills, or a drawer full of empty bottles, or letters from one of his mistresses. Mitch had a lot of sadness in his life. I didn't see things the same way, but I know it was difficult for him."

"I'm sorry, I don't want to pry, but did you say, 'mistresses'?"

"Oh yes, dear, there were quite a few. He couldn't seem to help himself, though he was always most contrite when his indiscretions would come out. And those were different times. There was a sort of acceptance that 'men had their needs' and there was nothing to be done. I think part of it was the company he kept. He would go down to Hayti and listen to jazz and drink, and there were women there ... well, you can figure out the rest. That also changed when he quit drinking."

"Were there reasons for this 'sadness,' or was it more like a clinical depression?"

"It's hard to say, isn't it? He always had reasons, though who knows if another person would have taken it so hard. We were never able to have children, and I think that was a disappointment for him. There was his work, for another thing. He was very ambitious, and he wanted to make his mark on Durham. He had a few major projects in the middle sixties, what with the freeway and RTP, then things seemed to slip away. He wanted so much more."

"Was Hayti part of that ambition?"

"That's right. He couldn't believe the city bulldozed everything and never followed through on any of their grand plans."

"Did he ever blame anyone in particular for what happened?"

She was suddenly wary. "What do you mean?"

"I guess I'm asking whose fault it was. Was it the developers? Was it the mayor? Was it somebody else in politics?"

The last question startled her, and Michael watched her wariness turn to fear.

"Mitch is dead, Mrs. Stanley. If you're still trying to protect him, there's no need."

"I know that," she said. "I know that." She sighed. "Mitch was involved with Congressman Randy Fogg. Congressman Frog, they used to call him. Do you know who Fogg is?"

"Yes, ma'am. He's famous even in Texas." Michael was thinking of the photos on Wilmer Bynum's wall.

"Congressman Fogg was a racist. He pushed hard for government money to tear Hayti down, then when it came time for new construction, he fought it until everyone gave up."

"Was Mitch involved with him somehow?"

She sighed again. "In the late fifties, when Mitch was first starting out, he wanted his own firm more than anything. Fogg was only a sportscaster then, but he had lots of connections and access to money. He offered Mitch financing and promised him all the work he could handle—government contracts, downtown renovation, even hints about a new corporate development, which turned out to be Research Triangle Park. Mitch was elated. He knew what sort of person Fogg was, but he considered that no more than another cost of doing business. He liked to think he could deal with the devil and come out ahead. 'I'm running with the big dogs now!' is what he used to say."

"What did Fogg get in return?"

"If there was a price—beyond a share of the business, which he was legitimately entitled to—Mitch never mentioned it. Still there was a sense, ever after, that Fogg didn't just own the business, he owned Mitch as well."

"How do you mean?"

"He would ask Mitch to do things for him. Things that I think were meant to humiliate him. I remember one night I had to drive Mitch to the airport to pick up a car that Fogg had left there. Mitch drove it to Fogg's home, with me following in my car, so I could bring Mitch back with me. Mitch was fuming."

"I know this is asking you to remember a lot. Is it possible Mitch got a call from Fogg on September fourth of 1969?"

"Goodness, that was thirty-five years ago."

"It would have been after midnight, and he would have had to call a couple of other people. My father would have been one of them, and Leon and Tommy Coleman. There was a cement mixer involved."

"Oh dear. I'm afraid I do remember that truck. He got the call very late at night and he had the dickens of a time locating one. I don't remember the date, but that sounds about right. And I remember him calling your father."

"Did you answer the phone? Do you know if it was Fogg on the other end?"

She shook her head. "Mitch answered it. He kept the phone by his side of the bed. I assumed it was Fogg. Mitch had that defeated look as soon as he heard who it was."

"Do you know why he called my father?"

"I assume because the Congressman told him to. My sense of your father is that he was very much like Mitch in some ways—very idealistic, very kind. But much more innocent. If there was wrongdoing involved, I don't think your father was part of it."

"There was wrongdoing."

"I have a dreadful feeling that you know what happened that night."

"A man was murdered. I don't think Mitch or my father had anything to do with killing him, but they were involved in covering it up."

"Literally? Covering it in concrete?" Michael nodded. "Is this related to that body that's been in the news, Barrett Howard? In the embankment of the freeway?"

"Yes, ma'am."

"The same embankment where Mitch killed himself?"

"I'm afraid so."

"Oh my." Michael watched the realization sweep over her. "Oh my," she said again, and tears rose in her eyes and gently overflowed down her face.

"I'm sorry," Michael said. "I'm really, really sorry."

"Mitch knew Barrett Howard," she said, "knew him and admired him. I can't believe that he would have gone along ... Excuse me." She took a tissue from the end table and patted at her chin and cheeks. She seemed determined not to surrender her composure.

"Mitch told me once that Congressman Fogg was a member of a hate group. I often discounted Mitch's wilder stories, though I suppose there could be some truth to it. If so, they killed Mitch as surely as they killed poor Barrett." The tears welled up again.

"I hate to keep asking questions," Michael said, "but do you know the name of the hate group?"

"Yes," she said, patting again with the tissue. "They're called the Night Riders of the Confederacy. They're bigger than the Klan in this area."

"They're still around?"

"Oh yes, you still see them on the news now and again. People talk about how far we've come, but it seems to me we've been moving backwards for far too many years now. Have you talked to the police?"

"I was the one who told them about the body. I found out about it from Tommy Coleman on Monday."

"I remember Tommy. How is he?"

"Well enough, I suppose."

"You'll tell the police about Congressman Fogg?"

"As soon as I leave here."

"Thank you. I hate to be rude, but—" Another flood of tears started. "This has been a bit upsetting. Would it be possible for us to talk another time?"

Michael stood up and held her hand. "I'm sorry to be the one to have to tell you this."

"That's all right," she said. "It's always better to know the truth. I seem to have been telling myself that for most of my life."

MICHAEL CALLED BISHOP'S cell phone, and Bishop agreed to meet him at headquarters. "How's the excavation going?" Michael asked, on the way up in the elevator.

"It's going well," Bishop said. His tone and his distracted stare failed to invite further questions.

Once in Bishop's office, Michael said, "I've got a lead on Howard's killer."

"Is this related to the tattoo?"

"I know who called Antree and told him to pour the concrete."

"I'm listening."

"Congressman Randy Fogg. He was a silent partner in Antree's construction business."

"And how did you come by this information?"

"Antree's widow."

"Christ. I thought she was dead. Do you have her address?"

Michael read him the information from his sketchbook.

"And she can positively identify Fogg's voice?" Bishop asked.

"Well, no," Michael said. "But it's obvious that's who it was. There's enough evidence to bring him in."

"We'll check into it."

"The people who tried to dynamite the body. They were white, right? Fogg is involved with a racist group called the Night Riders of the Confederacy. If they killed Howard, it would make sense that they would try to destroy the evidence."

Bishop leaned back in his chair and spoke in a soft, matter-of-fact voice. "Michael. I understand your emotional involvement here. But I have to remind you that you are not a police officer. You have no training. There is every chance you could screw up our chances of getting a conviction if you keep meddling in this case. You need to back away from this and let me handle it. Do you understand what I'm telling you?"

Like a few other genuinely tough people that Michael had met over the years, Bishop had a quiet, easygoing charm because he had nothing to prove. It was not a good idea to push people like that, and Michael saw that he had gone too far.

"All right," Michael said. "I understand."

HE ATE A QUICK LUNCH while he packed up his laptop at the hotel, then set it up again at a bookstore called the Regulator, near Duke's East Campus.

They had a café downstairs with a high-speed Internet connection and Michael had a lot of studying to do.

He started with nightridersoftheconfederacy.org, an object lesson in outmoded design techniques: repeating rebel flag backgrounds that made the text hard to read, flashing text, and a marquee that scrolled horizontally across the screen.

Michael found the content oddly masochistic and self-pitying, at the same time that it hijacked the rhetoric of reason. Southern whites were persecuted by the NAACP and other "racist hate groups" who stripped them of their flags and subjected them to other "heritage violations." The NRC believed in "diversity," in preserving the "rainbow of human colors," which was being wiped out by race mixing. There was much mention of God, Jesus, Christianity, and the Church, all of whom seemed to be major supporters of White Rights. The NRC was looking for proud whites to join the group, which it insisted was a "legal and law abiding" nonprofit organization, with no room for "drug users/ dealers, perverts, or those of immoral or unstable temperament."

The site's logo included a Celtic Cross, a cross with arms of equal length extending out of a circle. Michael stared at the symbol, feeling again the chill of connection. If the cross had smaller circles at the ends of its arms, it would be the Sign of the Four Moments of the Sun.

Links from the site pointed to the Southern Legal Resource Center (not to be confused, a note warned, with the Southern Poverty Law Center, an arm of the "Communist miscegenation conspiracy"), to the Heritage Preservation Association, and the Sons of Confederate Veterans. No links to the KKK, the Aryan Nation, or any other major hate group. Slick, Michael thought. And smart.

He moved on to Congressman Randy Fogg and pieced his story together from various sites. Fogg had been born in 1930 in Pine Level, North Carolina, a small town east of Smithfield. He graduated in 1953 from what was then still North Carolina State College in Raleigh, the alma mater of Michael's father, with a degree in Journalism. That got him a job at the *Durham Herald,* and later at the *Herald's* radio affiliate, WDNC, where he covered sports and did occasional pro-segregation editorials. In 1960 he moved to the more powerful WRAL in Raleigh, with its chain of stations in the so-called Tobacco News Network. From then until 1968, when he won his first election to the US Congress, Fogg did a five-minute editorial every day, railing against "the University of Negroes and Communists" in Chapel Hill, the "disgusting, filthy abominations" of homosexuals, the "socialist welfare state," and the part of "Yankee neo-carpetbaggers" in the "Communist miscegenation conspiracy."

The last quote stopped Michael cold. He double-checked it against the

NRC site, then searched the rest of the Web. Those were the only two places it occurred.

He got up and stood in front of a rack of books, not seeing anything on the shelves. It wasn't proof, he told himself. Whoever created the NRC probably admired Fogg, probably studied all his speeches. That was what Sgt. Bishop would say.

In his heart Michael knew that Fogg had written the content for the NRC. It walked the same line that Fogg himself did, trumpeting law and order at the same time that it flouted the principles of equality and tolerance behind the Constitution. And, Michael noted, both Fogg and the NRC demanded puritanical sexual conduct in spite of persistent rumors of Fogg's own adulterous, bisexual, interracial misconduct.

The rest of Fogg's career was in the public eye. He'd taken advantage of the arrival of C-SPAN in 1979 to regularly deliver long harangues to an empty House after the day's session was finished. Because the single camera remained focused on Fogg, viewers didn't know that the Representatives he was charging with Communist and homosexual sympathies weren't even present.

It was the birth of a new era of right-wing dirty politics, and the party rewarded Fogg well for it. By 1989 he was party whip and would probably have been elected Speaker of the House if he'd been willing to take the job. He claimed to prefer working behind the scenes; insiders said the party didn't want to provoke a serious investigation into Fogg's private life.

Rumors circulated every election that Fogg was planning to retire, and every two years he ran again, and won the 4th district hands down. And part of his appeal, Michael had to admit, was his refusal to be intimidated by rich corporate interests. "Nobody owns Randy Fogg," was his constant refrain. He attacked big business as viciously as he attacked big government, and he worked hard to get jobs and a better standard of living for the poor whites of North Carolina, even if poor blacks happened to benefit along the way.

The afternoon was gone. Michael bought the two books the store had on Hayti, one a collection of black and white photos and the other an informal history by Dorothy Jones, Denise's predecessor. The pictures gave him a feeling he found hard to explain, a painful nostalgia for a time and place he'd never known.

HE RAN, SHOWERED, ATE, and called Denise. There was a lot of noise in the background: whistles, squeaking, yelling, as she waited for Rachid's basketball practice to finish. She didn't know how long she'd have; she went outside so she could talk to him in peace.

Rachid was still not done by the time they'd made their arrangements, so they kept talking. Denise was hyper from work and the night of chauffeuring Rachid that lay ahead of her. It made her easy to talk to. She was like a standup comic, impersonating Rachid's friends, riffing on the upcoming election, making fun of her own ineptitude at household tasks. Michael sensed she was trying to charm him, and that only made her all the more successful.

He was a bit hyper himself after they finally hung up. He channeled the energy into work, finishing five pages that had been in various stages of completion. In the middle of it, Helen Silberman called to see how it was going.

He never knew how to respond to her. She was younger than Michael but seemed much older—MFA in Creative Writing from NYU, self-possessed, with a highly personal and expensive fashion sense that involved vintage stores, western wear, and Japanese designers. Her husband was a broker type, and they had a daughter who was less than a year old. Her hair was an unnatural shade of blonde, she was thin to the point of brittleness, and she burned cigarettes like incense, without ever seeming to inhale.

On the other hand, she had an easy laugh and had always been sweet to Michael. Even now, nagging him gently for being late, she was apologetic. Once he assured her there were pages coming, she was relieved and funny about it.

It was after 1 AM when he finished. He got a FedEx box ready and lay down with Dorothy Jones' book. Her attitude was relentlessly positive and left him feeling shortchanged. When he finally fell asleep, his dreams were filled with strange three-dimensional rotating puzzles that he twisted and turned and never quite managed to solve.

Saturday, October 23

HE DROVE TO DENISE'S apartment with half his attention. The other half mulled and anticipated and worried. He wore khakis, a carefully pressed white dress shirt, no tie, a corded silk jacket, black leather lace-up shoes.

Denise lived close to the Duke Medical Center, in an enclave of student and professional apartments. It wasn't until he got off the freeway that he realized the same headlights had been behind him since he left the hotel. At that moment the lights moved in, almost touching his rear bumper.

He was on Morreen Road, heading the opposite direction from Tommy Coleman's apartment, back toward Duke and the city. The Millennium Hotel was on his left and the road was well lighted, but he was suddenly afraid. When he eased his foot off the gas, hoping the car would pass, it slowed with him. He heard the throbbing bass of giant speakers.

He signaled and turned left onto Campus Walk, a long stretch of apartment complexes. The car followed. As it turned he saw that it was an oversized SUV, maybe a Ford Expedition. North Carolina, unlike Texas, didn't require a front license plate—not that he could have read it anyway, as close as the SUV was. He couldn't see anything beyond the glare of its headlights.

He noticed the address for Denise's complex and drove past, heart thudding. Campus Walk ended in a T intersection, and Michael turned left, remembering a strip center a few blocks away with a grocery and a video store. At least there would be witnesses there.

Suddenly, on his right, he saw the entrance to a gated community. There was no guard, but there would be a phone, he thought, and he could push buttons until somebody answered and then yell for the cops.

As soon as he pulled into the drive, the SUV hesitated, then roared away, speakers still pounding. The windows were tinted to a mirror blackness, and Michael caught himself in the automatic assumption that the occupants were black as well.

Don't do that, he told himself. Not tonight.

Lightheaded with relief and residual nerves, he looked both ways and then backed out into the street. The road behind him stayed clear. He drove straight to Denise's building and parked on the far side, where his car was invisible from the street.

Denise answered the door in black pants and a black sweater with a swirling gold design. Michael thought she looked elegant and utterly desirable.

"Whoa," she said. "What's wrong?"

"I'll tell you in a minute. Let me get my breath."

She brought him in and sat him on the couch. The overstuffed furniture and the dark orange walls made the room seem smaller than it was. There were piles of schoolbooks and papers, a pair of congas, two lovebirds in a cage, basketball trophies, pieces of a couple of different computers, a TV, a stereo, and shelf of records and CDs.

"I apologize for everything to do with this apartment in advance," she said. "I take full responsibility for everything, even though a lesser person would try to pass the blame to Rachid. Except the birds. Rachid is totally to blame for the birds." As if in response, the birds twittered briefly and hopped around the cage.

"I like birds," Michael said.

"Tell me what happened."

Michael told her, as plainly as possible.

"Why would somebody follow you?" she asked, sitting at the other end of the couch.

"I'm sure it was just some kids screwing around with me. I'm being paranoid, that's all. It's because I've been going around asking all these questions. About that tattoo. About Mitch Antree."

"Do you want a drink?"

"I don't drink, actually."

"Good, because I was bluffing. If I have anything at all, it's a bottle of Frangelico in the back of one of the cabinets that's older than Rachid. I wouldn't want to try it."

Michael's nerves had quieted. He liked the life and clutter of the room. He found he was able to very clearly picture himself kissing Denise. Before the thought could build to critical mass, Denise said, "We should get going. Who's driving?"

"I don't mind," Michael said. "It's a rental, we might as well take advantage of it." He paused. "Unless you're worried about my friends in the s u v."

"I'll risk it. My car is even more of a mess than the apartment."

On the drive to the restaurant they talked about painting. They had in common their regard for some of the artists at the Hayti Center and their contemporaries: Biggers, Gwathmey, Bearden. "I can see Klimt and some of the other Symbolists in Biggers," Denise said. Michael glanced at her; her smile bordered on a smirk. "Also Thomas Hart Benton. But the artists he reminds me of most are Leo and Diane Dillon."

"I love the Dillons," Michael said. "How the hell do you know all that? I thought you were a programmer."

"I read the Dillons' picture books to Rachid when he was little. The rest comes from being a fine arts minor."

"You didn't tell me." He looked again. She was definitely gloating. A memory popped into his head of his father, in a rare comic moment, telling a joke that he credited to Mitch Antree. The punchline, in black dialect, was, "I believe I is temporarily in love."

There seemed to be no end of racist garbage clogging his brain. And I'm supposed to be one of the good guys, Michael thought. Is there any hope at all?

"Do you paint?" Denise asked.

"Not yet," Michael said. "I mean, I have, and I do, but I feel like I'm working up to it. I'm still trying to get black and white right, still learning to draw lines."

"I want to see what you're working on now."

Michael reached into the back seat. There was a bundle of full-sized photocopies he'd made that morning before shipping the new pages off to New York. He handed it to Denise. "You can bring that in the restaurant with us if you want."

They were on a stretch of southbound freeway lit by periodic streetlights. She unfolded the bundle and Michael caught glimpses of the top page in the flashes of illumination, enough to see it as an abstract, something he'd found only partly successful techniques to do on purpose. It looked okay.

"Michael, this is beautiful. This is *art*."

"There have always been classically trained illustrators doing comics, guys like Alex Raymond, who did *Flash Gordon* in the thirties, or Hal Foster, who did *Tarzan* and *Prince Valiant*. And lots of people better than me doing it now." He stopped himself. "Um, I guess what I meant to say was, 'thank you.'"

"Stay left here, and take the exit all the way around and go north again, by where the mall used to be. So you're making a living at it?"

"Yeah, a pretty good one. More than my dad ever made."

"I don't know that many people who get real money for doing what they love."

"I'm lucky," Michael said. "I try not to lose sight of that. What about you? Do you miss programming?"

"It was a mixed blessing. When you build it and it goes out and does something useful, it's really satisfying. When it crashes and you can't figure out why, it can drive you crazy. And you always end up working too many hours."

"What about now?"

"I love the work. I'm not making enough money, is all, for somebody with a kid to put through college. From one month to the next they don't know if they're going to be able to keep me on. I'm trying to get as much oral history on tape as I can, while there's still a budget for it and these people are still around and talking. I hate having to put it on hold for all this ATC business, important as it may be."

"They must all hate my father."

"Not so much. There's plenty of blame to go around. It was the black community leaders who sold them on the whole redevelopment idea, and I think a lot of people are still angry at them. Then there's the Durham Select Committee, which was pushing for the freeway to get people to RTP easily, RTP being their big goldmine. I don't think your father's name has ever come up, though I could search the transcripts for it. Not this light, but the next one, turn right."

"Transcripts?"

"We don't have that many. It's what I do nights and weekends instead of watching TV."

"Can I look at them?"

"That's why they're there. Do you have a laptop? They're all on CD-ROM, and you can go through them in my office. Left at the next light. It's in that strip center, past the Kroger. Sitar India Palace."

The restaurant featured an upscale buffet of Southern Indian cuisine. Michael couldn't remember the last time he'd had a proper meal, and the smell of the food made him realize how hungry he was. He ended up making three trips through the line.

As they ate they made first-date conversation: tentative circling around previous relationships, lists of favorite movies and albums, rough sketches of childhood. Denise's father still ran a plumbing business in Queens and was part owner of his own apartment building as well as two others. Her mother did substitute teaching at the elementary level. Denise had been "wild" in high school and college, until a DWI in a borrowed car—trying to get an even drunker friend home—put an end to that. Within two months of her night in jail, she met her ex in her Russian literature class at Hunter College.

"Russian literature?" Michael asked.

"I took a bunch of Russian classes for a while, until I had to admit I had no aptitude. I was looking for something dependable that I could make a living at while I figured out what I wanted to do with my life. I thought there would always be a market for Russian translators. Then I discovered programming. Fortunately."

She married Joseph Brown the month they graduated, and Rachid was born a year later. She thought of herself as a romantic. Joseph was the only long-term relationship she'd ever had.

For his part Michael talked about why he was in Durham and about the dead ends he'd hit in search of his past. Then somehow he found himself telling Denise about his father's record collection.

He'd hadn't thought of it in years. His father had a shelf three feet long of jazz LPs, all in beautiful condition, with special plastic-lined inner sleeves he'd bought from a library supply company. They started with Charlie Parker and Dizzy Gillespie and went all the way up to a complete run of Coltrane's Impulse albums. In between were all the Miles Davis Columbia releases from *Miles Ahead* to *In a Silent Way;* Art Blakey with Lee Morgan and Wayne Shorter; Cannonball Adderley's quintet with brother Nat on trumpet and cornet; and on and on.

His father kept them to himself. Michael would find him sometimes late at night, listening to his old Harmon Kardon stereo with the tubes that glowed in the dark and the headphones so massive that as a child Michael couldn't bear their weight.

A handful of times, times that he remembered individually, his father had called him over and played him a solo or a song, and he'd listened dutifully, trying to understand what he was supposed to hear. Even as he was reaching out, in a way, his father seemed impossibly distant, withdrawn into a private and unassailable place.

Michael couldn't remember ever telling anyone the story before. Afterwards he felt more exposed than he wanted to. He tried to shift over into the relationship topic, where there was little to be said. After the plates were cleared away, Denise read the *Luna* pages more slowly, and he told her about Roger and the series.

They'd talked for two and a half hours, and there was only one other couple left. The waiters were lined up near the kitchen, watching them.

"So where do you see yourself in twenty years?" Denise asked. "Still doing comics?"

"I guess in twenty years I'd hope to be painting. I would love to do something like Biggers did, after he went to Africa and everything started clicking for him, the shotgun houses and the pots and the mythology. First I'd have to have something of my own to say."

"Everybody's got a story to tell."

"Maybe. I'm not even sure of that. Certainly not everybody is a storyteller. There are too many artists in my business who started writing their own stuff when they shouldn't have, because you can make a lot more money that way.

"Roger convinced me that it's not something you should dabble in. He's always talking about narrative as a double-edged sword. How it's got this kind of function that the shamans used to have in society, to explain and heal and preserve. But at the same time it also distorts and simplifies. It's always at least a little bit of a lie." He listened to his own words echoing in his head and said, "Sorry. Where are *you* going to be in twenty years?"

"I knew you were going to ask me that. I don't know. There are a thousand things I want to do. Collect and edit oral histories of places like Hayti. Get a master's in history. Get an MFA in art. Travel the world. It's just that when I try and think about twenty years from now, I keep coming back to Rachid. Where is *he* going to be in twenty years? Apart from the trouble he's going to have because of being black—increased risk of violence, of drugs, of going to prison—there's the everyday stuff that all of us have to face. AIDS, global warming, fundamentalist Muslims, fundamentalist Christians. I know I sound like my parents did in the seventies, but it seems like everything is going to hell—Presidents stealing elections, Enron, plagiarism, 'reality' TV—what kind of a world have we made? How much worse is it going to get in twenty years?"

Without letting Michael respond, she stood up. "That is absolutely the only gloomy thought I am going to allow myself in this perfectly lovely evening. Now it's time to go, before the waiters mutiny."

The check was long paid. Michael held the restaurant doors for her, and as they walked to the car his arm, all on its own, went around her and he felt hers just as easily slide around his waist. As simple as that. He unlocked the passenger door and she slipped quickly inside.

They didn't talk much on the way to her apartment, and Michael liked the ease of the silence. She seemed to be the kind of person who could be comfortable and happy in the moment, a trait he envied. It had, indeed, been a perfectly lovely evening, an antidote for the last month of grim fortitude.

As soon as he parked at her complex she said, "Can you come up for a minute?"

"Sure," he said. He could feel his own heartbeat.

He followed her up the stairs. When they got inside she said, "Wait here."

He didn't have time to construct a fantasy of her reappearing in a diaphanous nightgown; she was back in seconds, carrying a hardcover of *Sand Castles*. "Rachid had this. When I asked him about it, he said it was quote awesome end quote. I have to say, I was shocked when I looked through it. He was only 13 when he bought this. Obviously I should have been monitoring his reading more closely."

"Other than being shocked, what did you think?" Her answer, he realized, was more important than he wanted it to be.

"I thought the art was beautiful. I saw N.C. Wyeth and Whistler and Sargent in it. I thought the story was smart and also very cynical. And there was too much violence for me, and it bothered me that it was so … stylized."

"I was not even 30 when I started working on it. I didn't think anything about the violence at the time. It was like a movie or something. By the time I was done, it bothered me a lot. It was one of the things we talked about for *Luna*. Not that there would be no violence at all, but that it would have consequences, that it wouldn't be pretty, that it would be clear that it caused real suffering. It was one of the few arguments I ever won with Roger. I quoted his own rap about narrative and asked him what he was explaining and preserving with it."

"I'm glad. Do you think you could sign this for Rachid anyway?"

"Sure." Michael sat down and took his time with the inscription, then drew a quick Batman next to his signature. He watched Denise's expression while she read it.

She laughed, fortunately. "This is so he can show his friends, right?"

"The stuff about us drinking beer and chasing women together in Tijuana? Yeah, that's the idea."

"Thank you. He'll love it." She found a place for the book on the cluttered coffee table. "I noticed you didn't eat any of the meat dishes tonight. Are you vegetarian?"

"Yeah. It happened toward the end of *Sand Castles,* actually. I got to where I didn't want to see any more blood."

"Does it bother you that I still eat meat? I mean—" Though her posture didn't change as she stood by the table, he suddenly felt her nervousness. "It wouldn't put you off, or anything. The smell of it, or ... the taste?"

Michael could take a hint. He walked over to her. She watched him do it, and didn't look away as he stepped in and kissed her. He was very gentle about it. Her lips were cool and soft. She reached up as he did it and rested the fingers of her right hand on his cheek. He put both hands around her waist and drew her in until he could feel the full length of her body.

When he broke the kiss, she turned her head into his shoulder and said, "Michael."

"I'm sorry," he said. "I—"

"It's not like that. I just have to take this slow. Really, really slow."

"Okay," he said.

"Okay." She took his face in both hands and pulled him down for another kiss. There was desire there, but not the mounting passion that would have invited more.

It finished and, still holding his face, she whispered, "You should go."

"Okay." He started toward the door. "Can I come by on Monday and look at those interviews?"

"Yes." As he put his hand on the knob, she took three long steps and kissed him again, a big sloppy one. "Yes. Go. I'll see you Monday."

He could see her still standing in the doorway as he pulled into the street.

Sunday, October 24

MICHAEL WAS CARRYING a load of groceries up the stairs to his hotel room when his cell phone buzzed.

"He's dying," Ruth said.

"What is it?" Michael asked. "What's going on?"

"I can see it in his eyes. He's not fighting anymore."

"Maybe he just had a bad night."

"It's in his breathing, too," she said. "It's slowing down. I'm losing him."

"Have you talked to the doctor?"

"It's the weekend," his mother said. The weekend meant the Pakistani resident, whose accent she claimed to be unable to understand.

"Is he awake now?"

"Yes."

"Let me talk to him."

"This is your fault, you know. Bringing those police around."

"Just let me talk to him, okay?"

His father got on the phone. "Don't pay any attention to her," he said. "She always has to make a federal case out of everything."

His voice was weak, and Michael couldn't help but wonder if bringing in Sgt. Bishop had in fact hastened the end. "I'll be there as soon as I can."

"There's no point. I'm all right."

Michael wished that for once his father would ask him for something, if only for his company. Especially for his company. "I'm coming anyway," Michael said.

"Suit yourself. Did you want to talk to your mother again?"

"No," Michael said. "No, that's okay."

He spent an hour sitting in the hospital room in silence and saw that his father had been right. There was no point. His mother worked on a crossword, and his father flipped through the channels on the TV, dozing off for minutes at a time.

He talked to the charge nurse, who told him only that his father was stable and that he should talk to the doctor in the morning.

There was nothing more to do, no conversation to be had. He said goodbye to his mother, who gave him a resigned and disappointed look, and returned to his hotel.

He didn't know whether Denise's "talk to you Monday" meant not to call before then. He decided to take a chance and ended up with her voice mail. He hadn't prepared anything to say. "It's Michael," he said. "I was ... just thinking about you." Once he hung up he wondered if it was too much.

She had warned him about her schedule. Still he kept looking at the clock, coming up with reasons why she was just about to call.

Monday, October 25

As part of his expectation management, he made himself take the 15-minute drive to the impound lot in Raleigh on Monday morning. The metal door of the shed where Bishop had been working was closed and pad-locked, and the guard at the gate had no information. Michael felt Bishop had brushed him off, that the investigation was moving along without him.

He got back on the road to Durham. His emotions, he noticed, were running a bit high. It was one of the reasons he'd tended to fall into affairs at conventions, relationships that could be picked up or set aside as convenient. He was no good at the dance of exposure and withdrawal that dating required. He couldn't imagine any sane person enjoying it.

And yet, as he climbed the steps of the Hayti Heritage Center, he felt light-headed with anticipation.

Charles let him go downstairs unescorted. Denise smiled when he knocked on the frame of her open door, but she didn't get up, and her body language made it clear that she was on the job. "Rachid went totally nuts when he saw what you wrote. He took it to school today."

"That's great. When do I get to meet him?"

"That's going to require serious diplomacy. I have to be careful about freaking him out."

Michael was pleased that she believed there was something to freak out over.

Denise nodded to his shoulder bag. "If that's your computer, you can set it up here." She pointed to a newly bare corner of her desk. "See, I made room for you. You should be flattered."

She handed him a single slimline CD case. The words HAYTI ORAL HISTORY #1 were neatly lettered in Sharpie on the surface of the disc.

They talked as Michael unpacked his laptop. She didn't mention his phone call on Sunday, so he didn't either. He loaded the CD and found 14 MS Word documents with titles like "Ezra_Dawkins_b1948_ 20040317.doc."

He searched all the documents in the folder for the word "Cooper" and got no hits. For "Robert" the only matches were people other than his father, though Michael found himself getting caught up in some of the story fragments that he read in the process. Like Liza Mae Davis, born in 1931, interviewed in June:

"First thing I done when I got my own house—it was unheard of in those days for a woman that never had no husband or no children to own her own house all to herself—the very first thing I done was plant me a magnolia tree in the front yard, because I love me the sweet smell of magnolia blossoms in the summertime.

"I hadn't been there a year when the man from the city come around and says I got to sell up. Says the law give them the right to pay me a 'fair market value' for my house, which happened to be less than I paid for it. So I end up owing money on a house I don't even own no more. But what made me mad, I asked that man what about my magnolia tree? And he said I could go on and dig it up and move it with me to where my brother lived in Henderson, which is where I had to move because I couldn't find no place to live in Durham at that time. But I come home from my last trip taking my furniture out there, and they already got that bulldozer up in my yard, already got that tree busted up and buried under a pile of dirt with the pieces of the sidewalk.

"Now why would somebody want to do a thing like that for? The man in that bulldozer, he knew what that tree meant to me because I told him before I left that last time, I said, 'You be careful of that tree, I be coming back for it.' That tree never did no harm. It was just a baby. Had its whole future ahead of it, and they went and smashed it up like so much garbage."

Michael kept looking. He came up blank for "Antree" as well. It was Barrett Howard's name that finally struck pay dirt.

"There are some things I don't miss," a woman named Camilla Prentiss said. "I don't miss living across the street from that Barrett Howard's girlfriend. Always putting on airs with her French sounding name when she wasn't nothing more than a tramp. If it wasn't that troublemaker Howard over there, it was that white man, and if it wasn't that white man, it was some of her tramp friends. Never gave me a minute's peace."

He scanned the rest of the interview. It was short and seemed typical, except that Mrs. Prentiss thought she'd gotten a good deal on the sale. She was one of the lucky few; with her income and her husband's, she'd been able to rent an apartment further down Fayetteville Street.

Michael highlighted the paragraph about Howard and called Denise over to look at it. He was intensely aware of the warmth of her body as she stood behind him, and felt a jolt of pleasure when she rested one hand on his shoulder with easy intimacy.

"I remember her," Denise said. "She's only 61. She's living with her kids in a subdivision in Southwest Durham. Her son's at Duke Medical Center, doing well for himself. She's got an apartment over his garage. She's got a stake driven very deeply into the high moral ground."

"Do you think she'd talk to me?"

"Probably. You want me to call her?"

"Would you? I'm thinking the white man she's talking about might be Mitch Antree."

MRS. PRENTISS WAS AT her clerical job at Durham Regional Hospital. She had a lunch break at 11:30, she told Denise, and they were welcome to join her.

Her office was one of several that encircled a waiting area. Radiology outpatients would come in, give her their insurance information, and she would route them to the proper destination. She was five-ten, solidly built, with short hennaed hair in a kind of pageboy cut. She had a strong nose and crinkled eyes, and she was one of the privileged few hospital employees who got to wear a business suit instead of scrubs.

When she shook Michael's hand, she looked at him oddly, he thought. She seemed to shrug it off and said, "Let's eat. I'm starving."

They got cafeteria salads and settled at a table near a window that gave onto the lawns at the back of the hospital. "I can see," Prentiss said, "you're a polite young man that knows how to be kind to old ladies. Go ahead and ask your questions. You don't have to butter me up with chitchat."

She had a remarkable face, Michael thought. He doubted many had thought her beautiful, but her eyes flashed with sass and her mouth fought off one smile after another.

"I'm mostly interested in Barrett Howard," Michael said. "In your oral history you mentioned a girlfriend?"

"Lord, yes. Miss Mercy Richárd." She pronounced the last name ree-SHARD. "Short for Mercedes, though she was more of a Dodge Dart if you ask me. That was a car anybody could drive. At that time I was living on East Beamon Street, Hayti, North Carolina. I was number 108, she was 109.

"That woman had so many contradictions it was impossible to know what to think. She was what they used to call a high yellow gal, skin light enough that she could have passed if she wanted to. Long wavy black hair. Looked like one of those Italian actresses, Sophia Lollapalooza or whatever. Some said she had a double life, that she was passing in her day job. Some said she was white, passing for black, though why in the world anyone would want to do that is beyond me. Here she is going around with Barrett Howard, who was black as the ace of spades and shouting from the housetops about black power, and at the self-same time she's messing around with a white man."

Michael had brought the printout of the Antree obituary. "Is this the white man she was messing with?"

"No. I might have seen this man around at one time or another. She did have some wild parties there. But that's not the white man that was more or less living there with her."

"Can you describe him?"

"I don't have to describe him. Go look in the mirror, you'll see him."

MICHAEL TRIED IN VAIN to press her for details. Over the next 15 minutes his own emotions began to boil until they felt like a slow, muted screaming inside his skull, until he could barely hear what she was saying.

She had moved out in the summer of 1968, she said, long before the neighborhood went under the bulldozers. The first time she had seen Michael's father at Mercy's house would have been the summer before. She had no idea what had become of Mercy or where she had gone. She had never seen Michael's father again either. "He was your father, wasn't he?" she asked, and Michael numbly nodded. As for Barrett Howard, she had understood that he had sold out to the white man and gone to Mexico until she had seen his name in the paper on Tuesday.

MICHAEL DROVE DENISE back to her office with white knuckles and a blank stare.

"Michael?" Denise said. "Michael, please say something."

"I don't know where to start."

"You think this Mercedes woman could be your mother, don't you?"

"And my father could have killed Barrett Howard over her. It's the missing motive."

"What are you going to do?"

"I'm going to make him talk to me. I don't know how, but he's going to talk."

"Do you want me to come with you?"

He saw nothing in her face beyond concern for him. "That's sweet," he said, "but this is going to get pretty ugly."

"Honey, I'm from Queens. You don't know from ugly."

He reached over to squeeze her hand. "Thanks. I'll call you tonight and tell you what happened. If you're available."

"Call after ten. I'll be waiting."

He'd brought his computer when they went to lunch, not wanting Charles to get up to mischief, so he had no excuse to go inside. He parked long enough for Denise to get out, walk around to his side of the car, and put her hand on his cheek. "Good luck," she said.

"Luck hasn't been getting it," he said. "I want some answers."

HE SPENT HALF AN HOUR on the Internet at the Regulator, then made a call from his cell phone. Based on that information, he got the supplies he needed at a drugstore across the street. Then he drove to the VA.

His parents were just back from walking Robert up and down the halls. Ruth was tidying up the plastic containers from lunch, and Robert was in the bathroom. Ruth saw the determination in Michael's face and reflected it back to him as fear. "What?" she said. "What is it?"

"I'll tell you when he comes out," he said.

"Your father just had his exercise. He needs to get to bed and rest."

"This won't take a minute."

She walked warily over to her armchair and sat down. The toilet flushed, water ran, and Robert came out of the bathroom. Looking at him, Michael thought: *Not long now.*

"Hello, son," Robert said.

Michael nodded. Robert made his painful way to the bed and got in.

"I should have done this a week ago," Michael said. "As soon as all these questions started coming up." He reached into the Kerr Drugs bag and took out a package of sterile cotton swabs, the hospital kind, with the long wooden handles. "Two sticks each. Swab the inside of your cheek and give them back." He held out two swabs to Robert, who shrugged and took them. He offered two more to Ruth. His hand, he saw, was trembling visibly.

"No," Ruth said.

"I FedEx them to a DNA lab tomorrow. Pay a premium for overnight service and get the results Wednesday. Guaranteed 99.999 percent accurate for inclusions." He looked at Ruth. "Guaranteed 100 percent accurate for exclusions."

Ruth began to cry. "How did this happen? How did all this happen?" She blew her nose into a tissue.

Robert did one swab, then the other, and handed them to Michael. "Go ahead, test them. Your mother isn't going to cooperate, but this will tell you I'm your father. As should be obvious."

Michael put the swabs into a clean plastic bag and sealed it. He took a second bag, turned it inside out, and grabbed the used tissue from Ruth's lap with it.

"She's not my mother," Michael said. "They can prove it with this. Or with hair from her hairbrush back at the room. Or even from her toothbrush. It's over. No more lies."

His father's bravado collapsed. Michael realized then that he'd been waiting all his life to see it. The coldness, the distance, the unreasoning anger were gone, and there was only a wounded and dying animal underneath. Michael felt the dizzying exaltation of total victory even as he recoiled in shame from the violence of it.

"Talk to me," Michael said. "Please. I need you to talk to me."

"Ruth," Robert said, "go to the hotel. I'll call you later."

ROBERT HAD TO TELL HER a second time, with a forcefulness Michael had rarely seen. She left in tears. Michael closed the door, drew the curtain between Robert and his roommate, turned off the TV and dragged the chair over next to the bed.

And so, finally, they began to talk. With interruptions for meds and dinner, they talked late into the night. They talked through the next day and the day after that, with Ruth exiled to the lounge down the hall. Michael asked questions, and showed his father photos from the books, and prompted him with the few facts he had. He made inferences about the things his father would never be able to put into words.

And slowly, gradually, Michael began to see it in his own head: Hayti as it had been, Hayti as his father first saw it, Hayti in its raucous, swaggering prime.

ROBERT

1962-1970

ROBERT'S PARENTS had taken him to Durham as a boy, and in his memory the Hayti neighborhood was as mysterious and frightening as the Caribbean island it was named for.

This would have been in the years just after World War II. During the war, a riot in Hayti had injured four people, damaged thousands of dollars' worth of property, and required tear gas and machine guns to put down. Robert's father had seen it as a sign of the Last Days.

Robert remembered the tobacco warehouses that dominated the center of Durham, and the singing that came from the basement of the American Tobacco Company plant, where black men cut the stems from the tobacco leaves in murderous heat for inadequate pay. He remembered his parents rolling up their windows, and ordering him to do the same, before they drove through Hayti. Robert had stared out at the sea of dark faces, wondering if they meant him harm, and why.

At that time the Cooper family lived at the far western edge of North Carolina, in Asheville, where Commodore Vanderbilt's grandson George had built his dream house, a 250-room mansion on 125,000 acres of rolling, forested land. Robert's paternal grandparents were among the original servants at Biltmore House at the turn of the 20th century. Robert's father became a groundskeeper after the estate opened to the public in 1930. Robert had grown up in the shadow of vast wealth, though his family was poor. That proximity had given his father a belief in a social order that was already dead on its feet, and left Robert conflicted and eager to escape.

Robert was drafted after high school, in the summer of 1956. He hadn't bothered to apply to college, knowing there was no money for it, and was a few weeks into a construction job when the letter came. He served two years in Germany and then went to North Carolina State on the GI Bill to study Civil Engineering. The US was sprouting homes and skyscrapers and high-ways, and Robert wanted to be in the thick of it.

As a teenager he had looked at the towering façade of the Biltmore House and thought that there were things that man could make, and things only God could make, and that only God knew which was which. The Egyptians had used lime and gypsum to hold the pyramids together, and the Romans had built their aqueducts using slaked lime and volcanic ash, but for Robert's money it was the invention of Portland cement in the early 19th century that had truly given man the godlike power to create stone. Concrete was infinitely malleable when wet, and changeless once it dried. Depending on the mixture, it could be light enough to float in water or heavy enough to hold back the Colorado River. It held Biltmore House together and paved the roads that led out of Asheville.

Concrete was the answer to most of the questions that Robert asked himself.

In April of 1962, toward the end of his senior year at State, Robert answered an ad in the Raleigh *News and Observer* and landed an entry-level job at Mason and Antree in Durham. It was an important firm, with architects and engineers downtown, and an affiliated company that had a construction, paving, and precast operation east of the city limits.

Until that time he'd set his sights on the North Carolina Department of Transportation, where the state's highways were conceived, drawn up, and let out to contractors. But the Mason and Antree ad had specifically sought a highway engineer, and the salary was substantially higher than the state offered. So was the excitement level.

Durham was no longer the grimy boomtown he'd glimpsed in the forties. The tobacco companies had moved their headquarters to New York and many of the factories had gone to Richmond and points north. The textile mills had closed or flown overseas.

Now the city was picking itself up by the scruff of the neck and shaking itself awake. The hospital at Duke University had become world famous for its doctors and for its ability to secure grants. And people were talking about a revolutionary industrial development to be called Research Triangle Park. Believers said it would transform the region by bringing in the new computer and technology companies. If it happened, the Park would need roads and offices and factories as fast as people could design them and pour the concrete.

Robert's fiancée began to talk about a June wedding as if he had already agreed to it. It was typical of their courtship. He had met Ruth Bynum at a dance at Meredith College, down the street from State in Raleigh. She was from rural Johnston County, with an accent that put him off a little, but she was a looker, no question. A lush figure set off by a narrow waist, honey-brown hair that turned up at the shoulders, wide green eyes. If her lips were a bit thin, it didn't stop her from pouting and flirting with the best of them. And dancing. She could waltz, jitterbug, and foxtrot, and the memory of their slow dances made Robert sweat.

Robert had learned to dance at Biltmore parties, and she liked his lead. If she'd been more interested in him, or less, he would have felt only a passing attraction. As it was, she frustrated and befuddled him into something he confused with love.

In March she had taken him to meet her parents. Robert found Wilmer, her father, to be a strange mixture of ignorance and privilege. He lived, in his own small way, like the Vanderbilts. Though he did no work himself, the locals looked up to him as if he were a feudal lord. He rarely left the house, summoning the people and things he wanted to see. At the same time, his accent was so thick that Robert often had to mentally replay the man's sentences to make sense of them, and his paternalistic and condescending attitude toward Negroes made Robert deeply uncomfortable.

As for Ruth's mother, she seemed austere and not unkind, a hard woman honed thin by the years. Unlike other rich white families Robert had known, the Bynums had no servants, no cook, no maid. Ruth's mother prepared all the meals, and Ruth herself did the washing up. Ruth's mother seemed to like Robert well enough, and more than once he felt she'd wanted to tell him something, perhaps warn him away. It was not anything he was disposed to hear, and the words never came out.

They spent Sunday night in the ramshackle Bynum house, and some time after midnight Ruth came to him in the guest room—a room, she told him with some excitement, that used to be hers. It had taken Robert completely by surprise. He'd been convinced he would have to marry her, something he was far from sure he was ready for, before she would surrender to him.

It was not Robert's first time. Ruth told him it was hers, though there was no blood. The sheer surprise of it, the need for silence and hurry, had been exciting and had left Robert wanting more, though other women he'd known had seemed to take more pleasure in the act itself.

In the days that followed she rebuffed all his attempts to make love to her again, while treating him with a new possessiveness that seemed to take marriage as a given. He found himself referring to her as his fiancée without ever having proposed.

The wedding, inevitably, was at the Bynum home. Wilmer paid for a honeymoon in Jamaica and there, far away from farm, friends, and family, he saw a side of Ruth that he'd begun to think he'd only imagined. She gave herself utterly to him. These were days of skin against bare skin, desire that conquered exhaustion, ocean sounds and salt breezes and sweat-soaked sheets. He was the happiest he'd ever been.

They came back from Jamaica to a two-bedroom bungalow on Woodrow Street, north and west of downtown Durham, two blocks from the city reservoir. Wilmer Bynum had provided the down payment, after he'd sent his own inspector to look the place over.

Robert's parents rode the train in from Asheville on the Saturday before Robert started his new job. Ruth was at her most charming, and his parents loved the house and the quiet, tree-lined streets of the neighborhood. "We were in our forties," Robert's mother said, "before we were able to buy a place of our own." Her jealousy, Robert saw, was aimed at Wilmer Bynum rather than himself.

"Our boy has married well," was all his father said, beaming at Ruth. After the women retired, Robert and his father sat up late in the den.

"I've asked around a bit about this Bynum fellow," his father said. He stood at the picture window, looking past the sycamore tree to the neatly trimmed lawn. "He's no Vanderbilt or Rockefeller, but he does have a good deal of money and political influence. I don't want to interfere or in any way compromise your happiness. I only say anything at all because our family has a long history of service to the rich, and I feel I should warn you to be careful."

He turned to look at Robert. "The very rich tend to believe they own people in the same way they own steel mills and oil wells. It takes a certain coldness to amass a fortune and keep it. You have to see the feelings of others as being less important than your own."

Robert took his time in answering. "I know what you're saying. I don't trust the man. He's helped make things easier for Ruth and me, but I landed this job on my own. This is the start of great things for me. I'm going to make you very proud."

"We're already very proud. You'll be serving the needs of thousands, maybe millions of people. We want to be sure that nothing will interfere with that."

"Nothing will," Robert promised. "You'll see."

THE WINDOWS of the long room started at eye level and ran up to the twelve-foot ceiling. Gray metal fans hung down on long shafts and lazily stirred the morning sunlight. Three of the walls were old red brick and the fourth was yellow plaster, a shade darker than the linoleum tile floor. The room held five drafting tables in a rough circle around a sixth. Massive metal bases held springs and dampers that allowed the boards to rise, fall, and tilt with the touch of a lever. The boards themselves were covered in pale green vinyl, and their parallel bars sighed quietly as they moved, frictionless on their ball bearings, wires, and pulleys.

Draftsmen worked at four of the tables, and with a start Robert noticed that one of them was colored. He wore a striped short-sleeved shirt, red suspenders, and round, wire-frame glasses. His receding hair was cut short. Robert guessed him to be in his mid-thirties.

The center table bore a large, hand-lettered sign reading THE BOSS IS AL-WAYS RIGHT. Used coffee cups and open materials handbooks lay on top of a barely touched 24 × 36 sheet of Albanene tracing paper.

The remaining table stood bare and unoccupied, the small wooden stand next to it empty save for a brush, a new art gum eraser with its sides still sharp, an adjustable triangle, a lead holder, a lead pointer, and an unopened box of leads.

Mine, Robert thought.

"This place used to be a textile mill," Mitch Antree told him. Antree was Robert's height, a lean and hyperactive hipster type. He had jet black hair, sideburns, and the hint of a ducktail at the back of his neck. Robert could smell the Wildroot Creme Oil on his hair. He wore a reddish-brown corduroy jacket over a yellow turtleneck.

"The company went under in the Depression, and the building sat empty for twenty years. Fred and I remodeled it for a client, then the client went out of business. So we worked out a deal and got the dry cleaners next door to take half the space, and here we are."

Fred was Fred Mason, the architect half of the partnership, who worked out of his home in the pricey Forest Hills neighborhood. Robert had met him briefly at his second interview. Mason was in his sixties, a big man in advanced stages of decay. His hair was long and chaotic, reminding Robert of Beethoven, mostly white, with enough of its original red left to give it an odd, pinkish tone that matched the man's moist eyes.

"Fred thought the place was unlucky and didn't want to bid on it. People make their own luck, is my way of thinking." The dry cleaners, which was foundering, might have been inclined to agree with Mason.

"There's offices, rest room, coffee room, all that jazz, through that hallway. This is where the real action is. Step on up and meet the rest of the inmates."

Two were apprentices, in their late teens. The one named Carl had severe acne and a full-blown DA haircut. The other, thin and bookish, was Ernest. A fat man named Charles squinted around a lit cigarette as he shook Robert's hand, then turned back to the building section on his table.

"This is Maurice," Antree said, one hand casually on the colored man's shoulder. "Maurice Wilson. Meet Robert Cooper. Robert's just got his degree from State."

"Congratulations," Maurice said. Robert, on guard for irony, wondered if he'd heard any. He put out his hand, careful to do it no differently than he had with the white men. Maurice pumped it twice with faint enthusiasm. Robert wanted to ask him some sort of personal question to humanize the moment. His mind was blank.

"You'll be here in the office half the time," Antree said. "The rest you'll be in the field with the work crews."

"Sure," Robert said. "That'll be great." He cleared his throat. "I can do elevations, floor plans, any of the architectural drafting too. If you should happen to need it, I mean."

"Charles and Maurice do the architectural work. I need a senior man on the engineering side. Engineers are not second-class citizens in this firm." Robert nodded, wondering about Antree's choice of words in front of the Negro. "Fred's a good architect," Antree went on, "but it's the engineers that make those pipe dreams real. Don't ever forget that."

"No, sir," Robert said. "I won't."

"Hey, man," Antree said, "you don't need any of that 'sir' jive around here. Call me Mitch."

Robert nodded. He'd met a few people in college, beatnik types, who affected Negro slang. He'd never known how to react.

"All right," Antree said. "Now, dig that we've got long-term plans for you, and they're not going to happen overnight. You need to get experience with all the aspects of our business, including demolition, highways, apartment buildings, the whole deal. Taking those pieces of paper and making them into 3-D Technicolor structures. Think you can handle that?"

"Yess—yeah. Yeah, Mitch, I can handle that."

"Cool. Because we're about to have more work in here than we can handle. You know anything about Research Triangle Park?"

"A little. Some people seem to think it's a boondoggle."

"They're wrong, daddy-o. It's the future. Pharmaceuticals. Medical equipment. Computers. Scientific instruments. Guys like Ernest over there, in long white lab coats." Ernest, bent over his table, smiled without looking up. "They're out there buying up land between here and the airport right now, as we speak. There is going to be some serious bread on the waters, and I'm going to get us a substantial piece of it. How does that sound to you?"

Enthusiasm on demand came hard for Robert. "It sounds great," he said. The words fell flat despite their sincerity.

"Good deal, Lucille. Let's get you some piece drawings to do so you can start earning your keep."

AT TEN AFTER 5, Robert got into his '56 Mercury coupe, rolled up his shirt sleeves, and lit a Lucky. He was headed home. To avoid the worst of the American Tobacco traffic, he drove north of downtown, then cut across to Club Boulevard. The July heat was suffocating, and even with both front windows open, he couldn't build up enough speed to get the thick, wet air moving.

He finished the cigarette and started a second before he got to Woodrow Street and pulled into his driveway. The day had turned overcast, intensifying the green of the leaves and hedges and lawns. Crepe myrtles in a hundred shades of pink and purple exploded in every yard. Between the overhanging oaks and the breeze from the reservoir, it felt at least ten degrees cooler than downtown. Robert sat and smoked for another minute or two, listening to the whir of a push-mower two doors east, the popping of sheets on a line.

He hadn't been sure until that morning that the job was real. Now he had a place in the world, a fulcrum. Mitch Antree had an air of moral certainty that Robert associated with success, and that success could sweep Robert along in its wake. It was all he asked, really. A few basic comforts and a chance to make a difference.

He cranked up the window and went inside.

He could hear Ruth's voice from the kitchen as he let the screen door bang behind him. "Ooooooh!" she moaned. "I wanted to make you a special dinner to celebrate and it's all going wrong!"

He stood in the kitchen doorway and accepted a quick, puckered kiss as Ruth brushed self-consciously at her apron. It startled him to see this pose again, when only a few days ago things had been so natural and easy between them. He managed an equally artificial smile, enough to keep her from pouting and peppering him with questions.

"It went really well," he offered.

She whirled around to face the oven, which was emitting a thin, ominous curl of smoke. "Don't look!" she cried.

"I'll be in the den," he said.

He'd worked the entire summer after his freshman year at State to buy his component hi-fi system. He'd realized by then that he was never going to be a musician himself and had accepted that fact, more or less. The hi-fi was a compromise with ambitions he'd given up before he'd ever told anyone they existed. He'd struggled with the trumpet through high school, going off into the woods by himself to practice in the afternoons. His embouchure had never developed. The band director had offered to let him try saxophone or clarinet, instruments that didn't speak to him, except in the hands of a few geniuses like Parker and Goodman.

So he became, instead, an aficionado. A fan.

While the receiver warmed up he took out *Kind of Blue,* set it on the turntable, and cleaned it gently with an anti-static cloth, though it had never had a chance to pick up any dust. He flicked the needle with a brush and carefully lowered the tone arm. There was a slight hiss, then Paul Chambers' bass eased into the room, a presence more than a sound. Then the horns, staccato, stark, and quiet, playing just for him.

There was little furniture yet: a folding card table to hold the receiver and turntable, speakers on the floor in the corners. An orange chair with a piece of plywood supporting the cushion, and two gray folding chairs from the same yard sale.

This too would change. Once they had real furniture and some money in the bank, once they'd established themselves and become part of the dynamic future that lay ahead for Durham, he was sure Ruth would relax. As Robert's career grew more solid, her parents' hold on her would weaken. In a few years, it would all be there in his hands.

Something crashed in the kitchen. Robert chose not to accept the invitation. Instead he closed his eyes and let the music fill his mind until there were no spaces left.

A YEAR AND TWO MONTHS later, Robert found himself on his first job in Hayti.

Twenty or thirty Negroes stood outside the chain-link fence that surrounded the property, a large lot on Pettigrew Street near Mangum, a few blocks south and east of Durham's central business district. On one side was a grocery and on the other a coin laundry, both run down, both still in business.

As he slowed his Mercury, double-checking the address, individuals emerged from the crowd. He saw three old men standing together, a woman with an infant riding on her hip, a man Robert's age with a cigarette pack rolled up in the sleeve of his white T-shirt.

The peeling painted numbers on the side of the building matched the ones Antree had neatly lettered on a scrap of tracing paper. Robert drove through the gate, maneuvering around the crane, whose tank treads took up most of the asphalt parking lot. He pulled up next to a pale green Ford pickup from the 1940s that had somehow managed to tow in a generator. It was 7:30 on a late September morning in 1963, and the air was still and humid.

Three more colored men sat or leaned against the side of the pickup. These men, Robert saw, were there to work. One of them wore a hard hat with letters across the front in what seemed to be red fingernail polish. As he walked around his car toward the men, Robert saw that the letters spelled the name LEON backwards.

"Leon Coleman?" Robert asked him.

"Yes, sir," the man said. He was over six feet tall, thin and wiry, and his skin had a reddish cast, like stained mahogany. He looked to be in his thirties.

"I'm Robert Cooper. I work for Mason and Antree?" Robert wasn't sure whether to offer his hand. Leon's arms remained folded, so Robert put his own hands in his pockets.

"Yes, sir. Mr. Antree told me to expect you. I see you looking at my hat. Mr. Antree gave me this hat. Said, one of them damn buildings falls on me, I can look in the mirror, remember who I am."

Robert smiled. Leon's expression didn't change, nor did those of the men next to him. He glanced quickly at the crane. "I thought this was a building site."

"No, sir. Demolition site."

The building behind them was a one-story box made of "sticks and bricks," as the precast concrete men liked to say. It was in an advanced state of disrepair, every window broken, tufts of fescue prying apart the cracked sidewalk. Through the missing front doors, Robert saw a stained, slick-finish concrete floor from which cut lengths of pipe stuck up like the stumps of a metal forest.

Robert supposed he shouldn't have been surprised. The first victim of the renewal had been the former Boy's Club building on Fayetteville Street, demolished at the end of July. Antree, with Maurice in tow for publicity value, had led that crew himself.

A voice behind him said, "You in charge here?"

Robert turned to see an overweight white man with long sideburns and greasy yellow-white hair. He wore navy-blue zip-up coveralls like an auto mechanic, with the name "Steve" embroidered over the breast pocket.

"I guess so," Robert said.

"I'm Porter. Crane operator."

"Uh, okay. Good."

Porter held out an open tin of Copenhagen. "Dip?" The moist tobacco smell turned Robert's stomach, and he waved it away. Porter pointedly did not offer any to the Negroes. Instead he stuck in three thick fingers, rooted around briefly, then packed a wad between his lower lip and gum.

Robert felt a sticky sweat break under his arms. He'd never done any demolition work and he didn't have the vaguest idea of what came next. Porter, Leon, the Negroes lined up at the fence, all were watching him, all with blank expressions. Robert was sure they were laughing inside, waiting for him to make an ass of himself.

When Robert couldn't stand the silence any longer he cleared his throat and said, "Maybe we should get started."

Porter took a step back. "Union says I don't have to start till eight."

Having played his one card, Robert could only nod.

Porter spat a stream of dark brown juice onto the sidewalk. "Tell you what. I'm going to go wait in the cab." He sauntered back to the cabin of the crane, and moments later Robert heard country music through the closed windows.

Robert felt the humiliation burn his face. He coughed to give himself an excuse to look away, then he patted his shirt pocket for his Luckies. Better wait, he thought. His hands were shaking and lighting a cigarette would only make that more obvious.

To Leon he said, "You have to help me out. I don't know what to do."

"Mr. Antree said you wouldn't. He just need you here because that crane operator won't take no orders from no colored man." The younger of the other men made a noise that could have been a laugh but ended as a cough.

"This here's my nephew Tommy," Leon said, pointing to the coughing man, who wore a baggy, striped cotton railroad hat. He was still in his twenties, darker, with a round face and the beginnings of a mustache. He touched the bill of the cap with one finger.

Leon hooked his thumb toward the other man. "This my brother-in-law, Booker." Booker was short and heavy, bare-headed, balding, with bloodshot eyes. He nodded to Robert without moving his head more than a fraction of an inch. "Too early for Booker. Booker get going after dinner time."

"Do you know what this place was?"

"No, sir. This is Hayti, here. I live out on the north side."

"Do you know why all these people are here?"

"No, sir. Like I said, I don't live around here."

Robert looked at Tommy and Booker. Both of them stared at the ground.

"All right," Robert said. "I'll walk around and try to look important, and at eight o'clock I'll come over here and you can tell me what to say to the crane man."

"Yes, sir."

With the toe of his boot, Robert turned over a piece of a wooden sign that lay in the dirt next to the building entrance. It said URSERY. Inside, he saw that the far half of the roof had once been glass, shards of which glittered on the concrete floor like misplaced stars. The acrid tang of fertilizer still hung in the dead, damp air. It couldn't have been that long, he thought, since the place was in use. He lit a cigarette to cut the smell.

Just do your job, he told himself. Antree is testing you for some reason. You're going to come through fine, and good things will happen to you.

As he came back outside, he saw Leon at the fence, arguing with one of the old men there. By the time Robert arrived, Leon was shouting, "You get along home now, don't be hanging around here no more."

"Something wrong?" Robert asked him.

Leon was already walking away. "Everything fine. Let's tear this sucker down."

In the end there was not much to it. The bricks were no match for the wrecking ball and by lunch time, when the bulldozer and dump truck arrived, there was nothing left but a pile of rubble in the center of the lot. The dozer scraped the shattered bricks off the concrete slab while they ate, then Leon backed the generator up to one edge and fired it up. Tommy and Booker wrestled two pneumatic jackhammers out of the pickup bed and they began to batter the slab into basketball-sized chunks. They worked for 20 minutes, then took a rest.

Robert asked Leon, "Do you think I could try that?"

"Yes, sir, I reckon you can if you want. You need to be very careful with that jack. Mr. Antree have my black hide if anything happen to you."

In fact it was a perfectly simple machine. Robert relished its noise and power. The steel handles vibrated hard enough to make his palms tingle through heavy leather gloves. His first blows chipped and gnawed at the surface of the concrete, and for a moment he worried that he was doing it wrong, that the weight of the jackhammer alone was not going to suffice. Then, like magic, the first cracks appeared and the chisel point of the jack nosed its way into them and through to the dirt.

The machine wasn't fighting him, he saw. All it wanted was to break things, and Robert had only to stay out of its way. It brought him full circle, from creating stone to destroying it.

He smiled at Leon and took one hand away long enough to give him a thumbs-up. Leon shook his head and stomped over to pick up the other jack-hammer. "Damn if I can stand there and watch you work," he shouted over the roar of the generator.

Tommy and Booker convulsed with laughter. "Look at that!" Booker yelled. "You got *Leon* working now!"

"Shut up, fool!" Leon shouted. "I work you into the ground any day of the week!"

They took 20-minute shifts, Robert and Tommy alternating on one jackham-mer, Leon and Booker on the other. By four o'clock they'd broken up the entire slab, and the dozer had loaded the pieces into the dump truck. The truck, driven by a friend of Leon's, had then made a parade lap around the empty lot in an excess of enthusiasm while Booker and Tommy cheered and applauded.

Despite his initial misgivings, Robert felt a warmth independent of the pain in his lower back. At 8 AM the lot had been part of the past—decayed, useless, finished. Now it was clean, new, full of potential. Now it belonged to the future.

"I guess we're done?" Robert said to Leon as the others loaded the jackhammers into the ancient truck. The crane, dozer, and dump truck had all departed.

"Yes, sir. All done for today." He seemed to be waiting for something.

"That was a good day's work," Robert offered.

"Should have been two days' work, only I lost my head." Robert had yet to see Leon smile.

"Is there anything else I'm supposed to do? Mr. Antree takes care of paying you, right?"

"Yes, sir. Mr. Antree, he takes care of all that."

"Well, okay, then. You be careful, now."

"Yes, sir."

As he walked toward his car, Robert saw the old man that Leon had been talking to at the fence. The man was shuffling toward the freshly plowed earth, where it shone red-orange in the afternoon sun.

Robert trotted over to him. "Excuse me, can I help you?"

The old man looked Robert up and down. His face was cracked like old leather, and tufts of white hair stuck randomly out of his head and chin. "Just looking around."

"I'm afraid this is city property. We're locking up for the night."

"I know whose property this is. This was my place of business y'all tore down. I *know* whose property this is."

"Your place...?"

"Hamilton Nursery. Mose Hamilton, that's me."

"You mean you still own the place?"

"Hell no, you think I'd let you tear down my place of business if I still owned it? City owns it now, like you said. Condemned it and now they tore it down. See, I kind of wanted to keep the sign. They get all these slums cleared, city going to build me a new place. Thought I'd like to have that old sign still hanging inside. It ain't no big thing."

Robert's back was beginning to seriously hurt. Tiny spasms sparked up and down the long muscles of his waist. Still he was curious enough to ask, "How long were you here?"

"Opened up in nineteen and twenty eight. Thirty-four years it would have been next month."

"Hey, old man," Leon said, coming up fast behind Robert. "I thought I told you to keep the hell out of here."

"Ain't hurting nobody."

"Somebody be hurting *you,* you don't get on home."

"This was his nursery," Robert said.

"Yes, sir. I know he say that, but it ain't his nursery no more. It's Mr. Antree's now."

"I thought it was the city that bought it," Robert said, more puzzled than suspicious.

"Whoever owns it, Mr. Antree be the one responsible for it, and he don't want nobody trespassing."

"Forgive us our trespasses," the old man said. "As we forgive those who trespass against us."

"See?" Leon said. "His mind nothing but mush." He took the old man by the shoulders, turned him around, and gave him a shove toward the street. "Get going now, hear?"

"He maketh me to lie down in green pastures," the man said. He stumbled as he turned down Pettigrew Street.

"That's all for today, Captain," Leon said.

As Robert drove away he saw Leon in his rearview mirror, fists on hips, a fierce angel guarding vacant ground.

IT WAS THE SPRING of 1964. The office had hit its Friday afternoon stride, windows open to the late March air, cool flowering smells replacing stale cigarette smoke. Conversation had fallen off, and the room was quiet except for the hum of the fans, the zip of parallel bars, the slap of plastic triangles, the pop of the suction cup on the base of a lead pointer. When Maurice started humming, Robert wasn't consciously aware of it.

Maurice broke off in mid-note and looked at him. "What are you doing?"

"What?" Robert asked.

"Hey, boss," Maurice yelled in the general direction of Antree's office, where he'd been holed up since lunch. "Come out here!"

"Look, I didn't mean anything," Robert said. It was the opening riff from Coltrane's "Giant Steps" that Maurice had been humming, and Robert realized he'd been whistling along.

Antree emerged into the drafting room, collar open, pink shirtsleeves rolled to the elbow. "What's up?"

"Your boy here listens to Coltrane," Maurice said.

Antree squinted at Robert. "Is that true?"

"Yes," Robert said, pleased and embarrassed.

"Just Coltrane?" Antree asked. "Or anybody else?"

"Miles," Robert said. "Jamal. Dizzy, Bird."

" 'Bird,' " Maurice said, shaking his head. " 'Bird,' the man calls him. Who said you could call him 'Bird'?"

"Cool it, Maurice," Antree said. "Everybody calls him Bird. Robert, step into my office." Maurice followed without invitation.

Antree's office was cool and dark, with only a floor lamp in one corner for illumination. Thick drapes hid the window, and wall-to-wall carpet muffled their footsteps. There were framed prints by an artist Robert didn't recognize, full of distorted figures and odd blue colors.

"So tell me, Bobby," Antree said. "How long has this been going on?"

Robert shrugged. "My father was into the swing bands, the early cool stuff. I started listening to bop when I was in Germany. American bands were always touring Europe. Art Taylor and Donald Byrd, Bud Powell with Kenny Clark— they were living over there. I saw Miles in Paris in December of '57 at this tiny little club in St. Germain...."

Antree and Maurice looked at each other. "Definitely," Antree said.

"You ever hear Charlie Shavers?" Maurice asked.

"I've got one of his records," Robert said. *"Like Charlie?"*

"Well, tonight," Antree said, "you're going to be seeing him in person."

Robert's emotions felt like crickets, jumping in the cupped hands of his chest. "I can't," he said. "Ruth doesn't even like music, and—"

Antree slid the pointer on his metal address book to "C" and popped the lid. He ran his finger down the listings, then dialed Robert's home number.

"Mrs. Cooper? Mitch Antree here. I'm doing splendidly, thank you, how about yourself? Almost feels like spring, doesn't it? Well, I did have one thing. I asked Robert if he'd be able to work late tonight, and he expressed some concern as to whether that would be all right with you. Uh huh. Well, I'm afraid it might be very late indeed. We've got a very significant client in town that we need to have dinner and discussions with, and I expect it will be, oh, round about midnight before Robert gets home." Antree winked at Maurice, who made a face. "Oh yes, I wouldn't ask if it weren't important. No, I'll see to it that he gets a good supper. Why, thank you, Mrs. Cooper. The same to you."

He hung up and smiled at Robert. "Any other questions?"

"No," Robert said. "No more questions."

AT 6 THEY ALL got into Antree's Cadillac, with its factory air conditioning, leather seats, and 396-cubic-inch V8. Robert hung back slightly to see how the seating arrangements would fall out, and wasn't terribly surprised to see Maurice automatically take the front passenger seat.

They were in Hayti in five minutes. Antree idled on Pettigrew Street outside the Wonderland Theater while Maurice ran up to the box office to get tickets. Robert tried not to stare. Close as it was to the office, Robert had never been there on a weekend. At home, on Woodrow Street, a few of Robert's neighbors might sit out on their porches of an evening, cigarettes and citronella candles burning against the mosquitoes, while everyone else hurried inside to their televisions. Here the entire neighborhood seemed to be on the sidewalk.

It was like the stories Robert had heard about street corners in Harlem. Negro businessmen in suits stopped to shake each other's hands. Women wore skirts slit nearly to the waist, and blouses cut for maximum provocation. There were Negro GIs from Camp Butner, tightly creased and standing in clumps, school kids in striped T-shirts and bright jackets, old men with suspenders and canes and snap-brim fedoras.

Maurice got in the car and Antree edged into the traffic, crawling east to Fayetteville Street, where he found an open spot at the curb and parked.

"I suppose we're going to Elvira's," Maurice said.

"That jake with you?" Antree said.

"I expect I can take it if Robert can. How's your tolerance for grease, Robert?"

"Compared to what I get at home," Robert said, "I'm sure it'll be fine."

They locked the car, and Robert found himself swimming upstream through a river of black humanity. Along with the crowd came the sound, a chorus that rose and fell in slow waves, peaking when three or four voices surfaced momentarily into audible words, then fading again below the rattle of broken mufflers, the drumming of high heels on concrete, the chirp and whistle of distant radios, the claps and hoots and laughter and surprise.

It was impossible not to brush up against strange Negro bodies. Robert quickly got over his first shock and found nothing to be afraid of. No one seemed to pay him particular attention. I'm handling this well, he thought.

A couple of the storefronts along Fayetteville Street were boarded up, but when they turned the corner onto Pettigrew, business seemed good. They could hear the presses working inside Service Printing on the corner, and the *Carolina Times* next door was bustling. Next to Pee Wee's Shoe Shop was a big plate glass window that read ELVIRA'S CLUB DINE-ET. It was part of a contiguous block of storefronts whose second floor sat back a good ten feet from the first. Peeling white paint covered the bricks as high as the tops of the doors and windows, with plain red brick above.

"So what gives, here?" Robert said. "This place doesn't look like a slum to me."

"Keep your voice down, won't you?" Maurice said. "Some folks around here are not that crazy about the word 'slum' these days."

Robert felt his face heat up. "Sorry. You know what I mean. This isn't what I expected."

"Not enough winos in the doorways for you?" Maurice asked. "They'll be out later, never fear."

"I said I was sorry."

"It was different here, even five years ago," Maurice said. "Better. It was only when all this renewal talk started up that everybody gave up trying. Why put glass in that broken window when the appraisers are going to pay you the same for cardboard?"

Through the screen doors of the restaurant wafted smells of burning fat, yeast, cornbread, collards, and spilled beer.

"We can talk inside," Antree said, rubbing his hands. "I need me some soul food."

With one foot in the doorway, Robert had a sudden memory of the stories his father had read to him as a child. It was possible to come and go from Fairyland as long as you followed a few simple rules: Don't pick up any stray objects, don't make any wagers with magical beings, that sort of thing. Above all, never eat the food. Once you'd eaten their food, they had you forever.

For all its shabbiness, Hayti seemed a magical place. As he crossed Elvira's threshold he thought, What would it be like to belong here?

IN THE END the food was neither unpalatable nor particularly exotic. They all had fresh chicken fried in grease that was not so fresh, collard greens with bits of dried ham, white corn, and sweet potato pie. Afterwards Maurice accepted a Lucky, and he and Robert smoked while Antree drank a third beer.

Robert's feelings were complex. He'd been married for two years now, and a full-time employee for just as long. He had found moments of contentment standing in the morning mist and looking at his house, his lawn, his quiet street. There was still pleasure, on rare occasions, in bed with Ruth. Work alternately absorbed and bored him, and the excitement of rebuilding Hayti and creating RTP seemed to recede constantly into the future.

He and Ruth had little social life, and she had lost interest in dancing after the wedding date was set. Once or twice a month she would go to her parents' house for the weekend. Sometimes Robert would go along, spending long hours with her father and trying to stay awake through endless sports broadcasts, sometimes on television, often droning on endlessly from the radio. Wilmer Bynum's encyclopedic knowledge of players, statistics, and history was largely wasted on Robert. Lately he would drop her off at the farm and spend the weekend at work or alone in the house with his records.

He hadn't been to see live music since college. The idea of it stirred something in him, memories and longings, a sense of formless possibility, a tang of the forbidden. The libertine atmosphere of Hayti magnified the risks—not only the physical danger that lurked there, but the loss of control that beckoned from darkened doorways. It was, Robert thought, something like Havana before the revolution, a place where you checked your inhibitions at the door.

"Shall we?" Maurice asked, pushing back his chair.

"Yeah, man," Antree said. Robert felt like a teenager, dizzy with anticipation.

The Wonderland Theater was two blocks east, between Elvira's and the Biltmore Hotel. It was a three-story red brick cube, with a wide arch across the front that rose as high as the second story windows on either side. The words WONDERLAND THEATER were cut into the stone of the arch, and the box office nestled neatly inside the recess. The place still served as a movie theater, and glass frames held posters for *The Great Escape* and *Fun in Acapulco.*

A crowd had already formed, with an hour yet until showtime. Robert couldn't remember ever being among so many black people in such close proximity. The truth, he saw, was that he was at one end of a spectrum of skin colors, many of them no darker than his own. The crowd was mostly male, mostly in coats and ties, though there were some turtlenecks and open sport shirts. The main thing that struck him was the obvious care and effort that virtually every one of them had spent on his appearance: hats, slickly processed hair, brightly shined shoes, rings, cufflinks, tie tacks.

Then there were the women. Some wore furs and broad-brimmed hats, others simple linen dresses and dime store gloves. They had an ease with their own bodies, no matter what size or shape, that Robert found both alien and appealing. And some of them were simply stunning. He was unable to stop looking at one woman whose long, white silk dress clung to her hourglass figure as if static electricity was all that held it on. She had curly black hair past her shoulders, creamy tan skin, olive-colored eyes, delicate features, and a half smile that made her seem oblivious to everyone around her, as if she were turned inward to focus on the soft hum of the biological machinery that moved her so gracefully through the crowd.

They began to file into the lobby. The slightly threadbare, multicolored carpet there held the smell of popcorn, though at the moment the concession stand was serving liquor.

"You want something?" Antree asked. Robert shook his head, thinking he should keep his wits about him. Antree waded away through the crowd. Maurice didn't seem inclined to conversation. He was nodding slightly as people caught his eye, smiling occasionally. Robert put his hands in his pockets and tried in vain to look inconspicuous.

Antree came up behind him with two glass tumblers. "The only scotch they had was J&B, that all right?"

"You're buying, I'm not complaining," Maurice said.

"Look who I ran into at the bar," Antree said, and Robert turned around to find himself face to face with the woman in the white dress.

"Hi," he said, thinking fast. "I'm Robert."

She raised one eyebrow and let him take her hand, which she offered with fingers down and wrist bent. "Charmed, I'm sure," she said. She was not as tall as he'd thought at first. Her perfume was delicate, sweet, intoxicating.

"Barrett, how're you doing?" Maurice asked, reaching past Robert to shake the hand of someone standing next to the woman in white.

"Maurice. What you know good?" the man said.

Antree said, "Barrett Howard, this is Robert Cooper, my new engineer."

Robert forced himself to look away from the woman long enough to shake Howard's hand. The man's grip made a statement, Robert discovered. The statement was, "I can take you." He was six feet tall and looked like he lifted weights. His hair was unprocessed and grown out unevenly half an inch or more. His broad, dark face looked too young for the number of lines criss-crossing it. He wore a blue dress shirt, open at the throat, with a thin black tie hanging loose and a navy blue blazer on top. His pants were dark khaki, worn over suede cowboy boots with pointed toes. "Hey there," he said.

Robert had seen Howard's face on the evening news. "He looks like a gorilla," Ruth had said, and Robert had let the racist implications pass at the time. Newspaper and TV commentators portrayed him as a kind of monster, violent and threatening in an almost sexual way, not just an integrationist but a communist and a revolutionary. Randy Fogg, on WRAL radio, regularly referred to him as "Fidel" Howard, "The Red Negro," "The Black Stalin," and a dozen other epithets. Yet here he was, shaking Robert's hand.

"Nice to meet you," Robert said, then hated himself for the banality. Before he could redeem himself, Antree had his arm around Howard's shoulder.

"You going to talk tonight?" Antree asked.

"Nah, man, I'm here to listen to the music, like everybody else. Listen, I got to go."

"I can dig it," Antree said. "You be cool, now."

Howard nodded distractedly, scooped the woman up by her narrow waist, and pushed into the crowd.

"Who is she?" Robert asked.

Maurice looked at Antree. "Now see what you've done?"

"Don't even think about her," Antree said. "Don't even look."

"What's her name?" Robert asked.

"Trouble," Antree said. "Capital T."

"I know who Barrett Howard is," Robert said.

"I'm not talking about Barrett Howard," Antree said. "Forget that crap you see on TV. Howard's a pussycat. She's the one you have to watch out for."

Robert looked at him blankly.

"You know what a mambo is?" Antree asked.

"Sure. Perez Prado, 'Cherry Pink and Apple—' "

"No, man, I ain't talking about some Cuban jive. Tell him, Maurice."

Maurice cleared his throat. "The rumor has it that she's a voodoo practitioner. A mambo. Did you see her earrings?"

Antree said, "I think he might have noticed a necklace, if it hung low enough."

"What earrings?" Robert said.

"Those little heart-shaped things?" Maurice said. "That's hoodoo stuff. Same as on top of St. Joseph's church." He watched Robert's face. "You've never looked at what's on top of St. Joseph's church, have you?"

"You mean the cross?"

"Look again, daddy-o," Antree said. "That ain't no cross."

It felt to Robert like the first few weeks of junior high, when the older boys had mocked him for his ignorance of sex. He hadn't wanted to know what they were taking about, didn't care about the mystery. He wanted them to leave him alone. "Tell me her name," Robert said.

"Mercy," Maurice said. "Her name is Mercy. And if you have any sense at all, you'll leave it at that."

AT 8:15 THE DOUBLE DOORS opened, and the crowd made its way down the aisles. The seats had curved wooden backs and red velvet cushions, many of them loose. Robert could not have cared less. In the muted glow of the footlights he saw a black grand piano, a small trap set, a few microphone stands adjusted to varying heights. It was like the first sight of the ocean in summer.

They found seats in the tenth row. Though the show was not scheduled to start until nine, the room was filling quickly. Everyone seemed to know everyone else, as if Robert had crashed a private party of a thousand or so. Men stretched across rows to shake hands, women leaned over the railing of the balcony and shouted through cupped hands. Even Antree was getting into the act, calling out to people in the aisles, while Maurice slid ever lower in his seat, staring at his own knees.

After a few minutes Robert began to feel invisible, began to accept that no one was about to evict him or demand an explanation, and he was able to sit and smoke and observe. He watched Barrett Howard and the woman, Mercy, sail through the crowd like royalty, never lingering with any one group, finally landing on the front row. Everything was foreign, exotic, from the slang that, at its fastest, Robert found incomprehensible, to outsize gestures that were more like dance than anything in Robert's white world of economical movement.

And then, at last, the lights came down and from the darkened stage a man's voice said, "Ladies and gentlemen, welcome to Wonderland," drawing out the ends of the words, "where later tonight Durham's own native son is gonna cool this joint, and you know I got to be talking about Mr. Charlie Shavers and his horn of plenty. But first, from North Carolina College, let's y'all give a warm Wonderland welcome to the Manny ... Jackson ... Quartet!"

In the darkness another voice counted to two and then, twice as fast, to four, and the ride cymbal and standup bass took off in a breakneck shuffle. A single, dissonant piano chord broke over the rhythm section like an egg into a hot skillet, and then the lights came up and the tenor sax rode in fast and loose.

Jackson's quartet played for close to an hour. During intermission Antree went for more drinks, and Robert sat in a state of quiet euphoria. Then the Shavers quintet took the stage.

Shavers himself was short and thickset, with hair cut so close and jowls so big his head was pear-shaped. He had a pencil-thin mustache and charcoal gray suit and seemed to vibrate like a kettle on full boil, an impression borne out when he would lean back and point his trumpet straight up into the air and unleash a high-pitched squeal of pure joy.

What Robert was beginning to understand was that everything he had painstakingly figured out as he listened to his favorite records, the concepts of harmony and modality and counterpoint, all those ideas were not only true and correct, but in the live, red heat of the moment they were so obvious as to be inconsequential, no more important than Shavers' clowning on stage. All that counted were the pure emotions that the musicians were transmitting from their guts into Robert's.

When the last encore was over, standing in a knot of people outside the Wonderland, Robert knew that he had been transformed, the way heat and pressure turned dull gray shale into glittering mica schist. Secrets he could never put into words had been revealed to him. Some in the audience had heard them and many had not.

Antree, for one, had been largely unaffected. He stood talking to Barrett Howard, and Robert saw that Howard, too, had not been particularly moved. Maurice had. He and Robert looked at each other with the eyes of initiates and nodded and smiled. And Mercy, the woman in white, seemed to float as she walked up to them. Her face perfectly mirrored Robert's own emotions, and she acknowledged it with a radiant smile. As if in a dream, Robert felt her slip into his arms and rest her head against his chest for a heartbeat, then two. He didn't react other than to bring his right hand up and rest it below her shoulder blade, as if they were slow dancing. She was fully present in his arms. He could feel the pressure of her breasts and the heat of her breath through his shirt, smell the aromatic oils in her hair. Then she slipped away again and turned in a slow, elliptical orbit around Howard, lost to everything except the inner worlds the music had opened in her.

"Did that just happen?" Robert asked.

"No," Maurice said. "It most definitely did not happen."

They drifted leisurely down the street, still part of the concert crowd, Antree basking in Howard's attention, Robert tinglingly aware of Mercy as she took her own erratic course around and through them.

The crowd slowly melted away until the three of them were alone on the street next to Antree's Cadillac.

"Well, Maurice?" Antree said. "How's our boy?"

"He's fine, Mitch. Let's go home."

RUTH WAS ASLEEP when Robert got into bed, her back to him. An arousal came over him that was as dreamlike as the rest of the night, but far more urgent. Lying behind her on his side, he began to touch her gently through her nightgown. She responded to him without waking, and he slipped out of his pajama bottoms. She didn't come fully awake until he had entered her from behind, and then her first reaction was to press harder against him. A second later she said, "Robert? My goodness, Robert, what are you...?"

By then nothing could have stopped him.

Afterwards, as he collapsed onto his pillow, she rolled over and kissed him on the forehead. "My goodness, darling, I would have thought working late would have tired you out. You're like a man possessed."

The possession had left him. Sleep bore down on him like a train, and he couldn't manage to speak before it took him.

ROBERT TOOK MAURICE to lunch the day after the concert. They ate at Woolworth's downtown, and though Maurice got some hostile looks, the counterman was willing to serve him.

"So I'm thinking maybe I underestimated you," Maurice said. "Maybe."

"I'm not trying to prove anything," Robert said. "I'm not trying to impress anybody. I just love the music."

"I can see that." Maurice reluctantly unwrapped his hamburger and lifted the bun. A thick layer of chopped onions lay over the meat. "You heard me say 'hold the onions,' right?"

Robert nodded. "Mitch said something last night about Howard speaking. Does he give lectures or something?"

Maurice scraped the onions onto his plate and reached for the bottle of catsup on the counter. "He probably spit on it, too, when we weren't looking. Lecture isn't exactly the word. Rabble-rousing is more like it."

"If he was doing this somewhere, how would somebody find out about it?"

Maurice reassembled the burger, took a bite, chewed and swallowed. He ate a few rippled potato chips that lay next to the onion pile and took a drink of his Coke. "You don't have any more interest in hearing Barrett Howard speak than you have in living in Ethiopia."

"Sure I do."

"You're hoping Mercy will be there, so you can wake up crawling out of some graveyard, mandrake roots all over you, and go work in some swamp until the gators drag your numb, brainless body away."

"So does he do it in Durham much?"

"You want to know why Barrett got kicked out of the NAACP? He used to be the president of the Durham branch. Then he wrote a letter to Martin Luther King saying that he was in favor of pacifism as much as the next man, but if an armed white man came into his house without an invitation, he was prepared to, quote, meet violence with violence, end quote."

"I don't even own a gun."

"People make mistakes. For instance, I think you're about to make one. If you haven't got sense enough to be afraid of the woman, maybe you could manage to be afraid of the man."

"Mitch said he was a pussycat."

"Mitch sees things the way he wants them to be. I think Barrett puts up with Mitch for the same reason I do. He's what they call a holy fool. He thinks everybody in the world is like he is, and it makes him fearless. He thinks it's okay to try to be a big shot because he doesn't think anybody will get hurt by it, that it's all some kind of game."

"Isn't that what we're all doing? Trying to be successful? That's what this country is all about."

"I don't think most black people would see it that way. No offense. From where I stand, somebody always gets hurt. Look at those people in Hayti whose houses we're knocking down. Where are they going to go? A lot of them didn't get paid anything like what their property was worth. Most of those houses were better than anything they'd ever had in their lives, and there's no place left for them to move."

"That's temporary. You've seen the plans. There's that development with close to 2000 rooms. We can't build it until we clear the ground for it."

"Yeah." He looked down at the pile of onions on his plate. "That's what I keep telling myself."

APRIL ARRIVED, and Robert found that it added only five minutes to his drive home to detour down Pettigrew Street, through the heart of Hayti. Maybe ten. After the first time, he asked himself what he thought he was doing. Within two weeks it was part of his daily routine.

The dreams had been coming more often, three or four times a week. They lacked action and concrete images, consisting mainly of odors and textures and sensations that evoked female sexuality. Lurking in the background was an unseen presence, distinctly feminine without being identifiable as anyone he knew, not Mercy or anyone else. He could not say for certain that it was even human, only that its nearness brought him comfort and calm. Waking brought a drab, hollow feeling that lasted into the morning.

One afternoon he saw Barrett Howard outside the Donut Shop, two doors down from the Biltmore Hotel. He was arguing with another Negro on the street, a younger man in glasses and a dark brown suit. Howard looked violently angry, and Robert drove past without slowing down.

Mercy was nowhere in sight.

The next day, after work, he parked on Fayetteville Street, walked back to Pettigrew, and went in the office of *The Carolina Times.*

The paper came out once a week, on Saturday morning, and for the last three weeks he had driven to a corner grocery in the nearby Walltown neighborhood to pick up a copy. He told Ruth that Antree had asked him to do it, to gauge the reaction of the neighborhood to their work. In fact there was nothing in there about the renewal, nor was there any mention of Barrett Howard speaking anywhere. Most of the stories were about the difficult progress of the Civil Rights Act through Congress and the ongoing demonstrations in Mississippi and Alabama. The rest was local church news, or glowing reports of achievements by Negroes around the country.

A young colored woman sat at the desk in the front office. "Yes, sir, may I help you?"

His hands began to sweat and he had trouble finding his voice. "I was wondering if you knew a way to get hold of Barrett Howard. I understand he writes for the paper sometimes."

"He hasn't written for us in some time. He and Mr. Austin have some differences of opinion. May I ask what this is about?"

"No, I just ... I had some personal business that I wanted to see him about."

"Are you with the police?"

"Me? No, no, nothing like that."

A man stuck his head through the door that led to the back of the building. He looked to be about 60, with short, thinning hair, glasses, and piercing eyes. His nose looked like it had been broken and badly set. He wore a tie and a white shirt with the sleeves rolled up. "Is there a problem, Ellen?"

"No, sir. This gentleman is looking for Mr. Howard."

"You won't find him here, sir." The man gave Robert a look that drained the last of his resolve.

"Uh, okay. Thank you. Thank you both." He retreated to the sidewalk and made his way as purposefully as he could toward his car.

Then, without warning, he heard Antree's voice. "Bobby? What are you doing here?"

Robert turned to see Antree standing next to his Cadillac. "Mitch. I ... I was..."

"Bobby, are you okay?"

"Yeah, I'm fine." He couldn't think of a lie, couldn't avoid the question. "I'm looking for Barrett Howard," he said. With the admission came a sense of release. He hadn't truly relaxed, he realized, in weeks.

"You looking for Barrett, or for his chick?"

Robert shrugged.

"Man, you are way out of your depth." He looked Robert up and down. "I must be crazy to even bring this up. He's meeting some people at Mercy's house tonight. I can bring you with me, but you have to not fuck up. You understand what I'm saying?"

"I'll be good. What's the meeting?"

"Howard's talking about trying to start a union. He hasn't got a hope in hell, and I have to pretend to take him seriously. So don't say anything."

"All right. Thank you."

"Don't mention it. I mean really, do not mention it." He looked at his watch. "Elvira's? My treat."

THE RESIDENTIAL STREETS of Hayti after dark were not designed to make Robert feel at home. Beamon Street described a short arc east of Roxboro Street and south of the tracks. The houses there, Antree told him, had been built for tobacco workers in the downtown factories around the turn of the century. They were wood frame with a triple-A roofline, which was to say the transverse gable over the front door matched the gables on the sides. Most of the roofs sagged. Cars, tires, wooden crates, and tough scrub brush filled the yards. There were no streetlights.

Mercy's house had lights blazing, and Robert heard voices from inside as they pulled up. "You still up for this?" Antree asked.

Robert nodded and got self-consciously out of the Cadillac, careful to lock the door. Unlike some of the other, identical houses on the block, 109 had an actual sidewalk leading up to the front porch. Robert waited there for Antree, then followed him up the steps, through the screen door, and into the crowded living room.

The room was 20 feet long and 12 feet wide, sparsely furnished. The walls were a light pinkish-purple and appeared recently painted. There was a fireplace on the interior wall, where Howard stood with one arm resting on the mantel.

Another dozen or so men, all black, fidgeted in twos and threes. Robert didn't see Mercy. His emotions, running at high-school levels, began to sour.

He suddenly recognized Leon and Tommy Coleman, Tommy with his arms folded and his back and left boot to the wall. Robert joined them, offering his pack of Luckies around.

"Booker's not here?" Robert asked.

"No, sir," Leon said, waving the cigarettes away. Tommy took two, parking one behind his ear for later. "Booker be living large tonight," Leon said. "Friday night, payday night. Booker's eagle be flying tonight." Robert realized that Leon was nervous too.

Howard's voice was suddenly louder than anything else. "All right, let's start this thing." Conversations broke off and people shifted to face him.

"This is my show, so I guess I got to take the reins," he said. "I wanted y'all to come here tonight so we could talk about what's going on. I mean what's happening to our neighborhood, and what we can do about it. I wanted to talk to y'all, because y'all are the ones doing the real work that is going to make this new road happen. So I want to talk a little about roads and cars what all that means to you and me.

"The East-West Expressway started with Henry Ford. Y'all know that, right?"

A few people went along with him and shook their heads or said, "What you talking about?"

"Henry Ford," Howard said, "had the idea of 'a motor car for the great multitude.' He thought everybody should have one, because then everybody would be free. Well, and he would make a few dollars along the way.

"Thing is, there's all different kinds of freedom. Cars used to be about freedom, about being able to drive anywhere you wanted to go. Now cars is another kind of slavery.

"You don't have a car here in the South, you can't work. You can't get to the store to buy groceries. You're sick, you got to get your own self to the doctor somehow, because he don't make house calls no more.

"What are we building here but another superhighway, going to hook up with the Interstate system? I can tell you how that's going to turn out. Going to turn out the same as when they put the railroad through, or the first paved highways, or the first turnpikes up in New York. Where the highway is, businesses are going to grow—unless they already knocked them all down, like they doing in Hayti now—and everywhere else, the businesses going to die. So the cities get more and more spread out along the highways, and then you need more cars, more cars need more highways, and on and on."

Robert looked for Antree to see how he was taking it. Antree was by the front door, shoulder to shoulder with a man in a suit who looked like a preacher, and he was smiling.

"Henry Ford believed in the individual," Howard said. "But there's different kinds of individuals, too. When Ford cut his prices too much, his investors took him to court and won, because according to the law of this land, the purpose of a business is to make money for its stockholders.

"Because that is the individual that this is really all about, and in the end old Henry Ford, he saw it that way too. When the Depression hit, he cut wages below what everybody else was paying. And he fought longer and harder than anybody to keep unions out of his business.

"Thing is, it's the same idea at the heart of all this, whether we talking about freedom of the roads or freedom of the rich to make more money. When you say every man for himself, you can bet it's going to be the ruthless and the greedy come out on top every time. Every time."

As Howard got his cadence going, some of the men were nodding along. The preacher was one of them, like a drummer tapping his foot to another drummer's beat.

"I'm talking about your Rockefellers, your Carnegies, your Vanderbilts," Howard said, and Robert felt a twinge of guilt, as if, for the sake of his father and grandfather, he should stand up to Howard and argue with him.

"These are the people America looks up to as heroes," Howard said. "These are the men that created the oil companies and the steel mills and railroads that made America what it is today. They all got rich from it, too, not just a little rich, I'm talking about fifty-car rich, houses with rooms you've never been in rich. And all that money came from the labor of other people. Other people that they kept on the edge of starvation or shot down in the streets when they got uppity, shot them down with their own private police forces, like the Ford Service, which at one time was the largest private army in the world.

"These men never stood together without selling each other out. They were individuals, by God, and they had no friends and nobody they trusted, and nobody they could even talk to. And they were miserable, by all accounts, every one of them, and scared sick of losing their money. But they wrote the story of this country, and that is the story of the individual above all else.

"And that is why we are here tonight. On the one hand is the lie that America is built on, the lie that all men are equal, the individual is sacred, don't tread on me. Behind that lie is the rich man, the powerful man, the greedy man.

"On the other hand is the truth that when the poor, the black, the disenfranchised stand together, there is no force on earth can stop us. We outnumber the rich and always will. This is still a democracy, more or less, and we have the ability to vote with our brains and not some kind of mixed up idealism that makes us go against our own interest. And we can organize, so that when the rich and privileged don't keep their promises, we have a way to make them listen."

It was a tough crowd, Robert saw, and when Howard said the word "organize" they began to slip away. Unions smacked of the North, of communism and disloyalty and troublemaking.

Howard saw it too and regrouped. "Because we are looking at a world of broken promises. Integration is a broken promise, broken since 1954. Look at Mississippi and Alabama and tell me the promise of voting rights is not broken. And we got serious broken promises here in Hayti.

"They told us we were going to have new buildings for our businesses, new homes for our families, and all they do is tear things down. This federal urban renewal program that's paying for all this, it happened right after we won *Brown v. Board of Education*, and you can't tell me that was a accident

"For every step forward there has been a step back. After slavery there was sharecropping and Jim Crow. Now that we've got Jim Crow on the run, there is something else happening, something even worse, some kind of all out economic warfare, war against the black and the poor, and if we don't want that to turn into actual war in the streets, we have to do something."

There it was, the threat behind the rhetoric. Robert realized he had been waiting for it, hardly breathing. Now that it was out there in the room he felt sad more than anything else. The mood around him was uneasy. People shifted their weight, talked in nervous whispers.

"We have to get together and stand together," Howard said, and Robert heard the first hint of desperation in his voice. "We have to stand together and say, 'If you want this road, give us our houses and our businesses. Do that first, then we build you your road.'"

"We say that," asked a voice Robert didn't recognize, "who puts the food on our tables?"

"*If* we start a union, and *if* the union has a action, we don't have to be fighting alone. That's the whole point. The I W W been fighting actions like this for fifty years. I ain't saying it's going to be easy. I ain't saying I got all the answers. What I *am* saying is, we have to start talking about it. We have to start now, because otherwise it's going to be too late. There won't be anything left of Hayti, no place for any of you to spend the money you make on this job, no place for the black man in America except prison or living on the street."

Robert, strangely, found himself rooting for Howard. Don't leave it there, he thought. Give us some hope, some good news, something to believe in.

Instead Howard seemed to have run out of gas. "That's all I got to say, really. If y'all got questions, ask them. Talk to each other, talk to me. This is about all of us, and whatever you got to say, I want to hear. In the meantime, I think Mercy has got some coffee and cookies and things like that."

Robert's head jerked around at the sound of her name, and there she was, coming out of the swinging door that led to the kitchen, carrying a tray and a coffee pot. She wore a white cotton dress, the top tight and low cut, the short loose skirt buoyed up by petticoats, revealing long, bare legs. It took Robert a while to realize he'd stopped breathing.

She put the tray on the table with poor grace and set the pot next to it. When she went back in the kitchen her gaze swept over Robert without seeming to register him. A moment later she was out again with another tray, this one stacked with mismatched coffee mugs. She set those down too and then walked straight up to him.

"What did you say your name was?"

"Robert." He was amazed the word came out so clearly.

"Robert. Do you dance?"

"Yes." He had to clear his throat and try again. "Yes, I dance. I'm a little rusty."

"That's all right. Long as you don't have to sit out, you won't be too bored. Wait here."

She made her way through the crowd with a languorous walk that rolled her hips and took her shoulders up and down. The rest of the men in the room didn't seem to pay her that much attention, maybe out of respect to Howard. To Robert she had the power of a slow hurricane.

She blew up to Howard where he stood talking to Mitch Antree and the preacher. Robert couldn't hear any of the words, only saw Howard excuse himself and turn to her. With growing horror, he saw Mercy point to him and saw Howard stare at him with narrowed eyes. Robert held up both hands, miming his incomprehension. Howard shook his head in what looked like disgust and turned to Antree.

Robert watched Mercy walk past him, and he thought, with a hint of disappointment, that the crisis was over. Then she was back, clutching a white patent pocketbook and saying, "Let's go."

"What?"

"I said, 'let's go.'"

"What in God's name are you talking about?"

"There's a swing band at the Biltmore Hotel. You are my chaperone."

"Are you crazy?"

"Like the lawyer said, don't ask questions you don't want to know the answer to. Are you coming or not?"

"I thought you were Barrett's woman."

"You, and Barrett, and everybody else needs to understand that I am nobody's woman other than my own. I'm not taking you out to fuck me, I'm taking you out to dance with me." Robert felt his face catch fire. "As long as Barrett don't want to dance with me, who I dance with is my own damn business. And as long as I'm going, he's better off having somebody with me that'll watch out for me. Now, for the last time, as the singer said, is you is or is you ain't coming along?"

The Colemans had edged away from him, as if sensing danger. Robert himself did not need a slide rule to do the calculations. There was nothing he wanted more than to go dancing with this woman. Not his job, not his marriage, not his physical safety.

"As the lady said," he shrugged, " 'let's go.' "

He followed her out onto the porch. "I don't have my car," he said. "I came with Mitch."

"We're taking my car." She produced a set of car keys in a leather folder and tossed them to him. "You're driving."

SHE HAD A BROWN late model Impala sedan, four doors, white vinyl seats, a family car. "I was expecting a red MG," he said, opening the passenger door for her.

"I use this car for work. Which is why you're driving. I'm tired of it."

As he got in on the driver's side the irrationality of what he was doing hit him like a freezing wind. Antree had specifically told him not to screw up, and here he was. Once the car was rolling, though, the feeling passed. In its place came a sense of unreality, like lying between waking and sleep on a Saturday morning, when fantasies blended seamlessly into dreams and began to play themselves out. He glanced at Mercy, who had coiled into the juncture of seat and door and was sizing him up.

"Where'd you learn to dance?" she asked.

"It started with my mother. My father stopped dancing after they got married, so she taught me when I was little. She'd play big band records, and we'd dance on the linoleum in the kitchen. What about you?"

"Men taught me."

Best not ask, he thought, how many. "So where do you work?"

"Mechanics and Farmers. I'm the head teller." Next to NC Mutual, Mechanics and Farmers was the most successful black business in Durham. Its offices had always been downtown on Parrish Street, the so-called Black Wall Street, though they had a branch in Hayti.

"That's impressive."

"Once I finish my master's at NCC, they're going to move me into accounting." North Carolina College, formerly North Carolina College for Negroes, was on Fayetteville Road on the southern end of Hayti. "Then I'm going to get me a nice house in South Durham, maybe on Hope Valley Road, get me a white boy to mow my grass."

"You don't want a family?"

"What do I want a family for? So I can end up like all my friends from high school? Fat, broke, and miserable, with a bunch of screaming kids? I don't think so. Park anywhere along here."

There were no spaces on Pettigrew, and Robert had to circle the block and park on Dillard. He walked around to open Mercy's door. She swept out of the car like royalty and left Robert to lock up and follow along behind.

He could still, at this point, deny any serious wrongdoing. They weren't having an affair. Howard knew where they were, and Robert had called Ruth from Elvira's, so she knew too, more or less. When Robert looked into his own heart, though, he saw desire and betrayal beyond forgiveness.

The Biltmore Hotel was three stories of dark red brick and a striped awning over the main entrance. The music spilled out onto the street, where it had drawn a small crowd, some of them dancing on the sidewalk, some clapping time. Mercy reached for his hand and drew him through the lobby, then shifted impatiently while he paid admission to a man at a card table outside the ballroom.

The room itself was small compared to the Durham Armory and some of the other local halls. The floor was polished hardwood, and the band had an elevated stage at the far end. There were eight of them, including four horns and a girl singer, all Negroes. They were playing Basie's "One O'Clock Jump," and Mercy dragged Robert straight onto the floor, already crowded with 40 or more couples, saying, "All right, Robert, let's see what you got."

Instead of the wild energy he'd expected from her, Mercy danced with smooth economy, swiveling on the swingouts and throwing embellishments into her other footwork, yet always showing up where she needed to be, right on time. She followed well, and Robert struggled to come up with new moves to keep her amused.

Meanwhile, on all sides, he glimpsed dancing like he'd never seen outside of the movies. Women were tossed in the air, flipped into handstands, thrown over partners' backs and hauled up between their legs. And that was just the flashy stuff. Even the older dancers were hitting the breaks in the music, styling with their hands and arms, throwing out kicks and slides, stomping and clapping, cutting up and cracking up.

Robert managed to finish with a quick dip. As he brought her back to her feet, Mercy smiled and said, "Who's rusty?" Robert thought it was perhaps the best thing anyone had ever said to him.

The band went immediately into "Woodchopper's Ball" and Mercy made no sign to leave, so Robert picked her up and swung her out again. He kept an eye on the other leaders, and some of their milder stuff reminded him of moves he knew. He sharpened his timing, putting more leverage into his swingouts, more precision on his tuck turns, letting his right hand hover at shoulder level when he wasn't using it. He felt the dance get better, the balance of pressure and resistance seeming to come straight out of the music.

By the end he was sweating, exhilarated, and exaggeratedly aware of Mercy's body. On stage, the orchestra stopped to adjust its sheet music. Mercy showed him her smile again. "Not too shabby," she said. "Your mama taught you all that?"

"Not all of it," he said.

Then he felt her attention fade. She glanced around the room, as if looking for someone, and Robert felt a pang of rejection. Had he really expected her to dance with him all night long? A moment later a tall, thin Negro of about 60 appeared, wearing a white shirt, bow tie, and newsboy cap, his shirt sweated through to reveal a sleeveless T-shirt underneath. He tipped his cap to Mercy and nodded to Robert.

"Hello, Bernie," Mercy said.

"Evening." He looked at Robert. "Might I borrow this young lady for a dance?"

Robert looked at Mercy, caught her nearly invisible nod, and smiled with the best grace he could manage. "Certainly," he said, and stepped aside.

He retired to a folding chair along the wall as the band lit into a swinging version of "Perfidia."

Bernie began slowly, reeling Mercy in and out, turning in place. Unlike the leaders who hunched low as they worked, Bernie was casual, collected. He barely seemed to move, Mercy responding to the merest flicks of his wrist with big turns and spins. Now that he was on the sidelines, Robert saw how high her skirt flew when she twirled; the entire length of her magnificent legs was on display, all the way to the edges of her white cotton panties. The sight constricted Robert's breathing.

As the song went on, Bernie dug deeper. Mercy began to hop as she moved in, first sitting on his bent leg, then letting him swing her around his back. Toward the end, he threw her in the air and caught her on his shoulders. She pushed off and did a split in midair, then landed cleanly, taking his hat with her. She put it on and kept it for a minute or so, then Bernie finished with a dip so low the hat came off again. He snagged it before it hit the ground and put it back on his own head.

Mercy gave Bernie a hug, and then there was another man waiting. Robert wondered if he'd get another dance. There were more men than women in the room, and no white women at all. He was far from home and had no idea of the rules.

He finally managed to look away from Mercy and saw Bernie walking toward him. Bernie had a longneck beer bottle in one hand, and he eased himself down into the chair next to Robert. "Lord, lord, lord," he said, stretching out his long legs. "Getting too old to be dancing like that."

"It was amazing," Robert said. "I wish I could dance like that."

"I guess it's like anything else. It's not too hard once you get the hang of it."

On impulse, Robert said, "That move where you put her over your back. Could you show it to me?" Aerials were strictly forbidden at the dances Robert had been to.

Bernie looked at him hard and squinted one eye. "I might could. Wait till this dance over, see can we get somebody to help us out."

The entire room now knew that Mercy was there. Before the last notes of the song had died out, men were circling her in a feeding frenzy, and Robert worried that they might turn on each other. Bernie waded into the chaos and returned with a slight woman in a yellow sundress. Her slack expression added to the impression of childishness. "What you want with me, Bernie?" Her voice was a high chirp.

"Going to help out my friend here." To Robert he said, "Minnie don't weigh hardly anything. She'll be easy to learn on."

"Don't want nobody learning on me," she said.

"I'm Robert," he interrupted, offering his hand.

"Pleased to make your acquaintance," Minnie said, and curtseyed.

Bernie gathered her up in closed position. "I'll walk through it once as slow as I can. Thing is, you can't slow it down too much or you lose your momentum."

It took Robert ten minutes to get the basics of the move—the footwork, the lead, the mechanics of the lift, the follow-through. Minnie was stoic throughout. Finally he took her onto the floor and worked the pattern in again and again, having to abort the first couple of times, missing the timing on the next few, then, like a miracle, working it over and over.

When the song was over she shook his hand and said, "Thank you very kindly for the dance, but I believe you has worn me out." With great dignity she walked over to the chairs and sat down.

He went over to thank Bernie, and found him talking to a woman in her forties, heavier than Minnie, and yet not, Robert thought, out of the question for his new move. "This is my friend Robert," Bernie said. "Robert, this is Audrey."

"Hi, Audrey," Robert said. "Would you care to dance?"

After that the ice was well broken. He started to ask strangers. A few turned him down, and he smiled and moved on; others, especially the older women, gave him a chance and he felt he was able to show them a good time.

The band struck up "Moonglow," one of Robert's favorites. He was looking for a likely prospect when an arm slipped around his waist from behind. "Did you forget about me?" Mercy's voice asked.

He turned to face her. They were both hot, sweating, flushed. "No," he said.

She moved into his arms. The band took it slow, and she laid her head against his damp shirt. He smelled the perfume in her hair and the warmth of her body, like fresh ironed linen.

"I saw your new trick," she said.

"Bernie's a great teacher."

"Something like that," she said.

He wasn't sure what she meant, didn't need to know. The only thing that mattered was the pressure of her body against his, the music. They danced like old lovers who knew each other's every breath and heartbeat.

The reckless feeling that had been haunting him passed in the course of the dance. By the end he felt a quiet determination, something like destiny.

He dipped her long and slow on the final chord, one hand behind her neck for support. As he brought her up, she held him by the arms and didn't let go. "Want to show me your trick?"

"If you're willing to risk it."

"Like the gambler said, 'What's to lose?'"

Mercy ignored the two men standing next to her, waiting their turns. The piano player called for Charlie Barnett's "Skyliner," "on the tracks." She took Robert's left hand in her right and put her free arm on his shoulder. The band took off like a Redstone rocket. Robert got on board. The speed of the music made everyone crazy. Women flew, men hit the floor in splits and bounced up again, couples spun around each other like Tilt-A-Whirl cars. Robert put Mercy over his back and liked it so much he sent her over a second time, which earned him a "Whoooo" from her, nearly lost in the thunder of the band and the cries of the other dancers.

When it ended they were hanging on each other, out of breath. The piano player said the band would be back in 15 minutes and Mercy said, "Take me outside. I need some air."

The night had turned cold. Steam came off the dancers' clothes as they stood on the sidewalk, pointing at each other and laughing. Robert passed his pack of Luckies around. Bernie and Mercy and a couple of others helped themselves, and he lit them all with his Army Zippo. The talk was about the band, about the NCAA basketball tournament that had ended a couple of weeks before. Robert leaned against the bricks of the hotel and closed his eyes. When he opened them again Mercy was leaning against the wall next to him.

He tried to think of something conversational to say, then let it go. Ruth felt compelled to fill every silence with talk and it was peaceful just to lean. He knew more or less what she was thinking. There would be songs still echoing in her head, the pleasant hum of fatigue in her muscles, memories of weightless moments above the dance floor.

When their Luckies burned down, he pushed himself onto his aching feet and felt Mercy slide her arm through his. As they strolled inside, he wondered where he would find the energy to dance any more, at the same time that he knew he would, and in fact did, as soon as the music started again.

He danced again with all the women he'd danced with in the first set, and Bernie volunteered to show him another move, and Robert learned it, and it seemed like every third or fourth number Mercy was there to dance with him again, and she always found him for the slow ones. He neither sought her out nor questioned his fortune, simply accepted it for the gift it was.

At midnight the band took another break and Mercy said, "That's it. My dogs are barking." She limped alternately on both feet to make her point. I suspect your friend Mitch is long gone. How you going to get home?"

He hadn't thought that far ahead, hadn't thought how it would hit him in the pit of the stomach to say goodbye to her. "My car's down the street. You could drop me if you like."

She gave languorous hugs to some of the other dancers on the way out, and a kiss on the cheek to Bernie. She whispered something to him, and he looked at Robert and laughed. "My pleasure," he said. "Y'all be careful now, hear?"

They walked side by side to her car, close without touching. Robert was thinking about kissing her. He was pretty sure she would let him. He wondered what those wide, swollen lips would feel like under his. He felt as if he'd been waiting his entire life to find out.

She stepped into the street, toward the driver's side, and held out her hand for the keys. Robert passed them to her and waited for her to get in and reach across to unlock the passenger door. She started the car and said, "It hurts to work the pedals." Robert closed his door. "Where are you?" she asked.

"Fayetteville Street. South of Pettigrew." He savored their last moments together. He was calm and happy being near her, the way he felt in dreams. She was like one of those negative ion generators he'd read about in *Time,* that were supposed to make you feel like you were on a beach or next to a waterfall.

Cars slowly cruised the streets, windows down, radios blaring, young black

men leaning out to call to people on the sidewalk. It was utterly unlike the
world Robert had grown up in, yet it seemed comfortable, familiar. Maybe it
was the fatigue.

"It's the black Mercury there on the left," he said.

She stopped the car there in the street, halting traffic behind them, and
turned to him. "Thank you," she said. Her tough façade was nowhere in sight.

"My pleasure." He saw then that to kiss her at that moment would be pre-
dictable, and would thus surrender his only advantage. Still, it was more than
he could do to simply walk away. He put his right hand on her cheek, barely
touching it, then ran his first two fingers across the fullness of her lower lip.
She closed her eyes. He noticed, finally, her earrings, tiny scrollwork hearts.

"Take care," he said, and got out into the street. He stood next to the line
of parked cars and watched her drive away, half-blinded by the oncoming
headlights.

HE LAID HIS SWEAT-SOAKED CLOTHES across the washing machine
and showered before getting into bed. Unlike the last time he'd stayed late in
Hayti, he felt no desire for Ruth as she lay snoring gently next to him. Rather
he felt as if he'd wandered into the wrong house, and that if Ruth woke she
would fail to recognize him, would scream and call the police.

At the same time, the reality of what he'd done began to sink in. Undoubtedly he'd made an enemy of Barrett Howard, which could be disastrous for
Mason and Antree. Someone might have recognized him at the Biltmore or
on the street outside. Word could get back to Ruth, or, worse yet, her father.

Then he remembered the sensation of Mercy's arm sliding around him and
her voice saying, "Did you forget about me?" His face felt odd and he touched
it, finding it stretched wide by a smile he hadn't known was there.

He fell asleep to "Moonglow" playing in his head.

ALL DAY SATURDAY Robert worried that Antree would call. He might be
fired. How could be possibly explain?

In the early afternoon he made a weak excuse and drove to St. Joseph's
AME church in Hayti, remembering what Maurice had said. And it was true.
The thing on top of the steeple was the same symbol that hung from Mercy's
ears. The memory of his fingers on her lips, the heat of her breath on his fin-
gertips, made him squeeze his eyes shut, not to push it away but to hold on a
little longer.

THAT NIGHT HE TOOK Ruth to the country club for dinner. Afterwards
they danced to Lawrence Welk-style schmaltz delivered by a band of senior

citizens. After three songs Robert excused himself to stand out on the patio, light a Lucky, and stare at the gently rolling fairways of the golf course. He was alone except for a teenaged daughter of Durham society, who nursed a bottle of Coke and pretended not to watch him.

The eastern sky glowed with the lights of downtown, turning the clouds a smoky red. Hayti was over there, and Barrett Howard was probably out in it with Mercy. Her body was probably moving under her dress the way it would under satin sheets, the fabric soft and clinging, still not softer than her skin.

A waiter stepped out from the kitchen, dressed in white shirt, black pants, and a black bow tie. He was the same age as Robert. He carried a white towel over one arm and an empty tray under the other. "Beautiful evening, ain't it, sir?" he said. He began to clear glasses from one of the tables.

"Yes," Robert said. "Yes, it is. Won't be this cool much longer."

The man chuckled as if Robert had offered some profound wisdom. "No, sir, you got that sure enough right. Summer be down upon us before you know it. Ain't no doubt about that. No, sir."

Reflexively Robert offered his Luckies. The man held up one hand and said, "No, thank you, sir. Very kind of you, but we ain't allowed to smoke on the job."

The "we," Robert understood, referred not to the job description but the skin color.

"Anything I can bring you, sir? Drink from the bar?"

"No," Robert said. "Thanks. I need to be getting back in."

"Then you enjoy your evening, sir."

Robert nodded, deeply uncomfortable, at a complete loss for a way to bridge the chasm between them. I'm not who you think I am, he wanted to say. I was in Hayti last night, dancing at the Biltmore. How condescending did that sound? How many unwarranted assumptions did it make?

"Thanks," he mumbled. He flipped his cigarette into the thick, green lawn and went inside, back to the cool, clean arms of his wife, the tepid music, the loud voices of white men, the clinking of glasses, the life that was laid out before him like a narrow road with high, neatly trimmed hedges on either side.

ALL THE WAY to work Monday morning Robert dragged his anxiety behind him like an anchor. The night had been one long, anxious dream of lost piece drawings, desperate searches, waking, turning, falling again into nightmare.

He was at his desk by 8. Antree arrived at 9:15 and went straight into his office without speaking. It was a relief when, half an hour later, he finally opened the office door and called Robert in.

Too much coffee and too many cigarettes had left Robert feeling breakable. He sat with his elbows on his knees, shaky hands clasped in front of him.

"Howard is going forward with the union thing," Antree said. Nothing in his tone pointed to Robert's betrayal of Friday night. The feeling of relief was so powerful that Robert thought he could fall asleep where he sat. "Even Leon and Tommy were thinking about it. This could do us real harm."

"He's asking for what, more money for the workmen?"

"I don't care about the bread. There's enough of that around, and those men get paid pretty good anyway. The hassle is that Howard is asking us to come through on our promises. The shopping center, the apartments, the housing developments, everything."

"I don't understand. We're planning to do all of that, aren't we?" He finally met Antree's eyes and saw claustrophobia there.

"It's not up to me. I'm just a cog. Howard may single us out because of the expressway. He said at one point Friday, he said, 'There's not going to be an expressway until we get houses.' But then, you weren't there for that part."

Uh oh, Robert thought.

"He can stop the freeway if he has a mind to," Antree said. "We don't have the right of way yet, can't get it until DoT makes the route official. He can make that hard. Strikes, sabotage ... it could get ugly."

"Can't we build some houses?"

"That's not our contract."

"Whose is it?"

"I don't think that's been bid yet."

"The freeway contract you keep saying is ours isn't let either."

"Yeah, only that one is guaranteed to come our way. You may not think too much of me. I know a lot people think I'm a happy-go-lucky idiot. The thing is, this is a lot harder than it looks. It's a balancing act, every day. If it was just me I wouldn't care, but I got employees, I got overhead, I got the people in Hayti I made promises to, I got the future of Durham at stake, because if RTP doesn't work, this whole town could go under.

"I got into this business because I wanted to do some good in the world. I guess I was pretty naïve, all right. But I'm not ready to pack it in yet."

It was all Robert could do not to look behind him, to see if there were someone else in the room that Antree was performing for.

"There is a point to this," Antree said, "and the point is this. Howard seems to like you, God knows why."

"Really?"

"I'd be looking to kill you, myself, after Friday night. Apparently he's used to that kind of thing with her. Seems she told him she liked the way you handled yourself, that you were a quote unquote real gentleman."

Robert longed for detail that he knew Antree didn't have. He forced himself to concentrate on what Antree was saying.

"He wants to meet with you. Wednesday afternoon, one o'clock. Meet him in the lobby of the Biltmore Hotel. You know where that is, right?"

Robert saw the bait and refused to take it. He was keeping his night with Mercy strictly to himself. "Yes," he said. "Do you have any idea what this is about?"

"Haven't got the foggiest. And I'm counting on you to take mental notes. I want to know everything he says to you and the tone of voice he says it in. You dig?"

Robert stood up. "This is all too weird. What did I do?"

"I don't think what you did is the issue. It's more about who you are."

Robert shook his head. "Is that supposed to be mystical or something?"

Antree waved his hand and started looking through the papers on his desk. "Nothing," he said. "Never mind."

Robert reached for the door.

"One more thing," Antree said.

Robert froze, thinking, here it comes.

"You may have used your connections to get this job, but don't push it. You understand what I'm saying?"

"Connections?" Robert said, turning slowly to face him.

Antree stared. "Your father-in-law? And his pal, the voice of race hatred on WRAL?"

Robert sat down again. "What are you talking about?"

"No, you wouldn't know, would you? I was wondering how somebody so cold-blooded could pull off that innocent act so well. Only it isn't an act at all, is it? That's what Howard and Mercy and everybody else is so taken with. Me too, God help me."

"Are you talking about Randy Fogg, the sportswriter? I don't even know the guy."

"Maybe you don't. Ruth's father does."

"And what does Fogg have to do with you or this job?"

"Look, I'm sorry I said anything, all right? Forget about it. Forget I said anything at all."

All Robert could think of was the way he'd bragged to his father that he'd won this job through skill alone. What did he have, really, that was all his own? His skills as an engineer, which he'd barely used. A hi-fi and some records, an aging Mercury hardtop sedan.

"Get to work," Antree said, with a cheer that rang as false as his earlier melodrama. "Go on, now."

Robert stood and walked numbly to the door.

"And don't forget Wednesday," Antree said. "One PM sharp."

FOR THE REST of the day his mind circled between Randy Fogg, Wilmer Bynum, and Ruth. He'd told Ruth, naturally, when he applied for the job, given her all the details. She must have known about Randy Fogg's connection to Mason and Antree—whatever it was—and gone to her father.

For that matter, the idea that Antree was involved with a racist like Fogg was baffling, incredible. As badly as he wanted to know what the relationship was, he was equally afraid of finding something out that would make it impossible to go on working there.

Behind it all lurked his own sense of guilt. He was in no position to talk about betrayal after Friday night. Not to mention the thoughts he'd had since, more vivid and more credible now than they'd been the week before.

At five he left the office determined to have it out with Ruth, only to feel his will erode the closer he got to home. He ended up staring at the reservoir from Club Boulevard until he was late for dinner. He spent the rest of the night swallowing his feelings the same way he'd choked down the overcooked, tasteless pork chops, listening to Ruth prattle on, remembering the long, stoic silences of his father and not wanting to repeat them, unable to find a way to break the pattern.

By Wednesday the pain had dulled, and the need for reckoning lost its urgency. It was easier to carry the hurt than share it.

And by then it was time to meet Barrett Howard.

ROBERT GOT TO THE BILTMORE ten minutes early. Once he was sitting in an overstuffed chair, gazing into the ballroom where he and Mercy had danced, the tie he was wearing seemed too much. He pulled it off, folded it, and stuck it in his jacket pocket.

He'd lain awake for an hour that morning, watching the hands of the clock crawl toward 6:30. He'd pictured Howard taking him out into the countryside, pushing him to the ground and shooting him in the head. I won't kneel, he'd thought. If he's going to shoot me anyway, at least I can die on my feet.

In the light of day the fantasy had seemed ridiculous. It came back full force when Howard finally walked into the lobby, scowling, the stub of a cigar smoldering in the corner of his mouth.

Robert stood up.

"Sorry I'm late," Howard said, and offered his hand. His left eye was squinting against the cigar smoke, Robert thought, that was all. He wore jeans, a blue chambray work shirt, and a flowered tie. "Been waiting long?"

"No," Robert lied. "Not long."

"You up for walking? I want to show you some things."

"Sure. Okay."

They turned left outside the hotel and walked past the Regal Theater, then turned into the Donut Shop. The space was long and narrow, with a chrome counter and stools along the right hand wall and booths along the left. Older men in suits filled half the seats, teenaged girls in long dresses the rest. The air smelled of yeast and sugar, and Ray Charles was on the jukebox, singing "I Can't Stop Loving You." A middle-aged woman at the soda fountain flipped Howard a two-fingered salute, and he leaned across the counter to hug her. "Anybody in the Jade Room, Miss Ella?"

"Just let out," she said. "You want anything to eat?"

"Not this time. Showing my friend Robert around."

"Hello, Robert," she said, with a smile.

Even as Robert saw the "my friend" for the blatant manipulation it was, he couldn't deny the warmth it gave him. "Hi," he said, and smiled back.

A door at the far end of the shop led into a second, parallel room, even more narrow, done in pea-green wallpaper with pink trim. Square, unframed mirrors every ten feet or so gave the illusion of more space. Eight pedestal tables, side by side, ran the length of the room, covered with white tablecloths and the remains of lunch. Two middle aged women in elaborate dresses were fussing with their hats and gossiping as Robert and Howard walked in.

"Afternoon, ladies," Howard said.

Apparently they recognized him. Heads down and all but clucking their tongues, they squeezed past and bustled out the door.

"The Jade Room," Howard said. "Official meeting place of everyone from the North Carolina Lawyers Association to bridge clubs and kids' birthday parties. This is where community happens, here in this room."

His sincerity was palpable. Robert felt petty when he asked, "Why are you telling me this?"

"Because you need to understand what it is that you're tearing down. These are not just buildings. This isn't just history. This is a living, thriving culture with roots that go deep into this particular patch of ground. You cut the people loose from Hayti and you're not only taking away their homes and their businesses, you're taking away the glue that holds them together, that makes them strong. You're taking away their barbers, their babysitters, their mechanics, the faces they nod to every day even when they don't know their names."

"You act like I have some say in this. Like I have the power to stop it."

"Mitch Antree listens to you. He trusts you. Why else did he bring you to that meeting the other night?"

Because I ran into him on the street, Robert thought. Instead he said, "This is bigger than Mason and Antree, and you know it. If Mitch refused to do the work, they'd just get somebody else in here, probably somebody who'd take a lot more pleasure in it and get the job done a lot faster."

Howard slowly deflated. He settled into a chair and slumped forward. "Shit," he said.

"I'm sorry."

"No. No, you're right." Howard pushed his massive fingers through his thick, unprocessed hair. "All you have to do is look around, see what's going down everywhere else. Paradise Valley in Detroit, the Shaw District in DC, the Hill District in Pittsburgh. What the government hasn't knocked down yet they're going after."

"I could quit," Robert said. "You could work on the next guy Mitch hires, maybe you could get him to quit too. And the guy after that."

"No, that ain't no good either."

Robert sat down facing him. "Well, at least you could finish showing me around."

"Why?"

"Because I'm interested."

"You don't have to humor me."

"This is for real. I want to know."

Slowly Howard got onto his feet. "All right. Come on, then."

Robert followed him out to the sidewalk. They stopped at the Biltmore Drug Store, occupying a corner of the hotel lobby, to get Howard a fresh cigar. The woman behind the counter was the daughter of Gloria Pratt, "the most beautiful woman I ever saw," Howard said. "I used to come in here and buy a pack of Juicy Fruit every Friday afternoon, just to look at her." He smiled at the cashier. "You've got her eyes."

Robert hadn't known that Negroes could blush until that moment. "You're still going to have to pay for that cigar," she said.

"So you grew up here," Robert said to Howard.

"Born in Monroe, North Carolina, down by Charlotte." He took his change and held the door for Robert. "Moved here when I was four. Left when I was seventeen to live with my auntie in Chicago so I could go to school at Chicago State. Got a master's in sociology. Got tired of racism in the north and came down here to fight it at the source. Married once, too young. Got a son I don't get to visit. I like to bowl. Throw a decent hook and own a 201 average. Something about that little black ball and all those white pins. Anything else you want to know?"

There was a lot Robert wanted to know. Most of it had to do with Mercy and he wasn't ready to borrow that particular trouble yet. So he asked, "What do you do with a master's in sociology?"

"Teach. I got three sections at NCC, one freshman and two advanced. When I can, I teach some classes at Durham Tech. And the other thing you do when you're a black man with a sociology degree is, you have opinions. That's the problem with education. You get to thinking your opinion is worth more than some ignorant fool's."

"Any fool in particular?"

"If you're trying to get me to say Mayor R. Wense Grabarek, then I would ask you why you want to ask a question if you already know the answer?"

Howard's confrontations with the mayor of Durham were a recurring story in the *Herald,* and something in his tone made Robert let out a short, surprised laugh. Howard smiled, and for the first time Robert saw the vulnerability and need to please under the showmanship.

They were in front of the Wonderland Theater. "I know you know this place," Howard said. "I want you to know something about the man that built it."

"Tell me," Robert said.

"His name was Frederick K. Watkins. They called him 'the Movie King.' He built the Wonderland in 1920. He had a chain of theaters across the Southeast, and he lived here in Hayti. He went before the City Council in the thirties, trying to get black police officers for Hayti. Didn't get them, but he tried. He got his start in movies by making them himself and taking them around and showing them in schools."

They walked on. "When that place goes, won't be anything like it to take its place," Howard said. "You ever been to Europe?"

Robert nodded. "I was there in the Army."

"You know what I'm talking about, then. They got buildings there hundreds of years old. It's history you can walk around inside of, you know what I'm saying?"

People they passed called and reached out to Howard. Most of them were young, most of them male, but there were women too, and Robert had a strong feeling that Mercy was not the only one straining against the limits of the relationship. None of these people seemed to want anything more than the acknowledgement that Howard gave them—a nod, a handshake, the sound of their own names.

"Down at the end of the block, that's the *Carolina Times.* Louis Austin bought it in 1927, used to be the *Standard Advertiser.* That's thirty-seven years that man has been fighting. We don't always see eye to eye. He's a very religious man, which I am not. He got his positive message, which I sometimes don't think is justified. But damn. Two or three editorials every week, for longer than I been alive, going up against the Klan, the NRC, the City Council, the Durham Select Committee, never backing down, not even in the face of death threats, never giving up, never losing his faith. I cannot imagine that. If you was to read that paper—"

"I do read it."

That stopped him. "For real? Since when?"

"A few weeks now."

"Why?"

Robert shrugged, wishing he hadn't said anything.

"Jungle fever, that's why," Howard said. "You got the fever for Mercy."

"Are you sure you want to talk about this now?" Robert said. "Here in the street?"

"Why, you afraid I'm going to come after you? I ain't going to come after you. Not unless there's something I don't know about."

"No," Robert said. He felt a drop of sweat run down under one arm. Then, amazed, he heard himself say, "Except what's in my head."

Howard stared at him. "Man, you either brave or crazy, one."

Later, when he tried to explain it to himself, Robert thought it was the loneliness. He couldn't talk about Mercy to Ruth or Mitch Antree; not to anyone else at work; not to any of his casual acquaintances at the country club. Barrett Howard was the only man he knew who could possibly understand what he was feeling.

"Come on," Howard said. "Let's get this off the street." They were standing in front of Elvira's. Howard walked up to the door and motioned Robert in. They sat at a red vinyl booth, and Howard ordered two bottles of Schlitz.

"I have to go back to work," Robert said with little conviction.

"Antree knows you're with me. He ain't going to say nothing."

The waitress, a heavyset beauty in her late thirties, was already back. She ran her hand affectionately through Howard's hair as she dropped off the bottles.

"Drink your beer," Howard said.

Robert drank. The beer was as cold as freshly melted snow, so cold it tasted like nothing at all.

"So what are you trying to say about Mercy?" Howard asked. "Are you in love with her?"

"I don't know," Robert said. "I don't know what I'm feeling. I've never felt anything like it. I'm all knotted up when I'm not with her, and when I'm around her, if she's even somewhere in the vicinity, then I'm calm and happy."

"This is based on what, seeing her twice in your life?"

Robert had to stop to count. "Yeah. It's like she's a place and not a person. Like a tree house when you're a kid."

"I never had no tree house," Howard said. "not that many trees in most of the places I lived."

"How long have you known her?"

"Couple years."

"Where did you meet her?"

Howard thought it over for a second or two, then shook his head. "I can't tell you that."

"Is this that voodoo business?"

Howard fixed him again with a look that should have terrified him. "Yeah," Howard said. "Yeah, it's 'that voodoo business.' I went to her for instruction." He took a long drink and then put his left arm up along the back of the booth. "I don't know any of what you're talking about, that calmness and all. It was the power that got me. There is something about a powerful woman that does the trick for me, and I felt it the first time I saw her." Then, as if he couldn't help himself, as if he had to prove ownership, he said, "She felt it too. She was in my bed that same night."

Robert had to look away from him, down to the rings their beer bottles had left on the table.

"Look," Howard said, "you are in so far over your head you got no idea. You ain't got the idea of an idea. You think this is all about Bebop and the Lindy Hop. That shit ain't even a gnat on that woman's windscreen."

"You're wrong," Robert said.

"You're telling *me* I'm *wrong?*"

"I'm saying I know how she feels about the music and the dancing. I feel the same way. If you don't feel it, how can you understand?"

"Motherfucker," Howard said, and his voice was barely a whisper, "you want to understand, I'll give you understanding." He stood up and for a second Robert thought he might be in serious physical danger. "You be outside your house at midnight. You might want to be wearing old clothes. I'm a come pick you up. Be out there waiting, 'cause I don't want to have to come in there and wake your ass up." He threw two dollars on the table, finished his beer in one long swallow, and walked out the door.

ROBERT WENT BACK to the office. His hands felt weak and unsteady and he couldn't control his pencil. When he tried to roll the lead against the parallel bar it leapt out onto the page; when he tried to letter the point snapped off. He knew he should talk to Antree, but still jumped when he heard Antree's voice suddenly behind him saying, "My office."

Robert followed him in and closed the door. Antree's smile melted when he saw Robert's face. "What the hell happened?"

"Nothing," Robert said, his shrug stiff and unconvincing. "He wanted to give me a history lesson so I would stop knocking Hayti down. I tried to tell him it wasn't my decision."

"And then what?"

"What do you mean, then what?"

"You look like a college girl trying to smuggle dope through customs. What did you do?"

Robert shrugged again. "We talked about Mercy."

"Holy Christ. What did he say?"

"We just talked."

"The hell you did. Why does this always happen? Why does some chick come along, and everybody starts thinking with their dicks, and everybody else's hard work goes down the drain? Friends, business partners, employees, everybody turning on each other and burning everything down, and for what? A piece of ass? Something that will come and go and leave nothing but regrets?"

Robert thought it would be worth anything to avoid one of Antree's bouts of self-pity. Rare as they were, they seemed endless when they came. "It's not like that," he said. "He made me drink a beer with him in the middle of the afternoon and it gave me a headache. In fact, we're going to hang out some more later tonight."

Antree's emotions spun in a tight circle and came roaring back. "You're kidding. No shit?"

"It's true," Robert said.

"Why didn't you say so in the first place? This is great. I don't know how the hell you pulled this off, but it's groovy, dad. Take the rest of the afternoon off. You're going to need your wits about you." As Robert stood up, Antree came around the desk and put his arm around him. "You're the key to this whole deal," Antree said. "If you can handle Barrett Howard, man, we are home free."

ALL THE WAY HOME Robert tried to come up with a believable excuse for going out at midnight. His brain was sluggish. He had pulled all the way into the driveway, in fact, before he noticed the brand-new red and white Buick sedan parked in front of him.

Ruth met him at the door. "Oh my Lord," she said. "Is something wrong? I can explain about the car. What are you doing home? Are you sick? Is everything all right?"

"Whose car is it?" Robert asked, his thoughts leaping automatically to infidelity. He almost hoped it was true.

"It's mine. Ours, I mean. I was going to surprise you. Well, I guess I did surprise you. Daddy bought it for my birthday next month, and I've been keeping it parked down the street. I didn't think you'd be home—"

"Down the street?"

"Well, I know how you feel about Daddy's money, and him paying for the house and everything."

Not to mention buying my job, Robert thought bitterly.

"And so I was trying to think of the right way to tell you without you getting upset, or feeling like..." She broke off and attempted a smile.

"Like what?" Robert asked, keeping his voice calm.

"You know, like you can't take care of me or anything. In the style to which I'm accustomed."

Robert saw then that he didn't have to explain anything. All he had to do was walk away.

And, surprising himself yet again, that was exactly what he did.

"Robert?" she called after him from the front door. "Robert, where are you going?"

He got in the Mercury, headache gone, elation rising in his chest. I don't know, he thought. I don't know where I'm going. And I don't care.

He drove toward town out of reflex, then remembered that Howard was supposed to pick him up at midnight. He had no phone number for Howard or Mercy, no way to reach either of them other than driving to their house. So that was what he did.

He arrived a few minutes after four and parked behind a boxy black 1960 Ford Falcon on the street. Mercy's Impala sat in the driveway, and the sight of it excited him. He looked at his hair in the rearview mirror and finger-combed it away from his forehead, checked his deodorant, which had not yet given up, and got out of the car.

It was a beautiful afternoon, cloudless, hot, not yet suffocating the way it would be in July and August. Here in Hayti it was less beautiful than it was among the rich lawns and overarching trees of Woodrow Street. Life here was exposed, raw, transitory.

Robert climbed the steep sidewalk to the porch and knocked on the front door. There was no answer, so after a minute he tried again, louder. He hesitated a few seconds, then, suddenly self-conscious, started to turn away.

The door opened. Howard stood there in nothing but a pair of blue jeans, primal and imposing. Behind him, Mercy leaned against a doorway in a white terrycloth robe. She wore her usual abstracted smile. "Hello, Robert," she said.

Howard seemed more amused than angry. "I guess God really does look after fools and drunkards. I can't believe you come pounding on my door like this and I ain't killed you yet."

"I'm sorry," Robert said. "I didn't mean ... I didn't realize I was interrupting..."

"You didn't interrupt anything," Howard said. "If there had been something to interrupt, I wouldn't have come to the door. But I still have hopes, so tell me what you want and be on your way."

"We need to meet someplace else tonight," Robert said.

Howard turned to Mercy. "You go on back to the bedroom, honey. I'll be there in a minute."

He stepped out onto the porch and pulled the door to. "What happened, your wife throw you out?"

Robert shrugged, not yet ready to think through what he'd done. "You could pick me up at Elvira's or something."

Howard looked at him closely. "You all right?"

"I'm good," Robert said. "Really."

Howard started to go in, then said, "This thing tonight. Mercy don't know about you being there. It might be better for everybody if we kept it that way. You understand what I'm saying?"

Robert nodded, though he did not, in fact, understand. "Can you pick me up at Elvira's? Midnight?"

Howard nodded once, sharply, and went in the house. Robert tried not to think about him going into the darkened bedroom, slipping out of his jeans, opening Mercy's robe, peeling it back from her shoulders, her still smiling that mysterious smile.

He drove to the Kresge's downtown to eat, and while he was there, not knowing when or if he would go back to the house, he picked up a cheap white shirt and a change of socks and underwear. The defiance was liberating and a bit dangerous, as if he were a teenager running away from home.

He ate a hamburger at the lunch counter. None of the black people that shopped all around him were eating. Robert was still trying not to think of those other two black people and what they might or might not still be doing. Images from racy films he'd seen in the Army came unbidden into his head, with Howard and Mercy substituting in the lead roles.

Once cool, the hamburger lost most of its appeal. Robert grazed on the remaining potato chips and pickle slices, then surrendered to his impulse to return to the office. Outside of Ruth, his records, and his tentative new life in Hayti—none of which were available at the moment—work was all he knew.

The lights were all on and Miles was in the midst of one of the more dirgelike moments on *Sketches of Spain* when Robert opened the door. Mitch looked up from his central drafting table, blinking, as if he'd been asleep. His tie was loose and his collar open, his eyes puffy and his chin dark with stubble. When he saw Robert, he smiled. "Bobby! I thought you'd be home with the little woman."

Robert's innate caution kept him from saying anything about Ruth. He shrugged instead.

"You still seeing Barrett tonight?"

"Later. I got a few hours to kill."

"Hell, let's make some plans, then." It was a joke Mitch never tired of. "You want a drink?"

"That's okay."

Robert went to the drawers and took out the plans and elevations for a sub-urban bank branch that Fred Mason had drawn. Mitch went to his office and emerged with a highball. On the way back he took Miles off the turntable and put on Cannonball Adderley's *Them Dirty Blues,* leading off, appropriately, with his brother Nat's "Work Song." The change in tempo brightened the room.

Robert taped down the drawings and began taking sections through the walls, stopping at interesting intersections to lay out piece drawings for the individual members. It was work that occupied the part of the brain that worried while leaving free the part that listened to music.

Mitch kept the music coming, moving from Adderley to Duke Pearson's *Dedication,* then to *Ellington at Newport,* and finally back to Miles for *The Birth of the Cool.* He seemed to be rationing himself to one drink per album, a pace nonetheless sufficient to put him well in the bag by 8:30.

"That's it," he said at last. "Time to split this lame joint. The service is for the birds."

"You okay to drive?"

"Hell, yes. The day I have to drive sober, that's the day you should start worrying." Robert knew that Mitch was drunk, even if he couldn't point to clear symptoms. His hands were steady and his speech was clear, but his eyes were anesthetized. "Good luck with Howard. Don't worry about coming in on time tomorrow. Get a decent night's sleep."

Robert nodded, not sure such a thing was possible. A minute later he heard Mitch's Cadillac start up over the last notes of "Darn That Dream" and gently squeal its tires as it pulled out of the lot.

With Mitch gone, Robert's concentration faded. After 15 restless minutes he shut the office down and pointed his car south, past Hayti and St. Joseph's, past Beechwood Cemetery and out into tobacco country, one small farm

after another, the plants only a few inches high and pale green in the moonlight. At some point he pulled over and walked out between the rows. He
fired up a Lucky, the end product of all this effort, though it was no longer
made in Durham. Somewhere near where he was standing the new Interstate 40 would go, connecting the south edge of Raleigh to the south edge
of Durham and the north edge of Chapel Hill. Meanwhile I-85 would swoop
down and replace State Highway 70 across the north of Durham, meet up
with 40 on the far side of Hillsboro, and the two roads would run west together until Greensboro.

Durham's East-West Expressway would connect the two. When it was
done, it would split off from I-85 eastbound near Robert's house, cut
through downtown, then curve south to meet I-40 on the edge of RTP.
There was talk that the East-West Expressway might get designated an
alternate route for I-40, which would put them in the way of even more
federal money. Altogether the three highways represented millions of tons of
concrete that would change the face of the Triangle, of all of North Carolina,
wake Durham from its coma, bring jobs and money and the whole star-
spangled dream. Despite Barrett Howard's union speech, it was still a dream
Robert believed in, a dream where the jobs and the money weren't ends in
themselves but the raw materials of freedom.

However tainted his entry, the dream was his to be part of, if he could keep
his focus. His career would survive a divorce, if it came to that. If the improb-
able happened with Mercy, the thing that he believed in and Barrett Howard
insisted was his ignorance talking, Mitch would sympathize if anyone would.
And if he couldn't save Hayti, he would save all he could.

He drove slowly toward town, feeling the length of the day, the lateness of
the hour, and drank coffee at Elvira's until midnight.

HOWARD WAS LATE, and Robert began to let himself hope that nothing
would happen. Elvira closed up and put him on the street, and Robert was
thinking about where he was going to spend the night when Howard's black
Falcon jerked to a stop in front of him. It was 12:15.

"Get in," Howard said. Robert climbed in the passenger seat, trying to
judge Howard's mood. Not anger or triumph, but something more turned
in, private, determined. Once they were moving, Howard handed him a large
gray hooded sweatshirt. "Put that on. Once we get there, keep the hood up so
you won't be so conspicuous."

Robert had speculated that wherever they were going had to do with the
things Maurice had warned him about. The voodoo. He associated the word
with pins in dolls and mandrake roots and stealth and subversion. Something

in Howard's grim expression said this would be confrontational. Up until that moment he had assumed that being with Howard would keep him safe. He felt the first chill of real fear.

He sniffed at the sweatshirt. It smelled clean. Mercy washed this, he thought. The idea gave him comfort. He pulled it on over his short-sleeved white shirt.

Howard said, "One other thing. I can't let you see where I'm taking you. Obviously I can't drive around with a blindfolded white man in my car. So I need you to kneel down on the floorboards there and lay your head down on the seat."

"What, you mean now?"

"Now would be good."

Robert did as he was told. The Falcon had bench seats, and with his feet against the firewall, his knees were shoved hard against the base of the seat. He folded himself as tightly as he could, put his left cheek against the vinyl, and closed his eyes.

"Good," Howard said. "That's good."

Howard drove for a while in what seemed a deliberately random pattern, turning every few blocks, and Robert quickly lost all sense of direction. Then they were in the country. The air had a deep green smell, and Robert heard frogs singing to the wet spring night.

The road got rougher, turning first to gravel and then to rutted dirt. Robert thought it had been at least 20 minutes since they left Hayti, probably longer. They could be halfway to Pittsboro or Wake Forest.

Howard made a slow, bumpy turn and said, "Okay, you can get up now."

At first Robert thought there was something the matter with the car's engine. Then he realized that what he heard was drumming. He was familiar with congas and hand drums—Chano Pozo from Cuba had played with Diz and Bird even before the mambo craze of the fifties. But these drums were wrong. They were playing much too fast. They sounded like panic, and the feeling went into Robert's chest and legs.

Above the drums was the clank of metal, highly syncopated. The sound made Robert think of chains. And above that were the voices. Singing, ostensibly, though the highest voice, too high above the others, was more like a scream.

They tried to tell me, Robert thought. Maurice, Howard, Mitch. They all tried.

"Okay," Robert said. He was still on his knees on the floorboards. "I believe you now. Can we go back?"

"Put the hood up on that shirt," Howard said. "Get it down over your face. And keep those lily-white hands in your pockets or someplace."

Robert put the hood up and got awkwardly out of the car. The sound came from a wooden structure 200 yards away. The flat, sloping roof was corrugated steel. White light leaked out through the gaps between the vertical boards of the walls. Another 20 or more cars and pickup trucks had parked in the same empty field as Howard's Falcon. Except for that field and the long stretch of grassy ground between it and the shed, everything in sight was old-growth pine forest, dark and menacing. Haze muted the thin sliver of a moon.

Howard started walking toward the shed. Robert could not get his legs to work. "I ain't fooling with you, now," Howard said, looking back. "Let's go."

Robert stumbled forward stiffly. Like a zombie, he thought, without humor. He pulled the sleeves of the sweatshirt down over the unsightly paleness of his hands.

Howard waited until Robert caught up, then fell into step with him. "Once I get you settled, you do not move, you do not speak, you do not call attention to yourself in any way whatever. You have questions, you ask me later. You understand?"

Robert nodded.

"I can't hear you," Howard said.

"Yes," Robert said. "I understand."

An old black man, skin wrinkled like an elephant's, stood by the opening at one end of the shed. He had a shotgun and a walkie-talkie, and Robert realized there must have been other watchers along the road. The old man nodded to Howard, who pushed aside the blanket hanging in the doorway and gestured for Robert to go in.

The place was some kind of abandoned barn, too big for a tobacco shed, maybe 40 by 60 feet. The instant they were inside Robert began to sweat. The air was thick with humidity, and the drumming and singing battered him in tangible waves. What must have been a hundred candles lit the room. Their heat and the smell of burning only amplified Robert's fear.

Four drummers sat along the left wall, playing tall, tapering drums that looked like congas. One drum had a battered blue sparkle finish, another looked crudely homemade. Two of the drummers played with open hands, two with one hand empty and the other holding a forked stick shaped like an upside down checkmark. They were bare to the waist, pouring sweat, their eyes closed or rolling back in their heads. A fifth man tapped a black iron hoe blade with an oversized nail, swaying, rapt. The rhythm loped like feet running away, the way Robert's feet ached to run.

Five women shuffled rhythmically from side to side toward the rear of the shed. They wore loose white cotton robes and had white scarves knotted around their heads. They moved together like the fingers of a single hand. Dust from the hard-packed floor made a cloud around their feet. Whatever they were singing was not English. Maybe some kind of Haitian Creole, maybe something more ancient and African. The words came in a blur of speed, sometimes in call and response, sometimes in a jumble of frenzied chanting.

In the center of the room, a single post ran from floor to ceiling. It was white with a red stripe that spiraled up the length of it, like a perverse barber pole. Near it, a wooden model of a sailing ship, complete with paper sails, hung from a rafter. Opposite the ship was a smaller pole, three feet high, forked at the top. A woven straw bag hung from the fork.

Between the big pole and front door, drawn in the dirt and filled in with colored sand, was the symbol from St. Joseph's church. From Mercy's earrings.

Mercy herself was nowhere in sight. Robert's relief far outweighed his disappointment.

Twenty people sat on three rows of wooden benches near the entrance. Howard led Robert to the farthest corner of the last bench and settled him there. For an instant he thought Howard was going to leave him there and he let Howard see that fear in his eyes. Howard shook his head sharply once, silently greeted a few of the men and women around them, and finally sat down to Robert's right.

The drums roared to a finish, and the voices carried on without them for a few seconds. When the drums started again they were slower and more melodic. A man came in through the back of the building dressed in white pants, a loose white shirt, black belt and shoes, and a bright red tie. His head was shaved, and he showed a gold incisor when he smiled. His skin was a deep matte black. He carried a thin pine branch about three feet long and he was the only person in the room not sweating.

He went straight to the straw bag and pulled a bottle of rum from inside. He took a long drink and then started to draw in the dirt with the thick end of his pine bough. He drew a cross, then added circles at the end of one pair of arms and stars at the ends of the others. Then he added Xs and curlicues up and down all four arms.

"The crossroads," Howard whispered. "He's calling Papa Legba to open the way." Robert, as he had been told, did not answer, did not look at him, did not acknowledge him in any way.

The priest finished the drawing, stood up, and sprinkled rum over it, holding his thumb over the neck of the bottle. Then he reached into the bag and scattered peanuts, roasted corn kernels, and dried chunks of some orange substance, maybe sweet potato, over the drawing. Finally he began to chant. Robert heard the name Legba and words that he recognized from his college

French, including something about a *chapeau* and a *grand chemin*. Robert was starting to think that it was not so bad, that maybe he could endure it, when one of the women brought out the rooster.

He was speckled black and white and had a bright red comb. His feet were tied, his wings free, and unlike Robert he was giving voice to his fear. The woman could barely hold on, and the sight of him brought the crowd to its feet.

"Stand up," Howard said, and Robert stood.

The people around Robert were singing now, writhing where they stood, and the drummers began to hit accents that cracked like gunshots, making the muscles up and down Robert's legs twitch and jump. The priest took the rooster from the woman and made a complete circle of the room with it, the bird fighting him all the way. When he got back to the center pole he held the bird with his left hand alone, reached up with the right, and quickly wrung its neck.

Robert heard its death squawk over the drums, over the singing, over the pounding of his own heart. A spatter of white guano hit the dust at the priest's feet, and the crowd yelled approval.

The priest threw the dead bird aside and began to dance, taking hunkered, bowlegged steps, thrusting and jerking as if the spirit of the rooster had entered him. The drums changed again.

"Now Loco Atisou," Howard said. "After Legba, always Loco."

"*Va Loco Loco Valadi,*" the women sang. "*Va Loco Loco Valadi.*"

One by one the members of the crowd sat again. The priest drank from the rum bottle and sprayed more of it around the room.

The drums stopped.

As much as the drumming had frightened Robert, its absence was worse. The women were singing now, and the priest slowly backed out of the middle of the hut to stand behind the silent drummers. The women began to move in a new formation, a rocking step that took them two paces back for every one forward, clearing a path. Everyone stared at the space they'd opened, focused, waiting.

From the rear of the shed came a noise like a ship's foghorn, only higher, more hollow and mournful. At the first note the women stopped singing, and complete silence fell for the first time. Mercy stepped into the light carrying a conch shell the size of her head. Like the other women, she wore a loose, belted white dress and headcloth, except her dress was gauzy and loosely woven and seemed to drape over her in multiple layers, tantalizing Robert with hints of the flesh underneath.

She walked to the center pole and turned her back to them, holding the conch shell with her left hand all the way into the opening, bringing the broad, flat end to her mouth. She blew into it and released the loud, alien, fog-horn cry again before turning and directing a final blast toward the crowd.

Robert shifted until the woman in front of him blocked his view of Mercy's face, and then he looked down at the dirt floor. At first he had felt the warmth that the sight of her always gave him. Then he'd seen her eyes, which were as strange and distant as the sound of the conch shell.

She handed the shell to one of the dancing women, who took it to a long low table in the rear of the shed and added it to the pile there of cakes and bottles and embroidered flags and bits of iron and images of the Catholic saints. Mercy closed her eyes and began to sing. The language was again French or something like it, and her voice was high and sweet and true, not the voice that Robert would have expected to come from that lush body. Though he could not make any sense of the words, the yearning and passionate melody spoke to him clearly.

As if answering her call, a young man entered from the front door, carrying a straw mat loaded with objects. He walked slowly, formally, bringing his feet together with each step. He was in his early twenties, with short hair and acne-scarred skin of a deep, rich brown. He was barefoot and he wore white cotton pants and a white T-shirt.

He knelt at Mercy's feet and spread out the mat, revealing a bottle of white wine, a white enameled pot, a white paper bag, and two straw cages. In one cage were two white doves, in the other a white chicken. When he was finished he stepped away, and the priest came out from behind the silent drummers. The priest reached into the paper bag and came out with what looked like a handful of white flour, which he sprinkled over the mat. Mercy was singing all this time.

The priest reached for the cage with the doves in it, and Robert closed his eyes, expecting more blood. A moment later he heard the sound of wings and opened them to see that the priest had merely released them, and they were fluttering around the room, trying to find a way out.

The priest took the cover off the pot and poured some of the wine into it. He drank from the wine bottle, with an exaggerated show of pleasure that got a laugh from the crowd. Then he beckoned the young man toward him.

The other women began to sing behind Mercy. At first the melodies intertwined, then the other women became more urgent. They began to dance again, and gradually Mercy stopped singing and became very still.

The young man lay down on the mat. He was trembling, which Robert thought did not bode well. The priest dipped both hands in the wine and whatever else had already been in the pot and pantomimed washing the young man's head with them.

The drums were still quiet as the women's voices got louder and Mercy began to sway back and forth. Her eyes were closed, but not in relaxation. Every muscle in her body was tense, the tendons in her neck and hands standing out, the movements of her legs becoming stiff and awkward.

Howard's voice was in his ear again. "No matter what you see in the next five minutes, do not move from your seat or I will kill you."

It looked as if someone came up behind Mercy and gave her a hard shove from behind. She went down on hands and knees in the dirt, right into the heart-shaped drawing. She stayed there for a long second, then another and another as the singing stretched the moment tighter and tighter.

When she got up she wasn't Mercy anymore.

Something swelled inside her, something larger than she was, something of vast animal power. Whatever the thing was, it was female. Her movements were sinuous, erotic, as she swayed onto one knee, then to her feet. Her golden skin, sleek and damp in the blazing candlelight, was satin smooth, soft as a featherbed, warm as the sand on a summer beach. It cried out to be touched.

Robert's own skin tingled. He could feel where his shirt touched the hairs of his chest, like sunburn without the pain.

She began to dance. The thing inside her seemed to exult in finding itself in such a glorious body. Robert felt its joy. The display lacked all calculation or deliberate provocation; the gauzy wrappings of her gown were confining her, and it seemed the most natural thing in the world that she should pull them off, one after another, and toss them aside. There were six sheets of gauze, and when the last one fell, she was naked.

The man on the mat had come up on his elbows and turned toward her. He was breathing hard, and his erection was clearly visible through the white fabric of his pants.

Despite his fear, despite the freakish circumstances, Robert could not help being aware that this was Mercy's body, the body he had held in his arms, fantasized about, longed for. Mercy's full breasts, stiff dark nipples, gently rounded stomach, thick black tangle of pubic hair. Not innocently sunbathing or changing clothes, but sexually charged and provocative. Even as he was aroused he was embarrassed, repelled, angry, and jealous.

She circled the room, taking wide, strutting steps, and as she walked she twisted slowly at the waist, cupped her breasts and ran her hands down her thighs, seemingly oblivious to the eyes watching her.

When she finished her circuit she saw the man on the mat. She started toward him, walking with her legs spread wide, her toes pointed out, her crotch thrust forward.

Apparently Robert's need to look away was not strong enough. As the man on the mat watched, hypnotized, she lowered herself slowly toward him until she was on her knees and his mouth was on her sex. Now, finally, Robert was able to close his eyes, but he could not close his ears a long minute later when she cried out, less in passion than in triumph, and when Robert's eyes opened involuntarily he saw her rise again, laughing in unconstrained delight. The man had fallen onto the mat, eyes closed, a damp stain spreading down his trouser leg. The priest and another man came and took one arm each and helped him stagger dazedly out the front entrance.

She stood near the center pole, singing, now in a lower, harsh voice. Her eyes were wild and her chest was flushed, her nipples taut, her pubic hair wet and matted, the pink flesh of her cleft showing through. Robert's need to be away from her, from that place, from the blinding light and piercing sounds, was now stronger than his fear of Barrett Howard, or of the priest, or of the creature that Mercy had become.

With a final, shrill cry, she collapsed in the dirt. Two of the female dancers rushed to her with a white terrycloth robe. It looked exactly like the one he'd seen her wearing that afternoon.

He stood up.

"Sit down!" Howard said, his voice muted but furious. Robert ignored him. He pushed his way past the other people on the bench, and as he got to the aisle he saw Mercy out of the corner of his vision. Her eyes were open, and she was staring at him. Robert looked back at her for what he was sure would be the last time.

Then he turned and walked out into the night.

HE PULLED OFF the sweatshirt as he walked and threw it into the grass. He moved quickly, not running, borne on the relief of being in the clean night air, relief that grew stronger with every step. He was beyond fear, more or less indifferent to what might happen next, with one single desire in his heart: to return to the life he'd had six months ago, a life that was orderly and under-standable, with a small, tidy house, an alarm clock to wake him in the morn-ing, a newspaper on the lawn, familiar streets to drive to work, dinner waiting when he got home.

Finally he stopped and looked back. No one pursued him. He took a deep breath and reached for his cigarettes.

The drums took off again.

The cigarette pack flew from his hand. The sound, he thought, would make him physically ill. He went to his knees, located the white pack in the deep grass, scooped it up and got a cigarette lit.

For want of another plan, he found Howard's car and sat on the hood. He had no idea where he was, there were certainly armed guards on the roads, and if Howard wanted him dead there was no escaping it by running, not unless he kept going, out of Durham, maybe out of the country.

He sat there in something like a state of shock, arms wrapped around himself, smoking when he thought of it, for about 45 minutes. Finally Howard appeared, by himself, carrying the sweatshirt. "Get in," he said.

Robert threw down his cigarette and opened the car door.

"Face down on the car seat, like before," Howard said.

With mild interest, Robert processed the information. If it mattered that he not see where they were going, then Howard must mean for him to live. He got in the car and knelt on the floorboards.

Howard seemed completely without emotion. He cranked up the car, backed out, and drove over the same bumpy road they'd come in on. He was, Robert noted, driving faster. Robert grunted at a couple of worst lurches, as did the Falcon's suspension.

Howard didn't speak again until they were on hardtop and the cool night air was whipping through the open windows. "You got any questions?"

"Yes," Robert said. "One question. How could you ... How could you sit there, while that man ... while another man ... did that to Mercy?"

After a silence Howard said, "That wasn't Mercy. That was a *lwa,* the *lwa* Erzulie." He was quiet again for a while, then he said, "Erzulie was using Mercy's body, that's all. Riding her, they call it."

Do you really believe that? Robert nearly asked. The hesitation in Howard's voice was all the answer he needed.

When Howard told him to sit up they were in Walltown, a black neighborhood north of Duke's East Campus. They rode in silence through downtown and then, as they turned onto Pettigrew, Howard asked him where his car was.

They parked at the curb behind the Mercury. As Robert opened the door, Howard said, "I'm sorry."

"For what?" Robert said. It came out with a bitterness that surprised him.

"Everything," Howard said. "I'm sorry for everything."

Robert stood on the curb and watched him drive away. It was three in the morning. Robert stank of smoke and the sour sweat of fear. He had been given what he asked for. But when he reached for the door of the Mercury, he felt as if his hand could pass right through it.

HE DROVE TO THE HOUSE on Woodrow Street and parked in his tree-lined driveway, behind Ruth's shiny new Buick. The porch light was on. He turned it off and locked the door behind him. "Robert?" Ruth's voice called sleepily from the bedroom. "Is that you?"

"I'm home," he said. His voice sounded like someone else's, but Ruth seemed to recognize it. "I'll be there in a minute."

He stood under a hot shower until he realized that he could stand there for hours and it wouldn't remotely be enough. When he got out he found himself with hands planted on the marble countertop, searching the mirror in vain for some sign of the corruption that had lodged inside him.

Ruth was asleep when he got in next to her, and soon so was he. If he had dreams, he didn't remember them.

IN THE MORNING he had Ruth phone the office and say he was sick. He lay in bed until noon, dozing intermittently. He saw that he could go on that way all day, so he got up. Ruth watched him without asking questions. She was like a puppy that had been spanked and then fed. She no doubt assumed he'd gotten drunk, maybe gone to one of those places on Highway 70 and been with a prostitute. It disturbed him that she didn't seem to care.

He volunteered to grill steaks for dinner, and she was pathetically grateful. Somehow he made it through the day and night, and Friday morning he went back to work.

MITCH ARRIVED AT 10:30, jumpy and excited, and called Robert into his office. Robert was unable to summon either concern or relief. He was a drafting machine. If Mitch sent him out to do demolition, he would be a demolishing machine.

"Two things," Mitch said. "First, Howard cancelled the strike meeting he'd called for this afternoon. I heard about it from Leon. I don't know how you did it, but you are the golden boy around here until further notice."

Robert nodded.

"Here's the second thing." Mitch spun a copy of an offset-printed press release across the desk. It was two pages long and much handled. It had an IBM letterhead and a date of April 7, 1964, two weeks ago. It announced the company's plans to begin selling a new product to be called the System 360. It was the first mass-produced computer, designed to sit in businesses as well as college computing labs. You could buy one outright for five million at the top end, or rent one starting at less than three thousand dollars—the price of a new car—every month.

"Sounds like a big deal," Robert said. "Something like that could change the world."

"You ain't just whistling Dixie, Slim," Mitch said. "The world it changes could be your own."

"What do you mean?"

"Mass-produced. That means manufacturing. That means new plants. That means they need to be in RTP."

"You may know that, but who's going to persuade IBM?"

Mitch smiled and leaned back in his chair. "Let's just say a lot of people would be willing to go a long, long way to get IBM here. All the way up to the governor's office. This is strictly on the QT, but land sales have been dropping for years. This whole RTP dream could go in the toilet if we don't snag some major names, and fast."

"Are you trying to scare me?"

"*Au contraire,* cat daddy. I think we're about to have it made."

THAT DECEMBER HE and Ruth drove to Asheville to spend Christmas with his parents. Ruth fought the idea long and hard, but Robert's parents were older than Ruth's, and he hardly saw them, while Ruth's family was a constant presence, in spirit if not in fact.

Robert's father had retired that summer at age 60. He and Robert's mother lived in one of the cottages in Biltmore Village, outside the walls of the estate. These were the homes that George Vanderbilt had constructed for the workers who built his mansion in the 1890s, and that his daughter had sold off after World War I.

Ruth had never been to Asheville, never been farther west than Durham, and her delight was obvious as she saw the tall trees and narrow half-timbered houses, lit by moonlight and streetlamps, their tile roofs lightly dusted with snow. "It's like something out of a Christmas movie," she said.

The house smelled of fresh-baked gingerbread, the Frazier Fir in the living room, the blazing logs in the fireplace. Robert's parents were truly happy to see them, herding them into the kitchen for snacks and mulled wine before sending them upstairs to bed.

It was late the next morning before Robert managed to be alone with his father. They had gone to the basement, where Robert's father kept his model railroad layout, now more than tripled in size since Robert had last seen it.

It was HO scale, the tracks 5/8 of an inch wide, one inch in that world equivalent to more than seven feet in Robert's. The upper left side of the layout, against the back wall, was a miniature version of Biltmore Village in its prime, with a replica of the elegant station that head architect Richard Morris Hunt had designed. From there the tracks wound to the right around a sheer mountainside, passed through a tunnel, and came out in the post–World War I town of Boone, with its icehouse, People's Bank, and five-and-dime. Then they stretched across a four-foot long bridge over the Cape Fear River and descended, finally, to the Outer Banks at the far right. A pier jutted into glassy rolling waves, and sunbathers in antiquated costumes, less than an inch high, watched from beach umbrellas that bent before an intangible wind.

The front half of the oval layout led inland, and Robert noted that his father had added downtown Durham halfway between the beach and Asheville, complete with sidings where miniature workmen offloaded Brightleaf tobacco onto ramshackle trucks bound for nearby warehouses.

"Durham started with the railroads," his father said. "Durham Station, 1850, named after the doctor who donated the land for it." He was wearing a dress shirt and a burgundy cardigan, wool slacks and leather house shoes, and merely being in the presence of his creation seemed to kindle an inner glow. He lifted a hinged section near the beach and stepped into the open center of the layout, then knelt, taking care of his back, to plug the transformer, bolted to the underside, into the wall.

The trains and some of the props—the animals, the human figures, the autos, and some of the trees and shrubs—were storebought. Robert's father had meticulously constructed the buildings and the terrain himself with balsa, plaster, glass, and papier-mâché. The layout preserved forever the summer of 1919, when Robert's father had been 15 years old. When Robert had asked the reason for that year in particular, his father had rattled off a list of events from 1920: Prohibition, Hitler's first public speech, the division of Ireland, the first commercial radio stations in the US. Nineteen-nineteen was, his father said, "the last time when things were simple." Robert could only infer that he meant it personally as well as politically.

Now, as the tiny locomotive pulled out of the Biltmore Village Station, Robert felt the power of that nostalgia wash over him as well. His father had created a world without voodoo ceremonies or superhighways, a world without revolution, without any change at all beyond the occasional miraculous appearance of new, changeless towns or scenic views, where the perfect wave would never break on the shore, leaves never fall, birds never flap away into the sky.

"As best I can tell," his father said, "in 1919 it was still the Southern that provided passenger service through Durham, taking over the Richmond and Danville roads. Most of the freight was through the Seaboard Air Line, though why they called it an Air Line is beyond me."

This obsessive knowledge of railroad history was new, too. "You've changed your mind," Robert said. "Haven't you? About the highway system?"

"Maybe I'm getting old. When your mother and I went to Paris last year, we felt such a sense of community there. We never got in a car or a taxicab. We rode the Metro everywhere, and it was clean and safe and efficient. If we'd chosen to, we could have retreated behind a newspaper or a book, but we didn't, and so we talked to people we would never have met otherwise and learned of a marvelous flea market and a splendid Moroccan restaurant."

"America is different," Robert said. "Europe is old and gray and cluttered. America is wide open. You couldn't have enough trains to take everyone where they wanted to go."

"Perhaps," his father said. His father had always been a gentle man, as sure of himself as he was reluctant to impose that certainty on others. Robert's mother had been in charge of discipline.

The train pulled into Durham station, and Robert suddenly realized that he was standing where Hayti would have been.

"Who owns the world?" Robert's father asked suddenly.

Robert looked at him in confusion. "I don't know what you're asking. The rich and powerful, I suppose?"

Robert's father nodded. "I suppose. I would like to think that we all own it, in common. It's an interesting word, is it not, 'common'? It's a pejorative if applied to manners or dress, but as a plural noun it was the heart of the village. And a thorny problem. Who is responsible for the things we all hold in common? Like the air we breathe, or the oceans? If it's everyone, is that not the same as saying no one at all?"

"That's government's job."

"It would be, if we gave them the power to do it. We had a nationalized railroad system in 1919, did you know that? The United States Railroad Administration, which lasted a sum total of twenty-six months. It was because of the Great War, of course. The individual railroad companies could not bring themselves to cooperate, and it was hurting the war effort. They were still robber barons by nature."

"Did I just hear you say 'robber barons'? I'm stunned. Father, what's come over you?"

"Too much time on my hands, I suppose. Too much reading and thinking. I used to believe that the rich were the only ones with the resources and objectivity to provide for the public good. As I look around, all I see is that trust betrayed. When I read about the awful violence that these men perpetrated, the Commodore among them, or the stock manipulations that left hundreds of thousands destitute, all for no other purpose than the enhancement of their profits, I fear for the human race."

"That was a long time ago. We have anti-trust acts and incentives for small business. No one has that kind of power anymore."

"We can hope so. At any rate, yes, the government nationalized the railroads, got rid of the redundant routes set up by squabbling rivals, raised wages, particularly for the lowest on the ladder, and in the process designed a series of locomotives that became the de facto standard for years to come. Like that one, a USRA Light 2-8-2 Mikado."

He pointed to the locomotive now crossing the seemingly fragile bridge on the back of the layout. Robert understood that the numbers had something to do with the number of wheels on the various parts of the engine, though the parts themselves were somewhat vague to him. Mostly he liked that his father was so deeply immersed that he felt no need to explain.

"It couldn't last," his father said. "For Americans nationalization was Bolshevism, and so the roads went back to private industry, which has now all but destroyed them. I've heard rumors that the Southern is going to stop passenger service to Durham. That would break my heart."

Robert's father no longer drove on the highway except in cases of dire necessity, not trusting his vision or reflexes in high-speed traffic. His mother had never learned to drive at all. Losing the train would mean seeing his parents less. While his love for them did not have the intensity and demands of Ruth's love for her father, it was nonetheless strong.

"Yes," Robert said. "I would hate that too."

"When the day comes that there is no cheap, reliable public transportation in this country, something will have been lost forever. Once the commons is lost, swallowed up by private greed, how do you get it back?"

"I think you're letting yourself be seduced by the past," Robert said. "Things change, that's all. We're moving faster now, too fast for railroads. People are flying more and more, and the airline industry *is* regulated. Once the Interstate system is finished, it'll be cheaper and faster to ship by truck than by rail, and the trucks will pay their own way with gasoline and road use taxes."

"Perhaps," his father said.

"Do you think I should quit my job?" Robert said. "It would hurt me to think you disapproved of what I'm doing."

"No, not at all. You are serving the public, and the public has made its decision. As Carlyle said, 'Do the duty which lies nearest to you.' And it's the duty of the old to believe the world is going to hell. In that way we make it easier for ourselves to go."

"Not anytime soon, I hope," Robert said.

"No, I expect not. And don't ever think I'm not proud of you."

They stood there, separate but close, watching the train move through its dream landscape, and Robert suddenly felt it was possible to talk to his father about Ruth. As he was searching for the right words, the door at the top of the stairs opened, and Robert's mother said, "Lunch is ready, you two! Everybody off at the next station!"

•

IN THE SPRING, Robert found himself sitting in the audience at a press conference at the offices of the Research Triangle Institute, in the woods east of Durham. It was 11:30 in the morning and Robert was in the suit and white shirt Mitch had instructed him to wear.

Mitch himself was on the podium with Fred Mason and a host of movers and shakers that included North Carolina Governor Dan K. Moore and former Governor Luther Hodges, both pale, overweight, and white-haired. Hodges was now Chairman of the Board of the Research Triangle Foundation, a clear signal that RTP was going to happen.

Next to the politicians were three representatives from IBM: Clarence Frizzell, head of the systems manufacturing division; Arthur L. Becker, former general manager of the Rochester, Minnesota, plant; and Donald F. Busch, former manager of the Endicott, New York, lab. The IBMers looked like tyrannosaurs in dark suits and narrow ties, exuding willpower and monolithic vision.

At the back of the audience, silent, the object of much whispering and attention, sat local celebrity Randy Fogg: sportswriter, white supremacist, and mysterious associate of Mitch Antree.

Apparently all involved had done a good job of keeping the announcements secret. Once the IBM contingent got to the meat of the proposal, the bankers and developers and real estate agents in the crowd were audibly excited by figures like "$15 million plant," "400 acre site," and "over 1,000 employees," two thirds of whom would be local.

Frizzell had the podium. He was thin and jug-eared, with an uncomfortable smile. A temporary office would open within the next few days to start hiring, he said. They would be looking for highly skilled technical workers, and the number of major universities in the area had been a major factor in the decision.

"And finally," Frizzell said, "let me introduce to you the gentlemen who will design our RTP campus. Fred Mason and Mitch Antree, of Mason and Antree, Architects and Engineers."

Mitch and Fred both stood up. Mitch had for once foregone his usual turtleneck in favor of a tie, though he'd kept his sideburns and tinted fighter-pilot glasses. As the audience cheered, he looked straight at Robert, grinned, and pantomimed shooting him with his index finger.

As Robert had predicted to his father, the pace of change was accelerating, like the thrust of the new Chevy Chevelle SS he'd bought in January, a kick that he could feel in his gut. Robert no longer read the *Carolina Times*, but the news was all over the *Durham Herald* as well—Johnson's wholehearted push for the Civil Rights Act, Martin Luther King winning the Nobel Prize, the Bloody Sunday attacks on civil rights marchers in Selma the month before.

They'd been followed two weeks later by the first manned Gemini flight on March 23, the next step in a program that was supposed to put a man on the moon by the end of the decade. And if it happened, it would be made possible by computers like the ones IBM would be building at RTP.

Robert supposed it had been the same way for many men. There came a time when you made a decision that from that point on you were not a kid anymore. He hadn't been dancing since his trip to the Biltmore with Mercy, and it hurt sometimes to think he might never dance like that again. Other times he was able to look back on the madness of those days as if from a great distance, and take a quiet pleasure in it. He'd done things that no one else he knew had done and come through them intact. There was a good deal to be said for that. The vivid, sexual dreams that had haunted him were also just a memory. His life had become a paragon of the ordinary.

And then, like a ghost from those times, Barrett Howard walked into the press conference.

Like nearly everyone in the room, he wore a dark suit, white shirt, and narrow tie. He pushed past a commotion at the doorway and stood in front of the podium.

"When you talk about white collar jobs," he said, "you're talking about white-skinned jobs, am I right?"

Becker, who would be managing the plant, looked at Mitch Antree next to him. Mitch whispered something in his ear, and Becker nodded. "Sir," Becker said, "we fully support the Equal Employment Opportunity provisions of title VII of the Civil Rights Act." Becker looked like a retired cop, especially around the eyes. "IBM does not discriminate on the basis of race, color, religion, sex, or national origin. Beyond that, we have an Open Door policy that's well known in the industry. Employees can take their concerns all the way up to the Chairman."

"You reading that off a cue card?" Barrett asked. No one laughed, and none of the white photographers moved to take his picture. It was not his audience. Robert, embarrassed, stared at a patch of beige carpet between his feet.

"What special efforts will you be making to recruit black workers?" Howard demanded.

"We will consider any and all qualified applicants," Becker said. "We need workers. We are ready to get this show on the road."

The audience cheered and applauded. Topping it, Howard said, "How is a black man going to get the qualifications to build a computer?"

A chair scraped loudly at the back of the room. Robert braced himself and turned to look. Randy Fogg, all six foot four of him, had gotten to his feet. In a thick central Carolina accent, Fogg said, "This here is a press conference, Mr. Howard. What paper do you represent?"

"I'm here as a citizen."

"I believe you've had answers to your questions, Citizen Howard. It sounds to me like your people are going to get every consideration."

Howard winced at the words "your people." It seemed to Robert that Howard had only two choices: He could walk away with the remnants of his dignity, or he could go berserk and physically attack Randy Fogg. The temptation for the second option was strong, and Robert could see Howard fight it down. With one last look to the group on the dais, lingering longest on Mitch, Howard pushed his way out of the room.

Fogg sat down and Governor Moore stood up and a few more banalities were passed around praising the other fine businesses who had been pioneers in the park, and how that had helped sway IBM's decision, not to overlook the vision of the men like Luther Hodges who had created the park in the first place. The mood of self-congratulation and imminent wealth soon returned.

Robert's own recovery was slower. Howard, he reminded himself, and all the things that he and Howard had done, belonged to the past. All eyes were on the future now, and the past had no power to hurt him.

THAT AFTERNOON Fred Mason officially unveiled the plans for the IBM plant to Mitch's staff. The design was good enough, Robert thought, to have won on its own merits, and he hoped that in fact it had, with no interference from the Durham Select Committee or anyone else.

It was an open secret that Mason no longer did his own renderings, instead farming them out to a local painter who also did covers for science fiction paperbacks. In this case the artist seemed to have served both masters at once. The building was white, clean, and restful, at home in the woods it inhabited, yet quietly dazzling. The people who moved through its covered walkways and lounged in the grassy margins looked like a golden race from a distant future, where computer technology had brought human perfection.

It was only as an afterthought that Robert noticed that not one of them was black.

Mitch had consulted on the engineering, and whatever his other failings, he knew his business. The walls would be precast, pre-stressed, with Styrofoam panels laid into the concrete to reduce weight and increase insulation. The double-T floor/ceiling members were strong, thin, and elegant.

Maurice had made a start on some of the floor plans and elevations; Robert recognized his signature north arrow on the tracings. They were works of art, with a line quality Robert had never been able to achieve, and hand lettering that exuded style and confidence.

"Some of you may be wondering," Mitch said, "how we plan to handle this volume of work. So this is a good time to lay another announcement on you. We're going to be expanding in to the rest of the building and hiring more staff. We're on our way to being the biggest firm in the Triangle."

There was scattered applause. Robert didn't mean to spoil the moment, but the question seemed to pop out of his mouth before he had time to think. "What about Hayti?"

"What about it?" Mitch said. "We'll have enough staff to deal with Hayti if and when the time comes."

"Pah," Fred Mason said distinctly.

The room went completely quiet. Robert listened to the fans creak overhead.

"Hayti is over and done," Mason said. "And good riddance."

He was huge, lion-headed, invincible. He stared at Robert as if daring him to argue. After a few long seconds, Robert looked at the floor.

"Now," Mason went on, "as Mitch said, we're hiring. If you can recommend anyone, we'll be paying bonuses for referrals. And until we get to full staff, there will be plenty of overtime, at time and a half, for anyone who wants it."

Robert caught Mitch's eye. Mitch grinned and shrugged. It's none of my business, Robert told himself. As the man said, I'm all right, Jack. That turn of phrase evoked Mercy's voice unexpectedly, and there, in the midst of the celebration, Robert found himself counting his losses.

THE OFFICIAL GROUNDBREAKING ceremony was September 23, five months later. Luther Hodges was there, and so was IBM chairman Thomas Watson, Jr., sharing a strange little three-handled shovel with an IBM VP. Newspaper stringers took the obligatory photos while Randy Fogg watched from the crowd.

Within a month Robert was setting the bolts in the foundation that would hold the precast wall sections. It was good to be building something of substance, something monumental. Robert was chief of the erection crew, a title he found more than a little ironic, given the sexual famine that prevailed in the bungalow on Woodrow Street. He had Tommy and Leon Coleman as senior men, and up to a dozen day workers, white and black, as needed. He theoretically reported to the general contractor, a grizzled white man in his fifties who was missing three different fingers between his two hands, making him, to Robert's mind, someone who didn't learn from his mistakes. The new weight that the Mason and Antree name carried meant that the general was all smiles and accommodation, and Robert got everything he needed.

On a crisp November morning they gathered to bolt the first wall sections into place. The crane was there when Robert arrived, and the operator turned out to be Porter, the snuff-dipping union man from Robert's first demolition. Porter was surprised that Robert knew his name, and didn't seem to recall their first encounter. Robert felt no need to refresh his memory.

The job was exacting, and a cold north wind didn't help. The crane had to lift the multi-ton wall section upright by two steel rings that protruded from the top, raise it into the air, then delicately lower it so the men could guide the holes in its base plates onto the threaded ends of the bolts in the foundation. The bolts—four per base plate—were fitted with nuts and washers. Once the slab rested on the washers, the men made minor adjustments to the nuts below to bring the wall section plumb. At that point a second set of washers and bolts went onto the top of the plate. The final concrete floor would fill in around the bolts and create a structure that would be as strong and permanent as anything man had ever built.

In the meantime, somebody had to climb a shaky ladder in the biting wind and hang a plumb bob from the top of the wall, 20 feet up. They all took their turns, all except Porter, who sat and dipped snuff and offered advice. "It ain't my ass on the line," he would begin, "but if it was me, I'd have me a cutting torch here and cut them base plates to where them bolts really are instead of where some genius thought they might be." This after Leon had used a six foot section of pipe to correct the angle on one of the bolts.

It didn't help that Porter seemed to have trouble with the third panel he tried to lift. He'd barely gotten the top end clear of the ground when the butt end began to shift. He yanked hard on it, then suddenly slacked off, and the panel thrashed at the end of the steel cable like an angry fish.

Leon was standing next to Robert. "He keep jerking that panel like that, he going to pull the ring right out of it."

"He must know that," Robert said. "Right?"

Leon didn't answer.

Porter began hoisting again and got the panel nearly to vertical, then slacked off again. The entire crane shook as the weight of the slab hit the limits of the cable.

"That fool going to kill somebody," Leon said. "You better say something."

It was the last thing Robert wanted to do. He took a couple of steps toward the crane. "Porter?" he yelled. "Are you sure you—"

Porter stuck his head out of the open window of the crane cabin. Tension had driven his voice an octave higher than usual and made his thick accent barely intelligible. "Don't you be telling me how to do my job. You better stand clear of this piece of shit."

Robert took a step back as Porter shook the slab again, as if in spite. There was a sharp crack, like a rifle shot, and Robert heard Leon's voice behind him yell, "Run!"

Robert turned and ran. Behind him came a huge low sound like a crashing wave, magnified a hundred times. The earth shook, hard enough to throw him onto his knees, and for a few seconds he stayed there, bracing himself with one arm, getting his breath.

When he looked back, the panel was flat on the ground, smashed into four jagged pieces, a haze of dust floating over it. The steel rings, dribbling rubble, still hung in the crane's hooks.

"Anybody hurt?" Robert asked.

Leon shook his head. "Mr. Antree going to be none too happy about this."

Porter got down from the crane. "Goddamn cheap shit concrete. I bet that son of a bitch was cracked."

"I guess it's sure enough cracked now," Leon said.

"What?" Porter said. "You say something to me?"

"No, sir," Leon said evenly. "Talking to the Captain, here."

Porter looked at Robert. "You looked pretty goddamn funny, though. You run like a duck."

Porter weighed half again what Robert did. His flattened nose and red spotted cheeks suggested that he got numb-fisted drunk and fought to the point of blood on weekends for relaxation. Robert took a long breath and said, "Let's break for lunch."

Porter ate in the cabin of his crane. Leon built a fire out of scrap wood from the foundation forms, and he and Robert and Tommy and the two extra crewmen sat around it and ate and drank coffee from Leon's giant thermos.

"Going to be your turn on that ladder after lunch," Leon said to Tommy. "You think you can deal with it?"

Tommy shrugged.

"What's wrong?" Robert asked.

"Tommy a little nervous about heights," Leon said.

"He doesn't have to go. We can send up one of the crew."

"I don't like being up there myself. Don't none of us enjoy it. Tommy can take his turn like a man."

Porter was the only one who returned to work with no sign of the morning's misfortunes hanging over him. He managed to put the next member in place without damage and came down to watch Tommy on the ladder. He sensed, with a bully's instinct, Tommy's discomfort.

"What you shaking for, boy?" he shouted. "Must be cold at them high altitudes, 'cause you fixing to shake yourself right off there!" Nobody else laughed, but Porter more than made up for it himself.

Tommy lowered the plumb bob, like a child's top cast from steel, on a long nylon cord. Robert caught it and steadied it, blocking the piercing wind with his body. The slab was leaning forward two degrees. Leon put a wrench on the inside left nut, then put his pipe section over the wrench handle for leverage. He and one of the crewmen turned the handle clockwise, and the slab bucked as the base plate dropped a fraction of an inch. Tommy lunged with the movement, grabbing hold of the top of the slab with both hands and dropping the plumb line.

"Looks like you dropped something," Porter said.

"Porter," Robert said, "why don't you shut up?"

"I'm just being friendly," Porter said. "Hell, give me his ball and I'll run it up there for him." He walked over to the ladder and put both hands on the rails.

Robert let the plumb bob fall in the dirt. He walked around the slab. "Stand away from the ladder, Porter," he said.

"Hell, I ain't going to do the boy no harm," he said. "Want to make sure this ladder's set good." He gave the ladder a playful shake and Robert saw, in his peripheral vision, Tommy clinging to the slab in terror, his eyes squeezed shut.

The wrench Leon had been using lay at Robert's feet. The handle was as long as Robert's forearm. There was a roaring sound in Robert's ears and he could barely see to pick it up. He held it at shoulder level and moved to within striking distance of Porter. "Get away from the ladder, Porter. Now."

Porter's eyes narrowed and his lips barely moved as he said, "Put that wrench down and let's see who's tough."

Leon got slowly to his feet. He still had the pipe in his hands. "I believe the Captain asked you to step away from the ladder."

Porter looked deep into Robert's eyes and apparently didn't like what he saw there. He took two steps back from the ladder.

"Pick up your things and get off my job site," Robert said. "You're fired."

"You can't fire me. Contractor hired me, not no Mason Jar and Anthill or whoever the hell you are."

"Fine. You go get the general and bring him here and have him tell me he's overriding my authority."

Porter half turned, walking sideways toward the lot where their cars were parked. "I got the union behind me," he said in a high, nasal voice. "You're going to be kissing my ass tomorrow and begging me to come back to work."

Robert threw the wrench down and turned his back on Porter. The rage had boiled up in him so quickly he hadn't seen it coming. His hands were shaking and he saw himself standing over Porter with the bloody wrench in his hands, smashing it into Porter's grinning face over and over and over.

"Tommy?" Robert said. "Get on down from there. We're through for the day."

Leon said, "You shouldn't have done that, Captain."

"I'll see to it everybody gets a full day's wages."

"You know that's not what I'm talking about. Man like that, he's apt to make trouble. Come out here at night and tear things up. The way he was acting, it wasn't any kind of thing. We get worse than that every day of the year."

"Porter is a coward," Robert said. "He'll go home and beat his wife and that'll be the end of it."

"What I'm saying, Captain, is you seem wound up mighty tight. You might want to think about that, is what I'm saying."

ROBERT DIDN'T HAVE to think about it. The problem, the biggest one, was obvious enough. He and Ruth were living in a sort of armed truce. She spent nearly every weekend at her father's farm and every weeknight acting as if nothing were wrong.

Robert had gotten in the habit of going to the country club on Saturdays and drinking himself into a state of comfortable anesthesia. On more than a few nights he'd had company in the person of Cindy Berkshire, who lived down the street from him and whose husband Bill "traveled in lingerie," as his joke went. He was out of town more weekends than not, and Cindy had made two things quite clear to Robert. The first was that she and Bill had an "understanding," and the second was that she found Robert extremely attractive. "Your wife is a fool to leave a man like you untended to," was her refrain.

Cindy was in her mid-thirties, at least five years older than Robert. Her dark hair was cut short, but not severely so, and her skin was pale enough to seem blue from the veins that pulsed under it. Her large eyes protruded, and her wide mouth was usually turned down in annoyance, mock or otherwise. The overall effect was a certain wantonness that spoke to Robert's less sophisticated side.

Cindy was the demonstrative type, and her custom was to wrap Robert in a tight hug when she encountered him at the club. The Saturday after he fired Porter, as Robert's arms went around her taut body and he felt her small, hard breasts pressing into him, it was like the construction site all over again. His control evaporated before he knew what was happening to him.

"Okay," he said into her ear. She was wearing Chanel No. 5 and it might as well have been Spanish Fly.

"Okay what?"

"Okay, let's do it. I want you."

"Hallelujah," she said. "Your place or mine?"

"Yours," he said. "As soon as we can get out of here without making a spectacle of ourselves."

She left a few minutes later. Though the place was empty, Robert lingered another half hour, talking to the bartender and chain smoking to hide his nervousness.

He drove home, left the car, and walked the two unlighted blocks to the Berkshire house. He couldn't seem to remember how to walk naturally. Caution took him around to the back door, and before he could knock, it opened into the darkness of the kitchen. He stepped inside and smelled her perfume. Then she was in his arms, wearing nothing but a thin nightgown that Robert soon peeled away. Her mouth tasted of cigarettes and brandy and he couldn't get enough of it.

But once he was sitting on the edge of her bed, his clothes in a heap on the carpet, he was stricken with doubt. If I do this, he thought, things will never be the same. I will have given up the moral high ground, and for what?

There was a candle burning on the dresser, and by its light Cindy was trying to read his face. "I don't even care if we have sex," she said. "Could you just hold me for a while and put your hands on me?" Her eyes glistened. "I get so goddamn lonely."

The show of vulnerability seemed to be what he needed. It happened quickly after that, both of them sprinting for the finish line. Afterwards Robert felt distant and empty, like a sun-faded black and white photograph of himself. To ease the awkwardness he began to touch her again, and the second time was slow and tender. The third time, in the soft light of dawn, was entirely about the proximity of their sleeping bodies and the smells of the previous lovemaking that still clung to them, a simple and unconscious act, a last trip to the buffet table for no other reason than that he'd been hungry so long.

AFTER THAT THEY saw each other nearly every weekend. Bill's and Ruth's cars were the warning signals. In their absence, the coast was always clear.

Once Cindy said, "I stay with Bill because, in spite of everything, I really love the big lug. But I don't get you. Why don't you leave her?"

It was the summer of 1966. They lay apart, smoking, Robert savoring the moment more for its absences than for what was there: the lack of tension, of desire, of urgency. "It's hard to explain. I try to picture myself telling her, and all I see is her confusion. She would not be able to understand why I was doing it."

"She can't understand that you need sex?"

"She couldn't understand how that could be more important than having a good home. Or not disappointing her parents."

"And that's a reason to stay with her?"

"Evidently," Robert said.

They lasted through the end of the summer, not quite a year, and it was indifference that broke them up. Robert found her pleasant enough company, and the sex was exactly as good as the excitement he managed to bring to it. When the excitement failed to materialize, as it increasingly did, it left him frustrated and angry.

"This," Cindy said after one such occasion, "is not what it used to be."

"No," Robert said, "it's not."

He got dressed and went home.

After that she no longer hugged him when he came to the club, though he would on occasion buy her a drink and ask after Bill. By fall she'd taken up with one of the executives in Bill's office, or so the gossip went. It seemed a worse betrayal than sleeping with Robert, and hurt her in his estimation.

That gossip made him nervous, briefly, that Ruth would find out about his affair. If she'd heard, she didn't show it. And the winter of 1966 began to melt into the spring of 1967.

IT SEEMED TO ROBERT that the world had changed more in the three years between 1964 and 1967 than it had in his father's entire lifetime.

Having seen a glimmer of hope in President Johnson's push for civil rights, black people who were tired of obstruction and delays began insisting on full equality. Summertime had become the season of riots. The police action in Vietnam had turned into a full fledged war. The US, which had never lost a war, was now mired in one it couldn't win, and the issue was tearing the country apart.

People only a few years younger than Robert seemed to have evolved into a different species. Most of the weirdness was confined to the West Coast, but even North Carolina had its share of recreational drugs and ban-the-bomb symbols and scruffy clothes and music with guitars that sounded like power drills.

All these things, Robert saw, were symptoms of the same idea, the idea that change was possible, that the way things had always been was not the way they always had to be.

Mitch had been swept up in it, growing his hair and sideburns, wearing paisley and polka-dot shirts to work. As jazz splintered into factions, Mitch opted for the funky pop of Ramsey Lewis and Cannonball Adderley over the

new thing that Coltrane and Ornette and Sun Ra were doing. Robert himself
mostly listened to his older records, or went to flea markets and thrift shops
looking for more from the early sixties.

At 28 he was two years from the age where he could no longer be trusted,
according to the wisdom of the young. He and Ruth had a sizable nest egg,
enough that they could trade their house for a newer, bigger one, if Robert
had seen any point in it. They were not in it often enough at the same time
to feel crowded. For two weeks each summer they would dutifully go on
vacation, usually by car—to Mexico, to the Grand Canyon, to the Lakes
District in Canada. The constant proximity made Robert snappish and Ruth,
in turn, sulky.

The idea of change was as thrilling to Robert as it was terrifying. He didn't
know where to start. He tried to talk to Ruth about his frustrations, and she
met him with the incomprehension he'd expected. "I don't know what's
wrong with you," she said, "but I'm sure it will pass."

Robert didn't know what was wrong either. He was no closer to leaving
Ruth than he'd ever been, and for all Mitch's idiosyncrasies, he was a generous
and easygoing employer. Robert tried golf, tried learning chess from a book
and replaying famous games by himself, went through a phase of heavy drinking that only sapped his strength.

Then, in March of 1967, Mitch said, "It's time."

Robert straightened up from his table. "Time for what?"

"They're asking for sealed bids on the East-West Expressway. Finally."

"Bids?"

"Don't worry, it's in the bag. Was I right about IBM?"

"So we pull the plug on Hayti," Maurice said. Maurice had fought change
on every front and won. He was wearing newly bought versions of the same
clothes he'd had on when Robert met him. He had nothing but anger for the
Black Panthers; he was sure they were "going to spoil things for the rest of us."

"I didn't think you cared," Robert said to him.

"I don't," Maurice said. "It's a slum. Let's take it down."

"What do you mean, 'let's'?" Robert said. He knew that he was perpetually
on edge lately. He seemed unable to do anything about it. "It won't be you
that takes it down, it'll be me."

"Don't do it, then," Maurice said, bending over his work again. "I don't give
a Goddamn one way or the other."

"All right, you two," Mitch said. "Be cool. We been waiting a long time for
this. This is the road to the future we're going to be building, here. This and
Interstate 40 will open the Park right up. We'll be papering the walls with
money."

"Rah rah rah," Robert muttered. "Sis boom bah."

"Robert, you want to share that with the rest of the class?" Mitch said.

Robert didn't bother to answer. Mitch's good humor was unshakable and probably, Robert thought, chemically enhanced.

Mitch sat at his drafting table, rarely used these days, though still in the center of the expanded bullpen. He unrolled a single blue line print, still smelling of ammonia, that showed a section of highway. "The first stretch," he said, "begins at Chapel Hill Road downtown and runs east for two and a half miles."

"Two and a half miles?" Robert said, looking dumbfounded at the map. "What the hell good does that do anybody?"

"It's a start, Robert."

"It's a start through the middle of Hayti."

"This isn't exactly news. Yes, it goes through the middle of Hayti. Just like the residents of Hayti voted for four years ago."

"That was when they thought they were going to get new houses and a new commercial center and a whole new city. Only that's never going to happen, is it?"

"No, Robert, it's never going to happen. Now, the second stretch will turn south and hook up with I-40 straight into Raleigh. We should have that done in three years—"

Robert walked out. He sat on the trunk of his Chevelle and lit a Lucky. When he looked up, Mitch was standing in front of him. It was only March second. The sky had clouded over during the day, and the temperature had dropped into the forties. They were both in their shirtsleeves. The chill felt good to Robert, cooling him out, as the jazz men would say. Mitch had his arms folded.

"I don't know what's bugging you, man," Mitch said, "but you need to get a handle on it. Especially in front of the whole office. You know what I'm saying?"

"You going to fire me? Oh, that's right. You can't fire me. Your pal Randy Fogg might complain."

Mitch shook his head, refusing the bait. "Man, you are pushing it. If ever I saw a man needed to get laid, it's you. Seeing as how you've got a taste for the dark stuff, I could fix you up. Change your luck, man."

Robert thought his rage might overwhelm him. Before it could explode, Mitch held up one hand and said, "Whoa, brother, hold on. I got a better idea." He produced a thin, hand-rolled cigarette from his shirt pocket. "Smoke this. Get a little perspective."

Robert jumped off the car and backed away. "Jesus Christ! Are you out of your mind? What if a cop was driving by? Get away from me with that stuff."

Mitch shrugged and put the joint in his pocket. "Suit yourself. This is going to be legal in a few years. People won't bother with booze anymore. It's going to be a better world."

"For who?" Robert said. He brushed Mitch back with his arm and got in the car.

Mitch was still talking through the rolled-up window as Robert started the engine. "Take the rest of the day off," Mitch said. "Get your head together. As long as you bring your ass back here tomorrow. We got work to do."

THE WORK, not surprisingly, was more demolition. The time had come to go after the businesses on Pettigrew Street. Today it was the Dreamland Shoeshine Shop.

Robert got to the office at eight and Mitch sent him straight over to the job site. The crane company had learned its lesson and sent a dour black man in his fifties named Johnston. Leon and Tommy Coleman were already there, talking to a middle-aged black man in a rumpled suit.

"Jerome Harris," the man said, shaking Robert's hand. "This was my store."

"I'm sorry," Robert said. "You know it wasn't me that—"

Harris waved away his apologies. "They got me a place over to Tin City now."

Tin City was a row of temporary buildings around the corner on Fayetteville Street. The Hayti Redevelopment Commission, still pretending that a new shopping center would magically appear any day now across from St. Joseph's Church, had their headquarters there, and a few of the hardier Pettigrew Street businesses had moved in next to them.

"It's temporary, you understand. I've had to relocate four different times, but it's always been called Dreamland. Been my dream for forty years now to have my own shoeshine business. That's where the name came from."

It was hard for Robert to meet his eyes.

"When they build me my new place, I'll keep that name. Dreamland." He shook Robert's hand again. "I'll let y'all get on with your work. Man's got to be able to do his work. That's what the good Lord put him here for."

When he was gone, Tommy said, "I believe the good Lord put me here for something besides work, but I don't work, I don't get to do what the good Lord put me here for. So let's get it on." He looked at Robert. "You all right, Captain?"

"Go ahead," Robert said. "You know what to do."

Robert walked across the street and sat by the railroad tracks. From there he had a good view of the decay that had set in. At least a third of the businesses had closed and some of the buildings had been cleared, leaving gaps like missing teeth in an idiot's grin. The few people on the street walked with their heads down, focused on their destinations and not their surroundings.

Robert was still sitting there when a group of protesters rounded the corner, headed his way. They had signs reading, "Save Hayti" and "Keep Your Promises," all, sadly, looking as if they'd been painted by the same hand. There were 20 of them, with a few young white faces together at the back.

At the front was Barrett Howard.

It was the first time Robert had seen him since the IBM press conference, other than on TV or in photos in the *Herald*. He looked bigger and angrier, and he'd grown a bristling mustache and sideburns to match his large, lopsided Afro. He led the marchers straight to the Dreamland Shoeshine Shop and spread them along the sidewalk for maximum effect. Then he looked up and down the street, as if wondering where the photographers were.

Instead he saw Robert. A wave of uncertainty washed over his face, then he sucked in his stomach and walked across the street.

Robert sat where he was, on the low railroad embankment, and waited for him. The wind gusted, and a candy wrapper fluttered down the middle of Pettigrew, clinging briefly to Howard's ankle. Howard kicked it away and climbed the embankment to where Robert sat. He nodded and sat down. After a moment he said, "Hey."

"Hey," Robert said.

"I want you to know I'm sorry for what happened that night. I should never have taken you out there. It was wrong. I apologize."

"That was a long time ago," Robert said. "Besides, all you did was show me the truth. I had to see it myself to believe it."

They sat for a while in silence, and then Robert said, "How have you been?"

"Good. Busy. We've come so far so fast, and we still have such a long way to go. What about you?"

"Good," Robert said. "Busy. What happened with the union?"

"Union didn't work out. Folks in the South, some ideas they're not ready for. Which is a shame, because the alternative ... well, it's going to be a lot harder in the long run."

That last had an ominous ring that Robert didn't want to pursue. He let it slide into another silence and then found that he couldn't stand it any longer. "Is Mercy all right?"

"You're asking me?"

"Who else would I ask?"

"We split up. Been more than two years now."

A wild tangle of hope and joy exploded in Robert's chest, making it hard to breathe. "You split up?"

"She quit the religion, too. I stayed. I'm a *houngan* now. A priest."

"She quit?"

"She quit within a couple months of that night. All it was was the truth of things coming out, like you say. Her heart wasn't in the craft, and she'd about had her fill of me anyway."

"It looked like her heart was in it to me," Robert said.

"I told you before. That wasn't Mercy. That was Erzulie."

He had changed, Robert saw. There was conviction in his voice that hadn't been there before.

"She didn't seek you out?" Howard said. "I thought sure she was going to come to you."

"No," Robert said. "She never did." The idea, the unrealized possibility, the very words, thrilled him. "Do you know where she went?"

"I don't know that she went anywhere. It was her house. She threw me out. She's still there, for all I know."

Images cascaded across Robert's inner eye. Mercy in her short, white terry-cloth robe, in the white silk dress he'd first seen her in. Her face so close to his on the dance floor. He stood up and focused on the job site across the street to drive the pictures away.

"What's going to happen here today?" Robert asked.

"We wave our signs. Maybe somebody takes our picture for the paper. We get lucky, a TV crew shows up and we get thirty seconds on the 11 o'clock news. You knock Dreamland down and another piece of black history gets obliterated."

"You don't want to stop it?" Robert was smiling.

"Are you serious?"

"If you all were to stand between the crane and the building, I'd have to send my crew home."

"You wouldn't call the cops?"

"I don't need cops telling me how to run my job site. Today's Friday. Once word gets around, there'll damn sure be cameras and reporters down here on Monday."

Howard scrutinized his face, more in suspicion than gratitude. "Whose side are you on?"

"When I figure that out, I'll let you know. Are we going to do this? If so, we should do it." They walked across the street together. "Sooner or later, we'll have to go through with it, of course. If not Monday, then soon. It'll cost Mitch a few days' pay all around, which he can afford, and maybe Mr. Harris will get a new store out of it."

A young black man in the crowd looked familiar, and with a hot flash of embarrassment, Robert realized why. "That kid there—he was the one, the one with Mercy that night."

Howard nodded uncomfortably. "His name's Donald Harriman. He's very devoted to the faith."

"Yeah," Robert said. "Yeah, I guess he would be."

"Look, I got to get these kids mobilized. Maybe you don't want to be standing around here when I do that."

"No," Robert said. "I expect not."

The bulldozer and the first of the dump trucks arrived as Robert caught up with Leon and Tommy. They'd blocked off the eastbound lane of Pettigrew, and Tommy was directing traffic around the heavy equipment.

"They ain't going to cause no trouble, are they?" Leon asked.

"They might," Robert said.

"Is there something funny going on here that I don't know about, Captain?"

"It's spring," Robert said. "Don't you like the spring?"

Johnston had the crane in place, parked parallel to the curb, the wrecking ball ready to swing from right to left into the building. Leon stepped away from Robert and shouted, "Y'all people stand back from the crane. Don't no-body want to get hurt, here."

The protesters shifted around in apparent confusion for a few seconds, then dropped their signs and quickly lined up across the front of the building, holding hands. Howard and the Harriman kid were in the middle, the word "Dreamland" visible on the plate glass window behind them. It would have made a perfect photo if someone had been there to take it.

Leon walked up to Howard and said, "What the hell you doing?"

"Morning, Leon," Howard said. "I guess we're not going to let you have this one."

"Dammit, Barrett, don't do this."

"It's already done, man."

Leon returned. "What now, Captain?"

"I don't see that we have much choice. We'll come back Monday, try again." Robert walked over to the crane. "Okay," he called, "might as well—"

Johnston, the crane operator, had his window shut and he was staring straight ahead. As Robert watched, he worked the levers and the wrecking ball began to bob gently from side to side.

Robert climbed onto the running board and rapped on the window with his knuckles. "Hey!"

The wrecking ball swung out over the street and then dove into the front of the building.

He'd aimed high, Robert saw, well over the heads of the protesters, and at the sight of the incoming ball, they'd all run for it. Except Howard and the Harriman boy.

The building groaned as the ball hit. Fissures appeared between the bricks, followed by pinging sounds as the surviving windows cracked and popped loose and shattered on the ground. Dust sifted onto all their heads, including Robert's.

"Get away from there!" Leon shouted at Howard.

Johnston took the ball back for another go. Robert tried the door; it was locked. He pounded on the window with his fists.

The second blow took the weakened sections of wall apart with a massive crunch. Bricks clattered into the abandoned store. Of the few that fell outward, one caught Harriman in the head.

He collapsed across the sidewalk.

Johnston finally looked up. "Get out of there!" Robert shouted. "What the hell is the matter with you?"

Johnston gestured for Robert to step away, then got out of the crane.

"What the hell do you think you're doing?" Robert shouted at him.

Johnston shook his head and walked away. "Damn kids," he said.

Robert ran to where Harriman lay. Howard and the other protesters were kneeling and standing around him. Howard was talking to a white girl. "The ambulance first, understand? Then call the papers. You got dimes?" She nodded and sprinted away.

"How bad is it?" Robert asked.

"He's all right," Howard said. Harriman had his eyes open. Blood seeped through the layer of brick dust and chips on his left temple. "We'll get our coverage now."

BY THE TIME the ambulance and the cops and the newspapers had come and gone, it was after noon.

"It's my fault that boy got hurt," Robert said to Howard when it was all over.

"I want some credit," Howard said. "I had to do the actual work."

"Somebody could have gotten killed."

Howard stared at him as if he were a child or a simpleton. "What kind of stakes you think we been playing for? For the last four hundred years?"

Robert nodded. "I guess I'll be seeing you again, now."

"Yeah."

Robert turned to go.

"Robert? You going to see her?"

"I don't know." Even with the crisis, he'd thought about little else all morning.

"When you do, tell her I asked after her."

"If I do," Robert said, "I'll tell her."

HE STAYED in the office until after six. Mitch had used up the first part of the afternoon, going over the events of the morning again and again, until Robert managed to convince him that Howard had gotten what he wanted. There would be no lawyers, no police investigations. "Face it," Robert finally told him. "It was a black crane operator and a black kid. Nobody cares."

Later he had taken out the specifications and surveys for the East-West Expressway and tried in vain to picture the highway they implied.

Ruth had already departed for the weekend when Robert got home. She'd left fried chicken and mashed potatoes cooling on the kitchen counter, slaw in the refrigerator.

Robert set the chicken and potatoes next to the slaw and took a shower. When he got out he put Charlie Shavers' *Live from Chicago* on the turntable and stood at the window, looking at a small patch of green lawn that had just begun to recover from the winter's cold.

He'd spent most of his life in harness to principles. Some he'd gotten from his father, like importance of service, and the need to be independent and strong. On his own he'd discovered the power and satisfaction that came from realizing abstract ideas like home and shelter and commerce in terms of concrete and steel.

Now he wondered if things were not simpler than he'd ever imagined, so simple that every dog and bird and insect and fish on the planet could understand them. Avoid pain. Seek pleasure.

The music evoked in lucid detail his night at the Wonderland three years before. The sight of Mercy, the sound of the musicians on stage, even more powerfully, the feelings about the music that he and Mercy had shared, feelings that had stunned and overwhelmed him. Who but a fool would turn his back on feelings that strong? What obligations, what commitments, could be more important?

He took a bottle of brandy from the kitchen cabinet and set it, with a glass, on the table in the den. Mitch would not hesitate in this situation, he knew. Robert understood that thus far he had let events carry him along, and that if he went forward now it had to be by choice.

He was not a churchgoing man, but like his father before him he believed in a God of compassion and justice. A weakness like Cindy Berkshire God could surely forgive. A woman like Mercy, who worshipped demons and had given herself to strangers, was another story entirely.

He also knew that if he opened the bottle he would not stop after one or two drinks, and there would be many, many more nights of insensibility to follow. Surely God did not intend for him to live in a haze of anesthesia.

He took the bottle and glass back to the kitchen and turned the hi-fi up for a trumpet solo. In doing so, he saw that he had made up his mind. When the song finished, he carefully put the record away, turned off the receiver and turned out the lights, and drove to the house on Beamon Street.

IT WAS 8:00 when he pulled up in front of Mercy's house. Her Impala was in the driveway. He was so keyed up he was afraid of a coronary.

You have only Howard's word that she remembers you at all, he told himself. And that was three years ago. Most of all, you have no reason to believe there's not some other man in there with her right now. But with his decisions made and only the last few feet of the journey to go, he was in a hurry. He shut off the engine and locked the car, in concession to the neighborhood, then walked quickly up to the porch, oblivious to the night and everything around him.

He knocked, heard someone moving inside. The door opened on a chain. He glimpsed Mercy inside as the door closed and the chain rattled and the door opened again. Then, as on that night at the Wonderland, she slipped into his arms as if they'd been holding each other all their lives.

HE DIDN'T EMERGE AGAIN until Sunday afternoon. He was red-eyed from lack of sleep, freshly scrubbed, back in the clothes he'd barely worn. He wasn't angry anymore.

When she'd let him in, Coltrane's *Kulu Se Mama* was playing softly in the background. The lights were low and the air was sweet with scented candles. She was even more beautiful than he remembered, in bare feet and jeans and a black T-shirt. "I got so tired of white clothes in my mambo days," she told him later, "I haven't worn white since."

Robert knew from the first that the night would end in her bed. That certainty made it possible to talk, to move slowly, to answer some of the questions that fluttered like moths inside his head. He needed to put words to feelings, to understand what she saw in him, to believe that he was not just a victim of "jungle fever," as Howard had said.

"That first time, at the Wonderland, it was the music," she told him. "It was like a light shining out of you. Then, when I had my arms around you, it was like we were in a soundproof room, no clocks on the walls, nothing outside the doors."

It had been the same for him. The feeling you have on the second day of a long vacation, he told her, lying on a beach with all the time in the world. As he said the words, the thought of Ruth and Jamaica gave him a momentary pang of guilt. But the intervening years had taken the heat from the memory, and it had no real power over him.

Mercy had an astounding collection of records, and she'd played them one after another, save for those few hours when they'd slept in each other's arms.

They'd talked, a little, of race. Her skin was no darker than that of Spaniards or Italians he'd known. She could have passed for white, lived anywhere. New York, Paris.

"Only by denying my mama," she told him, "and I would never do that. Her skin is dark black, African black, and you can see my face in hers. It was my daddy that was white, or so she tells me."

"You don't know who he was?"

She shook her head. "All she would ever say was that it didn't matter, that I was her child and not his. All he gave me was his color. All he gave my mama was me. Whenever I'd ask about him, all she'd say was, 'That's old business,' and that was that. She wants that secret to die with her, and I imagine it will. Nobody changes my mama's mind."

Robert tried to imagine his own life without the towering presence of his father. "It must be hard," he said.

"A lot of kids my age were the same," Mercy said. "I wasn't the only one didn't even know who my father was. It bothered me from time to time, but there are some things in this life you just got to let go of."

They talked about that night in the woods, something Robert had not yet been able to let go of.

"My mama is what they call a conjure woman," Mercy said. They were still sitting on her couch. He had his left arm around her, and she was holding his other hand against her right thigh. Her long, fragrant hair fell in black curls around both of their faces. He hadn't kissed her yet.

"So I was around hoodoo, as she called it, all my life. Root work, charms, a mishmash of Catholicism and vodou. I grew up in it the way other people grow up Baptist or AME. When I went to college at NCC, I started to learn about the real thing. I was working part-time at a beauty parlor in Hayti then, to help pay for school. I fell in with some people that were still practicing it. They were descendents of the artisans that Dr. Moore brought over from the island of Haiti back around the turn of the century. I even got to meet one of the men who made the symbol for St. Joseph's. He was the one who first introduced me to Erzulie.

"It was so powerful. I'd never known anything like it. So I saved my money and I went to Haiti for six months and wrote about it when I got back. They call it independent study now, but they didn't have a name for it then. I pretty much made up my own curriculum from a mix of religion and anthropology, and they gave me a BA for it, which I used to get a job in a bank."

"But you believed in it."

"Do you believe in gravity?" Mercy said. "There's a force in vodou, a power you can feel. You felt it."

The sound of the drums came unbidden into Robert's head. "Yes."

"The thing is, it uses you. That's what I felt when the *lwa* left me that night and I saw you watching me. At first I was mad. I thought, I don't need to be seeing myself through some white man's eyes. White people don't have any magic of their own, all they want is to rob it from the people that do. But then, a few weeks later, I found myself thinking, What am I doing? As a black person, as a woman, what am I doing letting someone—some *thing*—use my body this way? Isn't that how it's always been?"

"You were able to just walk away from it? Nobody said anything?"

"There was trouble. A lot of people were upset, saw it as a betrayal. Barrett stood up for me, made them see they were trying to turn religion into another kind of slavery."

"Barrett still believes."

"He wants so hard to believe. He thinks black people aren't strong enough to win freedom on our own. 'Outnumbered and outgunned,' he always used to say. He thinks the *lwa* are our allies. That we need their power to get our rights."

"And you?"

"In real vodou, in Haiti, there's only one God. The *lwa* are like saints to a Catholic. They're a way to let you approach God, *Le Gran Met,* who can be a little hard to find sometimes. They're not an end in themselves."

"So you believe in God."

"I think that when someone does an act of charity, of unselfish kindness, that's what God is. God is the spirit that enters the person when they do that. But there are other spirits, too. There's Erzulie, who enters you when you give yourself over to sexual pleasure." She glanced at him then, with a smile whose implications left him dizzy. "There's Damballah, who is the desire for power over others, or Ogoun Feraille, the spirit of war and killing. There's a hundred different *lwa*. For me it came down to the question of whether I was going to continue to step away and not be there when all these things were happening to me."

"And you can control it? Erzulie isn't going to one day come and push you aside?"

"No. She's there. Like God, I think she's a part of all of us. But I'm the one in control." She looked at him again and didn't look away. "You'll see."

It was then that Robert did, at last, kiss her.

Later, still on the couch, both of them half-drunk with desire, Robert said, "I'm still married. I have to tell you that. The marriage is a travesty, but I don't know how to get out of it."

She shrugged. "Like Houdini used to say, when you're ready, you'll get out. I don't like it, but I'm not going to wait for her to be gone. I've waited long enough."

So had Robert. He stood up and held out his hand to take her into the bedroom. As on the dance floor, she followed his lead. But once in the bedroom, she said, "I'm going to show you how to give me what I want." They took off the last of their clothes and he lay down on the bed next to her. The sheets were dark blue and perfumed with the oils she used on her skin: jasmine, vanilla, and sweet almond. She took his penis in one hand and said, "This is very beautiful, and later I want to feel it inside me. But first I want you to touch me with these," she kissed his lips, "and these." She took both his hands and put them on her body.

He didn't need instructions. All words left his head. His self-conscious, supervising brain was evicted by a creature of the flesh that knew only desire and love and excruciating pleasure, tenderness and awe.

It was a long time before they talked coherently again. That too was intoxicating, and small coincidences took on profound significance. They had, for instance, both read the same Encyclopedia Britannica article about ancient Egypt. Robert was after hard facts about the pyramids. Mercy was caught up in magic and symbols, and had learned to write her grade school friends' names in hieroglyphics.

In October of 1950, Mercy's great aunt Cecilia had driven Mercy to Asheville. They'd driven through the grounds of the Biltmore Estate and seen the mansion from the outside, but Cecilia had declined to go in, despite the fact that the tours were integrated even then. She was a tireless booster of the Negro race who did not care to mingle with whites. There was also some question about the expense.

The idea that they had been so near to each other so long ago gave Robert an odd, melancholy sense of thwarted destiny. If Cecilia had come inside, and 10-year-old Robert had seen 9-year-old Mercy, would he have felt something? Could it have changed his future, magically prevented his marriage to Ruth?

Aunt Cecilia, as Mercy described her, was the opposite of Mercy's mother. She was vain, materialistic, fond of gin, and quick to laugh. She couldn't understand why Mercy's mother never wanted to leave home. So it was Aunt Cecilia who took Mercy to the Savoy Ballroom in Harlem at the age of 13.

Mercy couldn't remember the name of the band that played that night. Nobody famous, she said. What she remembered was the power of the jazz orchestra: the blaring wall of trombones, the booming tom-toms, the clarinets and trumpets soaring high above the rhythm. And the dancers. These were the best Lindy Hoppers in the world, filling the 10,000-square-foot dance floor and jumping, she said, "like human popcorn."

Robert had only been 6 when he saw his first swing band at the Biltmore, and the dancing hardly compared to the Savoy. But it was the week the war ended in the Pacific, and the mood of jubilation was like nothing he'd seen since. That feeling got tied up in his head with the music and the dancing.

For Mercy it was life-changing. Home again in Bentonville, she began to sneak out on weekends and hitchhike the 75 miles to Hayti. "I was crazy, out of my mind. I know I made my mama sick with worry, but there was nothing short of handcuffs and leg irons could have kept me in that house."

She'd been lucky. On her first trip to Hayti she'd found her way to the Biltmore Hotel. There she had fallen in with sober, married, churchgoing Bernie, who had showed her the basic Lindy footwork and then watched out for her. "Already at 13 I was pretty well developed, and there was more than one man wanted to take me upstairs. After a night of dancing, I might have gone, too, if it wasn't for Bernie."

For Robert there was deep cosmic meaning in his having learned to dance at the Biltmore Estate and her having learned at the Biltmore Hotel. The hand of destiny seemed to be everywhere.

Time and again Mercy would toss off a remark, turning away as she said it, or dropping her voice nearly to inaudibility, as if she meant it only for herself but couldn't keep from saying it aloud. Wordplay, quotes from songs, references to a made-up cast of characters that lived in her head, the inventions of a restless intelligence that thought no one was listening. Robert, also an only child, recognized the symptoms. He didn't catch all of it, especially at first; what he heard and understood showed a soft, goofy underbelly that charmed him as much as anything about her. She reacted to his laughter with a raised eyebrow at first, later with a tentative smile, and finally with a flurry of jokes. Robert saw in all of it a loneliness, a hunger to be understood, a fear of rejection.

The future was the hardest thing to talk about.

"Never thought I'd end up a banker," Mercy said. "I always thought I'd be some kind of doctor or *curandera* or something. But there's a kind of momentum gets going when you're good at something and they keep giving you raises and the people you work with are funny and decent."

"Is that where you see yourself in ten years?"

"I don't look that far ahead. One day at a time is about all I can manage." It was early Sunday morning. They'd woken up long enough to make love and now seemed to be headed toward sleep again, Robert idly rubbing her back, his sun-browned hand darker than the secret skin between her shoulder blades. "And you?" she said, turning her head toward him. "You seem to be more the master-plan type."

"My master plan didn't work out," he said. "So I guess I'm with you. One day at a time."

When the time came to leave he stood at the front door holding her. "I can come next weekend," he said.

"Hush now," she said. "Don't talk. Kiss me and go and don't look back."

He did look back, though, from the porch steps, to see her touch her lips with the tips of her fingers and smile before she closed the door.

WITH A CHURNING in his stomach, he saw Ruth's car in the driveway of the house on Woodrow Street.

He'd been thinking that he might tell her he wanted a divorce. With a few hours to work it through and prepare himself, he thought he might find the way. First he needed to be away from Mercy, so that his head would stop spinning.

Now he felt only panic. Despite the shower, he smelled of Mercy. The alibis he'd prepared seemed hopelessly futile.

Ruth was in the kitchen. She had taken the fried chicken and fixings out and set them on the counter. She was on the verge of tears. "You didn't even eat the food I cooked for you."

"I'm sorry, honey, I was working all weekend. I've only been home long enough to sleep." He wondered if she'd already noticed that the bed was untouched.

"There's so little you let me do for you anymore. Now you don't want my cooking. You make me feel useless!"

Sex, he nearly said. Physical contact. Intimacy. These were the things she could have given him. He didn't dare say the words, even in anger. What if she took him up on it?

"I'm hungry now," he said. He got down a plate and put a cold drumstick on it and spooned up some slaw. In fact he was starving. They hadn't found time to eat more than a few cold cuts and some eggs all weekend.

"Wait," she said, suddenly cheerful again. "Let me heat it up for you. You go take a shower and change clothes. You smell!"

ON MONDAY MORNING he drove straight to the job site, ready to play it by ear with Howard. He arrived to find a vacant lot.

Mitch didn't come into work until ten. Robert followed him into his office and closed the door. "What happened to the Dreamland Shoeshine Shop?"

"I sent a crew out Saturday to take it down."

"While nobody was looking."

"That's right."

"I'm surprised you didn't do it at midnight."

"I thought about it."

"And you didn't trust me to do it?"

"I tried calling you on Saturday morning. Very early on Saturday morning." Mitch grinned from his chair, hands behind his head. "You look different this morning, Bobby. More relaxed, somehow."

Robert walked away.

Sitting at the drafting table he thought, This is how lives go out of control. Secrets, lies, utter disregard for the niceties of society.

He couldn't wait for the weekend to see Mercy again. On Tuesday he called her at work, then phoned Ruth to tell her he would be late. He drove straight to Beamon Street at five o'clock and she met him at the door, already half-undressed.

IN OCTOBER, Mercy took him to meet her mother.

She lived in Bentonville, at the southern edge of Johnston County, 15 miles from the Bynum farm as the mockingbird flew, twice that distance by car. Bentonville was the scene of the biggest Civil War battle in North Carolina, as the Confederacy mounted one final effort to stop Sherman's army on its march north from Georgia.

Thickets of historical markers grew on every corner, and it seemed that Civil War tourism was the town's major industry. "Didn't it make you crazy to grow up here, with all these Confederate monuments all over the place?" Robert asked her. They'd taken his Chevelle, and she was tucked into his right shoulder.

"No. All I had to do was remember what happened here. The Confederates got their asses kicked."

In the mountains where Robert grew up, the Civil War was not the issue that it still was in the lowlands. "Ruth just calls it 'the War,'" he said. As always when he brought up Ruth's name, he felt awkward and wished he hadn't done it. "As if Hitler and the Kaiser and Vietnam and all those other wars aren't even worth discussing."

Behind Mercy's even tone he could feel her discomfort as well. "And the

South was just misunderstood, I'm sure. It wasn't about slavery, it was about economics, right? Like a cotton and tobacco economy could sustain itself for five minutes without slaves."

"It's one of the many things we don't talk about." He hated the resignation in his own voice. "Listen," he said. "I think I'm going to drive up there today."

"To the farm?"

"I have to tell her. Maybe if I do it there, with her family around and everything, it'll be easier."

"Are you sure that's a good idea? They might lynch you."

"I can't wait any longer. I have to do something."

"Turn here," she said.

Her mother's house was on the far side of town, hidden in live oaks and high grass. The wood-frame structure was covered in orange and black asphalt shingles, the kind of house that Robert had passed a thousand times on rural roads and associated with a desperate poverty impossibly distant from his own life. All his attempts to prepare himself didn't prevent the shock. This is what it means, he thought. If you're black in the southern US, this kind of house is somewhere in your family.

Mercy's mother was in her fifties. She'd had Mercy late in life compared to many of the girls of her generation. She'd never been married, never had a steady man, never, according to Mercy, showed much desire for the opposite sex or had regrets about the lack. "Something," Mercy said, "I did not inherit from her."

Her mother must have been watching for them, because she came out the front door before Robert finished parking in the rutted dirt driveway. She was thin and powerful, with shiny, defined muscle groups in her arms. She wore khaki slacks, a sleeveless blouse, and a white kerchief around her head. Mercy had told the truth about her face. It was beautiful, a dark, lined version of Mercy's.

She took Robert's hand and smiled and said, "Come inside."

The house had few windows and was dark even in the bright autumn sunshine. Oil lamps stood on the tables, and Robert realized with a mild shock that there was no electricity. The room had an earthy, musky scent, faint and not unpleasant.

"Sit down, sit down," she said. "I'll bring some lemonade."

Instead Robert was drawn to an altar in the corner. There he found images of the Virgin, from Byzantine to cloyingly sentimental, black and white and color, torn from books and pamphlets and magazines. There were bottles and tin cups and plates, holding rum and bits of cake and other substances Robert couldn't identify. There were tangles of wire, candles, bits of ribbon, chunks of wood, rocks, dime-store jewelry, all heaped together on a wooden table that could have dated back to "the War."

"You know not to touch, right?" Mercy whispered behind him.

"Yes, baby," Robert said. "I know." He reached back for her hand. It was hard for him to be in the same room with her without being in physical contact.

Other objects covered the walls. Pieces of tin with nail-hole patterns forming hearts, crosses, birds. Old farm tools. A painting on wood, highly stylized, of a voluptuous woman carrying a jug on her head with stars all around her.

"Where did that come from?" Robert asked.

"I brought that to her from Haiti. It's Erzulie."

Her mother came in with a tray of mismatched glasses and a pitcher of lemonade. "You have so many beautiful things," Robert said.

"Thank you," she said. She seemed wary, and Robert didn't blame her. Mercy had told her everything: that he was married, that he was white, that they were in love. On the face of it, he had to admit, he didn't sound like a good bet.

They all sat on the couch. Mercy asked about her mother's bunions, her mother asked about things at Mechanics and Farmers. Finally Robert said, "I should go."

"He's got an errand he's got to run while we're up here, Mama."

"You seeing your wife's family?" she asked. The look she gave him was frank and unemotional.

"That's right," Robert said, trying to sound casual. "The Bynums."

"The Bynums."

"You know them?"

"Everybody around here knows Wilmer Bynum."

Robert waited, but there was no more.

"Will you be here for supper?" Mercy asked.

It was not yet eleven in the morning. "I would think so. I could call if I get held up."

Mercy shook her head. No, of course there was no phone. "Expect me," he said, "but don't panic if I'm not here."

As sick with nerves as he felt, it was a relief to have made up his mind. The thought of being able to come home to Mercy every night gave him strength.

It took the better part of an hour to work his way through Bentonville, up to West Smithfield, then over to the Bynum place. He drove the entire way with his jaw clenched and both hands gripping the wheel.

Turning from the paved highway onto the dirt road into the farm, Robert saw that the house had begun to sprout another cancer-like growth upstairs. The roof extension was covered in tarpaper and the exterior walls were nothing but empty 2 × 6 framing.

As always, the house swarmed with activity. Children ran through the fallow fields, some barely old enough to stagger, others in their teens, some with baseballs and gloves, others apparently running for the sheer hell of it. Ruth's mother was hanging washing on the line, and two old men sat on the long front porch in rocking chairs. Ruth herself was perched on a child's swing at the side of the house, watching her cousin, Greg Vaughan, lead his dog through a routine of tricks.

Robert parked in a field adjacent to the house, next to a collection of old and new pickup trucks, Ruth's Buick, an ancient Packard, and a '57 Studebaker with headlights like jet intakes and a rocket body that ended in tail fins.

When Ruth saw him she ran up and hugged him and gave him a smacking, theatrical kiss. "What a nice surprise! What brings you all the way out here?"

Robert shrugged. Greg eyed him suspiciously, and his dog, a big-chested German Shepherd, growled and looked ready to attack. Greg was in high school now, tall and gangly, his hair cut so short it had no apparent color. He wore faded blue jeans with iron-on patches over the knees, a white T-shirt, and high-topped basketball sneakers. "Greg," Robert said formally.

"Mr. Cooper."

"Your dog doesn't seem to like me."

"Funny about that. Usually he only acts like that around colored folk." He gave Robert a penetrating look. "You been around colored? Maybe he smells them on you."

"I work with black people," Robert said, instinctively protecting his relationship with Mercy. Only then did he see the racist trap Greg had led him into.

"Duke here has been showing me some of his tricks," Ruth said. She stood three feet away from Robert, hands behind her back. "He can dance, and he can roll over while he's in the middle of running, and all kinds of things."

"That's pretty amazing," Robert said. "You trained him to do all that?"

"Not really," Greg said. "More the other way around. Everybody's got their behaviors and instincts. You pay attention, they'll show you what they like to do."

"Well, don't stop on my account," Robert said. "I'd like to see his tricks too."

Greg had never stopped staring at him. "I think he's tired now."

To break the uncomfortable silence, Robert said, "What year are you now, senior?"

"Junior."

"You going on to college?"

The boy shrugged. "I have some hopes."

"Greg is the star of the South Johnston High basketball team," Ruth said. "He's got his eye on a basketball scholarship to Duke."

Greg virtually cringed with embarrassment. "It's bad luck to talk about it."

"Well, I wish you luck with it," Robert said. "College would at least keep you out of the draft."

He half expected an argument, given the boy's conservative politics. Greg only nodded. "Uncle Wilmer says not to worry. He says he has a feeling I won't get picked." Wilmer's feelings were reliable; he was certain to have connections at the draft board like he had everywhere else in the county. He had officially adopted the boy a few years ago. Greg's mother had been a distant cousin of Wilmer's, and nobody ever mentioned his father, who had apparently abandoned the two of them.

The same way he was about to abandon Ruth, he thought guiltily.

"Your Uncle Wilmer is a powerful man," Robert said.

"You can't have too many friends, that's what Uncle Wilmer says."

"Well, I'm glad you don't have to go over there."

"Uncle Wilmer says they're making a hash of it. Politicians won't let the Army win. He doesn't want me getting killed because of a bunch of damned liberals over here. Besides, he needs me on the farm, when my basketball days are over." He looked at Ruth with unmistakable love. "He went and had all those girls and no sons, and there needs to be a man around here, somebody to learn from him."

The boy was spoiling for a fight, verbal or otherwise. Robert had to remind himself that if Ruth was the prize they were competing for, he no longer wanted it.

Greg waved a farewell to Ruth, ignoring Robert. Then he whistled to Duke, the dog, and walked away. Duke had a final growl for Robert and a look that said, "I'll be back for you later."

"That boy's in love with you," Robert said.

"Little Greg?"

"Little Greg's hormones are in full flower. He wanted to club me over the head, throw you over his shoulder, and take you to his cave."

"I think it's sweet that you're so jealous."

"I'm not—" Robert reigned in his irritation and reminded himself why he was there. Merely being around Ruth made him slip back into defensive jabbing. "I'm not jealous," he said.

"Is everything all right? You never come out here anymore."

"Yes, everything's—no. No, it's not all right. We have to talk."

"Go on." She looked vulnerable and afraid.

"Look, I don't have to tell you this marriage isn't working. We never spend any time together. You're out here every weekend. This is where your heart is, not with me."

"That's not true."

"You know it is. When was the last time we made love?"

"I don't know. I don't keep track."

"New Year's Eve. You'd had some champagne. That was over nine months ago."

"You make me feel pressured. I feel the pressure for sex all the time. I can't relax and be myself."

Robert felt his resolve bog down in absurdities. He took a deep breath. "I want a divorce," he said.

She ran to him and threw her arms around his chest. "No, Robert, no! Don't say that! It's not true."

"Ruth, I—"

"I love you. You're my husband. We have our beautiful little house and our life together, and we're happy! I don't know what's bothering you all of a sudden, but you can't throw away the happiness we have because you're having a bad day or a bad week."

The intensity of her belief was so strong that it nearly infected Robert. He took her by the upper arms and held her away from him. "It's been years, Ruth. Years. Understand that. The last three years I've been with you I've been miserable."

"Then I'll change! Tell me what you want me to do and I'll do it. Anything!"

He felt as if he were torturing a puppy. Her eyes were full of innocence and love and pain. "I can't ask you to be someone you're not," Robert said.

"Is there—is there someone else?"

Robert had braced himself for this, had meant to tell her the truth, but now, at the crisis point, he didn't have the strength. "No," he said. "This is about you and me. The marriage doesn't work. I want out."

"If there's nobody else, then you can at least give me a chance. Give me a month. I'll make you happy. Remember how it was in Jamaica? It can be that way again."

He did remember, and standing there in the autumn sunlight, with her so close, he couldn't deny that he was still physically attracted to her. He hesitated, and Ruth saw it. She put her arms around his neck and kissed him under the ear. "Stay the night. I'll give you what you want. Remember our first time? It was here at the farm, right upstairs."

He was aroused, painfully so. He found himself wondering if they could sneak inside now, tiptoe up the stairs. He imagined them naked, imagined himself thrusting into her, and then...

And then, spent and defeated, he would have to explain to Mercy what had happened. He would have to protect the lie he had just told, and the lies would build and build until they filled his entire life.

"No," he said.

"Robert!" She jumped back, startled. "Don't shout at me! You scared me." She began to cry. "I don't know you anymore."

"It's over, Ruth. You can keep the house. I'll move my things out this weekend. I'll see to it that you're taken care of. You have your family. You'll be okay."

Her mood changed again, and her voice was suddenly cold and clipped. "You will not take anything out of the house, do you understand?"

"What?"

"We are not getting a divorce, or a separation, or living apart, or anything of the kind."

Robert stared. He had never seen her like this.

"Listen carefully to me," she said. "Like Greg said, my father has many friends, many powerful friends. If you leave me, my father will use his friends to destroy you. You will lose your job, and you will not find another one in North Carolina. No one will rent or sell a house to you. If you leave the state, I won't answer for your physical safety."

"You can't be serious."

"I advise you not to test me."

"How can you want to live like that? Knowing that I don't love you?"

"I believe you do love me. I saw how you reacted just now. You're confused, that's all. Do you think I don't know about your nigger whore? I knew the first day you came home to our house stinking of her. When you have that out of your system, you'll come around to loving me again. And I won't let you destroy both our lives over her."

Robert's legs felt weak. He sat in the parched grass.

"You need to look on the bright side," Ruth said. "You've finally got your highway to build. You've got our beautiful house, and a wife who loves you more than anything. You can even keep your mistress, as long as you behave and don't embarrass me with her. But as far as the rest of the world knows, we have a happy marriage. Do you understand?"

Robert couldn't speak or move.

"Good," Ruth said. "We understand each other. I feel so much better already. Now stand up. We're going to go in the house and visit with my father. You'll stay for supper, and then, if you want, you can go."

•

IT WAS 9:30 by the time he got to Bentonville. Mercy took one look at his face and told her mother they had to leave.

Robert told her everything as he drove. She sat against the passenger door watching him as he talked, and when he finished she curled next to him. "So what happens now?"

"We can leave North Carolina. This guy Arthur that I went to school with is in Texas now. He says there's lots of work there."

"I don't want to leave my mother. Not now, not yet. And you don't want to give up your road."

"No."

"It's not so bad, baby. At least you don't have to pretend with her now. We're young yet, as the poet said. Something will work out."

BISMARCK HAD CALLED POLITICS "the art of the possible." For Robert it was the perfect description of highway construction. More factors went into the final decisions than in any other kind of work. To get federal funds, the design had to meet standards of lane width, materials, access, and dozens of other criteria. Acquiring right of way was hard enough for the main freeway; getting additional land for entrances and exits was even more difficult. Then there were the existing roads, and whether to go under them, over them, or break them in half.

While the actual design was done in the Department of Transportation offices in Raleigh, Robert had to know exactly where he could deviate and what aspects were sacrosanct. He had to constantly balance cost against benefit, grade versus additional length, time versus quality. It was the hardest, most satisfying work Robert had ever done.

At the end of it, one or two nights during the week and all weekend long, was Mercy. He left changes of clothes there and would go straight to work from her house on Monday morning. The days of swing bands at the Biltmore were over as the slow death of Hayti took its toll on the hotel, but there were occasional dances at the Durham Armory or the Stallion Club— the former mostly white, the latter mostly black—where they could disappear in the crowd.

Other nights they spent in the kitchen. Mercy cooked huge Caribbean meals—pork *griots* and tropical fruit from Haiti, *arroz con pollo* from Cuba, jerk chicken from Jamaica—and then distributed the leftovers among her neighbors. Robert would help with the prep work and then sit and drink beer and enjoy the smells.

Mercy didn't own a television and had refused Robert's offer to buy her one of the new Japanese portables. Instead they went to the movies most weekends. Durham's theaters were desegregated now, at least in theory, and Mercy would have had no problem in any case. Still they preferred to stay in Hayti, or go to the Starlight Drive-In, where Robert would not be recognized.

In the house on Woodrow Street, Ruth smiled and made dinner and slept with her back to him. This, Robert understood, was what they called an "understanding." It was not ideal, but he could live with it.

THE FIRST BLOW came on March 31, 1968. On national television, at the end of a long speech about his failure to achieve peace in Vietnam, President Johnson said, "There is divisiveness among us all tonight."

Mercy had gone to visit her mother, and Robert was spending a rare Sunday night with Ruth. Though Johnson's words were hardly news, it shocked Robert to hear them come from this paternal, kindly-looking man.

Johnson went on to say, "I have concluded that I should not permit the Presidency to become involved in the partisan divisions that are developing in this political year." Then, in the final words of the speech, he dropped the bombshell. "Accordingly I shall not seek, and I will not accept, the nomination of my party for another term as your President."

Ruth, who had no love for Johnson, had the grace to hold her tongue. Robert, always cynical about politics, felt a profound unease that no national news had given him before.

THE NEXT THURSDAY, Robert spent the day grading what would be the Fayetteville Street eastbound entrance ramp to the East-West Expressway. Robert's crews had dug expressway-sized canyons on either side of Fayetteville Street in the raw, red, ferrous clay. When he squinted his eyes, it became an overpass and not merely an earthen dam with a road on top. He thought a sculptor might feel something similar when a recognizable shape started to emerge from the marble. It was a life-size, dirt-road model of a freeway, and in it he could see the finished form.

He hadn't planned to go to Mercy's after work. It was after six when he finally left the job site, his clothes saturated with dust, his shoulder and leg muscles burning with fatigue. He had just turned onto Club Boulevard when a voice broke in on the radio with the news that Martin Luther King had been shot on the balcony of a Memphis motel room. Robert turned left at the next corner and headed for Mercy's house.

Robert found her sitting at the kitchen table, listening to her old Bakelite radio. She got up to hug him as he came in and stayed in his arms.

"This is bad," she said.

"Do they know who shot him?"

"They're not saying. It doesn't matter, really. I mean, probably it was some crazed cracker, but it could have been the Panthers. It could have been the government." In the last months, King had turned increasingly radical and disillusioned, opposing the Vietnam War and fighting for a guaranteed annual income. He'd recently threatened to shut Washington down with an army of the unemployed. "Whoever it was, nonviolence is over."

They listened for a while, sitting at the table and holding hands. There was not much information. King had been in Memphis in support of a sanitation workers' strike, which black radicals had broken up. He'd been working on a sermon in room 306 of the Lorraine Motel, and he and his entourage had walked out onto the balcony on their way to dinner. The title of the sermon he'd been working on was, "Why America May Go to Hell."

The phone rang. Mercy answered in monosyllables, then came back to the kitchen. "People are going up to Pettigrew Street," she said. "Nobody's organizing it, it just seems to be happening."

"Sounds like trouble."

"It could be." She paused, then she said, "I think Barrett's down there."

"Have you talked to him?"

She shook her head. Robert didn't doubt her. She'd given him reasons enough to believe that any relationship she'd had with Howard, sexual or otherwise, was long over. "My friend Wilma, works at the bank, said he was down there talking crazy," she said. "I'm worried about him."

"Yeah," Robert said. "Me too. Maybe we better go see."

"Do you mean it? Like you say, it could be dangerous. It could turn into a riot. And anywhere we go, one of us is going to be the wrong color."

Robert shrugged. "If you want to go, I'm going with you."

They took Robert's car and parked south of St. Joseph's Church. By that point the traffic on Fayetteville Road had ceased to move. Robert led her across the huge red scar of the coming freeway and into the ghostly downtown of Hayti. The abandoned and broken buildings, the cracked and plywood-covered windows, the missing streetlights and fractured sidewalks looked the way Robert felt inside. A freight train huffed by on the north side of the street, blowing a low and mournful whistle.

Barrett Howard was in front of the boarded-up Regal Theater, next to the Biltmore. He sat with his back against the wall, and at first Robert thought he was drunk. "It's over," he said as Robert and Mercy walked up. His voice was clear and strong, his eyes bloodshot red. "It's over."

Robert hunkered down next to him. "Let's go, Barrett," he said. "We'll take you home."

"Didn't ask for half of what we had coming," Barrett said. "Didn't get half of that. Even that was too much. So they taking it back." He looked earnestly at Robert. "Motherfuckers."

Mercy seemed more annoyed than sympathetic. "Come on, Barrett. You can't sit here in the street."

"Why not?" Barrett said.

A deep voice behind them said, "Barrett. What's happening?"

Robert looked up to see a knot of black men, all younger than himself, older than teenagers. There might have been ten or twelve of them. They wore T-shirts, work pants, jeans.

Barrett stared at them without apparent recognition.

"Barrett, man, we got to do something," said the baritone. He wore a checked shortsleeve shirt open over a sleeveless undershirt. He'd made a start on an Afro. He was over six feet tall, and the contours of his dark muscles shone in the headlights that crawled slowly by.

"Nothing left to do," Barrett said, looking away.

"Don't talk that way, man, I can't deal with this. We can't just sit here, let them do this to us. Come on, Barrett, stand up like a man." He kicked the bottom of Barrett's shoe.

"Stop that," Mercy said.

"Stay out of this, sister," said one of the other men.

So far, Robert knew, he'd been lucky. But this day had been waiting for him, inevitable as rain. He stood up. "We're friends of Barrett's," he said. "We're going to take him home."

"Ain't no wheyface no friend of Barrett's or any black man," said a voice from the rear of the crowd, high-pitched and fast, almost comical. Other voices chorused around it: "I know that's right." "Uh huh." "That's what I'm talking about."

A police car eased to a stop in front of them. Robert felt a surge of relief, then saw that its windows were rolled up and the officers inside faced forward, eyes glazed. As soon as the car in front of them inched forward, the police closed the gap.

If I try to run for it, Robert thought, I won't make it to the curb.

"What do *you* say, Barrett?" said the baritone. "These your friends, here? 'Cause I don't think I like them too well." The man started to shift his weight back and forth, working himself up to something.

We shouldn't have done this, Robert told himself. It was the only thought he could manage; fear held the rest of his brain hostage.

"Barrett?" Mercy said. "Stand up."

There was a power in her voice Robert had never heard before. Barrett felt it too. He reached for Robert's hand, and Robert pulled him to his feet. Mercy was staring at Barrett. Barrett blinked, put one hand on Robert's shoulder for balance.

"Barrett, what the fuck?" said a voice from the crowd. The nervous movement rippled through them all now, building momentum.

Barrett took his hand away and straightened his shoulders and the confusion left his eyes.

"Y'all look at yourselves," he said. "What y'all doing? Pissing in you own food, burning down you own houses, going to teach the Man a lesson?"

The baritone took a step back, glanced at one of the men next to him.

"Y'all go on home now," Barrett said. "You want to fight, fight somebody needs fighting." He pointed to Robert. "You don't know these people. You too ignorant to be anything but a danger to your own self and everybody around you."

The man took another step backward, wounded. "What about this cracker here, messing with our women?"

"She ain't 'your' woman, and he ain't 'messing.' They man and wife. Now get along out of here. You want to do something, be here tomorrow, 12 noon. Bring your friends."

"What happens then?"

"You be here, you find out."

The men moved on. Robert walked over to the brick wall of the theater and leaned against it. His relief was so profound he wasn't sure his legs would hold him.

"What are you planning tomorrow?" Mercy asked him.

Barrett said, "I don't know yet. All I know is, everybody's judgment likely to be better tomorrow than tonight. Speaking of which," he said to Robert, "what the hell are you doing here?"

"Looking for you."

"There's a line between good intentions and being naïve. You understand what I'm saying? You keep acting like this ain't serious, you going to wind up dead."

"I think I got the message."

"Y'all need to get out of here. The crackers all out celebrating with they dogs and guns, no telling what could happen. Only a damn fool would tangle with them tonight, and they plenty of damn fools around."

"Come with us," Robert said. Mercy's hand reached out for Robert's and he squeezed it. Barrett's eyes registered the gesture and Robert hated the sadness there.

"I'm all right," Barrett said. "I got work to do."

"Five minutes ago you were sitting on the street ready to give up," Robert said.

"I'm on my feet now. Y'all go on home. Go on, get out of here."

In the car, Robert said, "What did you do to him?"

"I used to hang out with some very powerful spirits. I guess you pick up a thing or two along the way. There's certain ways to talk to people when you need to get their attention."

Robert wound his way through back streets to avoid the worst of the traffic. "'Man and wife,' he said. I wonder where he got that."

Mercy slid over next to him in the seat. "From seeing us together."

"Someday," he said. "Someday, I swear to you."

THE NEXT DAY, April fifth, black activist Howard Fuller led a peaceful march from NCC to downtown Durham in tribute to King, under the eyes of police snipers on rooftops. The night before he had singlehandedly turned back demonstrators from NCC who were headed up Fayetteville Street with violent intent. There was no Howard Fuller in Raleigh, where that same night students from Shaw University had thrown rocks and smashed windows and been beaten down by the police.

If Barrett Howard had tried to orchestrate anything, it didn't make the news.

In June, Bobby Kennedy was gunned down in Los Angeles and died the next day. On August 8, Richard Nixon won the nomination at the Republican National Convention in Miami. Meanwhile, across the bay in Liberty City, a police attack on a black rights rally left four dead.

At the end of August, all-out war erupted between Chicago police and demonstrators at the Democratic National Convention. Robert was unable to watch the footage that aired on TV every night. The rage of the police, the screams of the victims, the clouds of teargas and the image trails from the arc of nightsticks left him sick and fearful.

Even as he knew that the East-West Expressway was part of the ongoing disaster that had once been Civil Rights, he allowed himself to be drawn more and more deeply into the work.

Mitch Antree, faced with the same contradictions, seemed not to feel them. "A highway is a separate space," he tried to explain. "I mean, that's why they call it limited access, can you dig? It's not a part of the neighborhood that it goes through. If you live near the expressway, the people that pass you in the night are not your neighbors. If you drive that highway, you can't say you've been to the places it passes through, not unless you get off the road and stop. When we drive, we are part of the journey, we inhabit another world."

Robert stared at him. Mitch was wearing a purple paisley shirt and an orange tie. His hair was combed down over his forehead, covering the tops of his yellow-tinted glasses.

"It's not the highway's fault that somebody knocked down the wrong buildings to clear the right of way. You can't blame the highway for the mistakes of the people that planned it.

"Once the Interstate system is finished, and all the expressways that feed into it, there's going to be one superhighway that covers the entire country, this one long, continuous, single piece of concrete. How amazing is that? The only job we have now is to build our part of it and make it the best highway we can, so people can get from anywhere they are to anywhere they want to be with the least possible friction."

Harebrained mysticism aside, it was what Robert himself wanted to believe. Otherwise the importance of the work, and the pleasure and fulfillment he found in it, were hopelessly tainted.

"Speaking of Hayti," Mitch said, "what do you hear from your pal Barrett Howard these days?"

"Nothing," Robert said. It was October 7, and the election was approaching. "I haven't seen him in months."

"Well, you might want to keep it that way. The word is out he's recruiting a private army."

"We have to find him," he told Mercy. "He's going to get himself killed."

"Donald would know where he is."

"Donald, the kid you…"

"Initiated. Yes. And he would tell me."

Jealousy had not been an issue since the affair started. Just the same, the mention of the Harriman kid brought back images that made Robert wince. "Do you know how to get hold of him?"

"No," Mercy said. "But I can find out."

It took her two days. She learned that Barrett's group met at 2 AM Saturdays in the shell of the old Biltmore Hotel, room 207, the former Honeymoon Suite. The plywood over the back door, Donald told her, was loose and allowed them to come and go.

Friday night before midnight Robert dressed in dark clothes and rubber-soled shoes. His hands shook as he put batteries into a massive steel flashlight.

"You have to protect Donald," Mercy said. "You can't let Barrett know that's how you found out."

"I know," Robert said.

"One more time I'm going to ask you to let me do this. They won't hurt me. They might kill you."

"Barrett won't let that happen," he said, wishing he believed it. "And I don't mean for anybody but Barrett to see me."

"Then will you at least think about taking the gun?"

Mercy kept a .38 revolver in the nightstand on her side of the bed. "Absolutely not. Who do you want me to shoot with it? Barrett? Donald? No, baby, I'm not taking a gun."

She walked up to him, and her arms went around his back the way they always, inevitably did. It did not strengthen his determination.

"I have to go," he said.

"I love you," she said.

"I love you too."

Ten minutes later he parked near the mouth of the alley that led behind the Biltmore. It took him five long, nervous minutes to figure out the trick with the plywood, which turned out to be an inner frame of 2 × 4s wedged into a matching frame around the door. Once he tugged at it from the correct angle the whole thing slid straight out toward him. He replaced the panel once he was inside, and then he turned on the flashlight.

A foot-long rat stared at him from the curling linoleum of old kitchen floor, then ambled off with arrogant deliberation. The place smelled of mold and urine; apparently Barrett's people were not the only ones who knew the trick with the plywood.

Swinging double doors led out into the ballroom. Sadness threatened to overwhelm him. The very notion of progress seemed hopelessly inverted. What good was a bright concrete future with no dancing, with no hand-sawn hardwood floors and deco archways? He tried to trace a couple of steps across the floor, his rubber soles clinging to the wood and keeping him from being able to pivot. He remembered dancing with Mercy to "Moonglow," and it nearly turned him around and sent him home.

Instead he found the stairs and made his way to the second floor.

The carpet was decayed. Doors to some of the rooms stood open, and in one of them a man lay face down on a bare mattress. Robert wasn't sure if he was dead or alive, and didn't attempt to find out. Suite 207 was double-locked, with both the hotel's original hardware and a shiny new hasp and heavy duty padlock.

Robert found a chair with a missing leg in one of the rooms, propped it against the wall, and made himself as comfortable as possible. He turned the flashlight off and rested it in his lap with his thumb on the switch. The thought of being alone in the dark with the rats and junkies was almost more than he could bear.

Despite his fear and best intentions, he must have fallen asleep, because a banging from downstairs woke him. Someone had entered the stairwell. Foot-steps shuffled up the stairs.

Robert stood up and flattened himself against the wall, staring at the shades of blackness in the hallway.

The second-floor stairwell door opened and closed. The glow of a flashlight appeared beyond the angle of the hall, bright as dawn, and a big man passed Robert's room. Robert thought it was Barrett, wished he were more sure.

He waited until he heard the jingle of keys at the lock of 207 and then whispered, "Barrett?"

The noise stopped and the light went out. "Who's there?" Barrett's voice said.

"It's me. Robert."

"Jesus Christ. Are you alone?"

"Yes."

"Are you out of your stupid mind?" Barrett's muffled steps moved closer. "Turn the flashlight on yourself."

Robert did, blinding himself. He sensed, but could not see, Howard stand-ing in the hall.

"All right," Barrett said.

Robert pointed the light at Barrett's feet. It took his eyes a few seconds to adjust, and when the spots cleared he saw Barrett pointing a military style .45 automatic pistol at his chest. "You can't be here," Barrett said. "You really can-not be here."

"We have to talk."

"How did you find this place?"

"Mitch Antree told me what was happening." Which was true as far as it went.

"Shit, goddamn. How'd he find out?"

"'Word on the street' is what he said. What's behind that lock?"

"That is the last thing you want to know. You understand what I'm saying? The last thing."

"Are there guns in there?"

"I need you to get your lily-white ass out of here before the rest of the brothers show up. Come on."

Barrett led him downstairs at a trot, through the ballroom and into the kitchen. As they arrived at the door, the plywood hatch groaned and eased back into the alley.

Barrett gestured with his flashlight, motioning Robert into a corner of the kitchen along the inside wall. Robert stood behind a rusting steel refrigerator and clicked off his light. Something rustled in the space under the refrigerator, and Robert curled his toes away from the ends of his shoes, breathing shallowly through his mouth, sweat dripping under his arms.

"Barrett?" From where he stood, Robert could see Donald Harriman in the reflected glow of Barrett's light.

"Go on upstairs, son. I got something to deal with, may be a few minutes."

"Everything all right?"

"Everything fine. Move on, now. You can leave that hatch open."

Robert watched Harriman's flashlight bob away. Barrett stuck his head out into the alley, then waved Robert forward. "Let's go," he said.

Robert followed him into the alley, and Barrett put the plywood back in place. "Go on now," Barrett said.

"Barrett, I have to talk to you."

"Yeah, all right, but not now."

"When?"

"Tomorrow."

"Tomorrow Saturday, or tomorrow Sunday?"

"Saturday. Later today."

"Where? Where are you living?"

"Nowhere. I don't exist."

"Then where do I meet you?"

"Seven o'clock Saturday night. Drive up to where Elvira's used to be. Wait five minutes. If I don't show up, come back at eight. If I'm not there at eight, I'll call you at Mercy's. Now go."

ROBERT WAITED at the curb from 6:58 until 7:07 and then drove away, convinced Barrett had never meant to keep the rendezvous. Then on Robert's second attempt, at 8:02, Barrett walked quickly out of the deep shadows between the surviving buildings and got into the passenger seat of the Chevelle.

"Where to?" Robert said.

"How about your construction site? Nobody bother us there."

Robert parked in the deep cut near St. Joseph's, within sight of the symbol on the steeple. Barrett was unshaven and obviously hadn't bathed in a while. He looked like a street person, dressed in the same clothes he'd had on the night before—pants, jacket, and shirt that were various shades of gray and beige. Robert had brought a thermos of coffee and some sandwiches, just in case, and Barrett tore into them.

"Barrett, what's going on?"

"The Revolution," Barrett said. "It's happening."

"When, you mean now?"

"Within the next year. Probably less."

"And when you say revolution, you mean..."

"I don't know how far it's going to go. I'm here to light the fuse and fan the flames. If it's up to me, I'm a burn it to the ground."

Robert thought about the hopelessness of his marriage, his conflicted feelings about Hayti, the smugness of Randy Fogg and his supporters, and for a fleeting moment he thought, let it burn.

But Robert knew that he would not survive the burning, and because of him Mercy might not either. All he truly wanted was to do his job and come home every night to the woman he loved, and maybe dance on the weekends.

"There's no other way?"

Barrett relaxed in the seat and closed his eyes, showing a weariness that came from more than late nights and physical exertion. "In August, in Miami, Nixon cut a deal with Strom Thurmond. Thurmond delivers the white South for Nixon, and in return Nixon rolls back integration."

"That can't happen. Nixon is a crook and a loser. The whole world knows that. He can't get elected."

"You sit there, having watched King and Kennedy get shot down, having watched the Miami and Chicago cops go nuts without even a slap on the wrist, watching the black men come home in body bags from Southeast Asia every day, and you tell me Nixon can't get elected? The Summer of Love is over, man. It was a freak. A hiccup. The white man got distracted, let a little slack in the rope, and he's taking it back now."

Barrett roused himself, reached for the coffee. Robert stopped Barrett's arm and pushed the sleeve up to reveal the tattoo that had peeked out from the edge of the cuff. It was the crossroads shape from the voodoo ceremony, a cross breaking out of a circle with smaller circles at the end of each arm.

"Legba," Barrett said. "And a Yoruba symbol of reincarnation."

"You're all going to die," Robert said.

"If we do, then that's how it is. Nothing to lose at this point. At least we got the *lwa* on our side. That's our edge." He drank off a cup of hot coffee and put the last plastic-wrapped half-sandwich in his jacket pocket. Then he stuck out his right hand, soul-style, like they were going to arm-wrestle. Robert took the hand, and Barrett squeezed his shoulder briefly with his left. "Take it easy, man. And take care of Mercy. I hope you come out all right when the shit comes down."

"Barrett, let us help you. Find you someplace to stay, make sure you eat. I could give you a job on my crew, nobody would look for you there."

"Too late for that now. I appreciate the thought and all, but the time for that is over. The war has already begun."

With that he opened the car door and was gone.

•

NIXON INDEED WON the election. He did it despite George Wallace carrying most of the southern states, proof enough that the worst predictions of white backlash were true. Overnight the legal machinery of integration ground to a halt, even as Nixon's "secret plan" to end the Vietnam War turned to smoke.

In the same election, Randy Fogg won a seat in the House of Representatives for North Carolina's 2nd district. It was one more disaster in a year of the worst setbacks the US had ever known.

In the spring of 1969 the city of Durham was still negotiating right-of-way for the East-West Expressway. The exact location of the roadbed was long settled, but a few crucial homeowners refused to sell, complicating the placement of on- and off-ramps. Equally stubborn were the *Carolina Times* and Service Printing, who refused to move off Pettigrew Street. Robert spent his days at the drafting table coming up with alternate traffic patterns or working on other projects.

"We could lose our federal money," Mitch said, "if we don't build this thing. RTP wants to know where the expressway is. I'm starting to freak, here."

"What do you want me to do about it?" Robert asked. "Knock down houses we haven't bought yet?"

"Accidents happen," Mitch said. "Right?"

Maurice, who hardly spoke anymore, looked up. "Is that supposed to be funny?" On three separate occasions Maurice had told Robert he was quitting, but Mitch had apparently offered him more money than he could dream of making elsewhere. Mitch's self-image would crumble, Robert knew, if he couldn't point to a senior black man in his office.

Mitch shrugged. "Sure, a joke, that's all."

At the end of February, Robert woke to the sound of Mercy throwing up in the bathroom, followed by the sound of her scrubbing her mouth with toothpaste. When she returned to bed, he said, "Are you okay?"

"I'm pregnant," she said.

It was dark, and he couldn't read her expression. His own first reaction was joy. He had long ago given up hope of conceiving a child with Ruth, and this seemed a minor miracle.

He gathered her in his arms and kissed her all around her neck and ears. "This is fantastic," he said. "But how...?" When they'd first started she'd assured him that she was taking care of protection.

"Like the undertaker said, 'Life is full of surprises.'"

He rolled over and turned on the light on his end table. "What's wrong? You're not happy?"

"How can I be happy? First of all, I got serious doubts about bringing a child into a world like this one is turning out to be. Secondly, I will not have a child that only has a part-time father."

Robert opened his mouth and Mercy blocked it with her hand. "I'm not blaming you for anything. I'm talking about the way things are. I already made the appointment to get rid of it. I'm barely six weeks along and it won't be a problem."

"Whoa, stop, wait. Don't. I love you. I want this baby. I want to marry you and live with you. We'll do whatever we have to do to make that happen."

"And what's that going to be?"

"We're within a few months of finishing the first leg of the expressway. When that's done, with that experience under my belt, I can get that job in Dallas easy. We'll bring your mother with us. If she really doesn't want electricity, we'll build her a little stone-age house in the yard."

"And what's Ruth going to do?"

"She'll have to get over it."

"She threatened your life."

"I can't believe she'd have me killed. Whatever else is true, I do believe she loves me. And I will not spend the rest of my life being blackmailed."

"Are you sure?"

"She can't be happy, living like this, no matter what she says. She was so convinced that you and I would burn out in a few weeks. She's got to see that I'm never going to get over you."

"You're doing it again."

Mercy insisted that words like "never" were bad luck. "Don't start with your superstitions," Robert said. "Not now."

"Are you sure you're still going to want me when I'm all swole up?"

"I don't know," Robert said. "I do know I want you now." His hands began to move over her body.

"Better get it now," she said, "before I get big as a damn house." She wasn't laughing, but Robert was so full of lust and love that he didn't care.

THAT NIGHT the haunted dreams began again. This time it was not Erzulie speaking to him, but his own fevered brain. The dreams were always of an expressway, and he was trying to route it around a series of impossible obstacles: a sheer cliff face, swampy ground that melted under his feet, rivers that constantly changed their courses and carved huge canyons overnight. What exhausted him was the intensity of his concentration, the desperate importance of the quest, the elusiveness of the solution, always just out of reach.

He would wake up at four or five in the morning with his pulse racing, and as he tried to hang on to whatever puzzle had been torturing him in the dream, one real-life crisis or another would take its place. What dire alimony would the North Carolina courts impose on him after he deserted a prominent white woman for a black bank teller? Had Ruth's threats been serious after all? How much longer would it take to finish the freeway?

ON MARCH 17, Malcolm X Liberation University, a longtime dream of local hero Howard Fuller, opened and closed within a single hour. The school had hoped to teach Afro-American History, Psychology of Racism, Political Science, and other "pragmatic" courses. Later Robert heard from Tommy Coleman that the plan had been that Duke University's black students would leave Duke en masse and enroll at MXLU. The students failed to materialize. In the photo accompanying the story in the *Carolina Times,* Barrett Howard was visible with his back to the camera, shoulders slumped in defeat.

IN MAY, ROBERT FLEW to Dallas overnight, keeping it secret from both Mitch and Ruth. His friend Arthur picked him up at Love Field and took him to an interview in Carrolton, a suburb north of the flat, sprawling city. Afterwards they drove west to the empty prairie between Dallas and Fort Worth where the land for the new airport had already been purchased. "The Spaceport," Arthur called it, as the specs required that the reusable space ships the government was talking about building be able to land there.

He stayed that night at Arthur's house, and after dinner Bill, the head engineer of the firm, called to make a tentative offer. The money was better than he was making in Durham, and the start date was to be some time "in the fall." Robert accepted, and took his first relaxed breath in longer than he could remember.

Robert and Arthur stayed up drinking Canadian Club after Arthur's wife and 2-year-old son went to bed. Arthur was six foot three and thin, with wavy brown hair and bushy sideburns. He'd had bad luck with women all through college, then had married a sweet and statuesque blonde soon after moving to Dallas and still didn't seem to believe his luck.

Robert told him about Mercy, and that Ruth would not be coming when he moved. As he laid out the bare bones of it, he watched Arthur's guarded reaction. In truth, Robert thought he sounded unstable even to himself.

"I don't think Bill is going to care about the race issue," Arthur said. "But I'd let all this settle out before you starting airing it in public."

"You think I'm crazy?"

"Not crazy so much as ... irresponsible. It's not something people look for in an engineer." Arthur was two years younger than Robert, having gone straight from high school to college. In the seven years they'd both been working, he had somehow made the transition to grownup, a condition that still felt alien to Robert. It was like Arthur had passed him and moved on to their parents' generation.

WITH THE PROSPECT of Dallas that much more real, Mercy began to have her own second thoughts. "I'll be leaving everything I know," she said. "I already don't know who I am. I used to be *mambo,* a woman of power. Now what am I? A bank clerk and a housewife to somebody else's husband. And now you want to pull me up by my roots and stick me in some foreign soil."

"It's a second chance. You could go to medical school, or work in a hospital, or find some other way to do the kind of work you've always wanted."

"Maybe."

"It's foreign to me, too. I don't know anybody there but Arthur."

"I'm scared, that's all. I don't even know whose emotions these are that I'm feeling. My body's like a haunted house."

They were naked; Robert put his hand on her belly and felt the pulsing life inside her.

"There's no history in Dallas," he said. "The place where they're putting the airport, there's nothing there. A few cows and some grass. We can leave Hayti and Randy Fogg and Mitch Antree and start clean."

"You can tell me about it once we're there. Right now, you and me are the only people in the world want this. All I can see is everything standing in the way."

He pulled her to him and held her gently. He held the two of them, mother and child, the bulge of her pregnancy nestling perfectly in the hollow of his abdomen, their three hearts beating together.

IN JULY, AS ROBERT battled the increasing frustrations of pushing through a freeway where it wasn't wanted, Mason and Antree lost a major RTP contract that Mitch had promised was "in the bag."

"We got underbid," was all he would say. "O'Farrell Brothers is going to screw up the job and everybody is going to be sorry afterwards, but there's nothing we can do about it now."

Mitch retreated to his office. Maurice motioned Robert outside for a smoke. It was hazy and stifling, humidity and temperature both pushing 100.

"Mitch is losing it," Maurice said. "He's smoking pot, he's drinking, he's chasing women, he's not getting the job done. Me, I'm waiting for a confirmation letter and then I'm gone. Thought you might want to make some plans of your own."

"I've made them," Robert said, feeling ahead of the game for once. "Thanks. I've got something lined up in Dallas." Maurice, he knew, would not confide in Mitch.

"Dallas, eh? There's a lot happening in Dallas, I hear." Maurice offered his hand. "Good luck."

IN AUGUST HE GOT a call from Arthur. "Everything's still on," Arthur said. "We're just running behind."

"How far behind?"

"Your start date will be in November. December first at the absolute latest. You know how it is, it's the construction business. Nothing is ever on schedule."

Mercy was in her final month of pregnancy and was, in fact, huge. Their sex life, which had been good through the first two trimesters, had dropped off to nothing in the last two months. Her breasts were too tender to touch, she couldn't get comfortable in any sexual position, and her own need had disappeared. She used her mouth and hands to give Robert what satisfaction she could, but Robert felt her discomfort and lack of desire, and it often left him unable to finish.

It made for an undercurrent of frustration they'd never felt with each other. Mercy had been forced to quit her job; her boss knew the baby was illegitimate and refused to hold the position for her. Then there were the delays in Dallas and the delays on the East-West Expressway and the endless, unrelenting heat.

The next blow came one morning as Robert was leaving for work. He was barely awake and he might not have seen it, except that Mercy had followed him to the door and he had stopped beside his car to wave goodbye to her.

She saw his expression and stepped out on the porch in her black silk kimono. "Oh," she said.

During the night the house had been vandalized with black spray paint. There was a swastika on one side of the door and a cross in a circle on the other. Splotchy letters read, DEATH TO MIXED RACE BASTARDS and, even more ominously, WHITE SEED DIES IN BLACK GROUND.

Robert climbed the sidewalk with long strides and put his arms around Mercy from behind.

She seemed hardly to care. "Celtic cross," she said, pointing to the left of the door. "That's our friends in the Night Riders."

"We have to call the police," Robert said.

"Why?"

Robert knew well enough what she was asking. When the police came to Hayti, it wasn't to help out. "Because I'm afraid. This scares the hell out of me. This isn't some random race-baiting. This is personal. They know about us, about the baby. I can't leave you here alone."

"Come inside," Mercy said.

She put her arms around him, and even with the fear and helpless rage boiling inside him it was all he could do not to be overwhelmed with desire for her. "This don't mean anything," she said. "It's just talk, is all, ugly talk. If they wanted to do something they would already have done it."

"What if they come back? What if I'm not here?"

"Anybody breaks in this house going to answer to Mr. Smith and Mr. Wesson. You know that."

For once he was glad she had the gun. "So you're saying you don't want to do anything about it."

"Nothing we can do. Outside of the house don't matter, it's the inside that's important. We got to try not to let it make things worse than they already are."

"I'll have a crew over here before noon to clean it up and repaint."

"You do that, they'll just come back."

"If they come back, I'll paint over it again," Robert said, letting her go. "Or maybe you'll get to use that gun. I can't leave it, and I can't come home to that at night."

They were poised for their first fight, and as high as Robert's emotions were running, it could have raged out of control. Robert saw Mercy choose not to let that happen. "Go ahead then," she said. "Do what you got to do."

They said their goodbyes again, and Robert drove to work knowing they'd given the bastards exactly what they wanted, that their hatred had seeped deeper into the walls than the paint, had added its weight to the load pressing down on them.

As he struggled to hold on to his happiness with Mercy, Ruth sweetly and quietly insisted that he spend at least one night a week with her. "We *are* still married," she said, smiling in a coy way that Robert found unsettling. "I want to know how your work is going, want to fix you dinner, want to know you're there. If you were home waiting for me when I got back from the farm on Sunday afternoons, I could at least pretend things were the way they used to be."

Robert had not forgotten the way she'd turned on him when he asked for a divorce, hard as it was to reconcile that image with this one. "All right," he said.

"You might as well sleep with her," Mercy said when he told her. "I'm no good to you in that department anymore. Like she said, you are still married to her. You got the right."

"I'd rather do it with a snake," Robert said.

"You say that now, but give it another month, you'll be out there at the woodpile, 'Here snake, here snake.'"

"You say that like you don't care."

"I never said that. Not caring isn't the same as understanding that things happen sometimes."

"Well, that thing isn't going to happen."

MERCY'S PHONE RANG late on a Thursday night. It was August 28, two weeks from Mercy's due date. Half asleep, Robert heard Mercy say, "Hello?" Then, her voice softening, she said, "Barrett? Are you all right?" She switched on her nightstand lamp and put a hand on Robert's shoulder. "Where are you?" she said into the phone.

Robert rolled over toward her, squinting against the light. She was shaking her head. "He only wants to talk to you," she said, handing him the phone.

"Hey, Barrett," Robert said. His brain was still struggling to its feet.

"Can you pick me up? Same place as last time?"

"When? You mean now?"

"If you can do it. I need to get to Raleigh. Can you drive me? Just drop me off there and you can come straight home. I wouldn't ask you if it wasn't important. And I won't ask again."

"Okay. I can be there in ten minutes."

"Thanks." The dial tone buzzed.

As before, Robert pulled up to the curb where Elvira's had been, and this time Barrett appeared immediately. He was clean, if scruffy, and his energy level seemed high. "Thanks, man," he said as he got in and shut the door. "This helps."

"Where do you need to go?"

"Shaw University, downtown. Is that cool?"

"Yeah, it's fine. What's it about?"

"You know I can't tell you that."

"No. I guess I don't really want to know."

Robert headed east on Business 70. After a few minutes' silence he said, "Are you okay?"

"Yeah, I'm making it. We're getting down to the nitty-gritty now, and after that nobody knows how it's going to shake out."

Something in his tone made Robert look at him. "Nitty-gritty?"

"I'm all nerves, man. I'm talking more than I should."

"There's about to be trouble, is what you're saying. A riot, like in Watts?"

"Watts was small time. Listen, I heard Mercy's pregnant. Is that true?"

"Yeah, it's true."

"You're standing by her?"

"I love her. We're getting away from here. Going to Texas."

"That's good. That's very good. The farther from here the better."

To fill the time, Robert found himself talking about the job in Dallas, the new life he hoped to start there. Other than Mercy, there had been no one he could confide in, and he'd been holding it in for months. The only thing that scared him was how unreal it all sounded, like the elaborate pipe dreams that old winos would tell to con somebody out of a quarter.

When the words ran out they drove in silence again until Barrett said, "I wonder sometimes if I did this whole thing wrong. That maybe it could still be me with Mercy, that I could have had a straight teaching job and a family and been a regular citizen." He glanced at Robert. "No offense, man. Just a little idle jealousy. I know it wasn't meant to be."

Robert nodded. He was long past seeing Barrett as a rival. If anything, he was jealous of his own early days with Mercy, before her pregnancy, before the world turned so sour.

Highway 70 had turned into Glenwood Avenue, and they were in Raleigh now. The houses along Glenwood were huge and set well back from the road, houses where blacks cooked and cleaned and maintained the yards. Durham was evenly divided between the races, while less than a quarter of Raleigh's population was black. Raleigh imagined Durham to be a city of constant crime; Durham saw Raleigh as rich, white, and arrogant.

Shaw University was a black college in the center of downtown, only a few blocks south of the Capitol building. As they drove through the wide, deserted streets, Barrett got increasingly restless. Finally he said, "Listen, man, I have to warn you. I didn't want it this way, but stuff is going to happen to your freeway."

"Stuff?" Robert said.

"A lot of people see it as a symbol, you know, of what happened to Hayti and all. There's going to be some shit come down there."

"What are you talking about? What exactly is going to come down?"

"I said too much already. All's I'm saying is, at night, for the next week, don't be working late. You'll be all right."

The parts of the expressway that were finished were either precast or poured concrete over reinforcing steel. There was little anyone could do to damage them with less than an atomic bomb. Even so, the threat felt personal and Robert didn't like it.

They'd come to the front gate of the college. Robert stopped the car. "Don't hurt my expressway," he said. "It's not right."

"It's out of my hands," Barrett said.

"I don't believe that."

Barrett opened the car door and left it open. "One second," he said.

The car was covered in dust from the construction site. Barrett stood on the sidewalk and used his finger to draw the crossroads symbol for Legba on the passenger side of the hood. Then he walked around to the other side and drew the heart-shaped ideogram for Erzulie. He wiped his hands on his pants and came back to the open door.

"A little extra protection never hurt," he said. "Thanks for bringing me." He leaned in the car to offer his hand.

Robert looked at it, anger and sadness and love fighting it out inside him. "Goddammit, Barrett," he said.

"Take my hand," Barrett said. "You never know when you're going to see somebody again. We're at the crossroads, man. You want to be at your best when you're standing in the crossroads."

Robert took his hand. "Be careful," he said.

"You too." Barrett closed the door, vaulted the gate, and was lost in the darkness.

Robert turned north at his next opportunity, shutting off the car's air conditioning and rolling the windows down to feel the damp air on his face, his emotions still churning. "Goddammit!" he said again, and pulled over under the next streetlight. He shut off the engine and found a rag in the trunk and used it to wipe the hood clean.

When he was done, he felt suddenly cold and alone. "Superstition," he said out loud, crumpling the rag. He threw it in the trunk and drove, carefully, back to Durham.

MERCY WAS AWAKE and waiting for him.

"He's going to do something to the expressway," he told her. "Him and his army."

"Oh no," Mercy said.

"What am I going to do? Am I going to just lie here and let him do it?"

"You already know the answer to that. You know you won't choose concrete over a man."

"Why do I have to make that choice at all?"

"I can't tell you that, baby," she said, stroking his shoulders. He tried to hold her and she tried to let him, shifting around in an attempt to get comfortable, but he saw he was hurting her and he moved away. "I'm sorry, baby," she said. "Not much longer. Another couple of weeks and I'll be a normal human again."

"Yeah, I know," he said. "I know."

•

HE WRESTLED WITH IT in his head all weekend. Sunday night, in the house on Woodrow, Ruth had felt his nervousness and rubbed his shoulders as he pretended to watch TV, asking him what was wrong. When he'd told her there were threats of sabotage, she'd gotten upset and wanted more details than he was willing to give.

"Are you in danger?"

"No."

"Do you swear?"

"I promise. It's just the freeway."

"Oh, Robert, if anything happened to you, I don't know what I'd do. I couldn't abide it."

On Monday he told Leon to spread the word among the crew: Nobody was to come on the construction site after dark.

"Why is that, Captain?"

"Just some rumors going around. Best to be safe."

"Yeah, I heard some rumors too."

"What did you hear?"

"Nothing, Captain, not really. Something about there might be trouble on the freeway site."

"Where did you hear it?"

"Not sure I remember exactly. Booker, maybe. Booker probably heard something at one of those bars he hang out at." Booker wasn't there to confirm or deny. Most likely Barrett had warned Leon himself.

They were working on the Fayetteville Street overpass. Fayetteville Street itself had moved 50 feet to the west while they dug out the old roadbed. Down below, in the cutout, they'd bolted one six-legged precast T on either side of the right of way, with a third T in the center. There was a raw wood framework most of the way across, nestling the tops of the Ts, floored with plywood, ready to take the concrete for the overpass itself. Below it stood a form for the north buttress, looking ramshackle and random, the way forms always did from the outside.

As he stared at the fragile wooden structures he felt a fresh wave of sweat break across his forehead. That would be the target, he thought. There, in the center of Hayti, under the voodoo weathervane on St. Joseph's. A few well-placed sticks of dynamite could set them back for weeks.

It wasn't just the company's money, or the wasted work. Part of Robert wanted to see the freeway open and cars driving on it before he left for Dallas. Losing two or three weeks would make that impossible.

He spent that night in his Chevelle, blocking the end of the overpass scaffolding on the St. Joseph's side. He'd parked a bulldozer at the other end. After nodding off half a dozen times, he quit struggling and curled up on the bench seat and slept for a few fitful hours. When the sun woke him he went to Mercy's for another two hours, so exhausted that even her restless turning couldn't keep him awake.

He did it again on Tuesday, but by Wednesday he couldn't face another night of it. He ate and showered and went to bed, only to have the phone wake him at 2 AM.

They had been getting a lot of crank calls, the caller hanging up as soon as Mercy answered. Those had all been in the evening hours, never this late. Robert heard her pick up the phone and mumble a hello, then say, "Who?" in an irritated voice. She passed the receiver to Robert. "Mitch Antree," she said.

Robert stared at her in confusion and took the receiver. Mercy moved the body of the phone onto the bed between them to keep the cord from cutting across her breasts.

"Mitch?" Robert said. "How did you get this number?"

"Put your pants on," Mitch said. "I need you here at the office."

"Christ," Robert said, thinking immediately of Barrett, "what did he do?"

"What did who do?"

Robert took a breath. "Nothing. What happened?"

"Nothing happened. Put on your work clothes and get down here. We're going to pour some mud down by Fayetteville Street."

"In the middle of the night?" Robert said. "I don't understand."

"I hope to God you never do," Mitch said. "Listen to me, now. The fun and games are over. You come down here to the office, don't ask any questions, and I mean no questions, and when this is done you go home and you keep your mouth shut."

Robert hung up. "I have to go into the office. Like, now."

"Is it Barrett?"

"He won't say. My best guess is he's cooking up some kind of countermove against him. You know how weird Mitch has been getting. This could all be the drugs."

"Robert, is this going to be dangerous? If it is, don't go. This baby has got to have a father."

"I don't think it's like that. It's nuts, but I don't think it's dangerous." He kissed her. "I won't let anything happen to me. I pr—"

"Don't," she said. "Don't."

He brushed the hair from her forehead and kissed it. "I'll be careful, okay?"

•

A CEMENT MIXER SAT in the Mason and Antree parking lot. It had a full load, and the barrel was turning. Mitch sat behind the wheel. He had the window down and he beckoned to Robert to get in the passenger side.

Robert got in. He looked at Mitch's face and saw that he would keep quiet, like he'd been told. In Germany, Robert's outfit had been required to make three parachute jumps. Mitch had the look that Robert had seen on one of the men before his first jump. He'd gone out the hatch, but the next day he'd filed for a transfer.

Mitch was already fighting with the gearshift, trying to find reverse. "I drove one of these after college," he said. Robert did not offer to take over. Mitch kept his gaze moving between the side-view mirrors and didn't make eye contact with Robert. Finally he jammed the gears into place, got the behemoth turned around, and lumbered south toward Hayti.

As they drove, Robert felt a chill spread from his stomach out to the ends of his fingers and toes. Part of it was exhaustion and the lateness of the hour; most of it was fear. Fear came off Mitch in palpable waves, a sense that the safe and normal world had tilted so far off axis that nothing would ever be the same. The feeling was so strong that it eradicated Robert's curiosity. Now he silently echoed Mitch's hope that he would never find out what was going on. He pulled in his shoulders and stared straight ahead, past the conical beams of the headlights, into the darkness.

They rode the temporary blacktop across the canyon of the freeway. Robert didn't turn his head to look at the glow of floodlights down in the cut. Mitch turned left in front of St. Joseph's and followed the track of the access road down into the construction site, then swung a wide U-turn back to where the overpass would be. Leon and Tommy Coleman waited there. Their postures were all wrong; they looked worse than Mitch did.

Mitch backed the truck up to the form on the north side of the overpass. One rear wheel collided repeatedly with something it couldn't roll over. Robert did not want to know what it was. Still without looking at Robert, Mitch said, "Stay here." He got out, leaving the truck idling. Something crashed and he got back in. He backed up another six feet and got out again.

Robert heard muffled voices, then the familiar sound of the chute swinging out and the slurry rolling into it, like a hailstorm on a tin roof. Leon fired up his vibrator, the single-stroke engine roaring like the chainsaw it resembled. The familiar sounds helped. We're just pouring some concrete, he told himself. Nothing unusual about that, except the hour. He could have gotten out and joined them, standing around the back of the truck like any other workday. Instead he stayed where he was.

With every passing minute that he didn't have to get out, he relaxed a little more. Still, the inside of his brain was white and locked down, as if pinned in a thousand watt spotlight.

He didn't look at his watch until the mixer was empty and Mitch had driven them back to the office. "Go home," Mitch said then. It was not yet three. "Tell yourself this was all a bad dream. Do not tell anyone, not Mercy, not your wife, not anyone, what you saw tonight."

"I didn't see anything," Robert said.

Mitch nodded. Apparently they were done. Robert got down and shut the door of the truck, and Mitch immediately pulled away.

Robert walked slowly to his car. He'd thought it was later, thought the sun would be coming up. The stars shone fiercely, like they were giving their all for the final time. A faint breeze told him that he had sweated through his clothes without being aware of it. The air smelled of tar and the dumpsters on the corner, but to Robert it seemed fine. He lit a cigarette and leaned for a moment against the driver's side of the Chevelle. His brain was starting to thaw. He refused to let it speculate.

Mercy was still awake when he got home. "I need to shower," he said, stripping off his damp clothes. "It was dusty at the site."

"What happened?"

"Nothing," Robert said. "We drove out to the site and back again. It could be Mitch was worried about Barrett and wanted me there. I don't know."

Though there was nothing strictly untrue in what he'd said, he knew he had just lied to her for the first time. He watched himself do it with sadness, and yet no other possibility seemed available. Later, maybe, when he knew more, they would talk. After the baby was born.

"Mitch is losing his mind," Mercy said, turning away from him. "Hurry up and come to bed. You need your sleep."

ROBERT WAS IN the office by nine the next morning. Mitch had phoned in sick. "Probably hung over again," Charles said. "He can't seem to get it through his head that he ain't twenty anymore."

Maurice was gone now, having made good on his threats at last, leaving Charles and Robert as the senior men in a bullpen of eager kids, none of whom had been out of college longer than three years. Charles was bigger than ever and had taken on Maurice's role as chief cynic. And, like in the commercial, he was smoking more these days and enjoying it less.

"I'll be at the site," Robert said,

Leon and Tommy were already there, putting a slick trowel finish on a fresh load of concrete that completed the north buttress.

"Captain," Leon said, not looking him in the face. Tommy didn't say anything at all, just dipped his trowel in a white plastic bucket and massaged the face of the concrete, bringing the fine, smooth grains to the surface.

Robert nodded to them and kept walking.

TWO WEEKS LATER they'd moved west to the Duke Street overpass. Late in the afternoon, as the sky had begun to cloud over, a runner from the office found Robert sitting on his haunches in front of a set of bluelines, the corners anchored by rocks. The runner had a pink sheet torn from a phone message pad that simply said, "Call M.R."

It was the code he and Mercy had agreed on. "Leon!" he yelled. "You're in charge!"

Leon said something he couldn't hear—wasn't meant to hear, most likely.

Mercy was waiting on the porch, suitcase at her feet, as he squealed up to the curb. She smiled as she stood up. "Be cool, baby," she said, as he ran up to the porch. "Nothing's going to happen for a while yet."

"Contractions?" He reached for her suitcase with one hand and her hand with the other.

"About ten minutes apart. About—" Her face contorted and she sat back down. "About a minute long. Shit."

He held her hand until the pain subsided. She stood up and said, "Wait, now I have to pee again."

Robert could not keep still. He paced the porch, needing a job to do. Mercy laughed as she came out of the house. "Home stretch, sweetie," she said, giving him a big, smacking kiss. "Like the jockey said. Now drive *slow.*"

She'd insisted on Lincoln Hospital, near North Carolina College. Robert had pushed for Watts Hospital in his own neighborhood, but she wanted to be with the doctors who'd treated her throughout the pregnancy. Robert only knew that Lincoln was old, dark, and septic looking.

Once she was in a semiprivate room, in a gown and in bed, she said, "There's something I want you to do for me. I promise I won't have the baby until you're back."

"Back from where?"

"I want you to bring my mama. I got word to her, and she'll be ready to go when you get there. Get her and bring her to me. Please?"

"I want to be here when—"

"You will be. Most likely it'll be another twelve hours. Will you do it for me?"

He understood that her desire for her mother should not make him jealous, despite his prickly temper. Driving would at least give him something physical to do. "All right," he said.

He drove fast, but not carelessly. Mercy's mother, as promised, had her own suitcase packed and was waiting by the front door. She was not one for small talk, and once she'd gotten an update on Mercy's condition, they had run out of things to say. Then, unexpectedly, half an hour into the drive, she said, "When Mercy told me you wanted to keep the child, that you would stand by her, it told me what kind of man you are. It was what I already felt about you, and it made me glad it was true."

Since the night of the cement mixer, Robert had felt that he was no kind of man at all. "Thank you," he said.

To cover his unease, he began to talk to her about Dallas. He knew that Mercy had brought it up to her as a possibility. Now Robert laid out the scenario in detail and asked her to join them.

She nodded. "It's time for a change. I've been all my life in this one place, and lately it seems like everything I see reminds me of how much better things used to be."

"Good," Robert said, surprised and relieved. "That's good."

"Being alone is not everything it was once cracked up to be either," she said, and Robert found himself opening up to her, telling her about the spaceport and pre-stressed concrete, and the vision of the future that had sustained him through the long and frustrating summer.

Mercy, for her part, was as good as her word. She was still in her room, though her nightgown was soaked through with sweat and she was biting her lower lip with pain. "I read up on this," she said, as her mother put one hand on Mercy's bulging stomach and the other on her forehead. "This is the time when I'm supposed to feel like giving up. And you know what? I do."

It seemed wrong to Robert that she should hurt this much, wrong that the doctors weren't investigating. He couldn't stop himself from wishing that he'd taken her to Watts Hospital instead.

At that moment a nurse and an orderly rolled a gurney up to her bedside. "Let's get you into delivery," the nurse said.

As they lifted her onto the gurney, Mercy said, "Can my mother come in with me? She's a nurse."

"We'll see what the doctor says." To Robert she said, "The floor nurse can take you to the obstetrics waiting room."

Robert caught Mercy's hand for a final squeeze as they wheeled her away, saw her mouth the words "I love you," and watched her disappear down the corridor.

THE DOCTORS, NURSES, and staff were all black. If they found it odd to see him there, they did a decent job of hiding it. That was more than Robert could say about the two other expectant fathers in the waiting room who eyed him suspiciously until each, in turn, was called.

By midnight Robert's anxieties had full control. Until that night his greatest fear had been the one he could never speak aloud, even to himself: the fear that the child would be black. He wanted to believe it made no difference, even as the very persistence of the question made him a liar and a hypocrite in his own eyes.

Now he was sure that Mercy, or the baby, or both, were dying or dead, and Mercy's mother was holding him responsible. He imagined the operating theater awash in blood, Mercy terrified in a room full of strangers. He sat in a hard plastic chair and paged through a tattered copy of *Ebony* again and again, taking nothing in.

Finally, at 2 AM, a nurse he hadn't seen before came in and said, "Mr. Cooper? Mother and son are both fine."

Mercy was alone with her mother when Robert got to the room. She was crying. Her mother was curled in a battered armchair by the window, asleep. He sat on the edge of the bed and took both her hands in his. He'd never seen her cry before, and now he thought the hospital had made a dreadful mistake. "Baby, what's wrong?"

"I'm just so tired, and relieved, and tired, and sore, and happy, and tired." She smiled, but the tears kept coming.

"It's a boy," Robert said.

"Had to be. Felt like a six-year-old, coming out."

He was exhausted as well, had hardly slept in three weeks, had hoped that her happiness would lift him up with her, only to find himself now wanting to cry too.

The nurse came in with a bundle of blankets. When Robert saw the pinkness of the ancient, wrinkled face, the tiny, pale, perfectly formed fingers, he hated his own feelings of relief.

WHEN HE CALLED in sick the next morning, Mitch got on the phone. "Did she have the baby?"

Robert didn't ask how he knew. "It's a boy," he said. "We named him Malcolm."

"Congratulations. Take Monday off, too. You owe me a cigar."

Mercy's mother had made herself a bed on the living room sofa. The next two days were disconnected fragments: sleeping, trying to sleep, driving back and forth from the hospital, watching the baby at Mercy's breast, learning to change a diaper, finding himself endlessly fascinated by the tiny creature's every movement, his rubbery face and twitching slumber.

Sunday afternoon Mercy saw him watching the clock and feeling his own needs and desires clash with his promises. "Go," she said. "There's nothing you can do here, and at least you'll get one good night's sleep."

ON MONDAY HE BROUGHT Malcolm and Mercy home from the hospital, and that afternoon he lay in Mercy's bed as she slept curled against his side. Her mother snored in the living room, audible through the closed door, and Malcolm snored in the crib next to them. Robert had never known that babies snored.

Mercy stirred, turned over, locked one leg around Robert's, and put one arm across his chest. They were in their underwear, and the overworked air conditioner in the window leaked a thin stream of cool air. Mercy opened her eyes, pulled herself forward, and kissed Robert on the mouth. It had been a long time since she'd kissed him like that, and his reaction was instantaneous.

She laughed and took hold of him. "Not much longer," she said.

He could barely speak. "How much, do you think? Longer?"

"I'm sorry, baby. I have to heal up. They gave me an episiotomy, you know."

"No. Is that the spinal thing?"

"It's an incision."

She showed him. The doctor had cut her from the bottom of her vagina all the way to her anus, and then stitched her up again. The sight of it made Robert cringe from his diaphragm out to the ends of his fingers. "Oh my God," he whispered.

"It's routine. Especially with a big baby."

"It's barbaric."

"I didn't want them to do it. They don't listen to you. They always think they know best."

He gathered her gently in his arms. "I am absolutely sure they don't do anything like that in Dallas. It's time to go."

She didn't say anything, just held him tight against her.

"FIRST OF THE YEAR," Arthur said. "That's definite. I told him you had to start then or take another job, and he put it in writing. You start January second."

"That's more than three months."

"You've still got the highway job. You can finish that up and have one last Christmas in North Carolina. Maybe you could go see your dad up in Asheville."

Robert had not yet told his father about Mercy. He couldn't find the words, couldn't picture acceptance on his father's stern, Puritan face.

"Just swear to me there won't be any more delays," Robert said.

"I swear," Arthur said.

ON A RAINY MORNING in early October, Mitch said, "What do you hear from your pal Barrett Howard these days?"

Robert was stunned. Once he got past the sheer shock value of the question, a bubble of hope rose up inside him. For Mitch to even ask the question meant that the thing Robert had been unable to admit to himself, the thing he'd kept bottled up since that early September night, might not be true after all.

"Barrett Howard?"

"You can't have forgotten him already. Big cat, very dark, used to be involved in local politics?"

"Cut the crap, Mitch. What are you trying to say?"

"I was wondering if you'd heard anything. There's some stories going around."

"What kind of stories?"

"Supposedly he's been doing some fundraising. Got money from the Panthers, from Cuba, from the Soviets. Quite a bit of money. Then a few weeks ago he's gone, and so is the money."

"And?"

"And now he's turned up in Mexico."

"Bullshit."

"There was a photo of him in a Mexican paper."

"What paper? You saw it yourself?"

"The guy I heard it from did."

"Who was that?"

"Nobody you know."

"It's not possible," Robert said. "Barrett had—has—more integrity than anyone I've ever known."

"Integrity." Mitch sounded it out like he'd stumbled across it in a dictionary for the first time. "Well, I guess you knew him better than me."

What if it were true? Robert thought. What if Barrett were alive and living it up somewhere in the wilds of Mexico?

IN NORTH CAROLINA, the rain refused to stop. Robert and Mercy and the baby all went together to take Mercy's mother back to Johnston County. It was the longest drive Malcolm had yet taken, the only time he'd been out of the house except for a routine checkup at the hospital. The motion seemed to calm him.

On the drive home, Mercy stared out at the rain. "It's never going to change."

"The weather? Yeah, it's grim."

"Nothing's going to change." Her voice was flat. "You're never going to get that job in Dallas. You're never going to leave Ruth. We're never going to be the way we were before I got pregnant. I wish I'd never told you. I wish I'd just gotten rid of it like I wanted to."

Reflexively, Robert looked down at Malcolm, asleep in her lap. A rush of love for the baby muted his anger at Mercy. "I don't," he said. "A lot of women get depressed after they give birth. That's all this is."

"Yeah, that's what the doctor said. He gave me a bunch of pills to make me stupid, like that's a solution."

"You didn't take them?"

"No. I don't take white man's pills so I can get up in the morning."

Robert sat in silence, seething over the "white man" remark.

"Maybe you should go back to your own house for a few days," she said.

His own house? Robert thought. Was she being deliberately cruel, or merely thoughtless?

"Having you around all the time is not making things better right now. I need to think."

"Think about what? Are you hoping to come up with more ideas that involve us being apart?"

She put her hand on his arm. As always, her touch calmed him. "Today's Wednesday. Stay at your place through the weekend, come back on Monday. I'll get out of this funk by then. Everything will turn around."

Dallas was supposed to be the way they would turn everything around. The two of them moving away, together. "Do I have a choice in this?" he asked.

"Yes," she said, and took her hand away. "You can choose to not give me what I'm asking for."

WHEN HE WALKED into the house that night at 11 o'clock, Ruth was childishly happy to see him. "Is everything all right?" was all she asked.

"Sure," Robert said. "Why wouldn't it be?"

They sat on the couch and watched the news together, Ruth making small talk. Robert missed Mercy, missed his son, but his pride was smarting and the two pains nearly cancelled each other out.

HE TRIED TO WORK late Thursday. The rain still poured down, and the emptiness of the office made him blue. Twice he picked up the phone to call Mercy, only to change his mind when he pictured the cold and distant reception he was sure to receive. When he got home, Ruth was taking a pot roast out of the oven. "I wasn't sure if you were coming or not," she smiled. "I thought I'd go ahead, just in case."

She was still not much of a cook, but she'd gotten a few recipes from Robert's mother down well enough to trigger his childhood memories. Robert ate hungrily and dozed afterwards on the couch until Ruth woke him and led him half-asleep to bed.

The rain let up on Saturday, letting Robert make a dent in the yard work he'd neglected all summer. He trimmed branches, raked leaves, pulled weeds, and tried not to think about what was happening in the house on Beamon Street. Ruth brought him fresh lemonade in a pitcher and a plate of cookies.

Sunday morning it was drizzling again. The house was cold, and Robert woke warm and relaxed under a pile of covers. He lay there for a long time, knowing there were thoughts waiting to crowd into his head, but able to convince himself that none were terribly serious.

He turned over and saw Ruth was looking at him.

"Good morning, sleepyhead," she said.

She was wearing fresh perfume, Robert noticed. He was suddenly and completely awake. Very, very slowly, Ruth took an arm out from under the covers and touched his face. He could see her bare arm all the way to her shoulder and up to her neck and realized she was not wearing a nightgown.

Oh God, Robert thought.

She touched his lips and then, very slowly, moved toward him. He closed his eyes, then opened them. She kissed him, softly and lingeringly, and then her tongue flicked at the corners of his mouth. Her eyes were open wide. She moved up a little in the bed and the covers fell away, revealing her breasts, full and soft and pale. Robert reached for them, unable to stop himself.

"Yes," she whispered. "Oh, yes."

Once he was inside her there was no going back. He tried to make it last as long as he could, basking in the warmth and softness of her flesh, feeling her hands dig into his back and pull at his hair, tasting her mouth and neck and breasts. Still he finished all too soon and shame and revulsion at what he'd done washed over him.

He tried to turn away, but Ruth clung to him. "Oh, Robert, I've missed you so much. So much." She covered his neck and chest with kisses, and even in his disgust and despair his body responded to her, and he began to make love to her again.

AFTERWARD HE TRIED to explain. "Ruth, nothing has changed. I didn't mean for this to happen. My—other relationship—it's not over."

"Oh," she said. "I thought—"

But you didn't ask, he wanted to say. He wanted to blame her though he knew it was his own weakness that had betrayed him. "I'm going back tomorrow."

"Oh," she said, looking as if she might cry, then slowly forcing a smile. "Well, at least we have today. It's something to keep me going a little while longer."

THE ALARM FAILED to go off Monday morning. Robert had lain awake much of the night, trying to find a position where guilt would not twist his muscles into knots. When he did wake up it was to more rain and Ruth's hand gently on his mouth, hushing him. "I turned off your alarm when I got up. I already called the office. You don't need to go in. You're going to stay right here and have a second honeymoon. Just like Jamaica."

The bed and their bodies smelled of sex. The word "Jamaica," whispered in his ear and followed by the caress of Ruth's tongue, drove the guilt away again. What was one more day? What difference could it make now?

ROBERT COULDN'T BRING himself simply to walk out of Ruth's house and go to Mercy's on Monday afternoon, or Monday night, not with the stink of his shame on him. Though a part of him wondered if she would even notice, a thought that prompted another spasm of guilt.

He woke frequently through the night and finally got out of bed before six on Tuesday morning. He would go straight to Mercy's house and tell her what had happened. There was no other way. Maybe, just maybe, it would break the maze of loneliness they'd built around each other.

Those were the only thoughts he allowed himself as he drove across town. Do this thing you have to do, get it over with, see what happens next.

He hesitated on Mercy's front porch, feeling as if he should knock. It was the longest they'd been apart since their first weekend together.

The need to talk to her, to fix things, to do whatever he had to do, was strong in him. He unlocked the door and went in.

IT WAS FUNNY, in a way. One drop of Negro blood, so they said, was enough to make you black. Yet he had never seen skin so white.

There was more than a single drop of blood, though. There was an entire bathtub full of blood, diluted to pink by the bathwater.

She was naked in the tub. At some point she had clearly turned onto her side to get more comfortable. It was like going to sleep, he'd heard somewhere. Her head was on her right shoulder, her eyes closed, her back turned to him where he sat on the closed lid of the toilet.

He wished she hadn't turned her back to him.

He didn't think it had been more than a few hours. There was no smell of decay from her skin. He'd only touched her the once, to look for a pulse, to make sure. Her body was cold, and the house was cold. He was sure the mix of blood and water in the tub was cold, though he hadn't put his hand in it.

Monday night, he imagined. The light was on in the bathroom, and the lamp next to the bed. That was where he'd looked first. He tried to remember what he'd felt like, back then. When he'd first walked in. Before he knew. Before everything changed forever.

He had her note in his hands. She'd left it next to the bed. Like calling the police, like the simple act of standing up, reading the note seemed more than he could do. It felt like giving consent.

In the end he had to do it, because Malcolm was nowhere in the house, and as much as he feared the answer, still he had to have it.

IN THE NOTE she blamed Robert for nothing, herself for everything. Her biggest fear was that Robert would not forgive her. She accused herself of self-ishness in resenting Malcolm, said no one could hate her more than she hated herself. "Things used to be one way and they changed," she wrote, "and I don't know why I don't believe they could change back but I don't."

Then she wrote, "I will always love you." She signed her name and then wrote a PS, saying that Malcolm was with Mrs. Invers two houses down.

Robert read the note over and over, until there was no meaning left in the words, like chewing a bite of apple until the juice was gone and there was nothing left but dry, tasteless pulp. Then he looked at his watch. It was 7:30. He'd been sitting there for an hour. He got up and called the police.

He went back and sat on the lid of the toilet again. Then he got up and called Ruth.

"She's dead," was all he said. He didn't know if Ruth would recognize his voice. He didn't think he would have.

"I'll be right there," she told him.

RUTH GOT THERE before the police did. The address was Hayti, after all. No one really cared if a black woman killed herself.

Ruth found him still sitting on the toilet seat. She took him by the arm and led him out to the porch. She sat him down on the steps and then perched next to him, not saying anything, even after she took the note from his hands and read it. In a minute the police arrived.

First there were two uniformed officers. One went in for a look while the other stayed to keep an eye on Robert. "She's in the bathroom," Robert said helpfully.

The second officer took Robert's name and address, and by the time he had that, the first officer came out and nodded. The first officer went to the squad car and talked into his radio. The second officer asked Robert what his relationship was to the deceased.

"They were involved," Ruth answered for him. She handed the officer the note. "They were having an affair." She took hold of Robert's arm again. To the rest of the world it might have looked like she was getting support from him.

"And you are?"

"I'm his wife. Ruth Cooper. Same address as Robert. He came over to break things off with her and found her like that."

"Thank you, ma'am. The detectives will be here in a minute and they'll get all that information from Mr. Cooper himself."

The ambulance came next. Two white men carried a stretcher into the house and emerged a few minutes later with something on top of it, covered in sheets, darkened in places with wetness. Robert watched the stretcher roll down the sidewalk, the only sidewalk on the block, watched the men load it into the back of the ambulance, watched them exchange a few friendly words with the uniformed officers, watched the ambulance drive away.

When the detectives took him aside to question him, he found himself telling the same story Ruth had. As he stood on the porch talking to them, he saw Ruth walk down the street, go up to a house, knock on the door, and speak with a woman in the shadows of the porch. Then she went to the next house and went inside. Half an hour went by. Robert told the truth about everything except when he said that he was breaking up with Mercy. By the time he'd said it a few times, it, too, started to sound like the truth.

Ruth came back. She was holding Malcolm. Malcolm was crying and Ruth was trying to calm him, but Malcolm didn't want to be calm. He wanted to scream.

Robert excused himself and took Malcolm away from Ruth. He cradled him where Malcolm could see his face and began to talk to him, a lot of nonsense about jazz musicians and the weather. Malcolm stopped screaming to listen, cocking his head and flexing his tiny fingers.

"Is that the deceased's child?" one of the detectives asked. They were both white.

"Our child," Robert said. "His name is Malcolm."

The two detectives exchanged a look. It seemed very rude to Robert, but before he could get around to telling them so, the idea had lost its urgency.

And then they were finished and they told him he could go home. They might have more questions later. There would be an autopsy and an inquest, but everything seemed straightforward. It was not yet ten in the morning. It didn't seem like enough, somehow.

Ruth had been arguing with a man in a suit. At one point she called, "Robert, is there a phone in the house?" He nodded, and the two of them went inside together. When Ruth came out she said, "Malcolm is coming home with us."

Robert felt a quick flicker of relief. "Okay," he said. Malcolm himself had nodded off.

"I'll take him," Ruth said. "You follow me. We have things to talk about."

ROBERT FOLLOWED HER to the house on Woodrow. They made a nest for Malcolm on the couch and then sat at the dining room table. There was a full pot of coffee already perked and Ruth brought cups.

"Now," she said. "We're keeping the baby, but we can't possibly stay here."

Robert looked at her in confusion.

"We're going to go ahead with your plan to move to Dallas. We'll start over there. No one will know the baby isn't mine."

Robert stared.

"Oh, yes," she said. "I know about your plans. I know everything. Everything. I don't imagine there's another woman alive who would put up with what you've done. But I love you. I love you so much that I'm going to take you back and start again." She touched his cheek gently and for a second Robert thought his defenses might collapse.

"Now," she said, and took her hand away. "Malcolm is no name for a white child. From now on his name is Michael. Michael Cooper. A plain, ordinary name for a nice, ordinary baby."

THE HOUSE SOLD in November, and they were able to lease it back through the end of the year.

No one ever called again about Mercy's death, and no one ever questioned Robert's right to the child. On some level Robert knew this was the work of Ruth's father, probably with assistance from Randy Fogg. The machinations remained invisible to him. If Ruth paid a price of her own for Robert's damage to the Bynum family reputation, he never heard of it.

Life began to go through the motions again. Robert went to work in the morning and came home to a bland dinner and an evening of television. Ruth's doctor gave him a prescription to help him sleep and Robert took it faithfully.

In the first days after Mercy's death, Michael would wake up screaming in the night. It wasn't hunger; sometimes he'd had his formula only minutes before. Nothing Ruth could do would comfort him. It took the sound of Robert's voice, his inane one-sided conversations about baseball or highway construction, to calm the baby down. Robert would often fall asleep in mid-sentence and wake again with nonsense words on his lips, still talking.

The bloodcurdling interruptions went on for over a week. Then one night Ruth grabbed Robert's arm as he was about to get up. "Let him cry," Ruth said. "If you keep going to him, he'll never learn to be normal."

"I can't listen to him cry like that. The poor little guy—"

"Yes, you can. Because if you get up I'm going to scream louder than he can."

After five minutes Michael showed no sign of letting up. His cries went deep into Robert's own pain and threatened to let it out. "Ruth..." he said.

"Hush," Ruth said. "He'll stop."

And, eventually, he did.

BY MID-DECEMBER the first leg of the Durham East-West Expressway was finished. The constant delays had taken them into serious winter weather, and they'd scheduled the final pours around cold rains and hard freezes. Fences, signs, and median rails were all on order, and such landscaping as they could do had all been done.

At Mitch's request, Robert drove him to the westernmost end, near the new NC Mutual Life tower. They stood in their overcoats in a cold wind on the Duke Street overpass, looking east as the highway rose, fell, curved, and disappeared over the horizon. The lanes shone fresh and white, the shoulders asphalt black.

"From here," Mitch said, "you can see all the way to the future." He pointed straight ahead. "Interstate 40." He jerked his thumb toward his shoulder. "Highway 70. Someday Interstate 85. Full of cars, taking people to Research Triangle Park, and home to the burbs."

He turned to Robert. "You made this."

Robert nodded. He wondered if he should pretend to feel something.

"You want to drive it?" Mitch asked. "You should have the first go. You can take it all the way to Alston Avenue and back. Fast as you want. No traffic, no cops."

"That's okay," Robert said. "Maybe another time." It seemed that he was feeling something after all, something so large and so dark that he didn't dare look closely.

"Man, if you don't want it, I do," Mitch said. Robert held out his car keys, but Mitch shook his head. "I'll come back later. Maybe tonight. The night time is the right time."

The wind rattled their coats and stung their eyes.

"When do you leave?" Mitch asked.

"Next week. We'll stay at Arthur and Ann's for Christmas, find our own place in the new year."

Awkwardly, Mitch tried to draw him into a hug. Robert, startled, submitted with the best grace he could. He patted Mitch on the back with gloved hands.

"This isn't how it was supposed to be," Mitch said.

After a long second Robert stepped away, and Mitch folded his arms across his chest. "We're young, right?" Mitch said. "Our best work is still ahead of us."

"Sure," Robert said. He turned his back on Hayti, on St. Joseph's, on Pettigrew Street and Beamon Street and Lincoln Hospital and looked west, toward the unfinished cut of the freeway, toward Dallas. "Why not?"

MICHAEL

2004

Wednesday, October 27

AT 9 O'CLOCK on Tuesday night, Michael's father began to describe finding Mercy's body. After a few minutes, Michael saw that he would not be able to take any more. He got up in mid-sentence and walked out of the hospital and stood for a long time watching the cars roar by on Erwin Road. He imagined he was a common enough sight; one more shattered person stumbling out of that house of pain, barely knowing where he was.

He located Beamon Street on the map in his car and negotiated a maze of one-way streets to get there. He was not surprised to see everything changed, the single-family homes long since cleared for public housing. He sat in the cul-de-sac at the end of the street, thinking about his father's weakness, Mercy's selfishness, himself as an infant, crying in the dark.

He could not bear to think about Ruth.

The next morning he was back at the hospital, asking questions that his father answered to the best of his ability. By 11:30 they were, more or less, finished.

"It took eight or nine months," his father said, "before I was able to feel anything at all. We had the house on Wildflower Drive then. All the boxes were unpacked, and we had new furniture that Ruth's father paid for. I had a straight shot up Webb's Chapel Road to work every morning.

"I don't know if you remember Bill Morris or not. I was working at his offices there on the square in Carrolton. We were starting to fool around with some design ideas for the airport, and I was doing the road through the middle of the thing, and all the clover-leaf intersections for the terminals.

"There was an A&P across the street from our office, and I would generally get a sandwich there for lunch. One day I saw a woman ahead of me in line who looked like Mercy.

"It wasn't like I hadn't thought of her. There hadn't been a day where I didn't think of her. I had to keep the lights on in my head all the time, you know what I mean? So nothing could surprise me. But that woman came out of a dark corner.

"After that I had a bad couple of years. I'd be thinking about anything, about, I don't know, going swimming in the neighborhood pool. And I would think, Mercy should be the one going swimming with me. And that would start everything again."

He shifted uncomfortably in the bed. "When it wasn't Mercy, it was Barrett Howard. I would see him, too, walking on the side of the road, maybe wandering around one of my building sites. It caught me out every time, every time it was bad.

"The both of them believed in voodoo, they both believed it could raise the dead. They were wrong. This is what raises the dead." He pointed at his own temple. "This is what keeps them walking around among us."

Michael was not yet ready to feel sorry for his father. "What about Barrett Howard?" he asked. "Who killed him?"

"You know that as well as I do. It was Randy Fogg or one of his henchmen."

"Then why didn't you call the police? Take him down?"

"For all I knew Randy Fogg owned the police, too. Maybe he still does. If I started making noise, I could have ended up in an underpass myself. And how could I explain being in the passenger seat of that cement mixer?"

His father began to cough. It was a terrible, violent sound, a sound of flesh tearing, a sound that a human body could not make and continue to live for long. He put a tissue to his mouth and it came away bright with blood. It took a minute or more for him to get the coughing under control. He drank a glass of water, his chest still twitching with aftershocks.

"If I could do one thing before I die," he said, "I would like to make him pay for that. I would like to go to my grave with the belief that there was some kind of justice in this world."

"Maybe there's somebody who can help you do that. Did you know Donald Harriman is still here? He's teaching at UNC. I talked to him a few days ago."

His father's face lost what little color it had. I'm taking hours off his life with this, Michael thought. And he doesn't have many left.

"He claimed to have heard of me because of my work," Michael said. "He knows a lot more than that, doesn't he? He knows all about you and Mercy."

His father nodded.

"I think you meant for me to learn all this," Michael said. "It really was you who put the idea into my ... into Ruth's head to recruit me for this trip, wasn't it? I didn't believe her when she told me."

Pain clearly made it hard for his father to keep talking. "If I had ... some agenda ... it was not conscious. I'm past playing games."

"Maybe Barrett Howard was your agenda. Maybe you wanted me to get Randy Fogg for you."

"Listen to you. You sound like some TV tough guy. 'Get' Randy Fogg? Who are you to 'get' anybody?"

As long as Michael could remember, his father had used words like those to hurt him and push him away. "Just once," Michael said, stinging, "I wish you would ask something of me. Ask me to do something for you."

His father closed his eyes, and for a second Michael thought he was going to die then and there. "Dad?"

His father's eyes opened, then winced shut again. "Tell your mother she can come back now. I've kept her out long enough."

Michael stood up. His father would die before he would stop referring to Ruth as Michael's mother. If there were such a thing as magic, if symbols were real, the cancer would have gone away once the festering secrets came out. Except in this world cancer trumped magic, and his father had waited too long. Thirty-five years too long.

MICHAEL STUCK HIS HEAD in the lounge on the way out of the hospital. "He wants you to come back now," he said.

Ruth nodded glumly without meeting his eyes.

He could not yet connect this frail, somewhat pathetic figure with the woman who had stood beside his real mother's corpse, with the seductress and schemer who had destroyed his father's dreams. She didn't seem like a plausible target for the rage and bitterness and sadness and loss swirling inside him.

Just as well, he thought, for surely she would not be able to withstand it.

He drove to UNC, feeling urgency without a clear purpose. A student waited outside Harriman's office, and Michael smiled at her and said, "I need a second with Dr. Harriman. It's urgent."

"I have an appointment?" she said. She looked and dressed like an African and sounded like the San Fernando Valley.

"I understand," Michael reassured her.

The door was slightly ajar. Five minutes later it opened to reveal a boy in flipflops, shorts, and an oversized T-shirt. Michael quickly slipped into the office and closed the door on the young woman's exasperated sigh.

"I don't believe you're Jennifer Brown," Harriman said, looking over the tops of his glasses.

"I think you'd better send Jennifer home," Michael said.

"You're that graphic novel artist, correct?"

"Let's skip the games. You know exactly who I am. You know my mother, Mercy Richárd. Intimately. She initiated you into the cult of Erzulie. And

I'd bet a substantial chunk of money that you've got that tattoo I asked you about, that Four Moments of the Sun, on your left wrist, above that high-dollar watch."

"I see." Harriman got up and went to the door. "Ms. Brown, I'm going to have to reschedule your appointment. I'll see you in class tomorrow and we'll make arrangements then."

He closed the door and sat down again. "I'm a tenured full professor, and the University is aware that I have firsthand experience with vodou. If your intent is to blackmail me, I would advise against it."

"What do you know about my mother's death?"

"She had what we recognize today as postpartum depression. It's not unusual. Unfortunately, for a working-class black mother, especially an unmarried one, psychological counseling was simply unheard of at the time."

"So she killed herself."

"She cut her wrists in the bathtub with a kitchen knife."

"You were in love with her. And that's all you can say?"

"I've had a long time to recuperate. Thirty-five years."

"Do you have a picture of her?" Harriman shook his head. "Can you, can you at least tell me something about her? What was she like?"

Harriman finally softened. He thought for a few seconds and then said, "I only saw her dance once. There was a period of about six months where I was obsessed with her, in ... I guess it was the spring and summer of 1967. I would loiter near her house, watching from my car. Sometimes I followed her and your father when they went out. I don't think they ever knew I was there.

"One night they went to a dance at the Durham Armory. It was the Tommy Dorsey band—in name only, of course. Mostly white kids fresh out of college, led by some old guy on trombone playing the Dorsey arrangements. That night Mercy wore a short black pleated skirt that flew up every time she spun around, and a black flowered blouse with one too many buttons undone. Her skin looked pale by comparison.

"I remember watching her and your father walk over to the chairs along the wall to change their shoes. Watching her was like watching a major league hitter in the on-deck circle. She was so focused and eager and yet so calm and confident, all at the same time.

"You know what a hovercraft is? They never got the technology down to a graceful size. If they had, it would have looked like Mercy dancing. Her feet were flying while her body floated above them like it was weightless. And the joy surrounded her, like the mist around a waterfall."

Harriman stopped, and then he said, "I hated your father for many years. First because he had Mercy and I knew I never would. Then, when she died, I blamed him for her death. How could he not have left his wife for her? How could he have let her kill herself?"

"I've been asking myself those same questions."

"He was human, is the answer. Those were different times. Divorce was not that common then, they didn't have no-fault divorce laws in North Carolina, and indeed, Mercy's father was not someone to take lightly."

"No, I ... wait. Did you say Mercy's father? I thought she didn't know who her father was."

"Ruth's father. Robert's father-in-law. Wilmer Bynum. I misspoke myself." Harriman looked terribly uncomfortable, more so than a simple verbal misstep could justify.

"No, I think you just slipped up. Wilmer Bynum was Mercy's father, wasn't he? So she and Ruth were what, half-sisters? Holy shit."

Harriman didn't answer.

"Tell me," Michael said. "Tell me, for God's sake. Was Wilmer her father?"

"Yes," Harriman said.

"And she never told my father?"

"She didn't know it herself. Perhaps she suspected as much. Her mother refused to tell her, and I only got it out of her after Mercy's death."

"Why did she tell you?"

"With Mercy dead, she had no reason to keep the secret any longer. She wanted to hurt your grandfather, and hurt anyone who had any part in Mercy's death."

Dazed, Michael realized that Wilmer Bynum was back to being his grandfather. "Is Mercy's mother still alive?"

"No. She died in 1989."

"So my father still doesn't know that Mercy was Bynum's daughter."

"I don't see how he could. Ironic, though, isn't it?"

"I'm not exactly in the mood for irony. This is not academic to me."

"I apologize."

He seemed sincere. "What other secrets are you keeping? Do you know who killed Barrett Howard?"

"Know? I don't know for a certainty. Randy Fogg is certainly the obvious suspect."

"Was he—is he—head of the NRC?"

"Today the grand dragon is a man named Herbert Strong. He lives in the mountains near Asheville and is tied in with the militias out there. As for the sixties, I don't know. We assumed it was Fogg. It was much more of a secret society then."

"We?"

"The group that Barrett started."

"Do you have a name?"

"It's past tense. Everything fell apart after Barrett disappeared."

"*Did* you have a name, then?"

"No. To be able to put a name to something gives you power over it, places limits on it. We believed we would be stronger without it."

"Can I see the tattoo?"

Harriman hesitated, then slowly removed the cufflink from his shirt and folded the cuff over twice.

His skin was lighter than Barrett Howard's, and he had the advantage of not having been dead for 35 years. Other than being more clearly visible, the tattoo was identical to Howard's.

"What was he planning?" Michael asked.

"Nothing less than the Revolution. With a capital 'R.' That, we did have a name for."

"You had guns in the old Biltmore Hotel?"

He seemed surprised at the extent of Michael's knowledge. He nodded and said, "M-16s with grenade launchers. Browning Automatic Rifles. We had dynamite. Handguns, shotguns, .22 target rifles."

"How many of you were there?"

"Close to two hundred."

"Doesn't seem like enough to start a Revolution."

"Two hundred angry black men with guns? It surely would have started *something*." Michael had not seen this fire before. As quickly as it flared, it cooled again. "No. Evidently it was not enough."

"What happened to the weapons?"

"I don't know. I suspect they were sold off for drugs. That's pretty much what happened to all the revolutionary movements of the sixties. Everyone was jailed, killed, run out of the country, or ground down and disillusioned to the point of giving up. As a generation, we beat our swords into hypodermic needles."

"Do you know where any of the others are?"

"A few. One of them is a salesman for a Toyota dealership in Durham. Another works at the *Herald-Sun*. Another is a master sergeant at Fort Bragg. A good number of them have been killed or incarcerated, which is what this country does to black men whenever possible."

"Do you know where my mother is?"

"I don't understand. Your mother is dead."

"Is she buried? Does she have a grave?"

"The grave is in Beechwood Cemetery. There's an office there. They can show you how to find it." He shifted forward, clearly ready to stand and usher Michael out.

"Are you trying to get rid of me?" Michael asked.

"Yes. In all honesty. This has not been a pleasant conversation for me, as you might imagine. And you are disrupting my office hours."

Michael held back a sarcastic reply. "Do you have a cell phone?"

"Yes."

"Give me the number, and I'll leave you alone. For now."

Harriman wrote the number on a sticky pad and handed Michael the top sheet. "Can I trust you?" Michael asked.

Harriman took a cell phone out of his pocket and pointed to the land line on his desk. "Call it," he said.

"No," Michael said. "That's good enough." He was suddenly ready to be somewhere else. "I'm sorry to have put you through this."

Harriman offered his hand. "I'm sorry too. More than you will ever know."

MICHAEL CALLED DENISE as soon as he hit the street.

He'd talked to her every night after the conversations with his father, and she'd done her best to help him keep perspective. "So if your mama was black, that makes you black, right?" she'd said. "That is going to be a relief to my own mother, who's been ragging me about dating a cracker."

She listened to the latest revelations and said, "I know the supervisor over at Beechwood from my research. Let me call him up now, because he's about to go home for the day. I'll find out where your mom is, and we can go over there together."

It was strange to feel all the urgency of a new relationship and yet have it be so overshadowed by the rest of his life. She was on his mind constantly, an anxious question that he couldn't answer. What was she feeling? Did he know what he was feeling himself? Even the powerful memory of their first kiss was subject to interruption by an image from his father's narrative.

She was waiting for him on the steps of the Heritage Center. It was all he could do not to grab her as she slid in next to him. "I missed you," he said. The three days had crawled by like weeks.

"Me too," she said. She stared at him intently.

"Do you see him?" he asked.

"Who?"

"That black man lurking inside me."

"I'm sorry. You'd think I'd know better."

"It's okay," Michael said. "I've been doing the same thing."

He'd stared in the mirror until his vision blurred. The conundrums of race were no longer academic. Why did a single drop of African blood make you black, but a single drop of European blood not make you white? Did that heritage make him different than he would have been if Ruth had been his mother? Was his penis bigger, were his hands better able to catch a football, did he have more natural rhythm? If that was the fantasy, the reality included the possibility of sickle-cell disease and increased risk of prostate cancer and diabetes.

In high school, most of his generation's role models were black, from Michael Jordan to Michael Jackson, from Prince to Eddie Murphy to Mr. T. White boys in North Dallas had aped black slang and gestures, copied black fashion, listened to black music, maybe had a black friend. Now he'd been granted the implied wish, with no magical bonus of cool or toughness or style.

And what of his own children, if he ever had any? How would he feel if he fathered a black child with a white woman? What would the neighbors say?

"How are you holding up?" Denise asked.

"Not sleeping as much as I'd like to. I have all this frantic energy, and I don't know what to do with it. I feel like climbing a ladder and shouting at people on the street, only I don't know what I'd say. 'Hey, look at me, I'm black and my mother's dead'?"

He turned left on Fayetteville Street and they drove past the remains of the Victorian houses where John Merrick and Aaron Moore and C.C. Spaulding and the rest of the elite of Hayti had lived, now broken up into apartments or knocked down altogether; past the Lincoln Community Health Center, a squat, utilitarian clinic in front of a parking lot where Lincoln Hospital once stood, the hospital where Michael had been born; past the sleekly modern NCCU campus; past a block of beautiful turn-of-the-20th-century red brick bungalows; past Fayetteville Street Elementary to Beechwood Cemetery, where Merrick and Spaulding and Shepard and so many of the others had ended up.

Denise directed him to a narrow driveway leading through the high chain link fence and then west for a few hundred yards, to the far end of the cemetery.

Section D, like most of the other sections, was stark, flat, and treeless. The headstones, most the size of the Durham phone book, lay flat on the grass, many with attached vases and fresh flowers. Mercy's grave was in a thickly populated patch, the graves laid end to end and side by side with barely room to walk between them. A handful of other people wandered around nearby, most of them old, all of them black.

A polished granite marker listed her name as MERCEDES RICHARDS with the dates 1941–1969. Michael knelt in the still-green grass and put both hands on the stone. Denise stood beside him, her fingers lightly touching his neck.

So this is it, he thought. The end of the search. Apparently he was not going to cry, nor was he going to find closure. What he did feel was a painful finality to the name carved in rock, and more powerfully, a kind of comfort.

"I know I've probably talked myself into this," he said, "but something about this seems right. In exactly the way that everything about Ruth always seemed wrong."

Denise nodded encouragement.

Until that moment he had never understood why people would want to put their bodies in a box in the ground to rot. Now he saw the value of having some part of them still there, essence seeping into earth that he could touch with his hands.

He felt no urgency to leave. Instead he let his thoughts drift, thinking of the way Harriman had described Mercy dancing, the way his father had felt so calm around her. These secondhand memories, already worn smooth by others, were all he had of her.

When he finally stood up, Denise hugged him loosely and said, "Better?"

"I don't know. Maybe. Do you have to go back to work?"

"Not really."

"Can we get something to eat? I'm starving."

She directed him to Fortune Garden, a Thai restaurant near his hotel. The name seemed lucky, and in fact they arrived just as it was reopening for dinner. The inside was red vinyl booths and wood paneling, the food cheap and plentiful and good. When it was gone, Denise said, "So first Ruth was your mother, then she was no relation at all, and now she's your aunt?"

"Yeah. I think my emotions are on strike. 'Give us a call when you can get your story straight.'"

"Are you going to tell your father?"

"I don't know yet. I think I'd better sleep on it."

Denise looked down at her plate. "Speaking of which..." She seemed nervous. "Where were you planning to sleep?"

"Are you making an offer?" Now he was nervous too.

"It doesn't have to be, you know ... sex. You can just stay the night. Rachid is at a friend's house, and..." She looked up at him. "I was just thinking..."

Michael took her hand. "Yes. I'd like that a lot."

"I thought you might want to maybe stop by your room and get a change of clothes and a toothbrush. And condoms. If you happen to have any. Just in case."

THEY STARTED ON the couch, talking. They were both so nervous and distracted that Denise finally said, "This is ridiculous. Come on." She led him to the bedroom door and said, "Take it slow, okay? Really slow."

It had been a long time for her, long enough to be painful for her when he first tried to enter. That in turn made Michael self-conscious and afraid of hurting her again. She let him know there was no hurry. Michael loved touching the clean, compact lines of her body, feeling the sweet silk of her skin against his lips. Eventually, with her hand on top of his, she helped him bring her to a climax, and after that he fit inside her perfectly and she took him to his.

"Now you'll sleep," she said, and he did, so heavily that it seemed only minutes later when he woke up to sunshine pushing hard at the blinds.

"Is that your phone?" Denise said. A buzzing noise came from the pile of clothes on the chair in the corner.

"Mmmmmm. It'll stop."

"It could be your father."

Michael got heavily to his feet, put his glasses on, and fished up the phone. He was too late; the voice mail system had picked up. He looked back at Denise and saw her grinning at him. She was wearing a thin white T-shirt and white cotton underpants, the basic talking points of her anatomy barely disguised.

"You're beautiful," he said. More than anything he feared her regret. He didn't see any in her eyes.

"Don't you even think about kissing me until I've brushed my teeth," she said, getting up.

"I'm thinking about a lot more than that."

"I can see that. If I'm late to work, people will talk..."

"That doesn't sound like 'no.'" He followed her toward the bathroom.

The phone rang in his hand. Once he saw that the call came from the hospital, he'd missed his chance to ignore it. He switched it on, said "Hello," and heard only silence. "Ruth?" he said. "Ruth, is that you?"

Finally she said, "He's gone."

Michael sat on the edge of the bed. "When?"

She didn't seem to have heard him. "Where were you? Why didn't you answer your phone?"

He tried again. "When did it happen?"

"I don't know. Some time in the night. I was sleeping in the chair next to him, and I got up in the night and when I checked on him, his skin was cold ... oh my God!" She began to cry.

"He died in the middle of the night?"

"I've been up since 4 AM taking care of this."

"And you waited till now to call me?" Denise's clock read 8:17.

"There's been too much to do. I didn't have time to stop and call you."

Michael let it go. "Where is he now?"

"Still in the room, waiting for the funeral home to pick him up."

He saw Denise in the doorway, toothbrush in mouth, register his expression. She ducked out again and he heard her rinsing her mouth.

"I'll meet you there," he said, and switched off the phone.

Denise came and sat beside him. "Bad?" she said.

Michael nodded. "He died in the night."

She put an arm awkwardly around his shoulder. "I'm so sorry, Michael."

"It's not like it's a surprise or anything. Except that it is. It's a total shock."

"You were just starting to get to know him."

"Yeah," he said. "I have to go. Can I ... I mean, are we...?"

"Yes," she said. "Yes, we are, and you can. You'd better, in fact, whatever it is. Now put your clothes on and get out of here."

THEY HAD DRAWN the curtains around his father's bed. His primary care physician, Dr. Zeigler, had come off rounds to look at him herself.

"You folks can request an autopsy if you like," she said. "I doubt we'd learn anything. In terms of cause of death, there's no question about that." She was in her forties, trim, businesslike, yet gentle.

"No," Ruth said. The accusation Michael imagined he heard was probably his own guilty conscience.

"Can I see him?" Michael asked.

"Well, yes," Zeigler said. "In my opinion, you might be better off remembering him the way he was."

"No, I want to see," Michael said.

"I can't bear this," Ruth said. "I'll be outside."

Zeigler drew the curtain. Michael saw what she meant; his father looked like a bad wax dummy of himself. His eyelashes looked like crude stitches across his eyes, and the skin around his mouth had puckered like rotten fruit. It was not credible that this side of meat had ever walked around under its own power, that intelligence had lit its eyes.

"Do you know what plans he'd made for his ... disposition?" the doctor asked. Michael looked at her blankly, and she tried again. "Was there a funeral home?"

"Oh," Michael said. "Ruth will know all that. Whatever she wants to do is fine."

"He was an interesting man," Zeigler said. "I never heard anyone speak so passionately about concrete."

MICHAEL SPENT THE DAY with Ruth, wading through paperwork: death certificates, insurance, the funeral home, one obituary for the *Dallas Morning*

News, another for the *Durham Herald-Sun.* She spoke in a monotone, ignored any food or drink he put in front of her, and lost all animation in her face when he wasn't asking her questions. She'd never been physically affectionate, and she rebuffed his attempts to get her to talk about what she felt. She too, he realized, must have believed in magic, believed this day could be held back indefinitely if she only loved enough.

He saw her through dinner and took her back to her hotel room, where she suddenly became a ball of nerves. "I can't possibly sleep here alone," she said. "You can stay the night, can't you?"

Michael hesitated, torn between guilt and self-preservation. "No," he said at last. "I'm sorry."

If she'd softened, pleaded with him, he would not have been able to refuse a second time. Instead she said, "I'm still your mother, you know."

He stared at her. I'm going to wake up in the middle of the night, he thought, with the exact words on my lips that I should be saying now. "I'll see you tomorrow morning," he said. He hugged her, and she accepted it stiffly, arms at her sides. "Try and get some sleep."

He sat in the parking garage with his car windows down, letting the cool night air roll over him. Beyond his numbness and exhaustion he felt only the residue of the day's work, the nagging of unfinished business. There would be no mourning yet.

He called Denise.

"How are you holding up?" she asked.

"Hanging in there. Can I see you?"

"Rachid's home."

"I don't care, I want to meet him." He could hear her mulling it over. "It's got to happen sooner or later," he said.

"I'll ask him." She muffled the ensuing exchange with her hand, then said, "Okay, come on. Have you eaten?"

"For some definition of the word. I had to take her to Applebee's."

"I'm sure there's something here you can eat. You understand you have to behave, right?"

"I'll do my best."

Rachid turned out to be as tall as Michael, and thin in the way of hyper-active teenagers. Denise kept her distance as she introduced them. Rachid shook hands quickly, then his arms dropped to his sides like dead weight. "Hey," he said nervously.

Comic conventions were ideal training for dealing with the terminally uncomfortable. "Hey," Michael said. "You doing all right?"

"Yeah, yeah, good," he mumbled. Despite bad skin and posture, he was quite

handsome and clearly had his own sense of retro style, wearing his hair in a
scraggly natural cut that stood out an inch from his head.

"So what comics do you read?"

"Batman," he said. "X-Men." It was comfortable ground, and he showed the
first signs of relaxation. "You know the Black Panther?"

"Yeah, the Black Panther's cool. Marvel's got a Black Panther movie in development, did you know that?"

"No shit?" He glanced quickly at Denise. "I mean, no kidding?"

"I heard it was Wesley Snipes' company. Nobody's saying if Snipes is going
to play T'Challa, but he probably will, since the Blade movies did well."

"Blade was awesome."

"Why don't you guys sit down?" Denise said. "I'll see if there's anything to
drink around here."

Michael managed to keep Rachid talking for half an hour. He worked hard
at it. Rachid was a likable kid, a little too smart for his own good, a little alien-
ated, a little lost in his inner universe, the way Michael had been at his age.

Finally Denise sent him off to do his homework. "And you," she said to
Michael, "go this way."

"You're sending me home?"

"No," she said. She pushed him onto her front balcony, where she kissed
him fiercely. "Okay, Mr. Smartass, you impressed me."

"He's a good kid."

"You don't have to tell *me* that. Just be very, very careful. I don't want him
to get too attached until we know where this is going."

"What about you? Can I let you get attached?"

"That's the battle I'm fighting right now."

"Throw in the towel," he said, and kissed her again. "Let me stay the night."

"No," she said, and he saw how she could control a boy twice her size. The limits were clear and strictly enforced. "Sorry. I warned you it would be complicated."

"It's okay," he said. "I understand."

She reached up and combed through his hair. "I could probably get away
for a while tomorrow afternoon. I'll call you, and we can meet at your hotel
room for sex. It'll be cheap and tacky and thrilling."

"It's a deal," he said.

Back inside, they sat on opposite ends of the couch. They had entire lifetimes to catch up on. Michael talked about his father, how at times Michael's
very presence had seemed to make him angry or depressed, for reasons that
were now obvious. Michael had tried to win his approval at sports, where he
was a dismal failure, and schoolwork, where he was only marginally better. In
the last three days he'd found himself rereading his childhood, now that he had

the key, and all kinds of things were starting to make sense. Too late, of course, to undo the damage.

It was harder for Denise to open up. Michael gently pried loose a few facts. She'd been a good student, bright and eager to please. She'd never liked sports. She'd dreamed of being a dancer, but there was no money for classes. By high school she was barely five feet tall and filled out to the point that everyone told her to forget it.

"Ballet, modern, what?" Michael asked her.

"Anything," she said. "I would see Broadway dance numbers on Ed Sullivan when I was little and try to memorize everything they were doing."

"It's not too late," Michael said. "We could take some swing classes or something."

"Swing dancing? Where did you get that idea? Is it because of your father?"

"Possibly. He made it sound like such a blast."

"Michael, you're not trying to relive your father's life through me or anything weird like that, are you?"

"What do you mean?"

"I mean..." She let out a sigh. "I mean, you come to Durham, you start poking around in your father's past, and you get involved with the first black woman you meet."

"I've been in Durham, which is full of black women, for a month, and you're the first person I've asked out. And I didn't know about Mercy when I met you. Are you saying you don't know why I would be attracted to you?" He lowered his voice. "After last night you can still ask that?"

"I don't know. I'm confused. It's all happening so fast."

"Those are the words women say before they say things like, 'We should back off a little.' Are you running away from me?"

"It doesn't help for you to lump me with the entire female species."

"No," he said. "You're right. I'm sorry. You're scaring me, is all."

"I'm scared too. Obviously." She stretched out her hand and Michael, after a second, took it. "Maybe this wasn't a good idea," she said. "It's hard to be natural with Rachid only a few feet away." She rubbed her thumb along his palm. "I want to touch you, too."

It was not the time, Michael saw, to push. "It's late," he said. "Maybe I should go."

When she nodded, he realized how much he'd hoped she would argue with him. She let go of his hand and stood up. Michael walked to the door, and she stepped outside with him. He put his arms around her, and she rested her cheek against his chest. "I'm sorry," she said. "It's been such a long time for me. I'm not used to all this."

"Are we still on for tomorrow?"

"I'll call you," she said. It wasn't a yes or a no. She kissed him softly, lingeringly. It could have been a promise or a farewell.

He walked down the steps, forcing himself not to look back. When he'd started the car and come to a stop at Campus Walk, he yelled, "Goddamn it!" and shook the steering wheel with both hands. "You think I'm used to this? How could anybody be used to this?"

Friday, October 29

RUTH CALLED AT 7:30. He'd been up late, first calling Roger to tell him the news, then working on *Luna* until after two, nodding off with the blue pencil slipping from his fingers, descriptions from the script morphing imperceptibly into dream.

She'd had a terrible night, she said. She didn't trust herself to drive. She needed to see to the cremation, to go by the funeral home, buy a dress, and then she would need his help making phone calls in the afternoon. Had he checked the paper for the obituary?

"I just woke up," he said.

"Oh," she said, and went back to her list of tasks.

"Give me a few minutes, all right? I'll call you back."

Finding his way back to sleep already seemed an impossibility. He washed his face, pulling at the skin to erase the lines that made him look like his father. Then he poured a glass of orange juice and had time for one swallow before Ruth called again.

RUTH HAD PLANNED the memorial for that Sunday, two days away. Halloween. The funeral home, Hall-Wynne of Durham, had found them a 9 AM time slot. Michael had failed to convince her to delay it for a few more days. Ruth wanted to return to Texas as soon as possible, a reasonable enough desire in the circumstances.

Michael had not yet told her he was not going with her.

By three o'clock he had checked his watch so many times that Ruth asked, "Do you have somewhere you have to be, dear?"

"Maybe," he said, hope fighting it out with fear. They were in Ruth's room at the Brookwood, and Michael was making the calls to Robert's friends and family that Ruth said she was unable to put herself through. Robert's friend Arthur, with whom he'd been in business for years, broke down and it was all Michael could do to hang on to his own composure. Arthur's grief seemed so much more real than his own.

On the other end of the scale, Ruth's one surviving sister, Esther, took the news with little comment. Michael had only spoken with her a few times in his life, in keeping with his father's policy of ignoring Ruth's family. He sensed she was disappointed—though not surprised—that Ruth herself hadn't called.

It was nearly 4 when his own phone finally rang. Michael took it out on the room's tiny balcony. "Hello?" he said.

"Whatcha wearing?" It was Denise.

"Oh, the usual. Leather thong, some handcuffs."

"How far are you from your hotel room?"

"I can be there in fifteen minutes."

"If you get there before I do, go ahead and take your clothes off. You won't be needing them."

FOR ALL HER BIG TALK, she was shy at first, once they were alone in the room, the door locked, the curtains drawn. Michael didn't ask her how much time she had. Enough, apparently, to make love a second time as the sun was going down. Michael was hovering on the edges of sleep when she finally extricated herself. "What time is it?" he mumbled.

"Eight-thirty. I have to go. Can I put the light on?"

"Sure."

She gathered up the bits and pieces of her clothes, which lay on a path from the door to the bed. "I want you to spend the night tomorrow. Okay?"

"Yes. What about Rachid?"

"He'll be there. We talked. He's pretty grown up. And of course you charmed him."

"That was the idea."

"He wants to know what I'm going to tell his father. I said it was none of his father's business. I know it won't be as simple as that."

"He'll be jealous? Rachid's father?"

"He won't admit it. There will be remarks. Nothing I can't handle, and it's time I started acting like a normal adult with a life of my own. I may not be as uninhibited as I was this afternoon. You'll be patient with me, right?"

"Yes. Will you come to the funeral with me Sunday?"

She hesitated. "Are you sure?"

"Of course I'm sure. Why wouldn't I want you there?"

"Am I going to be the only black person there?"

"Other than me, you mean?"

"Other than you."

"Tommy Coleman will be there for sure. There may be others. Harriman, maybe. Does it matter?"

"It shouldn't matter. But you've only been black a few days. There's a lot you don't know yet."

"That sounds like the punchline to a bad joke."

"I'm serious, Michael. I don't want to minimize the shock of what you're going through, but you're not black the way I am, and you never will be. You look white, you were raised white, you have that sense of privilege totally ingrained in your personality. You don't know what it's like to walk into a big room full of white people and wonder if you're going to make it out without something happening. A look, a word, a man brushing his arm against your chest." She pulled on her red silk T-shirt as punctuation.

"Yeah, okay," Michael said. "I guess I had that coming. I still want you there."

"Then I'll be there. I'll get to meet your ... Ruth." She hesitated again. "You don't want me there just to shock her, do you?"

"Are you still going to be questioning my motives ten years from now?"

"Ten years should be close to enough. She *is* going to flip out though, isn't she?"

"Yeah," Michael said. "And maybe I do want that. What if you're right? What if I'm just using you somehow? I would hate that. How can I be sure my motives are clean? Can I even trust my own feelings?"

She sat on the edge of the bed and picked up his hand. She was fully dressed except for her shoes, fully separate from him. "It felt pretty real this afternoon. I wouldn't be here if I didn't trust you. Still, it probably wouldn't hurt for both of us to keep asking questions."

She pulled her shoes on, stood up, and kissed him. "Call me tomorrow afternoon."

"I'll miss you," Michael said.

"You, too." She blew another kiss from the doorway and was gone.

Saturday, October 30

LATE SATURDAY MORNING, Ruth called and begged him to come take his father's clothes away. They still smelled of him, she said, and it made her think he would be standing there every time she turned around.

It took him two trips to carry the clothes down to his car. He was painfully aware of his father's ashes, sitting on Ruth's bedside table in a brown plastic container the size of a hardcover book. He felt his father's presence in them. Though he knew it was a projection of his own feelings, he couldn't shake the idea that his father had after all wanted something from him, something he had never been able to ask.

He drove the clothes to Thrift World, a cavernous space in a run-down strip center a few miles from the hospital. His cell phone buzzed as he was carrying the last of the clothes through the back door.

It was Roger. "I don't mean to be in the way or anything," he said. "I'm at the Sheraton out by the airport if you've nothing on at the moment."

"You're here? In North Carolina?"

"Thought you might need a bit of moral support at the funeral."

"Wow." Michael was deeply touched. "That's really ... I'm glad you're here. Is it just you?"

"You mean, did I bring the trouble and strife? Not likely, mate. So do you know your way out here?" As usual, Roger was not to be diverted. Michael got directions and promised to be there within the hour.

He finished up at the thrift store and decided he didn't need to go back to the Brookwood, where Ruth would only find more busywork for him. He wound his way to the Durham Freeway and fought heavy traffic to the Page Road exit from I-40.

"Sit anywhere," Roger said as he let Michael in. As always, he wore black jeans, black sneakers, and a black T-shirt. If he got cold he would add a black leather jacket. His thick black beard was always a shock, at odds with his young, pale blue eyes. "Be with you in a tick, trying to lay hands on some notes I had a minute ago..." He began to circle the room, rifling his possessions.

The room had high ceilings, muted gray-on-white wallpaper, thick carpet, solid hardwood furniture. It made Michael's suite look like a doghouse. Or it would have, had Roger not already cluttered every available surface with fallout from the chaos that constantly swirled around him—books, magazines, cameras, cell phone, clothes, used towels, unfinished food and drink, piles of photocopies, notebooks, scraps of paper with images, dialog, addresses and phone numbers, in one case just a single word, "arachnotype," scrawled on a bar napkin with a fine-point black Sharpie, the only pen Roger ever carried. All of it smelled faintly of cigarette smoke.

Michael moved a Discman and a stack of CDs out of an armchair and sat down. The CDs were all field recordings of vodou ceremonies from Haiti. Michael picked one up and turned it over.

"I brought those for you, actually," Roger said. "Thought you might want to hear what that sort of racket sounded like. Here." He took the case from Michael's hands and put the disc in the player, fussing with a pair of battery-operated speakers until he got a loping, chaotic mix of drums and chanting voices to emerge.

"Do you have all this in your house?" Michael asked. "Filed away some-where, on the off chance that you might need it some day?"

"Yes, why?"

"How do you keep track of it all?"

"I'm very well organized." Roger seemed unaware of any irony in the state-ment. "Sod it, let's talk." He perched on the edge of the king-size bed, facing Michael. "Tell me some more of what your father said."

Despite the distraction of the music, which made his stomach flutter, Michael summarized the high points. It took fifteen minutes. Toward the end he found himself drawing the story out, enjoying the novelty of having Roger listen to him for a change.

When he was done, Roger said, "I can't imagine pulling all of that out of him and then having him die. It's like the old myth of the killing joke, only not funny, and turned in on itself."

"Ruth blames me for him dying."

"Yeah, she would do, wouldn't she? He was all she had."

"I don't know how to respond to her. We've never been physically comfort-able around each other, you know? Even when I was a kid. That's not a good basis for a mother-son relationship, and it doesn't give us a lot to go on now."

Michael paused and then said, "There is one more wrinkle. It turns out she is related to me after all." He told Roger about Harriman's revelation.

"Christ, this is amazing, isn't it? Hang on, let me get some of this down."

"Get it down?"

"Just a few notes."

"I thought you were here to give me moral support."

"I am. Without question. You have to admit, though, this is bloody great material."

"It's not *material,* Roger. Look, I don't think I want you using this."

"All right, no problem then, not if you don't want me to."

"Okay, good."

"All I'm saying is, you ought to think about it."

"Roger—"

"This is primal stuff, and the next bloke that comes along with a dead father—and that's all of us, sooner or later—could learn a lot from this."

"Learn what, exactly? That it sucks to find out your mother is your aunt, your real mother's dead, you're black, and now your father's dead, too? How big is the demographic for that, Roger? How many millions of lives is this go-ing to save?"

"Look, you're upset, obviously. This is not a good time—"

The voices on the CD player were screaming, tearing at Michael's nerves.

He jabbed the STOP button and said, "I'm upset? *I'm* upset? Like I'm the problem here?"

"This is not like you, Michael."

"Not like me to stand up for myself? Not like me to object to being the doormat?"

"Now you're starting to hurt my feelings. I can't believe you would want to do that, when I've come all this way."

Everything Roger said, with his calm tones and injured innocence, made Michael crazier. Worst of all was feeling like he was only seeing what had been in front of him, unacknowledged, all this time.

Michael stood up. "I have to go."

"I'll call you later," Roger said, as Michael crossed the vast room toward the door. "To make sure you're okay."

TRAFFIC WAS UNREASONABLY HEAVY on the short stretch of I-40 between the Sheraton and Michael's hotel. The reason proved to be a wreck at the Durham Freeway split, where somebody in an SUV had tried to change his mind at the last minute in front of an 18-wheeler. The legacy of the Interstate Highway System, Michael thought. Urban sprawl, pollution, crowding, hurry, frustration, mutilation, death. This is what my father's dream has become.

A shower and clean clothes failed to dispel his mood. It still clung to him as he rang Denise's doorbell for dinner, carrying his shaving kit and his suit for the funeral.

Dinner itself was pleasant enough. Rachid held forth through most of it about school, friends, the basketball team, television, and anything else that flitted through his hyperactive mind. Afterwards, Michael and Denise sat on the couch as Rachid, to Michael's amazement, did the dishes with only minor prompting.

"Am I naïve?" Michael asked her.

"Yes," she said, without hesitation. "Is that what's been eating at you tonight?"

"Was it that obvious?"

"Yes. So why are you asking?"

He told her about Roger, and then said, "Listen to me. It sounds like I've been nursing a grudge for years."

"Sounds like he's been taking advantage of you for years."

"It feels weird, like waking up one morning and realizing you're married to somebody who never loved you."

"I happen to know exactly what that's like, if you ever need a point-for-point comparison."

"The thought of not working for him anymore is … it's too strange. I can't wrap my brain around it."

"Don't think about it, then. Not now. You've got your father's funeral to-morrow, you've got all this other chaos in your life, you can leave this part of it alone for tonight."

Michael closed his eyes, nodded, and let himself slump on the couch.

"Whatever happens," Denise said, "you're going to be okay. Whether you keep working for Roger or not." She raked her fingernails through his hair, which calmed him as if he were a nervous cat. "You've got your skills, you've got the person you are inside. The chaos will pass. It always does."

"My God, that feels good."

"Let's go say goodnight to Rachid and I'll show you something that *really* feels good."

"Don't we need to make a show of staying up with him for a while?"

"The weekends are the only time I let him play video games. He couldn't care less about us."

Sunday, October 31

DENISE'S ALARM buzzed at 7. She shut it off, rolled over, and put her face on Michael's chest. "How long have you been awake?" Her voice was still slurred with sleep.

"An hour and a half," he said. He'd woken up hard, heart racing, thoughts jostling and bumping against each other in his head. Roger, Ruth, his father, Mercy. Memories of himself as a child, pointing a cap gun at Ruth and firing six shots, and Ruth bursting into tears. The panels he'd already drawn and let-tered in the current *Luna* that exploited his relationship with his father. The image of Mercy floating, cartoonlike, above a blur of whirling feet. There was no chance of falling asleep again, so he'd propped himself up and watched sunlight slowly leak into the room.

"Are you okay?" Denise asked.

"I don't know. I don't think I want to do this."

She pushed herself up on one arm. "Michael, you have to go to your father's funeral. Now get up and get going."

Her will power got him up and dressed and out the door with coffee and a piece of toast in his stomach. Denise drove.

"How should I introduce you?" Michael said. "As my girlfriend, or what?"

"Why don't you just tell them my name and let them figure out the rest for themselves?"

The funeral home was on Main Street, a few blocks west of downtown, in a 1920s-era brick building with a vast parking lot and its own freestanding chapel. Ushers led them to a long parlor in the main building with a sofa, stuffed chairs, and a tasteful floral pattern on the far wall.

Ruth sat on the sofa with Roger next to her. He held her hand in an odd, Victorian way, as if it were a cup and saucer. With a jolt, Michael realized that the willowy blonde standing next to the two of them was Helen Silberman, their Vertigo editor. He'd only seen her twice before, at comics conventions. On a chair by herself some distance away was Mitch Antree's widow, Frances Stanley. Tommy Coleman stood uncomfortably in the middle of the room with another late-middle-aged black man.

The other eight people in the room Michael guessed to be members of Ruth's extended family. Greg Vaughan, the dog lover, was in the middle of them, and their brown suits, wide ties, and 1970s haircuts all cried out Johnston County.

Tommy Coleman was relieved to see Michael. He took Michael's hand, then pulled him into an awkward hug. "I'm real sorry," he said. "I never should have started all this. Look what it's come to."

"This wasn't your doing," Michael said. "We talked a lot there toward the end, and I could tell he was relieved to finally get all that business out in the open. I think it helped him go easier."

The man with Tommy was short, very heavy, and wore a large hearing aid attached to the earpiece of his thick glasses. "This here is Booker," Tommy said. "Booker knew your daddy. Ain't that right, Booker?"

"What's that?" Booker said. He was squinting at Michael through the glasses.

Michael introduced Denise, and then Booker shook Michael's hand. "Thought you was the Cap'n," Booker said. "Give me a turn."

Out of nowhere, Michael suddenly thought he might cry. He made excuses to Tommy and Booker and led Denise over to Frances Stanley. After the introductions she said, "I told myself I wouldn't go to any more funerals. Yet here I am."

"Thank you for coming," Michael said. "It means a lot to me."

A voice behind him said, "Michael?"

He turned and saw Helen Silberman. "I'm so sorry for your loss," she said.

"Thanks. I had no idea you might be here. This is really ... when did you get in?"

"Last night," she said, and something in the sound of her voice gave her away. She'd flown down to be with Roger, Michael saw, leaving her husband and child in New York and Roger's wife in California. How very convenient this all must be, he thought.

Before Michael found anything to say, Roger stepped in next to Helen and slipped one arm around her waist. "How're you holding up, then?" he asked, as if the day before had never happened.

"I'm fine," Michael said. "Roger, Helen, this is Denise."

Denise shook Roger's hand and said, "I've heard a lot about you."

Roger mimed surprise. "I wish I could say the same."

Denise gave Michael a smile that warmed him from the center out.

"Listen," Roger said, "are you going to talk to your mother or not?"

It was Roger more than Ruth that made him say, "My mother's dead."

"Oh, don't let's quibble. You ought to say something to her."

He'd been headed that way, but Roger's commandeering the situation stoked his resentment. As the inappropriate replies lined up in his mind, nothing emerged from his open mouth.

"I think Michael needs to take care of himself today," Denise said. "If he feels like talking to her, fine, if not, then he won't."

Michael reached for her hand and squeezed.

"Bravo," Roger said, looking her over in an exaggerated and, Michael thought, condescending way.

A commotion at the front door broke the tension. Two white men in dark suits and sunglasses stalked into the room like a parody of Secret Service agents, scanning the thin crowd. One nodded to the other, who went back outside. A minute or so later, having successfully drawn the attention of everyone in the room, he returned with US Representative Randy Fogg.

Fogg was in his seventies now, with thinning white hair, pink skin like an albino's, and jowls that sagged to his chest. He carried a huge belly in front of him like a load of firewood, weighing down his every step. He came into the center of the room, looked around, and nodded his approval.

As soon as he'd finished his entrance, the funeral director appeared, as if on cue. "The chapel is open now," she said. "If you'll all come this way."

Fogg made his way to Ruth and offered his arm, though he seemed barely able to support himself. Ruth blushed, got nervously to her feet, and walked with him toward the side exit.

"Is that who I think it is?" Denise said.

"Yes."

"Did you tell me he was a friend of the family?"

"He was a friend of Ruth's father. My father couldn't abide him."

"This feels pretty weird, if you don't mind my saying so."

They filed into the chapel through a side door that brought them in front of the first row of pews. The room had a high ceiling and a wine-red carpet, 20 rows of wooden seats, and a recessed area in front with a lectern and a microphone.

One of the fantasies that had played out in Michael's head as he waited for dawn

had him making a speech in which he revealed himself as the bastard offspring
of his father's adulterous, interracial love affair, then accused Fogg of murdering
Barrett Howard. It ended with his being wrestled out onto the street by Ruth's
outraged relatives, Fogg admitting his crime in the heat of his anger, and the police
arriving to take Fogg away as he foamed at the mouth and cursed the African race.

In the cool, dim sanctity of the chapel Michael saw that he would do nothing of the kind. He would endure it as best he could and leave.

The funeral director gently took his arm and led him to the front row,
where Ruth sat by herself. Fogg was in the row behind, flanked by his body-
guards, with Greg Vaughan at the end. Michael sat down next to Ruth and
said, "This is Denise." Denise extended her hand across him. Ruth took it
briefly, then looked confused. "Are you with the funeral home?"

"She's with me," Michael said.

"Oh," Ruth said, clearly not understanding.

Everyone was seated now and music began to seep out of the speakers.
Bach, Michael thought. Doubtless to be followed at some point by the
Pachelbel Canon. Not *Sketches of Spain* or Charlie Shavers or anything that
might dare to evoke his father's memory.

He stopped himself. Let it go, he thought, or you'll never get through this.

The music faded and one of the Johnston County crew took the microphone, a short, balding man the same age as Randy Fogg, with a huge mole
over his left eye. "I never knew Robert Cooper," he began, and Michael saw
then that it was going to be as bad as it could possibly be. "But," the man said,
"I have known Ruth Bynum since I first became pastor of Mount Calvary
Baptist Church in 1963. I know her to be..."

Michael leaned forward and put his head in his hands. Surely that was allowed at a funeral.

When the pastor finally wound down, he had used up over fifteen minutes
of Michael's life. He then introduced, at length, "a man who needs no intro-
duction, Congressman Randy Fogg."

As Fogg lumbered toward the stage, Denise whispered, "You owe me.
Big time."

Fogg withdrew a sheaf of folded papers from his suit pocket, arranged them
on the podium, and adjusted his glasses. "I hope y'all will forgive me for jot-
ting down a few thoughts to share here today. I don't believe any of you would
enjoy it if I just got up here and rambled on as I've been known to do." There
were appreciative chuckles from Fogg's supporters.

"I'm here today to pay tribute to Robert Cooper, who was more than
a personal friend—he was a man of vision who helped shape the city of
Durham that we know today."

"My father hated you," Michael said, under his breath.

Fogg went on in that vein for a while, talking about the Durham Freeway and RTP as if Michael's father had been an equal partner in the planning and design and not merely a hired hand. Then he said, "Many of you remember what Durham was like before Robert Cooper. There was a blight on the edge of our downtown, a slum, a home to the worst elements in the city. Shiftless welfare parasites, reefer peddlers, and communists."

Michael looked at Denise, half expecting her to get to her feet and answer Fogg. Instead she seemed amused, in a bitter way. "Did he say 'reefer peddlers'?" she mouthed.

"Not only communists," Fogg went on, "but revolutionaries, violent, ruthless men bent on destroying the American way of life. We all owe Robert Cooper more of a debt than we know for burying that threat under the Durham Freeway."

"My God," Michael said, his voice lost in the murmur of approval on all sides. He looked at Denise again. "That was practically a confession."

"Shhhh, baby," Denise said. "We need to be very cool, here. This is getting scary."

Fogg went on, now praising Ruth, and Ruth's father, and the fine humble working men who were still the backbone of this country. Michael barely listened. He was giddy, angry, and not a little afraid himself.

Finally, when Michael believed he could not stand another minute, Fogg wrapped up and called Ruth to the stage. She dug through her purse, pulled out a wad of hotel stationery, and got unsteadily to her feet. She took Fogg's place at the microphone, tears now running down her face, and fumbled with her papers.

"I tried to write some things down last night," she said. "A few memories and things." Then, as if suddenly remembering, "Thank you, Congressman Fogg. You have always been a dear, dear friend of our family."

Michael looked down again. And saw, protruding from the purse she had left behind, a #10 envelope with Michael's name on it. The writing was his father's.

Michael plucked it from the purse. The flap had been sealed and then torn open again. Inside was a sheet from one of the blue-line graph paper pads that his father had always used.

The letter was dated Wednesday night, the night before he died. "Dear Son," it said. "I'm trusting Ruth to pass this on to you if she should find it before you do. I am also trusting her not to read it before she gives it to you."

The words, Michael thought, were meant to shame Ruth if she read that far. Clearly they hadn't worked.

"I have one last request, which I know is not going to sit well with her. I have purchased two grave sites in Beechwood Cemetery for her and myself, and I would like you to see that I am buried there. Obviously this represents something of a change of heart on my part. I have thought a lot about the things you said to me, about the reasons I wanted to come back to Durham, and I see now that you were right."

Michael couldn't remember his father ever having made an admission like it. Come back, he thought. I want to talk to you.

"I needed to be here, and I see now that I would like to stay here. Do this for me, son, if you can.

"Your father"

Michael handed the letter to Denise.

From the podium, Ruth suddenly noticed what he was doing and broke off in mid-sentence. "Michael?"

Michael stood up. He was aware, though he couldn't see them, that everyone in the room was staring at his back. "Did you mean for me to find this?"

"I was going to give it to you," Ruth said, into the microphone.

"When, exactly?" Michael asked.

He felt a hand on his shoulder and turned, shaking it off. Randy Fogg was on his feet now too, staring at him with red, watery eyes. "Mind your manners, son."

Before he could respond, Denise touched his arm and gave him back the letter. "Maybe we should go," she said.

He started to refuse, then saw the wisdom of it. "You're right," he said. "We're going."

Everyone in the room seemed to be whispering. It sounded like distant surf. "You can't leave," Ruth said. "I forbid it." She was too close to the microphone, and there was a short whistle of feedback.

Michael folded the letter and put it in his jacket pocket. He nodded to Denise.

When he got to the side door, he found Greg Vaughan blocking it. "I think you should go back in there and apologize to her."

"This doesn't concern you," Michael said, fighting a tremor in his voice. "Now if you'll excuse us..."

Vaughan did not move. "Ruth's feelings concern me." He smiled in what almost seemed a reasonable, friendly way.

"Then maybe you should go take care of her," Michael said. "And get out of our way."

Vaughan looked at Denise, then back at Michael, and shook his head. "Like father, like son." The words were barely audible.

Michael's face burned. "What's that supposed to mean?"

Vaughan dropped the smile. "Keep your voice down, college boy."

Michael's emotions were out of control. The last week of turmoil had built up to this moment. Vaughan, despite being in his fifties, was tough and wiry and undoubtedly dangerous. Michael wanted very much to kill him with his bare hands. "If you have something to say to me, say it," he said.

Vaughan took a step closer. "I don't take orders from you, boy." He was barely audible. "If you think you're man enough to do something about it, then you and me can go along over to the parking lot and have this out. But not here, not in front of Ruth and the Congressman."

"Michael," Denise said. She pointed with her chin toward the back of the chapel, where the main doors opened onto the street. "Let's go this way."

"Better do what she says, boy," Vaughan said. "You're out of your league."

Denise physically inserted herself between the two of them, forcing Vaughan to take a step back. She turned Michael by the shoulder and pushed him toward the other exit. "Go," she said. "Now."

She got Michael by the arm and led him down the left-hand aisle, past the rows of embarrassed mourners, most of whom looked away, and into the foyer and down the steps to the sidewalk. "Keep walking," she said. "Don't think, just walk."

They got in the car. Michael clenched his fists until they screamed with pain.

"I don't know what he said to you," Denise told him, "but I can make a pretty good guess. The guy is a cracker asshole and you have to not let him control the level of the discourse. Michael. Look at me."

Slowly, painfully, he made his head turn until he was looking at her. Every muscle in his body was rigid.

"When I first came down here from New York, I nearly gave myself an ulcer. It took me a while to figure out that there is power in walking away. You have to not let them make the rules."

He looked at his hands and willed them to open. Eventually they did.

"We need to go to Ruth's hotel room," Michael said.

Denise cocked her head.

"I think—I hope—my father's ashes are still there."

Denise smiled. "That's my boy."

MICHAEL COULDN'T SHAKE the idea that Ruth had second-guessed him and dispatched her cousin Greg to intercept them. He left Denise in her car with the engine running and sprinted upstairs, his key card in hand.

The ashes were there. Michael grabbed them and got a Ginsu knife from the kitchenette. He took the stairs down, two at a time, and arrived at Denise's car out of breath.

"Beechwood?" Denise asked, putting the car in reverse as soon as he got his door shut.

"Beechwood," he said.

Crowds were sparse at the cemetery. The rush would come, Michael thought, after church let out. He carried the ashes and the knife to his mother's grave and knelt in the grass by her headstone. He sawed the top of the plastic box halfway off, then wrenched it open. The ashes were grainier than he had imagined them, not the smooth texture of the ones he'd carried out of his parents' fireplace for so many years. He shook them out into the grass, moving the box back and forth, as if he were pouring detergent. When the box was empty, he spread them with his hands until they disappeared.

He clapped his hands, then looked at the graphite-colored stain his father had left on his skin. "Oh, man," he said. "Oh man."

"Are you okay?" Denise asked.

"I keep hearing Bugs Bunny saying, 'Of course you realize, this means war.' She's never going to let me get away with this."

"You did get away with it," Denise said. "There's no way to put the ashes back in the box. They're gone. Your father would be proud of you."

Michael started to cry. Denise sat next to him and held him. He cried for a good long time while Denise stroked his head. When it was over he said, "Wow. That was weird."

In silence, Denise offered him a tissue from her purse.

"It's funny," Michael said. "Watching you with Rachid, I can see what it would have been like to have a real mother."

"Was it really that bad?"

"You don't know what you're missing when you're a kid, you don't know that other families are different than yours. Then by junior high, high school, it gets pretty obvious. She was always so awkward around me, like I was some kind of gross, foul-smelling animal that had gotten loose in her house. She didn't know how to touch me. She would try to go through the motions, but it made me wonder why she was doing it."

"What's going to happen to her now?"

"I don't know. I do feel sorry for her. She devoted her entire life to my father. Everything was always about him. That was another thing that used to make me crazy—she would always take his side over mine, even when he was clearly wrong. She's going to have to fill that hole with something. At least she's got all her friends in Dallas, and her bridge club."

"And you?" Denise asked. She looked down at her hands. "Will you be going back to Texas, too?"

"No," he said, carefully. "Not any time soon. I have a lot to do here."

"Aren't all your friends there?"

"They're all over the place. I spend way more time on the phone or writing email than I do face to face with anybody. I can do that just as well from here."

She raised her eyes again. "So what are all these things you have to do here?"

He took both her hands in his. "I want to be with you, for one thing."

"Okay, that's one."

"I want to find some more people who knew my mother. I would like to know who killed Barrett Howard. And..."

"And?"

The thought had just come to him. He saw from the first that he would not be able to resist it. "I want to go back to my grandfather's house. This time without the tour guide."

THAT AFTERNOON DENISE organized a picnic. She improvised a hamper from a cardboard box and packing tape and stuffed it with potato salad, slaw, fresh fruit, bread, and cheese. They lured Rachid out of the apartment with only token protest on his part and drove to Jordan Lake, a few miles south of Durham.

Michael appreciated the gesture, even if he could not get his whole heart into it. Denise didn't push him to feel more than he was able. Part of it was his father. Mostly it was the idea of going back to Johnston County, an idea that, as he'd anticipated, was not fading.

It was the single most dangerous thought Michael had ever had. Goading him on was the anger and humiliation he still felt from Greg Vaughan's bullying at the funeral. He knew he was not a physical match for Vaughan. He had an objective understanding that might and intimidation did not make right. Nonetheless it galled him to retreat from it. A certain defiance was required.

Beyond that, he was convinced that Wilmer Bynum's house was hiding secrets. Why else would Vaughan be preserving it like some kind of temple? The entire time he and Michael had been inside, Vaughan's nerves had been stretched tight.

Denise suggested an early night and Michael found that, as advertised, sex was made all the sweeter by the presence of death. After Denise fell asleep he lay on his back, and his thoughts circled again to the Bynum farm.

Vaughan was probably comfortable with the idea of killing trespassers. On the other hand, he might be reluctant to shoot up the Bynum house, or Bynum's own grandson. Michael was kin, and if there were secrets in the Bynum house, he had the right to know.

•

Monday, November 1

AT HIS HOTEL the next day, sitting at the breakfast bar with his drawing board, he could not make himself concentrate. He saw that he wouldn't sleep decently again until he either went through with it or gave up on the idea altogether. Giving up seemed the harder of the two.

After lunch he went to a Home Depot and bought a putty knife, window putty, latex gloves, a glass cutter, a flashlight, a utility knife, and a roll of white duct tape.

"Doing some breaking and entering?" the cashier asked.

"That's right," Michael said. "Watch for me on the news tomorrow." He hoped his smile looked more natural than it felt.

At Thrift World he bought a dark brown pillowcase to hold everything. Then he went to his hotel room and watched TV, unable to say afterwards what he'd seen.

He ate dinner with Denise and Rachid. After Rachid went off to do homework, Denise tried to talk Michael out of going, then retreated into a hurt and angry silence.

Michael decided to wait for midnight at his hotel. As he left, Denise said, "If you do this, I want you to call me as soon as you're away from there. And if you change your mind, call me too."

Michael nodded, realizing that he had turned his cell phone off after the funeral to avoid Ruth and never turned it on again. "It'll be late," he said.

"I'll be awake," she said, and closed the door on him.

HE GOT ON THE ROAD by 12:30. The car's heater couldn't take the chill out of his hands and feet. All the landmarks from his first trip had faded in the darkness, and once past West Smithfield it got increasingly hard to find his way. The Bynum house was on him before he knew it so he drove past for a couple of miles, then turned around and drove slowly back. He turned his lights off before he was in sight of the house and pulled well off the road into a patch of weeds and dried grass.

He closed the car door soundlessly and left it unlocked. He was wearing black jeans and a navy blue sweatshirt. No ski mask; he wanted Vaughan to recognize him if it came to that, rather than be shot as a burglar or, God forbid in rural North Carolina, a terrorist. He had the bag of tools in his left hand, which was now sweating.

Henry was the first obstacle. If he was wrong about the dog, it was all over before it began.

He'd barely entered the driveway when Henry started to bark. Michael stood still and waited, heart pounding. Hurry, he thought, get over here before you wake Vaughan.

The moon was past full, the skies clear, and Michael saw the huge Shepherd galloping across the field toward him in full cry, a bounding blur of gold and black. "Henry!" Michael said, a shouted whisper. Two hundred yards away, Vaughan's trailer was still dark. "Henry!" he said again, louder, suddenly afraid the dog could not hear anything over his own barking.

The dog was 50 feet away and closing fast. I'm going to die, Michael thought. Right here. He stood his ground and one last time said, "Henry! Heel!" And, remembering, snapped his fingers twice.

Henry threw on the brakes, his hindquarters sliding around on him as he backpedaled. By the time he stopped he was facing the other direction and needed only a few minor adjustments to end up in heel position on Michael's left side. He looked up at Michael and panted. Michael leaned over to scratch the dog's chest. "Good dog, Henry," he said. "Good dog."

A light went on in the trailer.

There was a ditch to the left of the driveway. Michael snapped his fingers once and said, "Henry. Go." Then he scrambled into the ditch and lay on his stomach with his face pressed into his tool bag.

The night was full of noises: wind in the dry leaves, crickets, the deeper chattering of frogs. Even so he heard the creak as the trailer door opened. Vaughan's voice called, "Henry? Henry, what are you doing?"

"Go," Michael whispered, and Henry ran toward the trailer.

Michael forced himself to lie still despite a sudden, overwhelming need to urinate. You were fine ten seconds ago, he told his bladder. You're bluffing.

"What have you got out there?" Vaughan said.

Henry barked, once.

Please, Michael thought. Please don't come look.

"That didn't sound like a rabbit bark. Were you chasing rabbits? Were you chasing rabbits, boy?" Vaughan's voice had gotten husky, nearly crossing the line into baby talk. Michael pictured him roughing up the dog's fur.

If he knew I was listening, Michael thought, he'd be humiliated. He'd kill me for sure.

"You want me to come see? Is that what you want?" Henry barked again. "You want me to come see what you've got?"

The voice sounded closer. It could be the wind, Michael told himself.

"Well, I don't want to see what you've got. I want to go back to sleep. Now you run along and be a good boy." Henry gave one final bark, a simple cry of joy from a being whose life was black and white, who had only to distinguish between friends, intruders, and food. Michael envied him.

The trailer door closed. Michael lay still as long as he could, which in fact was not long at all. He put the shed between himself and the trailer, hurried to the trees on the far side of the driveway, and let his bladder go. Tears of relief came up in his eyes.

He zipped up and turned back to the road, where Henry waited for him, tail wagging. Michael snapped his fingers twice, and Henry fell in step with him. "Traitor," Michael said. "You'd have given him my name and the license number of my car if you could talk."

He retrieved his bag of tools and approached the rear of the house. He had the thought that he could turn around and go to his car and be safe in bed at the hotel in an hour. He pushed the thought away.

He sat on the back stoop, dried his sweaty hands on his pants leg, and put on a pair of latex gloves. Then he fished around in the bag for the duct tape. Everything made too much noise: the clink of metal on concrete as he set down the bag; the ripping sound as he slowly peeled away a strip of tape. He wrapped the loop of tape around one hand, sticky side out, and cut it free from the roll. He stuck the loop to the glass pane nearest to the lock and pressed it firmly in place. Shielding the flashlight with his left hand, he looked at the glass. It was secured with quarter round and covered with multiple layers of paint, so plan A, where he scraped away putty and replaced it when he was through, bit the dust.

That left plan B, the glass cutter. He'd cut a lot of glass for frames at Pratt, and it didn't take him long to get the hang of it again. He cut out the entire pane, as close to the frame as he could. It took the longest five minutes of his life, and when he finally lifted the glass free, his nerves had terminally frazzled. He set the glass on his tool bag, reached through the hole, and had his gloved hand on the inner knob when his confidence failed.

Vaughan hadn't turned off an alarm when he let Michael into the house that day. Maybe he activated one at night? A few feet away, Henry scratched himself. No, Michael thought, there's his alarm.

He cranked back the deadbolt, twisted the button on the inner knob, and opened the door.

Silence.

He was sweating so hard his eyes stung from it. He cut another long strip of tape and cut it again lengthwise. With the two narrow pieces of tape he put the windowpane back in the frame. The tape was a reasonable match for the white paint on the door, at least by flashlight. Unless Vaughan looked closely, or had some reason for suspicion, it could pass for a while. He peeled off the other tape he'd been using for a handle and put it in his tool bag.

He made sure everything else was in the bag and then stepped into Wilmer Bynum's kitchen. Before he could close the door, Henry whined a complaint from the porch. "Don't embarrass me," Michael said as he let the dog inside. "I'm trusting you, here."

The house had few windows, so he felt safe enough taking a quick look around with the flashlight. In the dark again, he oriented himself by the greater darkness of the doorway that led to the dining room and made his way to the front hall and the stairway.

Henry followed in patient silence as he climbed the stairs. At the top landing he risked the flashlight again, masking the glow with his fingers. A hallway ran down the center of the second floor. The first door on the left led to what must have been Wilmer's room. It held a king-size bed, a big screen TV, and a dresser full of argyle socks, white boxers, and old-fashioned tank top T-shirts. Wife-beater shirts, a girlfriend of Michael's used to call them.

In the top drawer was a German Luger. Michael stared at it for a long minute. The temptation nearly overwhelmed him. What better antidote for his fear than a gun in his hand? Then his better judgment kicked in, and he made himself close the drawer and turn away.

The walk-in closet was full of clothes, the polyester pants and wide-collared dress shirts that so many old men ended up in. They smelled of detergent and the cedar that lined the walls. The shoes, neatly arrayed on the closet floor, reflected the glow of the flashlight.

He found Regina's room across the hall. Doilies and framed photos of Wilmer sat on top of an empty dresser; her closet held only cleaning supplies.

Next to the bedrooms were two gleaming tiled bathrooms, across the hall from each other, then two bedroom additions. Michael couldn't help but wonder which was the guest room where his father had spent his first night at the farm, where Ruth had come to him in the night and sealed the peculiar relationship that had, in the end, cost him everything.

Despite their haphazard exteriors, the bedrooms perfectly matched the rest of the house: hardwood floors, double-hung windows, crown molding all around. It was evidence of Wilmer Bynum's contempt for appearances and the surface of things. Given that Michael shared his genes, he was glad to find something in the man to admire.

Still, it was not the revelation he'd been hoping for. He'd found someone else's memories, lovingly and bizarrely enshrined, but no secrets. Every moment he stayed put him more at risk. He'd proven his point, shown his flag of bravery, and that was going to have to be enough.

He moved quickly down the stairs and through the dining room, Henry's nails clicking the hardwood beside him. He opened the back door and then stopped with his hand on the outside knob.

Why were all the cleaning supplies upstairs instead of in the kitchen?

He turned back, opened the pantry door, and leaked light past his fingers. No shelves, no brooms, no cans, no water heater. No dog food. The floor was an empty square, four feet on a side, set back into the wall of the kitchen. Henry sat and stared into the emptiness, tense and alert.

No, Michael thought, something is not right here.

At that moment he heard Vaughan's voice, faintly, outside. "Henry! Where you at, boy?"

The dog's ears went straight up and he bolted out the open back door. Michael, blinded by panic, fought the urge to follow. He didn't know where Vaughan was, didn't know if he could see the rear of the house. Instead he eased the door closed and turned the lock, putting it back the way it had been. Then he stepped into the pantry and shut the door.

Don't come into the house, he thought. Please do not come in this house.

He was sweating again. He pushed the stem of his watch to light the dial. It was 2:25. Fifteen minutes, he thought. If nothing happens by then, I'll try slipping out the back.

He lowered himself to a sitting position against the back wall. As he eased down, he put his left hand against the side wall for balance.

The wall moved.

At the same moment he heard Vaughan's voice on the front porch and the sound of a key in the lock. Vaughan was talking to the dog again, though Michael couldn't make out the words.

Michael risked the flashlight. There, at waist height, where the left hand wall met the door jamb, there was a button: white-on-white, virtually impossible to see from outside. Michael pushed it and felt the left wall of the closet open out into darkness. A damp, earthy smell hung in the cooler air there. Beyond the opening he saw stairs leading down.

Vaughan and the dog were now in the foyer. "What are you trying to tell me?" Vaughan said.

He wants you to meet his new best friend, Michael thought. So we can all play games together. He switched off the flashlight and choked up his grip on the pillowcase of tools to keep it from clinking. In absolute silence he got to his feet, slipped through the door, found a handle on the other side, and closed it behind him.

He felt his way down the stairs in darkness, and only when he got to the bottom did he try the light again.

"Holy shit," he whispered.

The room was wider and longer than the house above it, 100 feet by 80 or so. The suspended ceiling was low, barely eight feet from the green linoleum floor. The walls were cheap paneling for four feet, then white paint over sheetrock the rest of the way up. Chairs folded along one wall looked like they could seat a hundred people.

Across the front wall spread a gigantic rebel flag, 9 feet long and 6 feet high. On either side were banners emblazoned with the Celtic Cross and the logo of the Night Riders of the Confederacy. In one corner stood a seven-foot high, plain wooden cross; in the other a US flag—substantially smaller than the Confederate—drooped from a pole.

There was a six-inch high platform in front of the rebel flag, supporting an antique wooden lectern. In the corner by the US flag was a plain wooden door, locked with a deadbolt. Along the wall opposite the chairs stood two metal cabinets with triple padlocks. The cabinets smelled of machine oil and Michael involuntarily pictured the guns inside.

He felt physically ill. He wanted out of that room more than he could remember ever wanting anything before.

The desire was in inverse proportion, he knew, to his chances of getting away. Already Vaughan and Henry were standing at the closet door above.

Briefly he considered lying in wait where the stairs emptied into the room and trying to bash Vaughan over the head with one of the folding chairs. Even if he got away with it, Henry would certainly turn on him. It was a comic book idea, not worthy of him. Why hadn't he brought the gun from upstairs?

There were no alternatives, no hiding places, no dark corners, no emergency exits. Only...

The ceiling.

He held his flashlight in his mouth and put his tool bag on top of one of the cabinets. Both cabinets were bolted to the wall, solid as bedrock. He hooked one arm over the top and braced his foot against the molding of the half-paneled wall, struggling to keep from banging the hollow metal with his knees. Lying on his back, stretched across the two cabinets, he used both hands to push one of the acoustical tile squares upward and to the side.

There was room for him. Barely.

He put the bag of tools in first. He could hear Vaughan at the top of the stairs, working the latch of the inner door. "You think somebody's down here, boy? I think you're crazy. I think you've been eating loco weed again. That what you've been doing?"

Michael slithered into the space between the ceiling tiles and the heavy wooden joists that held the floor above.

He'd worked for a record store the summer after his freshman year at Pratt, and he'd had to go into the ceiling to hang displays. Like this one, it had been filthy with dust and insulation, crowded with ductwork. He'd learned to negotiate the metal framework that held the tiles, a framework like the one under him now, suspended from the joists above with strands of wire the thickness of coat hangers.

Sweat flowed into his eyes, turning his vision red. He blinked it away and shifted himself around, feeling blindly for the loose tile, lowering it into its frame just as the lights clicked on in the room below.

The effect was eerie, blades of light stabbing up around the edges of the tiles. It made Michael feel conspicuous. He switched off his own light and settled slowly into the most comfortable position he could find.

His chest heaved. He opened his mouth wide and felt the sweat rain off him. Even Vaughan is going to smell me at this rate, he thought.

Henry certainly did. Michael could hear him on the linoleum below as he trotted in circles around the room, whining.

"What is it, boy? What do you think is down here?"

Henry tried to answer, clearly frustrated at Vaughan's inability to understand, his voice modulating from whine to growl to bark.

"Henry!" Vaughan said, the dog quieted. "What are you looking up for?"

They were directly underneath where Michael knelt. This is it, he thought, and willed himself to not exist. Nobody here, he thought. There's nobody here.

"When we was upstairs, you wanted down. Now you want up again?"

Reacting to Vaughan's tone, Henry barked once in affirmation.

Good dog, Michael thought.

"That's it," Vaughan said. "I've lost enough sleep over you tonight. I'm going to bed."

MICHAEL STAYED in the ceiling, in darkness, for another thirty minutes. His sense of relief was so powerful that he drifted momentarily into sleep, waking disoriented and panicky.

Taking one step at a time, deathly afraid of making a mistake in his eagerness to be gone, he finally switched on the flashlight, worked the tile free, and lowered himself to the cabinet.

He was filthy, the dust and sweat having formed a thin layer of mud over his exposed skin. He cleaned his glasses as best he could, then took his sweatshirt off and used it to mop tile crumbs and footprints and dirt from the top of the cabinets. He swept the residue underneath, then put the shirt on and started for the stairs.

Something made him hesitate. Partly from curiosity, partly from fear that Vaughan might still be lurking upstairs, he swept the flashlight around the room. The linoleum was scuffed and worn, the wooden panels warped and faded, the ceiling tiles gray with age. This was not some recent addition that Vaughan had made; it had to date back to the fifties or earlier.

Next to the locked wooden door was a 2004 calendar, poster sized, with a marker pen hanging on a string. The first Wednesday of every month was circled. The meetings were still going on, then. The next one was in two days.

The only other date marked was November 6, the coming Saturday. There was a black X through the date. Some hated anniversary? Michael wondered. Not MLK's birthday; that was in January. The day the Supreme Court decided *Brown v. Board of Education*? Or something more sinister?

Whatever it was, Michael had to leave. He had begun to tremble all over. The tension was catching up to him, and he couldn't allow that to happen, not yet.

He climbed the stairs and let himself out of the pantry. The house was quiet. When he stepped out the back door, Henry was waiting for him, scampering back and forth with excitement. Henry barked again, and Michael jumped. "Henry, heel!" he whispered, and snapped his fingers twice. He turned the lock on the doorknob and pulled it closed. Then he knelt and rubbed the dog's chest fur. "You ratted me out, you bastard," he said. Henry licked Michael's face, untroubled by the dirt and sweat, eager for more adventure.

Together they walked to the end of the driveway. And it was there, as he stripped off the latex gloves, that Michael realized he'd left his bag of tools in the ceiling.

"Henry, sit," he said, with a finger snap. Henry sat. Michael looked back at the house and thought about doing it all over again, peeling the tape from the window and unlocking the door, climbing into the ceiling, cleaning up after himself. It wasn't worth it. What were the odds that Vaughan would ever find that bag? And what difference would it make if he did?

Michael took one step toward his car, then another, fighting the urge to run that might have made Henry chase him. Henry whined. Michael looked back, said "No," and kept walking.

When he got to the car he fumbled the keys, dropping them twice in the dirt before he remembered that the door wasn't locked. He got behind the wheel and turned the keys in the ignition, breathing the plastic-scented air, comforted by the quiet ping as the electrical system sprang to life and the engine turned over.

He pulled onto the narrow tarmac and coasted past the driveway, where Henry still waited with a forlorn expression, before switching on the lights. Then he found himself going too fast and had to take his foot off the gas.

The rearview mirror was clear. He put the windows down and sucked cold, clean air into his lungs.

At highway 70 he turned his cell phone on. The display announced seven new messages. He called Denise.

"Thank God," she said. She sounded weak with relief. "I almost called the police three times. Are you okay?"

"I'm fine," he said.

"Did you find what you were looking for? Was it worth putting me through this?"

"I think my grandfather used to host the Night Riders of the Confederacy in his basement. And now my cousin Vaughan is continuing the tradition." He told her what he'd seen.

"Oh my God. And you're sure he didn't see you?"

"I'm sure. If he'd seen me I wouldn't be here now."

"Michael, you have to walk away from this. The NRC is not some joke. They are still killing people and getting away with it. They've got members who are cops, politicians, business people. They're everywhere."

"I'm done," Michael said. "I'm telling Sgt. Bishop everything I know tomorrow, and that's it."

"Are you sure you can trust him?"

"Am I positive? No. But he's been straight with me so far. And I have to trust somebody."

They talked another 20 minutes, until Michael hit the Raleigh city limits, and then he had to hang up and pay attention to the road. By the time he got to his hotel he was beyond exhaustion. He passed out twice in the shower and was asleep within seconds of hitting the bed.

Tuesday, November 2

HE WOKE HARD at seven o'clock, thinking of the brown pillowcase of evidence he'd left behind. He spent half an hour telling himself that it made no difference, no one would ever find it, and if they did, nothing in it would identify Michael.

Gradually his breathing slowed, and he was on the verge of sleep again when he remembered the receipt. He'd taken everything from the plastic Home Depot bag and transferred it to the pillowcase, there outside the thrift store. Everything? The receipt would tell Vaughan where he'd bought it and when. It would lead Vaughan to the clerk, who would remember Michael because of the breaking and entering joke.

He sat up in bed. He'd thrown the plastic bag in a trash can outside the thrift store. If the receipt was in the bag, it meant it wasn't in the pillowcase. He tried to picture it in his head, a ribbon of white paper in the bottom of the bag as he crumpled it.

The memory wouldn't come.

He might have put it in his pocket. He got up and searched his khakis from the day before, then went through the filthy black jeans he'd worn to the Bynum farm.

Nothing.

He got dressed and went downstairs. No receipts in the rental car.

If they hadn't emptied the trash outside the thrift store, the bag might still be there. He drove to the Durham Freeway and took it north through downtown, noting absently that they'd finished work on the American Tobacco complex, with signs and lights and retail businesses in place. He caught a glimpse of fountains and green lawns between the rows of former warehouses.

Then he was exiting, curving south again to Lakewood. The stores in the center were still dark, meaning no one would be watching him. This seemed like a good thing, as Michael was operating on nerves and three hours sleep. He parked at the curb and got out onto stiff legs. The trash can lid was brown, with a V-shaped flap. Michael took it off and looked inside.

Empty.

At least, he thought, it saved me the indignity of standing here on the sidewalk, going through a couple of days' worth of garbage.

He stood for a while under overcast skies, listening to the breath move in and out of his body. This is ridiculous, he told himself. Get some sleep and you'll realize what an idiot you're being.

HE SLEPT RESTLESSLY until 2:30, then called Bishop's mobile.

"Michael," Bishop said. "I was sorry to hear about your father."

That caught him off guard. "How did you..."

"I saw it in the paper. I tried to call, but your cell phone was out of service."

"Thanks," Michael said. "I appreciate your thoughtfulness."

"Is your mother all right?"

"You're behind the curve, Detective. Have you got time for me to come over and fill you in?"

"If you come now, I can spare a few minutes."

The skies had cleared, and the temperature was near 80. It seemed crazy to have this kind of heat wave in November. Michael thought of Roger;

whenever the subject of global warming came up he would point out that bad kings always brought bad weather. "The time is out of joint," he would quote from Shakespeare. "O cursed spite, that ever I was born to set it right."

Roger was probably there in his voice mail, with Ruth and Bishop, yet another call he didn't want to take.

Bishop met him in the lobby, as before, and Michael began his story on the elevator. He talked about Mercy and his father, his birth, Mercy's suicide. He talked about the weapons in the Biltmore Hotel and the revolution that failed. For reasons he didn't entirely understand, he didn't mention Donald Harriman.

By that point they were seated in Bishop's office. "So you don't think anymore that your father was involved in Howard's death."

"No, except as an accomplice after that fact. I'm more convinced than ever that it was Randy Fogg. Who showed up at the funeral, by the way, to make a speech about the debt Durham owed my father for knocking Hayti down and burying Barrett Howard under the expressway."

"In those words?"

"He didn't mention Howard by name. And his contingent of NRC pals was there to cheer him on."

"Not in hoods, I hope."

"They might as well have been. Did you know that they meet at Wilmer Bynum's farmhouse, like they've been doing for years, the first Wednesday of every month?"

Though Bishop hadn't moved, his attention had snapped into focus. "How do you know that?"

"Can you prosecute me for what I say here?"

Bishop spoke carefully. "I won't talk to you off the record. I won't promise you immunity. But if you confess that you threw a candy wrapper on the street or ran a red light, I don't think the State is going to care."

"I broke into Wilmer Bynum's house." It was a relief to confess it. "There's a giant basement underneath that's a meeting hall. I've seen it with my own eyes."

"Did you take anything? Damage anything?"

"No. And it is my grandfather's house. That gives me some right to be there."

"I thought you said Ruth Bynum wasn't your birth mother."

"Wilmer Bynum was Mercy's father."

Bishop leaned back in his chair, the light glinting off his glasses. "All right, Michael, I'm impressed. You've obviously got some detective skills. Let me point a few things out to you. First of all, there is no law against being a member of the Night Riders of the Confederacy. There is, however, a law against illegal entry. Not only can I not keep you out of jail if you persist with this kind of crap, there's no guarantee that you won't get killed."

"There's more," Michael said.

"What do you mean?"

"They're planning something. An action or something. This Saturday."

"What kind of action?"

"I don't know. I saw it marked on a calendar."

"Maybe it was somebody's birthday."

"No. It's going to be something big. I think lives are at stake."

"This is what, a hunch?"

"Yes."

"Okay. I respect hunches. I wish you'd give me more to go on."

"What's happening Saturday? Someplace where there might be a lot of people."

"There's football. Duke's away at Florida State, UNC's playing Virginia Tech here. State's at home against Georgia Tech. There's no big concerts or special events. There's live music at the clubs, maybe a race angle there..."

Michael shook his head. "That's the kind of stuff that happens every week. I'm thinking something really unusual."

"I'll follow up on it," Bishop said. "I promise—if you'll give me your word you'll back off. I don't want to get called out to a crime scene and find your body."

Michael stood up. "Something's going to happen. I don't think you're taking me seriously enough."

Bishop got up too. "Believe me, I do not like the words 'I told you so.' It gets in the papers, people remember, the whole department ends up looking bad. I will pursue this. You have to understand that all I'm working with here is a date circled on a calendar."

"It wasn't a circle," Michael said. "It was a big, black X."

HE CALLED DENISE from his car, bypassing the alert for new voice messages.

"I'm working late tonight," she told him. "It's going to be leftovers and bed for me."

"You don't want company for the second half of that?"

"I can't tonight, baby. It's too crazy right now."

"Is this because of last night?"

"It's work, is all it is. I told you I'm really swamped."

"Okay."

"I'll call you before I go to sleep, okay? Just for a few minutes. Right now I got to run."

When he switched off the phone, Michael felt sick to his stomach. Maybe everything was all right with Denise, he told himself. If he started a list of all the reasons he had to feel bad, he could go on forever. Lack of sleep, stress, his father's death, *Luna* pages overdue, hiding out from Ruth and Roger, on and on.

He started the car, drove to the Durham Freeway, and merged with the scant traffic. As he topped the hill overlooking downtown, it all clicked in his head.

He didn't trust himself to drive and talk at the same time. He pulled into the breakdown lane and called Denise again.

"Denise Franklin."

"It's me."

"Michael, I'm serious, I don't have time for this now."

"This is important. That opening at American Tobacco, that's what you're having to work late on, right?"

"Yes, that's what I—"

"When is it? When does it happen?"

"Didn't I tell you?"

"I don't think you did."

"This Saturday. November sixth."

HE CALLED Bishop again.

"Michael, I thought we had an understanding—"

It seemed like no one wanted to talk to him. "I know where it's going to be," Michael said. "The American Tobacco complex is opening this weekend. They're billing themselves as the fulfillment of the Hayti dream. It's run by a black-owned consortium. This is it. I know it."

"Christ, I'd forgotten about that. Yeah, that makes sense. Do you have any hard information to back this up? Or is it more of the same hunch?"

"It feels right. You said so yourself."

"All right. I'll get some extra people on it. And you're done now, correct?"

"What else is there for me to do?"

"You tell me."

"Nothing."

"Good answer."

"I'm done," Michael said. "I'm going back to my hotel and draw comics."

HE MADE an honest effort. He ate a lonely meal at Fortune Garden and returned to the stack of overdue script pages that sat on the dresser, accusing him.

He got into bed with his drawing board and script. The next scene had

Louann writing in her journal with an architect's lead holder. There was a long explanation about how her suspected father had gone to a technical college and learned drafting there, how he'd taught her to use a lead pointer at an early age, and now the mere thought of it had her on the edge of tears.

Michael had somehow missed this when he'd made his first quick pass through the script. Roger's loyal fans, he was sure, would choke up as they read it. For Michael it was like he'd seen the pulleys and wires at the magic show. Or, he thought, more like feeling empathy for the cow being slaughtered to make his hamburger. It took his appetite clean away.

He didn't remember telling Roger about his father and the lead holders, though obviously he had. Beyond Michael's personal sense of violation was something more objective and disturbing, the way Roger had labored so mightily to bring in this irrelevant moment of purloined sentiment.

Michael had brought a complete run of the series with him for reference. He took out the first issue and found, with some relief, that it still read well. By the third issue, though, the plot had started to meander, and by issue seven Roger was coasting.

He put the comics in a neat stack and set them on the breakfast bar. Then he sat up in bed and stared glassy-eyed at the wall in front of him. How much could somebody lose and not fall apart? The mother he had never known was dead. His father, whom he'd only started to know, was dead. His relationship with Denise had turned uncertain. And now the thought that would have been completely unthinkable a week before was right there in front of him.

Quitting *Luna*.

Just finish this page, he told himself. Maybe momentum will take over. No matter how hard he willed it, his hand refused to pick up the blue pencil. Instead it reached into his pocket and took out his cell phone. As soon as he switched it on, it began to ring, flashing the ID "Roger cell."

"Hello, Roger," Michael said.

"Where have you been? I've been calling for days."

"Something came up."

"We need to talk, yeah?"

"Yes, we do."

"Helen and I had some lengthy discussions—"

"Is that what you guys call it?"

"Michael, you don't sound yourself. Are you ill?"

"Oh, let's not be so concerned about me all the time. What did you guys talk about?"

"Now, it's not like there aren't extenuating circumstances, and God knows no one is blaming you. We're only concerned about number 25."

"And here I was thinking you were only concerned about number one." Michael felt giddy. It wasn't every day you got to throw away the only thing you had left.

"Have you been drinking?"

"You know better than that."

"Can we be serious for a moment, then? You haven't by any chance finished the book, have you?"

"No. You've got everything I've done."

"Twelve pages, then. Half."

"That's right."

"Helen wants to bring a fill-in artist on board. Just until you're back on your feet."

Michael stood up. "I'm on my feet now."

"Michael, you're making this extraordinarily difficult. It's hard enough as it is."

"Oh, sorry, there I was being selfish again. So who is she talking about?"

"Sean Phillips has offered to pitch in. He's got a similar style to yours, not quite as good, maybe, but still a first-rate—"

"So she's already set it up."

"Well, merely on a contingency basis—"

"I'm going to make this very easy for you, Roger. You can't fire me, I quit."

"Michael, don't be absurd. We'd only use him for an issue or two. You're crucial to the book and as soon as you're ready—"

"You'd go right back to using me. I guess I'm feeling used up at the moment."

"Michael, what is all this?"

"Among other things, I don't like you stealing my life and putting it in *Luna*."

Roger's annoyance finally broke through. "D'you think you're the only one with paternity issues? D'you think this isn't personal for me? You should try being on the other side of the equation sometime."

"What? What are you talking about?"

"Nothing. Forget I said anything."

"You're talking about Helen's daughter, aren't you? You're her father. Jesus. Does her husband know?"

"Michael, I've never told this to anyone before. I hope you appreciate the amount of trust I'm showing in you." That was Roger all over, Michael thought, always telling you how you were supposed to react.

"So after everything that's happened to me," Michael said, "you're going to torture that little girl with the same lies and doubts and confusions that I went through?"

"It's not that simple," Roger said.

"Yes it is," Michael said. "It's very simple. I don't think I like you anymore, Roger. And I don't want to work for somebody I don't like and don't respect."

After a silence, Roger said, "I'm sorry you feel that way."

"Yeah," Michael said. "Me too."

He switched off the phone, packed the script and Bristol board, and washed out his brushes and lettering pens. It took 40 minutes.

When he was done, the room seemed oppressive. He got in the car with no destination in mind, ending up drawn to the gravitational pull of the Durham Freeway. He got off on Fayetteville Street and parked in the Hayti Heritage Center lot, next to Denise's car, and walked across the overpass and down to the freeway. The city had patched the retaining wall where Barrett Howard's body had been, and the new concrete was a light gray against the existing dark beige.

Michael sat on the grassy slope and watched the sun ease below the horizon. At one point a cop car slowed to look at him. Michael ignored it, and it drove on.

Around 6:30 he saw Denise walking across the overpass, headed toward him. He loved to watch her move. Beneath the grace and sensuality was a New Yorker's swagger. She sidestepped down the slope and sat next to him.

After a few seconds Michael said, "I just quit *Luna*."

Denise slipped under his left arm and held him. "Because of Roger?"

Michael nodded.

"You're too good for him," Denise said. "I'm glad you finally figured that out."

"It's so hard. I helped create all those characters. I'm the one that brought them to life. It's like walking out on your family." He thought that over. "I guess that's what it would be like, if I'd ever had a family."

"I expect there'll be a feeding frenzy once word gets out that you're available."

"Maybe. I wouldn't put it past Roger to badmouth me around the industry. And I don't want to go draw superheroes anymore. I want something more ... real."

Denise didn't try to cheer him up, for which he was grateful. They sat in silence for a while, then Michael said, "What's going on with us?"

"I don't know. I went out to the parking lot, on my way to get something to eat, and when I saw your car there, I felt this ... pressure."

"Uh oh."

"I really like being with you. You're smart and talented and you've got a wonderful heart. And you're a sweet and patient lover."

"But...?"

"But Rachid and I have been on our own for so long that this is all very strange to me. Sometimes I feel like you need more from me than I've got to give."

"Do you want to break up with me?"

"No." She sighed. "I don't *want* to. I get these compulsions to run away sometimes."

"Don't listen. Your compulsions don't know what's good for you."

She squeezed him tightly for a few seconds, then let go. "I have to get back to work."

"You didn't get anything to eat."

"It doesn't matter." She got slowly to her feet. "Charles is working late too, I can send him out for something." He felt jealousy as a physical pain, then, like a stitch from running too hard. It eased when she raked her fingernails through his hair in the way that he loved.

"Denise?"

"What, sugar?"

He shook his head, unable to find words.

"It'll be all right," she said. "This too shall pass."

"That's what I'm afraid of," he said.

"I'll call you before bed if I can."

He watched her walk away, and once she was gone he felt the evening chill for the first time.

THEY WERE WAITING for him in the parking lot. There were four of them, and they carried the shadows with them when they stepped into the light. They wore sweat clothes with the hoods up, in anonymous gray and navy and black.

He was still ten feet from his car when they moved into a loose circle around him. "Say, man," said the one to his left. "You got a smoke?"

"Sorry," Michael said, his voice dry with sudden fear. All four were black, all over six feet tall. The one who'd spoken carried a 16-ounce plastic bottle of Coke; otherwise their hands were empty. Not that they needed anything more than their hands.

Michael nodded and smiled and made as if to push his way past the man in front of him. The man didn't give way. Instead he stared at Michael and said, "Yo, wait up a second."

Michael couldn't see inside the hoods, nothing beyond a broad nose, the flash of a gold crown.

"We just want to talk to you for a minute," the first man said.

If I start yelling, Michael thought, this will go to the next level, whatever that might be. Escalation didn't seem smart.

"So what do you want to talk about?" he asked, failing to make his voice sound relaxed.

"What you doing in this part of town?" the first man said.

Michael went with the first idea that came into his head. "My girlfriend works here."

"His *girl*friend," the third man said, from behind Michael's back.

"Your girlfriend black?" the second man said. He seemed genuinely surprised. "You trying to change your luck or something?"

"I'm black too," Michael said. "My mother was black." Just like you, he wanted to say. Only he wasn't black the way they were. Denise was right. He never would be.

"Don't look black to me," the second man said.

"Come on," the third man said. He sounded nervous. "Let's get on with it."

"Look white to me," the second man said.

"My grandmother was black," Michael said, feebly.

"Motherfucker," the first man said, "we *know* who you are."

The words chilled him. This wasn't robbery or casual sport. Now or never, he thought, and he tried to dodge between the two men in front of him. The second man gave way, and for an instant Michael thought everything might turn out all right. Then the first man swung him around by the shoulder and hit him in the stomach.

It was a serious punch, and though Michael tried to fall away from it, still it took him to his knees. His lungs emptied and refused to fill again, and his vision narrowed to a two-foot radius directly in front of him. Then somebody shoved him from behind, and he went face down into the asphalt, scraping his chin, nearly smashing his glasses.

"Hold him," said the first man, and Michael made it onto all fours from sheer panic before two of them caught his shoulders and pushed him to the ground.

"Help!" Michael shouted. A passing truck covered his voice.

The first man knelt next to him and grabbed him by the hair. "You yell again and I smash your face into that curb over there, knock every tooth out your stupid head. You be still, this be over with in a second." He let go and stood up. "Get his legs."

The fourth man lifted Michael by his ankles. When he felt the hands go around his waist and start to unbuckle his belt, Michael tried to thrash and kick himself free. His arms were coming out of their sockets, and the first man kicked him in the ribs, hard enough to make everything go gray again. Stunned, he felt his pants and underwear slide down his legs.

"Damn, man, your asshole stinks." Michael no longer knew which voice was which. "Don't you wipe yourself?"

"Probably shit hisself."

"Shut up and give me that. And hold him tight."

In spite of the roaring panic in his ears, partly claustrophobia and partly the more conscious fear of rape, he did register a strange, liquid noise above and behind him. Then he felt a hand parting the cheeks of his bare ass.

He began to scream. It was not a high-pitched, horror movie scream, but something low and ragged from deep in his guts. Then a fist hit him in the side of the head, right over the metal stem of his glasses, and the pain was so intense that he stopped struggling and lay passively as something wet and burning exploded across his rectum.

Then the pressure was gone and the men were laughing, slapping each others' hands, from the sound of it. Still he lay on the asphalt, meaning to get up, unable to remember the muscle sequence required to do it.

Part of his mind still functioned, analyzing what he'd felt, thinking, hoping, that it hadn't been an ejaculation—there had been too much liquid at once, no penetration, only the sudden heavy spray.

The first voice said, "Time to go back to Texas. You understand what I'm saying?"

"I don't think he hear you," another voice said.

"Nod your head if you hear me, so I don't have to hurt you again."

Michael found that he could nod.

"See, he hear me all right. You go back to Texas, there be no more trouble."

The voices, still laughing, moved away. When he could no longer hear them, Michael rolled onto his side. He reached between his legs, and his hand came away covered with thin, sticky brown fluid. He sniffed at it. Coca-Cola. The empty plastic bottle lay a few feet away.

For a second he was giddy with relief, then he began to feel the pain—in his raw chin, in his ribs and stomach, in his temple, in the sockets of his arms. He pulled up his pants and looked around to see if there had been any witnesses. The streets were empty. He saw Denise's car, thought of her sitting inside a few feet away while they worked him over, and the image was so humiliating that he had to push it away.

He got in his car and locked the doors and started the engine. Then, as he was backing out, he saw a movement in the darkened upstairs gallery of the Heritage Center. Too tall for Denise. What was his name?

Charles. How naïve he'd been to let Charles see the drawing of the tattoo. No wonder he jumped when he saw it. He probably had one himself.

He drove to the hotel with both hands on the wheel, eyes on the road, thoughts churning. He felt one leg already stiffening as he climbed the stairs.

With the door double locked, he emptied his pockets, took off his belt, and stuffed his torn trousers in the kitchen trash. He put his underwear in after them, then his T-shirt and socks as well.

He started the hot water running in the bathroom and did a quick assessment in the mirror. There was a patch of dried blood the size of a shirt button on the point of his chin that burned without his touching it. His lower lip was split in the middle. His left temple looked bigger than the right, and bruises were already showing dark pink on his left ribs and abdomen. Both knees were scraped, the right worse, neither bleeding badly.

He showered for half an hour, washing his crotch repeatedly, shampooing twice, mostly letting hot water beat down on his neck and shoulders. When he got out he treated the scrapes with peroxide and Betadine and put band-aids on his knees. He took three aspirin and held a baggie of ice against his temple. I can take care of myself, he thought. The way I always have.

He called Southwest Airlines and converted his open return ticket to Austin into a reservation for 12:55 the next afternoon. Then he turned off his cell phone and unplugged the room phone in case Denise should call. He put on a clean pair of drawstring pajama bottoms and got into bed and turned out the lights. After a minute he got up and turned the bathroom light on and left the bathroom door open wide enough that he could see into all the corners of the room.

Only then did he begin to shake.

Wednesday, November 3

HE SLEPT, EVENTUALLY. His nightmares were not explicitly about the assault. He was trapped in the back seat of a driverless car rolling downhill. Later, he needed to get to an urgent destination and found himself in turn on a bicycle, a scooter, on foot, eventually crawling on his belly.

He was packed and ready by nine o'clock. He drove to the airport and turned in the car and checked his bags, then sat at the gate and pretended to read *Rolling Stone*. He had to hold his right knee out straight, and he wore sunglasses to hide the blackening at the outside of his left eye. He'd been unable to shave. His ribs, though he was reasonably sure they were only bruised, hurt every time he breathed.

This too shall pass, Denise had said.

Eventually they called his flight. He was in the first boarding group. To his surprise he failed to get in line. The second and third groups boarded, then the standby passengers. When Southwest paged him, he didn't respond. The flight seemed to have nothing to do with him. When they closed the door to the jetway, it was 1:05.

At the main counter he arranged for his luggage to be flown back to RDU. He was a veteran of lost luggage and canceled flights and so had two days' worth of clothes in his carry-on. The woman was not sure if she would be able to refund his ticket. He told her it didn't matter. She asked him twice if he felt all right.

The rental agency gave him the same silver Echo, newly vacuumed and scented. Michael sat in the lot and turned on his cell phone. The voice mail alert flashed at him. He called Donald Harriman's cell and got Harriman himself.

"Surprised to hear from me?" Michael asked.

"I'm sorry?"

"Surprised I'm still in town? And not on a plane to Texas?"

"I'm afraid I don't know what you're talking about."

"Where are you?" Michael asked.

"I'm walking home from campus. I intend to have a late lunch and grade some papers."

"Why don't you give me your address and I'll meet you there?"

"As I said, I have papers to grade, and this afternoon is not really convenient—"

"I think you'd rather talk to me alone than talk to me and the cops, but it's your choice."

"What do the police have to do with it?"

Michael heard the nerves in Harriman's voice. "Four men attacked me last night. I got a chance to pull one of their sleeves back, and I saw your tattoo." As bluffs went, it felt like a good risk. "What do you call it, the Four Moments of the Sun? So I think your group, which supposedly has no name, is still going strong. And Charles at the Hayti Heritage Center is a member, as are you. I don't think it would be hard to prove once somebody knew where to look."

"What do you want?"

"Information. And I've got some to trade."

THE ADDRESS HARRIMAN gave him was across the street from the UNC campus, off a labyrinth of narrow lanes that were more like alleys. Michael parked behind a maroon BMW that was either new or maintained at considerable expense. The house itself was a sprawling one-story ranch in tasteful gray brick. He rang the bell, and a moment later Harriman let him in.

The marble-tiled foyer opened into a dining room with a cathedral ceiling that carried through the living room beyond. There was a lot of low mahogany furniture, with cushions covered in rough fabric of black, gold, and green. The far wall was mostly glass and looked out on birds, exotic landscaping, and a fountain.

"Do you want a drink?" Harriman asked.

"I'd like to sit down. I hurt in a lot of places."

Michael took an armchair that faced Harriman's massive green leather re-cliner. As he sat, Harriman said, "I had nothing to do with the attack on you."

"The rest of it's true. Your group is still active, and you're still part of it." He watched Harriman's reaction, then he said, "Even if you didn't have anything to do with the attack, you knew about it, didn't you?" Again, no denials. "So, was it Charles's idea?"

"I'm not going to admit to anything. What deal did you want to propose?"

"The NRC is planning something big, probably violent. I know when and where. I went to the cops with it, but I don't know that they're willing to do what it takes to stop it. As they like to point out, the NRC is a perfectly legal organization."

"And why do you care so much what the NRC does?"

"Because my mother was black. Because my grandfather was part of the NRC and I want to make up for that somehow. Because I know something bad is going to happen and I can't just stand by and watch."

"And what do you want in exchange?"

"I want your cooperation. Not just yours, I want your entire group to help me. And no more bullshit like last night."

"Help you how?"

"Help me get answers to my questions. About my mother, about Barrett Howard."

"And if I say no, you call the police. And because we're a black organization, we won't get the same protection the NRC gets."

"That's right. These days they might even call you terrorists. You could wind up in Guantanamo."

Harriman looked out the window, pondering. Michael was impressed with the man's control over his emotions. Michael himself was ready to fall apart at a moment's notice, to start smashing furniture or curl into a fetal ball in the middle of the floor.

"I won't make you any guarantees," Harriman said at last. "As you implied, there is something of a power struggle taking place at the moment. Charles, and the younger members, against myself and the old guard. Charles sees no point in vodou unless he can use it directly as a weapon. I think perhaps he's seen too many cheap horror films. Whereas myself and some of the older members respect the discipline and understand that it provides a vital adhesive that binds us more than our shared goals or heritage."

"I think Charles would welcome a confrontation with the NRC."

"No doubt. Tell me what you know."

Michael told him, in detail, about the secret room under Wilmer Bynum's house, the date on the calendar, the opening of the American Tobacco Campus.

"That's the only evidence you have? An X through a date on a calendar? I can see why the police were not impressed."

"It all fits. The Black Star Corporation is billing itself—"

"Yes, I know. Hayti rises again. The NRC would love to make it fall all over again. I don't doubt you. And I don't doubt that Charles would, as you say, welcome a confrontation. It would help if we knew what they're planning. Maybe it's not a demonstration. Maybe it's something more ... explosive. Like in Oklahoma City."

"Can you find out? Don't you have people in high places? Like in the cops?"

"We might. We'll look into it. Now what's your end of the bargain?"

"If my father had a last wish, it was that Randy Fogg go down for killing Barrett Howard. I want enough proof to put him in jail."

Harriman shook his head. "We'd like nothing better than to prove the same thing. We have no love for Randy Fogg. Unfortunately, there's no evidence to tie him to the murder. He was in Washington when it happened, with dozens of witnesses. Believe me, we checked. And there's no way to prove he ordered it."

"Prove the NRC did the killing and that he was Grand Poobah of the NRC."

"Dragon. They use many of the same titles as the Klan, but without all that precious K-L nonsense—klaverns and klockards and such. We've tried for thirty years to prove Fogg was Grand Dragon of the NRC and never succeeded."

Michael said, "We know he and Wilmer Bynum were practically blood brothers, and Bynum was hosting his NRC meetings for him."

"You've made a long chain of suppositions and provided no facts."

"I want to see what the Durham police got from Barrett Howard's autopsy. I want to see the whole file on Howard. I'm the one that brought Tommy Coleman in. They would never have found that body if not for me. I'm entitled."

"You expect me to smuggle you into police headquarters and get you a few hours alone with Barrett's file? You can't be serious."

"You must have somebody in the department. I want them to make a copy of the file."

Harriman's eyes shifted as Michael watched. Michael leaned forward, ignoring the pain in his ribs. "You already have a copy, don't you?"

Harriman looked away.

"Where is it? You have it here, don't you?"

Harriman sighed. "If I show you the file, will that satisfy you? Will you then go away and let us handle this?"

"No," Michael said. "In the last few days I've lost everything. My father, the woman I thought was my mother, my girlfriend, my job. There's nothing left. I want to be part of this. I *am* part of this." He stopped and took a breath. "But we can start with the file."

HARRIMAN'S STUDY was expensively and impersonally furnished, like a high-dollar law office. A dark rolltop desk held a green blotter and a banker's light. A swivel chair in matching wood sat on a forest green Persian rug that ran to the baseboards in all directions. Small African carvings and masks filled in the spaces in a floor to ceiling built-in bookshelf.

Opposite the shelves stood a brass-handled combination safe the size of a refrigerator.

"I must ask you to wait in the hall while I get the file out," Harriman said.

"What have you got in there, guns?" Michael had intended it as a joke, but Harriman's scowl told him he'd guessed correctly.

"I must insist," Harriman said, and Michael backed out as Harriman closed and locked the study door. Through the door Michael heard the sounds of tumblers and handles and the sigh of the opening safe. When Harriman let him in again, the safe was locked, and a plain manila folder lay open on the desk.

Rather than the chaotic pile of odd size papers he'd reflexively pictured, it consisted of a tidy stack of 8 1/2 × 11 photocopies.

It opened with an incident report by Sgt. Bishop, followed by transcriptions of his interviews with Tommy and Michael. Tommy's interview held no surprises, though Michael couldn't help noticing the haste and errors in the transcription.

Reports followed on the excavation of the corpse and the attempted bombing. He paged through expense reports for the ground-penetrating radar, the jackhammers, the food and beverages consumed by the student workers. Another report summarized 1960s newspaper stories by and about Barrett Howard from the *Carolina Times,* followed by pages of barely legible printouts from a microfiche reader. Michael had heard about the asphyxiating quantity of reports involved in police work, and this was worse than he'd imagined.

He skipped forward to the autopsy. The State Medical Examiner, who worked out of the UNC Medical Center in Chapel Hill, had handled the case personally.

The report ran to 11 pages of word-processed text. Page one summarized the contents, listing the probable cause of death as a "single sharp force injury" to the chest, penetrating the heart.

Most of the rest of the report followed the course of the autopsy, step by step, with a detailed description of the mummified remains, what was left of Howard's clothing, his injuries, and the lack of toxicology results due to the dehydration of the body. After 30 years the internal organs were barely recognizable and could not be weighed.

Essentially what remained was dried skin shrunken down over a skeleton. However, the mummification had preserved a remarkable amount of detail beyond what would have been found in a body that had been buried in the ground for the same period. For example, a skin defect was visible on the back of the head, with an underlying skull fracture. The indications were consistent with blunt-force trauma from an object such as a bottle.

A stab wound in the chest pointed to bony injuries in the rib cage. A sharp instrument appeared to have penetrated the ribs in an area over the heart. The location and angle of the blow was likely to be fatal. No indications of post mortem lividity survived.

Through a happy accident, the ME happened to have a copy of *Paleopathology in Peruvian Mummies* on his shelves, and he'd used the rehydration techniques in the book to restore several skin samples. A photograph showed the Four Moments of the Sun tattoo, the skin remarkably smooth and the pattern clear; the harsh lights of the autopsy room and the high contrast of the photocopy had bleached Howard's skin to a pale gray.

A second photo showed the deformation in the skull from the blunt trauma, and a third showed the patch of rehydrated skin that included the stab wound. The skin wound did not show much detail, but a fourth photograph showed the impression of the sharp force instrument as it nicked a rib in passing. It looked like the planet Saturn in profile—circular, with a fine cut extending slightly to each side.

The incidental findings on the last page of the report identified small particles of leather clinging to Howard's clothes.

The next document transcribed an interview between Sgt. Frank Bishop and the ME where Bishop had pressed for more detail on the murder weapon.

"Given the extraordinary conditions," the ME said, "and the fact that the date of death was over thirty years ago, we can't do much more than make a few wild guesses."

Bishop had asked him to do so.

"The findings are contradictory. The weapon could have been an ice pick, or it could have been an extremely thin-bladed knife. Frankly, it looks a bit like both."

Michael stood up.

"What is it?" Harriman said.

Despite the pain in his body, Michael felt like dancing. The sensation was so delicious that for a moment he didn't want to share it.

At last he said, "I know what the murder weapon is. I've seen it with my own eyes."

"Go on."

Michael poked the file with his index finger. "It's a shoemaker's awl. That's why the leather particles. Some of the NRC thugs lured Howard into an abandoned shoe repair shop in Hayti and hit him over the head. Then they brought him out to my grandfather's farm, along with a cobbler's awl they found in the shop. And my grandfather killed him, and then he had the nerve to go and put the awl in a trophy case in his living room where he could look at it for the rest of his life, whenever there was a time out in the Duke basketball game.

"Then he called his best pal Randy Fogg to tell him the good news, and Fogg pulled Mitch Antree's strings. The thugs put the body in the form, and Antree buried it in concrete."

Harriman frowned. "You say the awl is still in the house?"

"It was two weeks ago, when my cousin Greg showed it to me."

"Greg Vaughan?"

"You know him?"

"He's on one of our lists somewhere. Was he involved in the murder?"

"No. He was in California, in basic training, about to ship out for Vietnam. Look, I have to call Sgt. Bishop and tell him." He pulled his phone out and was switching it on when Harriman grabbed his wrist.

"Wait," Harriman said.

Michael looked at him.

"How are you going to explain having seen the autopsy report?"

"It doesn't matter. I saw it, that's all."

"It does matter. Bishop isn't stupid. He'll know there's a leak in the department, and it won't be that hard for him to figure out who it is."

"What are you saying?"

"I'm asking you to wait. Wilmer Bynum has been dead a long time, and Barrett even longer. You don't need to close the case tonight. You said you wanted to be part of this group. Is that still true?"

Michael thought about it. Solving Barrett Howard's murder was well and good, but the threat against American Tobacco was immediate. "Yes," he said.

"Then you have to place the needs of the group ahead of your own. Are you willing to do that?"

"What are you asking?"

"We do have, as you suggested, people in high places. We will see to it that

Barrett gets whatever justice he can at this late date. I assure you that I have a personal interest in seeing that done, perhaps greater than yours. As for American Tobacco, we have been training and disciplining ourselves for many years to be ready for a major confrontation. If this is it, we will be there, and we will know what to do."

"And you want me to stay out of it."

"If you're serious about joining us, then your day will come. But not yet."

"In other words, I should go back to Texas."

"I don't agree with the way that message was delivered. And you don't need to go as far as Texas. But I would advise you to stay well clear of the American Tobacco Campus on Saturday."

Michael turned toward the door.

"Michael," Harriman said.

Michael stopped, his back still to Harriman.

"We owe you an enormous debt of gratitude. First for bringing Barrett's murder to light, and for everything you discovered about the circumstances. And for the warning about American Tobacco. Please know that."

Michael nodded, once, and let himself out.

As HE GOT IN his car, his emotions were upending themselves. Beyond his disappointment was a sense of relief, a readiness to go back to picking up the pieces of his life and career. Beyond that was something darker, a sense that he had forgotten something, as if he'd left home with the stove on. Nothing he tried to match against the feeling seemed to fit—the unanswered calls from Denise on his cell phone, the unresolved situation with Ruth, his need to find work. The very attempt to figure it out depressed him.

He picked a new hotel, a Holiday Inn Express on Miami Boulevard. It was a few miles east of his previous location, equally close to the Durham Freeway. This was a tall brown building so new that Michael thought he might be the first to stay in his room.

He unpacked his shaving kit and change of clothes and eased his aching body onto the bed, trying to remember his Aunt Esther's married name, which he'd read out of Ruth's address book a few days before. Not Peterson but Pedersen, with a D and Es all around.

Information found a listing in Richmond. Michael dialed it and immediately recognized the voice that answered—feminine, but harsh and low. "It's your nephew Michael again," he said.

After a long pause, Esther said, "Michael, I wasn't expecting to hear from you again so soon." The tone had softened, and at the same time grown wary. "It's not Ruth, is it?"

"Ruth is fine as far as I know. She's gone back to Dallas. I need to ask you some questions, for my own piece of mind."

"Oh dear. What sort of questions?"

"It's about your father."

Esther sighed. "When Jack got transferred to Virginia, I almost didn't come with him. I was afraid of being as close as a day's drive from the farm. I knew that some day it was going to come back to haunt me." Unlike Ruth, Esther had shed every trace of her Johnston County accent.

"Did the Night Riders of the Confederacy meet in your basement?"

"Yes," she said. "Once a month, unless they had to go burn a cross or an innocent man's house down somewhere. From the time I was old enough to know what was going on until I was old enough to leave."

"Was Congressman Randy Fogg head of the NRC?"

"Randy Fogg?" She sounded amused. "Wherever did you get that idea?"

"Fogg is a racist, he was close to your father, he had virtually the same agenda as the NRC—"

"Fogg is a completely political monster. He knew better than to associate himself with the Riders. It was too risky, and Fogg never took a risk, never showed an ounce of courage in his life."

For a moment Michael was confounded. Finally he said, "If Fogg wasn't the Grand Dragon, then who was?"

"You really don't know? You knew about the basement and you don't know that?"

"No," Michael said. "Please tell me."

"My father was. Your grandfather. For forty years."

"Did everyone know it?"

"All the other Riders knew it, as you would expect. Unlike the Klan, however, the Riders never went out in public without their hoods. One of the catchphrases that they bandied around to intimidate people was, 'We could be anyone.' Anyone white, that is."

"And you're sure about Fogg? He wasn't in the background somewhere pulling strings?"

"It was Fogg's strings getting pulled. My father practically had to call him in the morning and tell him to wake up. The heart went right out of Fogg when my father died. I guess 'heart' is not the word. The clarity. The clarity of his intentions. He's been like one of those radio controlled cars with nobody driving it ever since. Bumping into the furniture, spinning his wheels. People are only afraid of him now by force of habit."

"Did you hate your father that much?"

"Words cannot convey the depth of it."

"Because of the NRC?"

"That, and so much more."

"Tell me."

"No." Her voice was flat, final.

"I beg your pardon?"

"There are things that I have never talked about, and never will. I don't expect I have all that many years left, and I plan to exit with my last few shreds of privacy intact. This conversation has been more painful for me than you can possibly know, and now I'm going to have to say goodbye."

"One more question, please. A simple yes or no."

"Go ahead."

"Did your father kill Barrett Howard?"

"Who?"

"He was a black activist in Durham in the 1960s."

"That would have been after my time. As far as I know, my father never killed anyone with his own hands. But I would not have put it past him."

"And there's nothing more you're willing to tell me?"

"If you want to know more, ask your mother."

Michael played his last card. "Ruth is not my mother."

"Ah."

"You don't sound surprised."

"She was not supposed to be able to have children. I always wondered how it happened that she did."

"You never had any children yourself."

"No. Nor did Naomi. We didn't have the examples of child-rearing that would incline someone to try for themselves."

"But Ruth did want kids. And she didn't hate her father."

"Each of us deals with what life throws us as best we're able. I wish you luck, Michael, with whatever it is you're searching for. I would be happy to hear from you again if the subject matter were different."

"I'm sorry this hurt you, Aunt Esther."

"I expect I'll survive." She paused, then said, "Talk to Ruth."

THE TV FAILED to hold his attention. He got a sketchpad out of his bag and let his subconscious dictate a few faces at random. Wilmer Bynum, Randy Fogg, his father. The desire came to draw Denise, and he pushed it away. Finally he found himself sketching a face that he could not at first put a name to. Then he remembered the hospital cafeteria and her story of living across the street from Mercy. He'd scrawled her name across an earlier page of the book: Camilla Prentiss.

He turned to a new page and let her face completely fill it, blanking his mind so the details would come on their own. At first he worked in his usual clear, strong lines, then suddenly found himself using the side of the lead and blending it with his fingers, picking out highlights with a corner of his eraser.

It got to be eight o'clock. On the freeway outside his window, red tail-lights shrank and faded into the cold and dark. Denise was probably wondering where he was. Or maybe she wasn't, which was enough to keep him from calling.

He phoned Southwest Airlines instead. They had his luggage and offered to send someone out with it. He told them he would pick it up himself.

He stopped on the way to the airport for a sandwich, parked in the multi-story lot by Terminal A, and got his luggage at the service desk. Then, without conscious plan, he stopped by the main ticket desk and put himself on a flight to Dallas the next morning.

Thursday, November 4

MICHAEL TOOK HIS SEAT on the plane and began to clean out his cell phone.

The first few calls were from Ruth, first angry then devastated, pleading with him to return his father's ashes. Her last message was cold, telling him she was leaving for Dallas, if he cared.

The calls from Roger overlapped the last from Ruth. He hoped Michael would reconsider. He trusted Michael would not make use of any confidential information that might have come out during their last talks. He felt that Michael's continued silence was passive-aggressive and quite immature.

With each deleted message Michael felt lighter, more relaxed. Then the messages from Denise began.

The first few were short. "Michael, where are you? Are you all right?" "Michael, please call me."

Then they got longer. "It seems like you don't want to talk to me. I hope to God it's nothing worse than that. I went by your hotel and they said you'd checked out. This feels like it's all my fault."

It hurt to listen, but once he'd started he couldn't stop. Maybe the next message would be definitive, would tell him what to feel. He melted when she said she missed him, then cooled when she said she didn't want it to end this way. How, exactly, did she want it to end?

The final message was from 7:32 that morning. "Michael, I know I shouldn't keep calling. But I'm a little freaked out. There was this ... thing outside my door this morning, sitting on my balcony. It's like a, like a brown pillowcase or something. And it's got these tools inside."

HE PUNCHED IN her work number from memory, his hands shaking.

"Denise Franklin."

"Thank God," Michael said.

"Michael? Where are you?"

"I'm on the runway at RDU, on my way to talk to Ruth. Never mind that. Are you okay? Did anyone follow you to work?"

"I don't know. I don't think so. What's this all about?"

"I have totally screwed up and now you're in the middle of this."

"In the middle of what? Please slow down, you're scaring me."

"I need you to be scared. And this plane is going to take off any minute, so I have to rush. Do you have anyone you can stay with, not a relative or somebody obvious? Just for a day or two, until I can get back there?"

"Yes, probably, but why?"

"That thing on your porch was a message from the NRC. They know I was in their meeting hall, and they're telling me they know about you. Rachid needs to stay with friends too. Promise me neither of you will go back to the apartment without a police escort."

"Okay."

"I want you to call Sgt. Bishop right now and tell him what I told you. He knows I was trespassing on the Bynum farm. He's going to be pissed that Vaughan found out, but that won't stop him from giving you protection." He gave her the number of Bishop's cell.

"Okay, I'll call him as soon as we finish. What about you? They must be looking for you, too. Do they have people in Dallas that can find you?"

"I won't be in Dallas long. Overnight, maybe, no more than that. Then I'm coming back to Durham."

"You are?"

He tried to read the emotion in her voice. It sounded like hope. "Yes," he said. "I'm going to have to lie low until Saturday. After that, one way or another, the NRC should be slowed down for a while."

"One way or another?"

"I've learned a lot in the last couple of days. The short version is, Barrett Howard's activist group is still around, and Dr. Donald Harriman is up to his ears in it. I told him the NRC is going after American Tobacco. If the cops don't stop them, Harriman's people will."

"Oh my God. People could be killed."

"Maybe," he said, stung. "If the cops can't control it. What else was I supposed to do? I can't let them get away with whatever it is they're planning. It could be a bomb, a riot, I don't know what."

"I'm not blaming you. The NRC started this. It's just terrifying to think about open race warfare on the streets of Durham."

"It *is* war. I never saw it before because I was a bystander. It's been war ever since Lincoln told the South to give up their slaves. I don't see any end to it."

"I've never heard you this angry. Is this because of me?"

Michael forced himself to take a long breath. "Maybe," he said. "I'm also scared, and I don't know what my life is going to look like if I make it through this. I'm tired of living out of hotel rooms and I'm tired of being alone."

It was out. In the silence that followed, the flight attendant announced that they were about to push back from the gate and that all cell phones needed to be turned off. Michael said, "Are you still there?"

"Yes," Denise said. "I don't like being alone so much anymore either."

"What do you want to do about it?"

"Can I ... can we see each other? Talk face to face?"

"You know I want to see you more than anything. I'm not the one with the conflicts and the questions." The words seemed harsher than he wanted.

"I told you from the beginning we needed to go slow."

"Slow is fine. As long as we're both going the same direction."

After another long silence she said, "I don't want to be without you, Michael."

"Okay, then. That's what I needed to hear."

"I miss you."

"I miss you too. Can I call you tonight?"

"Please. It doesn't matter how late."

The attendant was standing over him, a sympathetic look on her face. "I have to go," Michael said. "I'll call you."

ANOTHER AIRPORT, another rental desk. His father's house was in a subdivision of upscale custom-built homes near White Rock Lake in East Dallas. Michael took Mockingbird Lane all the way, the route so familiar he could drive it in his sleep, yet now also strange, dreamlike.

He parked in the driveway, careful not to block the garage door. The lawn had yellowed from lack of water and the house seemed unkempt, like someone who slept in his clothes. His father had designed and built the place himself in the early nineties, an upper floor at street level and a lower floor that grew out of the hillside and extended down toward the creek. He'd put his office in that lower section, in a room with windows on three sides, surrounded by willows, looking out on feeders for birds and squirrels, the creek visible in the background.

It helped to think of his father in that room full of light, alternating between working on a set of piece drawings and watching the animals. He must have found moments of peace there, even with Ruth upstairs, even with the cancer and the secrets eating away at him.

Michael got out of the car and rang the doorbell. He could hear a TV tuned to a talk show. Ruth's heels clacked across the tile, and the light behind the peephole went dark.

When the door opened, the chain was on it. "What do you want?" she asked. The wedge of sunlight coming through the door lit up one shoulder of a pale blue jogging suit, a thin silver watchband. Beyond that, it seemed she'd had a permanent and was fully made up.

"We have to talk," Michael said.

"What about?"

"Your father."

"Did you bring Robert's ashes?"

"They're in Beechwood Cemetery in Durham."

Ruth closed the door and Michael heard a deadbolt snap shut.

He raised his voice. "If you don't talk to me, I'll go to the newspapers."

After a long moment the door opened again, still on the chain. "What are you talking about?"

"'Local farmer headed hate group for forty years.' It could make the national wire."

"You wouldn't."

"I've got nothing to lose. Are you going to let me in?"

This time when the door opened, the chain was off. Michael followed her into the living room, where he found the remote and shut off the television. "They only had crackers on the plane," he said. "I'm going to make a sandwich."

She led the way into the kitchen, then sat on the stepstool by the phone and watched him go through the refrigerator. "You're limping," she said. "And your face is torn up. What happened?"

"I cut myself shaving," he said. He found peanut butter and jelly and made two sandwiches. As always, there were single serving bags of Fritos in the cabinets. What had changed, he realized, was that she had removed the few traces of his father that had marked the upstairs—awards from the shelves above the TV, framed drawings from the dining room walls.

"Michael, you have changed so much lately that I would hardly know you. You have become cruel, sarcastic, spiteful, and withdrawn. It started the day you moved out of the Brookwood. I don't know what brought it on, but it has hurt me more than I can say."

It was true. He'd seen a dark and petty side of himself in the last few days and weeks that he didn't care for. "I'm sorry," he said. He stood there awkwardly in the middle of the kitchen, holding his plate. "I didn't set out to hurt you. The lies and the secrets got to be more than I could stand."

"You act like it was all me. Your father had more than his share of secrets as well."

"Then how about this? Let's start over, as of now, and tell nothing but the truth. Can we do that? Talk to each other honestly and openly, without anger or fear or blame. Clear the air, once and for all. And then see where we are when we're done."

She thought it over. "I'm not sure if I can trust you."

"That's fair enough. I expect we both need to earn each other's trust at this point. And either one of us can back out at any moment."

He took her silence as provisional agreement. "I would really like to hear you talk about your father," he said. "Anything you wanted to tell me."

"Why?" she asked. "Why this sudden concern with a man you showed no interest in for your entire life?"

He was careful with his answer. "You know what it was like around here. Whenever the subject of your father came up, it seemed to make Dad angry. Kids watch things like that, and they learn not to talk about them."

Ruth nodded. "Adults too. He made me ashamed of my own family. You still haven't answered my question. And we're supposed to be telling the truth, right?"

"Okay. I think your father may have murdered Barrett Howard."

"You must be joking."

"I think some of his fellow Night Riders brought Barrett out to the farm. Your father killed him there, maybe in that secret meeting room downstairs."

"You've been busy, I see."

"The murder weapon was a cobbler's awl that he kept in that glass case in the living room."

Ruth shook her head. "Sit down and eat. I'll fix you some iced tea."

Michael sat and tore open the bag of Fritos. He was so tense that the chips scattered across the tabletop.

As she poured the tea, Ruth said, "There was no glass case in the living room, and no cobbler's awl, not that I ever saw. Not on all my trips to the farm, not even on those few I had the gumption to take after we moved to Dallas. My father never killed this black man. He was many things, but he was not some savage that would take pleasure in an act like that. He was a leader. There were things he ... I didn't always..."

She didn't finish the thought. "People loved and respected him," she said, "and they did anything he asked them to. But he never ordered them to kill this black man either."

Michael started to say something, and then understanding came to him in a rush, like a map unfolding in his head. Bright red lines like Interstate highways connected all the small, isolated stories, and together they made a pattern that could not be contested.

"He had friends," Michael said, "at the Army Recruiting Office in Raleigh, didn't he?"

"He had friends everywhere."

"These particular friends were willing to backdate a few enlistment forms, weren't they? To please Wilmer Bynum and get themselves a healthy, white, high-school graduate athlete to send to Vietnam?"

Ruth didn't answer, didn't need to.

"It was Greg Vaughan that killed Howard," Michael said. "And your father put him in the Army to get him out of town and give him an alibi at the same time." He had a sudden memory of Vaughan at the stove in his trailer, a flaring match lighting a fatal hunger in his eyes.

"And the Army taught him all kinds of skills," Michael went on, "like how to blow things up. Skills that he used to firebomb Service Printing and the *Carolina Times*." And, he thought but did not say out loud, skills he's going to use to set off a bomb on Saturday at the American Tobacco complex.

Ruth sat down on the far side of the table, her back to the sliding glass doors and the willows. "My father didn't know about the killing. Not until Greg came to him and told him what he'd done. My father was very angry, and Greg had only done it to please him. He knew how much my father hated that man."

"It was your father that called Mitch Antree."

"He called Randy Fogg in Washington and made him do it."

"Who put the body in the form?"

"Greg and some of the older men. They knew how to ... clean up afterwards." Michael was sure that they did. "What about the fire bombings?"

"Well, we were here in Dallas when all that happened."

"Yes. And...?"

Ruth looked down at the table. "Greg wrote me about them. Nothing direct. He said that he was carrying on the work. It wasn't hard to figure what he meant, when I heard about the fires."

"Do you still have those letters?"

Ruth fluttered her hands. "I don't know. Maybe. Somewhere."

"Never mind," Michael said. "It doesn't matter. Keep talking. Tell me everything. Everything."

RUTH

1940-1970

ALL LITTLE GIRLS love their fathers, but it seemed to Ruth that none of them had ever loved the way that she did.

From the time she was 4 she understood that her father was the most important man in Johnston County. Her older sisters told her so, when they weren't tormenting her, stealing her toys, and telling her she was adopted. She understood even then that they were jealous of the special love her father had for her.

No grownup life could compare to the childhood she had. She was able to run for hours in any direction and never leave her father's land. The whole world came to her, including the ice cream truck every Saturday in the summer, even during World War II when other people had to do without. There were horses in the corral, ducks in the pond, pigs and chickens in their pens, cats and dogs everywhere, all of them living off her father's bounty.

At night they would sit by the radio and listen to the comedy and variety shows, all except for her mother, who disapproved. Ruth always sat next to her father on the big couch. Her favorite program was *Make Believe Ballroom,* where she imagined she was dancing for hours in her father's arms.

Sometimes parents who came to visit would bring their children. The mothers would go into the kitchen and the fathers would go in the study with Ruth's father and close the door. The other fathers were usually downcast and sometimes ashamed going in; most of the time they had big smiles by the time they came out.

The little girls treated Ruth and her sisters like royalty. Ruth would show them her dollhouse and her dolls and all their clothes, or take them down to the swimming hole, where some of her father's friends had dammed the creek for her, or out to the swings and monkey bars and the real tin-floored slide at the side of the house.

Boys required a different strategy, often staying in their fathers' pickup trucks wearing sullen faces. Still Ruth could usually coax them out to see the new John Deere Model B tractor, with cultivator and hay rake attachments, and the high seat where she would ride on her father's lap.

•

SHE COULDN'T REMEMBER the first time she saw a Negro. Most likely it was on a trip into Smithfield with her mother. Milk and groceries were delivered, her mother made most of their clothes, and their church was near them in the countryside. That left little reason to go to town, which suited Wilmer perfectly well, if not Ruth or her sisters.

Negroes were as alien to her as crawfish. Her mother told her that she must be kind to them because their lives were hard. Ruth pictured them doing the labor that animals did, dragging plows, pulling stumps, carrying loads of firewood on their backs.

Later she understood that many people had Negroes who worked in their homes, cleaning, cooking, doing yard work. One night, when it was her turn to do the dishes, Ruth asked why they didn't have somebody to do them for her, like her friend Mary had.

"We do our own work here," her father said. "Every one of us."

RUTH WAS 5 when Orpha was born. It was not the brother she had hoped for; instead it was another girl to have to share her father with.

"Look who's not the baby anymore," her sister Esther told her. "We'll see how *you* like it now."

It didn't help that Ruth had to start kindergarten before Orpha was a month old. To be separated from her father as her father was preoccupied with this little drowned rat of a child was too cruel. On top of that, they put Orpha's crib in the room Ruth had formerly had to herself, the room her father had built especially for her. It reminded Ruth of the Bible story where Adam and Eve had to leave the Garden of Eden, only Ruth hadn't broken any rules, at least not any big ones. At night she would ask God to take Orpha back to Him, and then curl up and hide under the covers in shame at her own evil thoughts.

When Orpha "failed to thrive," as the doctors called it, Ruth was tortured by guilt. One day she heard her father tell a hired hand that Ruth's mother had been too old to have another child, and that he didn't know if Orpha would ever have a normal life. In his tone of voice she heard him pulling back from the sickly Orpha, and her instinctive thrill of triumph brought on more nights of torment.

Meanwhile, school proved not so bad in the end, and less emotionally complicated than home had become. She quickly had the run of the place. Once the girls found out who her father was, they all wanted to be friends, and the boys—well, boys were always easy.

WHEN SHE WAS 8, Ruth found a den of foxes near the creek. She tried to pick up one of the kits and the mother attacked her, biting her right hand and arm.

The foxes were gone by the time Ruth took her father to the den, so she had to have rabies shots in her stomach. On their first trip to the doctor her father said, "Let that be a lesson to you. The daddy fox would probably have tried to scare you off. Females don't kid around. They'll fight to the death to protect their family."

"I wasn't going to hurt them," Ruth said. Bandages covered her entire hand and half her forearm, the wounds aching and stinging and itching all at the same time.

"I know that, honey. That mama fox was doing the only thing she knew how to do. You don't want to blame her too much for that."

SHE AND HER FATHER remained close, and by sixth grade, when she was 11, he would come sometimes and cuddle with her at night in the room she shared with Orpha. He had many burdens to carry, like little Orpha, who caught every disease known to man and now had tuberculosis. Ruth's mother slept in her own bedroom and was no longer a comfort to him. When Ruth worried at first that it was not her place to be so much like a wife to him, her father assured her that it was all right.

One morning in seventh grade she got up in the night to go to the bathroom and felt blood running sticky down her legs. If there had been blood there before, that memory was now cloudy and confusing. She lay awake the rest of the night in fear, a wad of toilet paper jammed in place, sure that God was punishing her for her evil thoughts toward Orpha.

Her father had raised her to be strong and independent and not to ask too many questions. On subjects like where babies came from and why men and women were kissing on television, he referred her to her mother. Her mother's answer had always been "There will be time enough for you to learn about that later on," often followed by a reading assignment from scripture.

She was afraid to tell her father and afraid to do nothing, so she went to the school nurse with a story about having seen another girl with blood there. The nurse laughed at her and gave her a belt and a box of pads and a pamphlet with line drawings in it that she could take to her "friend." Ruth threw the book away and bought her own pads in secret on her next trip to town.

She had barely gotten used to the idea of bleeding every month when there came a month that she didn't. Then a second month, and she was sick to her stomach, so sick, so often, that it was hard to hide. If the bleeding was bad, this was far worse, and she knew she couldn't talk to the nurse about this.

In the end, it was her father that she told. There came a night when she was barely able to choke her supper down, breathing through her mouth and moving the food around with her fork after her first few bites. As soon as she could, she asked to go and play, and her father had found her out by the swing set, throwing up.

He was angry at first, wanting to know why she hadn't told him about the bleeding in the first place. That had made her cry and he'd hugged her then, promising that everything would be okay and warning her that she must never, ever say a word about it to anyone, or it would mean she didn't love him anymore.

The next Saturday they'd gone to see a doctor in Smithfield, a stranger to Ruth, though her father seemed to know him well. She'd never seen anyone look at her father the way this doctor did, as if her father had brought a bad smell into the office on his shoe. The doctor put her to sleep there on the examining table, with her father holding her hand, and when she woke up she felt sore and empty. She was bleeding again, "spotting," the doctor called it. He said it was normal, though it didn't sound like he meant it.

Ruth saw from the way her father held himself that she was not to ask questions, so she didn't.

After that things were very bad for a while. The operation had gotten infected, and the doctor wanted her to go to the hospital in Smithfield. Her father refused. She was in bed for three weeks, the first week with an IV drip in her arm and a catheter down below. The pain was unlike anything she had ever known, and it changed the way she saw the world. The world she had grown up in didn't have room for that kind of pain in it, especially not for young girls whose fathers loved and protected them.

Eventually she was able to go to school again. She told the other girls she had come down with a flu that came from Pakistan and that no one had ever had before. She also had to go back to the doctor for a checkup, which terrified her, though her father told her if she didn't go she might get sick again. That was when the doctor told her that everything was fine now, but that she would never be able to have children of her own.

She understood that this was God's will. That was what her father said, when she told him on the drive home. She began to harden herself to the idea, to make herself strong and not care, the way her father had hardened his heart against Orpha's illness. It was the end of the change in her that the pain had begun. And when her father didn't come to her anymore in the night, she hardened her heart to that as well.

SHE COULDN'T REMEMBER a time when she hadn't known about the men in white robes. When she was very little her older sisters had tried to tell her they were ghosts. When she repeated the story to her father, he had spanked Esther and Naomi both. The visitors were men, her father explained to Ruth, and they were also like angels. Once a month they came together to find ways to do good in the world. She should feel safe and special because they were always around her, but she should never try to talk to them or interfere with them, because when the men wore their angel robes they were very powerful, and it was dangerous to get too close.

One night after midnight she had woken to the rustling outside and gotten up to watch the angel men through the upstairs window. They flowed toward the house through the fields and the trees, silent and swift. After they had all arrived, Ruth crept down the stairs to see them all together, only to find the house empty. After that she knew that they truly were angels.

It was Orpha who spoiled the mystery, and so much else, on a Tuesday in the summer of 1953.

Orpha had learned to make her weakness her strength. Gaunt and pale as she was, no one was willing to punish her, to make her keep to the limits the other girls had to honor. She always whined one more question after being told "That's enough," always took up the toy she'd been told not to touch, always unwrapped the piece of candy she'd been told she couldn't have, and did it all with a pathetic defiance, daring anyone to add to her already overwhelming misery.

The day Orpha found the staircase, Ruth was 13 and Orpha nearly 8. Their mother had gone to a church meeting, as she did more and more frequently. Their father was in the tractor shed, tinkering with one of his projects. Naomi had married and left home the year before, and Esther was with her girlfriends in town.

Ruth came in the kitchen to find Orpha standing over a bright red stain in the middle of the tile floor, a box of Rit dye open in the sink. Orpha looked up with a vacant expression, her eye sockets as black as a raccoon's, her cheeks hollow and her jaw sagging open.

"Oh my Lord," Ruth said. "Daddy is going to kill you."

"Don't take the Lord's name in vain. Help me clean this up."

"That's Rit dye. That's not going to come up. What were you doing?"

"I wanted a red shirt. I wanted something *pretty*."

Ruth opened the broom closet and got out the mop and bucket. She started to fill the bucket at the sink. "What about vinegar? Would vinegar take it up?"

"I don't know."

"There's some in the closet," Ruth said. "Go look."

As soon as Ruth started to swab the floor, the dye turned the strands of mop red as well. Though it had all been Orpha's fault to start with, now Ruth had gone and ruined the mop as well. When her father came in he would be too angry to control himself, she knew. Yet nothing would happen to poor little Orpha; nothing ever happened to poor little Orpha.

When she looked up, Orpha had emptied the entire closet onto the kitchen floor. The box of Tide was now sitting in the edge of the puddle of red dye, soaking it up into the box. Ruth moved the box and brought the stain with it onto a new part of the floor. She began to swing the mop with furious energy, and watched with horror as the dye spattered onto the wood of the lower cabinets. She ran to get a sponge to wipe the cabinets, and now the dye was on her sneakers and she was tracking it across the floor.

"Orpha!" she yelled, and eight years of frustration, jealousy, and anger went into it.

She looked up, then, and saw Orpha standing in a doorway that had never been there before, a doorway inside the closet. Orpha had turned at the sound of Ruth's scream and in the process lost her balance. Her perpetual look of suffering and world-weariness was gone, and in its place Ruth saw shock and horror.

For the rest of her life, Ruth would go over that moment in slow motion, trying to piece the truth out of the disjointed images. When she rushed at Orpha, had she done it with fists raised and murder in her heart, willing Orpha to go backward over that threshold of darkness? Or had she stretched her fingers out trying to save her, and been too late?

She stopped when Orpha fell, that much she was sure of. And she turned and ran for her father, her voice screaming and her insides freezing cold.

RUTH WAITED in the kitchen as her father raced down the stairs, then came up carrying Orpha's broken body in his arms. He stopped to shut the door after him, though, the inner door, the one that led to the stairs.

"Call the doctor," he said, very quietly. "Then put everything in the pantry and close it up."

"It was Orpha spilled the dye," Ruth said fiercely, stubbornly. "I was only trying to clean it up."

"This is very important," her father said, and looked at her in a way she understood, a way that meant that this was one of their secrets. "If anyone asks, she fell down the other stairs. Do you understand? She was upstairs, and she lost her balance and fell down the big stairs."

"Yes, Daddy," Ruth said, and she was warm inside again and not afraid anymore. "I understand."

The ambulance took Orpha to the new Johnston Memorial Hospital in Smithfield to set her broken leg and X-ray her skull, then her father brought her home again. "If she wakes up," her father said, "she might be okay. But she has a concussion, and for somebody as weak as she is, well, it's not good."

It took Orpha two days to die. Ruth's mother sat by Orpha's bedside in perfect stillness, not so much as holding Orpha's hand, not reading, not praying, just sitting. Once Ruth was there when her father walked in, and her mother gave him a look she might give a piece of gristle before she scraped it into the garbage.

Ruth prayed continuously those two days for Orpha to wake up and be better. Mostly she did it in her mother's room, where she had moved for the duration; sometimes she did it beside Orpha's bed. Her mother ignored her, and, in the end, so did God. Ruth understood that she was being punished, and that God was not obliged to answer the prayers of sinners.

The day after Orpha died, which was two days before the funeral, some men came and put down a new floor in the kitchen. The men moved the refrigerator out into the dining room on a long extension cord, and for two days the neighbors brought them food and they ate it off paper plates. It was a terrible time; even so, Ruth's father let her know with a wink or a squeeze of her shoulder that he was counting on her, and she thought that if her father had forgiven her, then surely God would have to as well.

In time, Ruth's curiosity overcame her fear and took her down the hidden stairs. The room she found at the bottom was a disappointment; both for its emptiness and for the answer it gave to the riddle of the disappearing angels.

To HER SURPRISE, Ruth became beautiful, far more so than Esther or Naomi ever had been. She "blossomed early," which was her mother's way of referring to her breasts, fully formed at age 14, and to her narrow waist and shapely hips. A body and a face like Ruth's were a curse, her mother said, a constant invitation to lasciviousness. The high-necked sweaters and long skirts her mother forced her to wear failed to help; the boys stared at her as if they could see clear through them.

Ruth had no interest in the boys at South Johnston High anyway, not even the boys who played basketball or football, the Trojans. Ruth never understood why they would name their sports teams after a brand of French letters, and it put her off the whole idea. None of these boys began to compare to her father, and the few dates she went on ended in a chaste kiss on the cheek.

SHE WAS IN HER SENIOR YEAR when Greg Vaughan came to live with them, taking over Esther and Naomi's bedroom. Greg was a year younger than Orpha had been when she died. Where Orpha was weak and sickly, Greg was already as hard and self-contained as the old men who sat by the river in downtown Smithfield, pretending to fish but really just staring down the day in silent defiance. Ruth's heart went out to this little boy who had never known a father, whose mother was now dead, who nevertheless refused to ask for anything, who accepted the smallest kindness only with difficulty, who would have slept under the porch with the dogs and never complained.

The dogs took to Greg immediately, all the animals did, and the way he treated them, with such plain affection and dignity, spoke highly of him in Ruth's eyes. The first Christmas that he was with them, Christmas of 1958, she used her own money to buy him an AKC Certified German Shepherd pup from a breeder in Raleigh. She would never forget the way he looked at her when he realized what she'd done, the pure, strong love that shone out of his face the way it sometimes still shone from her father's.

Greg had a hard time at school. He didn't like being inside all day, he told her, though clearly more was at stake. Despite her attempts to help with his homework, his grades were never good. He came home with bruises and cuts, refusing to say how the fights had started.

She had a notion it might have to do with an argument she'd overheard between her parents. Ruth was in the hall when she heard her mother in her father's bedroom, a rare event by that time.

"How long do you mean to keep your bastard here living with us?" she asked him. Her voice was quiet and hard.

"Language, Regina."

"There's nothing wrong with my language. It's in the Bible. Deuteronomy, chapter 23: 'A bastard shall not enter into the congregation of the Lord; even to his tenth generation shall he not enter into the congregation of the Lord.'"

"He's just a boy, Regina. He had nothing to say about the circumstances of his birth."

"No, *you* had the say over that."

"He's got nowhere else to go. We can afford to feed another mouth. We could feed more mouths than his. And should, if we really listened to that Book you're always quoting."

"What am I to make of that? Am I to be grateful you didn't force me to take in his harlot of a mother as well? How many more bastards have you sown across the county, black and white?"

"That's enough, Regina. The boy stays. That's final."

Ruth barely made it to her room before she heard the crisp cadence of her mother's heels descending the stairs. A few seconds later her car pulled away with a spurt of gravel.

I have a brother, Ruth thought. She held this new secret tight inside her, her childhood wish come true.

ESTHER AND NAOMI had both left home as soon as they graduated high school, Naomi marrying a gawky boy with glasses who couldn't believe his luck, Esther winning a scholarship to a teacher's college in Kansas that no one knew she'd applied for.

Ruth was not about to run away. She was torn, though, between a desire to spend the rest of her life on the farm and the hope of finding a man of her own, a man like her father, but less inclined to harlots. She persuaded her father to send her to Meredith College, a girl's school with an impeccable reputation.

She made good grades, and still found time to meet the cream of Raleigh society and report back to her father on Sunday afternoon. Meredith, he decided, was not such a bad investment after all. On one occasion he had Ruth tell the daughter of a former Raleigh millionaire, now strapped for cash, to have her father get in touch. On another, he was able to help the owner of a large sausage factory in Columbus County deal with his labor problems. It was her father's love of sports that made Ruth approach radio personality Randy Fogg. Though she found him personally repellant, she convinced Fogg to come to the farm for her father's sake.

In what seemed an act of impossible daring, she learned to play contract bridge. Her mother believed playing cards were engraved invitations to Hell, conceived in witchcraft and propagated by confidence men, idlers, and fools. Ruth was fascinated by the coded communications between the players and the speed with which she was able to master the strategy. She refused to play for money, and quickly discovered duplicate bridge, which removed the factor of luck.

Her second rebellion was a ballroom dancing class—once she'd made sure that her mother would not find out. The men at the Friday night dances were more than willing to help her with her moves. These were far better looking men than the Trojans from high school, with sleek cars, spicy colognes, and Brooks Brothers suits they bought on trips to New York. On more than one occasion she'd been tempted to let one of them have what he wanted so badly, just to see what it might be like, knowing there was no danger of getting pregnant. Still she held out, knowing she was waiting for something, not knowing exactly for what.

Robert proved to be the answer.

She noticed him the first time he came into the room. He'd been in the Army, she found out later, making him older and more experienced than most of the other men there. He was handsome, not in a movie star way, but in a way that had to do with crinkled eyes and a strong nose that wasn't ashamed of itself, with a mouth that slipped into a smile every time it wasn't doing anything else. He was tall and carried a strength in him that was more than muscular.

He danced the way he did everything else. What he wanted wasn't complicated, and he was completely clear about communicating it. She loved dancing with him because she never had to think. One move followed the next
inevitably. It was what she had always imagined it would be like to dance with
her father, if her father had danced.

She found herself telling her father about him before Robert had even
asked for a date. Her father particularly liked the idea that he was studying to
be a highway engineer.

"This Interstate Highway business of Eisenhower's," her father said. "It's going to completely change this country. Once this gets started, it can't ever stop.
The more highways we get, the more we'll need. Highways will decide what
towns prosper and what towns die, the way the railroads used to. They'll decide where people live and work, not the other way around. This man Cooper
is getting in on the ground floor. That's a smart place to be."

Robert had impressed her father without even meeting him. That made
Ruth take note. For the next dance she bought a new dress, tight, black, and
low cut, unlike anything she had ever worn before. Her hands trembled at
the sight of herself in the mirror. When Robert saw her, his mouth opened
and no words came out. That night he came to her for dance after dance,
and afterwards he walked her to her dorm and invited her to dinner the
following night.

A month later Robert was still wavering, so Ruth brought him home to the
farm. Her father was eager to meet him, not put off that Robert's family had
been in service. This was America, where a man was what he made of himself.
Some of the Vanderbilts' breeding had rubbed off on Robert, and his courtly
manner charmed Ruth's mother and put her father on his best behavior. Even
Greg got drawn in, asking question after question about Germany.

After Ruth showed Robert to her old room and left him with a lingering
kiss, she went downstairs to ask her father what he thought. He nodded once,
closing his eyes, and that was good enough for Ruth. She did what she had to
do to make sure Robert wouldn't slip away. And if it was a sin, she was doubly
damned for the thrill she took in it.

NO ONE KNEW how much money Wilmer Bynum had. He didn't trust
banks, and Ruth heard stories about her father having bags of cash squirreled
away all across Johnston County. He never spent much himself, and he made
all his investments through third parties.

Like Randy Fogg.

The weekend after she'd brought Robert home she was back at the farm
without him. Her father was celebrating the ACC tournament with a barbeque,

though Duke had failed to make the finals. Fogg was there, partaking a bit too heavily of the white lightning that made its way around the party in unlabeled Mason jars.

Toward sundown Ruth had been sitting on the swings, talking to two Duke players, when Fogg wandered by, sweating and unsteady. The players soon excused themselves, stranding her with him.

"I don't know that I ever properly thanked you for introducing me to your father," Fogg said. He sat heavily in the swing next to hers. "It is truly an honor to know him."

"Glad I was able to help," Ruth said, staring straight ahead at a flock of starlings, noisily swarming from one tree to another and back again.

"And I'm grateful I've been able to help him in one or two small ways myself."

"Is that so?"

"Just this afternoon I became the owner of a hundred acres of land near the Raleigh airport. In name only, of course. And last year I bought a piece of a car dealership and the year before that I started a young engineer in his own business. Your daddy has trusted me with a sizable amount of money, no doubt about it."

That was how her father worked. He put nothing on paper and left everything to his memory and character judgment. Character being a virtue subject to many different definitions. Her father's character, if you believed the same people who talked about bags of cash, did not balk at harlotry. Many of the women were supposed to be Negroes, and her father's business associates had the run of them.

"I think maybe my father would not appreciate your discussing his business in public," Ruth said.

"This isn't public," Fogg said. "And he can't object to my letting his favorite little girl know what a fine man he is."

"And by extension what a fine, trustworthy man you are yourself?"

"Why, I would never say that."

"Neither would I," Ruth said with a big, bright smile that blinded him to the cut. "Shall we return to the party, Mr. Fogg?"

That Sunday evening, before leaving for Raleigh, she found her father in his study. "Daddy? Is it true you bought part of an engineering company?"

"Where did you hear that?"

"Your friend Randy Fogg was in his cups and trying to impress me."

"Was he, now. Did he say or do anything improper?"

Her father hadn't moved, but she suddenly had his acute attention. She was tempted to make up a story and see what might result; though Fogg had done nothing, his desire was plain enough. She would never lie to her father, though, and he had told her many times that Fogg was part of his plans, that he would be carrying the good fight to Washington someday.

"No, Daddy. He was just bragging."

"Well, I'll soon cure him of that."

"You didn't say if it was true or not."

"And if it is?"

"Robert's going to graduate in May."

Her father laughed. "I wish I'd had a son with your instincts. Don't worry about Robert. He'll have his part in this."

"Is he going to be one of your angels, Daddy?"

"I don't really see him as angel material, honey. But he too will serve."

GREG VAUGHAN WAS 11 that year, five foot ten and 120 pounds. Ruth couldn't tease a smile out of him. He was at the age of taking himself too seriously, and his feelings for her had clearly become more complicated. He had affected a thrift-store version of her father's style of dress: worn blue jeans, western shirts with pearl snaps, pointy-toed cowboy boots. If he had friends, he never mentioned them and she never saw them.

Her father's loves were Greg's. He had memorized the entire history of Duke basketball, including players' names and statistics. He had a basketball goal on a wooden post near the swing set, and sometimes she would hear him there for hours at a time on weekends, the ball pinging against the hard-packed dirt and banging against the backboard.

Her father had also given him his own acre of land to tend, and Greg had planted it in tobacco, cotton, and peanuts, a miniature of the Bynum farm. He knew more about farming than the NC State agriculture students she'd met at Meredith mixers. If her father had let him, he would have quit school and farmed full time.

And Wilmer Bynum's enemies were Greg's enemies. Greg talked not just about "the niggers," but used the rest of the vocabulary that went with it: "northern agitators," "pinko liberals," "communist miscegenation conspiracy." His wholeheartedness was not deterred by the fact that he could barely get his mouth around half the words.

It was the part of her father that she was least comfortable with. It didn't fit well with the man she knew to be strong, loving, and generous. Still, as the world came to a boil in the late 1950s, that side of him increasingly began to dominate.

The Northern courts had banned segregation in 1954; the decision had made little difference at first. A few Negroes tried to get their children into white schools, and there had been a sit-in at the Royal Ice Cream parlor in Durham in 1957 where the participants had quietly been taken away to jail.

Then in February of 1960, four Negroes in Greensboro insisted on being served at a Woolworth's, and within a few months the lunch counters at dime stores in Raleigh and Durham were having to close. There were picket lines, lawsuits, sit-ins, and demonstrations. The television was full of angry people shouting and throwing things.

Ruth, not entirely sure where she stood on integration, did not see how such behavior made things better for anyone.

"We worked hard for everything we've got," Ruth's father said. "Certain elements think they should have everything for nothing. Well, that's not the way this country works." He was never angry, never impatient, just smiled and went to work.

With his friends and supporters, he got the job done. If a boycott forced a department store to hire a black salesclerk, two months later that salesclerk would be in the basement cleaning toilets. If demonstrators forced a lunch counter to seat Negroes, those Negroes would arrive a week later to find all the seats taken out.

For Greg it was not enough. Those who made trouble should answer for it, he told Ruth, fists tight in front of him, so skinny he could barely stand up to a strong breeze. Ruth respected his inflated sense of dignity too much to laugh at him the way some of the men did, calling him "Cassius Clay" after the Negro Olympic boxer and braggart, which never failed to put Greg into a rage.

Ruth worried that unless he found a way to let off steam, he was going to get into serious trouble. She tried to encourage his dreams of playing basketball for Duke, sometimes sitting on the swings and watching him practice. Though she was not a sports fan herself, she could see that he needed to play with other boys instead of practicing alone. When she tried to talk to him about it, Greg insisted that he didn't need anyone. Ruth could not make him see otherwise; he was a very hard, very angry little boy.

As for her own life, Ruth could not imagine a better one. Two hundred people came to her wedding: politicians, sports figures, church deacons. She also brought in members of Raleigh and Durham society that she had met either on the dance floor or at the bridge table. Only the absence of her sisters cast a shadow, and that was a small one.

When the want ad appeared for an engineer for Mitch Antree's company, Ruth showed Robert the paper. She waited out his insistence that he needed to work for the state and let him realize for himself the potential benefits. And she made sure he applied, all without him seeing her father's hand in it. With that good job in his pocket, they moved into a perfect little house in Durham with grass and trees and a garden and a country club down the street.

The first hint of the trouble that lay ahead came when Robert went to work in Hayti. When he told her of the plans to clear the slum, she remembered a conversation she hadn't thought of in years, that she'd been too young to understand properly at the time.

She'd been in junior high, playing with one of the dogs by the tractor shed, when she'd heard voices inside. It was her father and another man, a man she didn't know except that he was rich and from Durham and on some Council or Committee or something like that. The man was saying, "—ever actually been there? They dress up in suits and ties and drive new model cars. They got their own businesses and go to the picture show and eat ice cream. It's like watching that chimpanzee on the *Today* show, all dressed up, you know what I mean? It ain't natural somehow."

"We've had our eye on Hayti for some time," her father said.

"No offense, but I think it's time you had more than your eye on it. Right there in the shadow of downtown. People coming in on the train have to look out on their little jungle main street."

Her father seemed to be thinking over his next words carefully. "You will not have to worry about Hayti much longer."

"What exactly do you mean, not worry about it? Could you be a little more specific? Because I have other people to answer to, you understand."

Her father was silent an even longer time, and then he said, "We will wipe out the businesses. We will level the buildings. We will flatten the houses and trees, we will plow it under and we will sow the earth with salt." His voice was calm and quiet in a way Ruth had learned not to provoke. "Do you think that will be good enough for the people you answer to?"

"Yes, sir," the man said. There was nervous laughter in his voice. "I would say that was more than good enough. Yes, sir."

Ruth had already begun to move away, and broke into a run as soon as she thought it was safe. She did not want her father to find her eavesdropping when he was in that kind of mood. At the time she didn't know what Hayti was, only knew she never wanted to go there, never wanted to pass close by. A wrath was going to descend there like it did on Sodom and Gomorrah, and she hoped she would be far away when it happened.

Now Robert was the reluctant hand of that wrath. She knew it didn't sit well on him, and she wished she could ease his mind. It wasn't like there was another way for this to turn out. Durham needed the highway so people could get to the new business park. The city would die without it. The highway was going to displace somebody, anywhere you put it. It only made sense that it was poor people that had to move. It would cost a hundred times more to buy up rich people's houses.

They told Robert a new, better Hayti would rise from the ruins, and he wanted to believe it. Ruth let him, and never said a word about her father's prophecy. Between the word of Mitch Antree and the word of Wilmer Bynum, she knew which would prevail.

THOUGH THE NUMBER of Ruth's mother's years would eventually prove to be two more than her allotted threescore and ten, she came from a time when that was a rarity. People didn't expect all of their children to grow to adulthood, and adulthood itself was precarious, what with farm accidents, poor nutrition, and epidemics like the Spanish Flu that killed both her own parents in 1919.

She raised Ruth with the attitude that adulthood was a brass ring to grab as soon as you had the chance and hold onto for dear life. Once you had it, all the emotional upheavals, the games and preening, late nights and jealousies of youth were no more appealing than the strained prunes you ate as a baby.

Robert, however, seemed unready to put aside childish things. He still preferred the Lindy Hop to the foxtrot, even at the cost of his dignity. He wanted to listen to his jazz records rather than adult music. And he would rather sleep in on Sunday than go to church.

Even so, Ruth was devastated when she found out he was having an affair.

They'd been married little more than three years. They'd had their ups and downs like all couples did; sadly, Robert's reaction to any sort of trouble was to run away, stay out all night dancing like a college boy, and leave his sweaty, perfume-tainted clothes for her to wash.

Of all the possibilities he must surely have had, he had chosen Cindy Berkshire, as close to a harlot as Willowhaven Country Club had to offer. She didn't have Ruth's looks, manners, or bearing. All she had, apparently, was a willingness to satisfy Robert's physical appetites, which were far greater than Ruth had ever bargained for.

Bad enough for Ruth to walk into the club and hear the silence fall like a blanket over the dining room. Bad enough that she had to endure Cindy Berkshire's feigned friendship, a brazen attempt to cover her sin. Bad enough that she would come home from church and Sunday dinner with her parents to find him listless and red-eyed from his indulgence.

No, what really stung was the pain of betrayal. Robert was her reason for living, the only man other than her father that she had ever truly loved.

Through that fall and winter and spring, Ruth gained a new appreciation for her mother's strength. Men were, as her father had always said, part angel and part animal. What Ruth now saw was that women were merely human, and they were the ones left to clean up after the animal and the angel both.

IT WAS HARD to describe 1966 and 1967 to anyone who wasn't there. It was like a nightmare she'd had as a child, where she would find herself on stage in an absurd and complex play whose script she had never seen. Once she thought she'd seen and heard everything, some new audacity would spring up where she least expected it. Men with hair to their waists, women in see-through blouses. Negroes with berets and guns making obscene threats. Music that was no more than howling and screaming, sexual jokes on TV, magazines glorifying illegal drugs. Riots in ghettos all summer long, body counts from Southeast Asia climbing ever higher, antiwar and civil rights protests in every city in the country.

Her father showed the strain as well. "It's war," he said on a Sunday morning in June of 1967. He threw the newspaper he'd been reading in the middle of the dining room table, barely missing a platter of poached eggs. "Loving, can you believe it? *Loving* versus Virginia."

"Daddy, what are you talking about?"

"I'm talking about the Northern Supreme Court saying that interracial marriage—miscegenation—is perfectly fine. That not Virginia, or North Carolina, or anybody can pass a law against it." He didn't usually talk about such matters with her, let alone at table. He seemed too exhausted to contain himself, worn down by a world careening out of control.

"You'd think," he said, "that they would be able to see the obvious. The more they hand over to them, the more they want. Johnson gives them the Civil Rights Act, and they disrupt the Democratic Convention. So he gives them the Voting Rights Act and the very next day, in gratitude, they burn down half of Los Angeles. So he gives them Affirmative Action, and they start the Black Panthers. Now they've as much as said that any black man can do anything he wants to any white woman, and we're just supposed to stand to one side and watch."

"Daddy, I can't believe they said *that*."

"You don't think so?" His voice had quieted below the level where it was safe to talk to him, so Ruth didn't answer. "You wait. You wait and see what happens next."

He pushed his chair back and went around the corner to his study. The door clicked shut in the otherwise perfect silence.

Greg, who always sat at Wilmer's right hand, shook his head. "You shouldn't antagonize him."

Anything she said in her own defense Greg would find equally objectionable, she knew. "Are things really that bad?"

"They're worse. But I would dearly love to see a nigger try anything like that when I was around."

"Greg," Ruth's mother said sharply, "we don't use that word at table."

Greg walked out, slamming the screen door.

He was 16 now, finally filling out under the supervision of his basketball coach. The Trojans had won their division that spring. Though he was only a sophomore, Greg had been the second highest scorer for the year. He would doubtless have been first if he hadn't fouled out so many times or spent so much time on the bench for poor sportsmanship. South Johnston High had finally succumbed to integration, and Greg made no secret of his resentment toward the one black player who'd been allowed on the team, a boy from Greg's class named Harvey Boyette.

Black players on opposing teams fared even worse. In one of the last games of the season, Ruth had come with her father to watch Greg play. Late in the final period, Greg had run a Negro player from the visiting team into the seats, where the boy had fallen and broken his arm. Greg had said something to him then, inaudible on the far side of the court where Ruth and her father sat. After the game the black boy's teammates had ambushed Greg and beaten him badly.

Ruth had been the one to bring him home from the emergency room. High on painkillers, ribs taped, one eye blackened and stitched, he swaggered proudly into the house, only to be met by Ruth's father. They looked each other over briefly, then Ruth's father beckoned Greg into the study. Whatever her father said to him calmed him for a few days, though it did not change him.

He was like an overloaded electrical outlet, all heat and sparks, waiting to burn the house down.

THE ONLY GOOD THING in those years was that Robert gave up his mistress, and from the summer of 1966 to the summer of 1967 he was all hers again. If they did not spend a lot of time together, many marriages were like that. Robert had never had any desire to learn bridge, though Ruth had become a highly sought-after partner at the country club. For her part, she had no interest in jitterbugging until all hours at smoky, dangerous nightspots. The important thing was the commitment, and she hoped Robert had learned his lesson.

Robert's company thrived, and he was finally doing the highway engineering he'd dreamed of. He worked long hours, and beneath his fatigue she thought she could see real satisfaction.

Then came the fall.

Cindy Berkshire, she discovered, had been far from the worst thing that could happen to her marriage. Ruth would have given up all her worldly goods to have Robert back with the Berkshire woman.

Worse yet, it was Greg who delivered the news. It was September 23, and Ruth had volunteered to drive him to a Saturday basketball practice. His rattletrap 1949 pickup, which he'd been driving since Ruth's father arranged a hardship license for him at 15, was in the shop. She'd tried to make small talk, difficult as that was with him. He took offense at trivial and unpredictable things, sometimes put out by the very idea of conversation.

Even asking about his chances for a Duke scholarship failed to get a rise. To keep away the silence, she'd been talking about Robert's work on the highway. Greg had slid lower and lower in his seat, head turned to the window like he wasn't listening. Ruth let her voice trail off. After what seemed forever, and still without looking at her, Greg said, "Your husband's got a nigger girlfriend."

In shock, Ruth watched the gray asphalt rush toward her. The late summer sky was pale with clouds, the trees stunted, the grass yellow. There were any number of reasons, she thought, that Greg might say a thing like that. The complicated feelings he held for her shaded all the way into jealousy where Robert was concerned. She'd never told Greg about Cindy Berkshire; she might, however, have said enough that his imagination could fill in the blanks. Certainly from the time of the Berkshire business Greg had grown more antagonistic toward Robert, and more defensive toward her.

"He stays at her house," Greg said. "One of the brothers saw him there with her. You know who she is? She's the girlfriend of that big gorilla nigger, Barrett Howard. Him and Robert share her between them."

Ruth felt a lurch of nausea. She swallowed hard.

"That's why they saw Robert. They watch that house, to keep an eye on Howard. She's a real looker, too, they said. High yella gal, could pass for white."

"That's enough, Greg," she managed to say.

"Your daddy didn't want to tell you, but I thought, that ain't fair. She ought to know. I mean, him sharing a woman with Howard is practically like having Howard right there in your—"

"Shut up, Greg. Or I'll tell my father."

"I know it ain't nice to hear. You'll thank me one day."

He was quiet after that. Ruth could not wait to get to Four Oaks, where the high school was, so she could be alone to let her feelings out. Ten endless, silent minutes later she pulled up in front of the gym. Taking his cheap leatherette bag by the handles, he opened the door and said, "I'll get a ride home. You don't have to come back for me."

By the time she was on the highway again, Ruth had gone cold inside and neither tears nor sickness would come. She drove straight to Durham and called her mother to say she wasn't feeling well and would miss church the next morning.

Robert didn't come home that night, and her last hope—that Greg had been lying—slipped away.

Despite her churchgoing, Ruth had been feeling distant from God for some time. Part of it was Robert. He claimed to believe, though he didn't care for church, and Ruth thought God might not have felt too welcome in their house lately. With Robert gone, in the long hours before sunrise, Ruth found the words to pray for strength and said them over and over.

Eventually the strength came, along with the words of David's song to the Lord. "For thou hast girded me with strength to battle: them that rose up against me hast thou subdued under me." My love is stronger than this other woman's, she thought. My love will endure and hers will not.

And with that she was finally able to sleep.

IN APRIL OF 1968, Martin Luther King was shot in Memphis. That was a Thursday, and the next day Ruth drove out to the farm for the weekend.

She knew her father hated King above all other Negroes, and she understood, objectively, why. Much of the chaos of the last decade had been at his urging, the result of his terrible impatience, his unending pressure, his manipulation of the press. He had all but publicly admitted to being a Communist. And Ruth was personally repelled by the stories of his harlotry.

And yet, watching him on TV, Ruth found herself oddly moved by him. His emotions seemed so close to the surface, and some of them Ruth could not fail to recognize: humor, love, sorrow, loneliness.

And so she entered her father's house with her feelings already muddled, only to find him buoyant, barely able to restrain his joy. At the supper table he said, "The tide has turned, now. You'll see."

Something in his voice alerted Ruth. "Daddy, did you have something to do with this?"

"Directly? No. But if you wish and pray for something long enough, I suppose you can take some credit for it when it happens."

Ruth's mother stared down at her plate, loading her fork carefully with one morsel from each of the foods there: pork chop, collards, mashed potatoes, cornbread, redeye gravy. Her insistence on a civil table had worn away to nothing, and she had retreated into her own increasingly strange habits.

"You don't give yourself credit," Greg said. He too was grinning uncontrollably.

"Hush, now," Ruth's father said. "Mind your tongue."

Ruth's appetite withered. She ate what she could and listened to the talk of sports, weather, the tobacco and cotton planting coming up at the end of the month. Her mother would not meet her eyes.

Later, as she and Greg did dishes alone in the kitchen, he said, "Your daddy don't want it to get around, but he did a lot more than pray where King was concerned. The Lord helps those that help themselves."

Ruth did not point out that this sentiment was not scripture. "What are you saying?"

"I ain't supposed to talk about it. The brothers don't completely trust me as is."

Ordinarily it amused Ruth to hear Greg talk about "the brothers," the same way black people talked about each other on television; this night she could not get past her unease. The smells of the food scraps and the lemon scent of the detergent were too strong, stomach-turning. She didn't answer, and after a minute or so Greg couldn't hold himself back any longer.

"There was a man through here last winter name of Raul. Your father put him up down in the basement. This guy was weird, said he had people all over the South, and one of the places he named was Memphis. Said he had a guy there ran a bar, could hire a guy would take care of King next time he was in town, if the money could be put together for it. I guess he convinced your daddy, because your daddy kicked in."

Ruth took her hands out of the dishwater and dried them on a towel. "We don't know that it was this man," she said. "Do we? I mean, it might have been somebody else."

"That's true," Greg smirked. "Maybe it wasn't him at all."

"Can you finish up?" Ruth said. "I need to go sit down."

Greg suddenly softened. "You all right?"

"Fine," she said. "Just tired from the drive."

She sat on the swings in the warm April night. Frogs down at the creek were singing their hearts out, a high-pitched, clattering roar. Ruth thought about her childhood and the way her father had seemed to her then, wise and just and strong and calm. They had both changed, she supposed, though the thought made her terribly sad. He had become the kind of person who would help pay for a murder, and she had become another man's wife.

The change had been slow, and she hadn't really seen it until now. Until tonight she had still been divided in her love; now she saw that Robert was all she had. And Robert had gone astray.

THE SUMMER OF 1968 was endless, with riots in ghettos across America and riots at the Democratic convention. White America, her father said, was standing up and making it clear they'd had enough of Black Power, hippie protestors, communists, deserters, and all the other traitors. It was Armageddon, he said, the Final Battle, and the angels were winning.

"Richard Nixon is going to take this election, guaranteed. And once he does, that's the end of integration in this country. He will turn back the clock to happier times."

She still drove to the farm every Friday and stayed through Sunday afternoon, though it felt now as if she were only going through the motions. The one weekend she'd spent in the house on Woodrow she had been haunted by Robert's absence, unable to stop thinking about where he was and what he was doing. It was all out in the open now, had been since the previous fall when he had tried to leave her. Her one consolation was that he had lied to her face, denying the other woman. On that denial she pinned her belief that he would betray his affair in the end.

THE WEEKEND AFTER Nixon's "surprise" victory in November, Ruth's father finally relaxed. "If somebody would only do for Barrett Howard what they did for Martin Luther Coon," he said at Sunday dinner, "my satisfaction would be complete."

Ruth looked at her mother, who was listening to another, more ethereal conversation. Greg, of course, had no objection.

"Daddy!" she said.

He held up both hands and smiled as if, like a beloved but clumsy infant, his forgiveness should be taken for granted.

That fall was the start of Greg's senior year. In mid-December, a scout from Duke came to several of the practices. Everyone knew. Greg had been on his best behavior, he assured the family. Passing off the ball, working close to the net on defense, hitting over 80 percent of his free throws.

At the next Friday's game against Smithfield-Selma, Ruth drove up from Durham to watch the Trojans overpower the Spartans 85 to 66, with the Duke scout in the audience. Greg was the game's top scorer. He handled himself well, except for one play early in the second half when a black player for the Spartans elbowed him in the kidney as he went up for a shot. Greg turned in the air and landed with his fist pulled back, inches away from gut-punching the black boy. Then he remembered where he was and stepped away and let his hand drop to his side. He was so rattled that he missed his free throws, but surely, Ruth thought, that was a small thing, not even to be noticed.

Afterward, in the parking lot, Ruth and her father watched Greg get into a brand new Cadillac Seville with the Duke scout and Harvey Boyette, the black boy from Greg's class.

"This is a happy, happy night for me," Ruth's father said. He showed it less in his smile than in the relaxation of his shoulders, the broad gestures of his hands. "That boy has made me very proud."

"He loves you very much," Ruth said.

Her own life was no source of pride for anyone. As winter turned into the spring of 1969, Robert was more or less openly living with his black harlot, only coming home to Woodrow Street on the one night a week she demanded. Then, just as she believed things could get no worse, they did.

After dinner one Friday night her father called her into his office the way he'd summoned Greg and so many others, the way he'd called her in as a child to receive punishment. As the gloom and foreboding settled over her, she thought about the way those childhood feelings were always with you, waiting to ambush you when you least expected them. At that moment she found herself suddenly thinking of Orpha, and the memory was so painful she pushed it away and concentrated on the physicality of closing the office door and sitting in the wooden visitor's chair across from her father's desk.

"Does the name Mercy Richards mean anything to you?"

"Yes," she said. "I know the name."

"Robert's mistress," her father said.

"I've heard that. Never from him."

"Robert's *black* mistress."

She didn't answer.

"Well, now it seems Robert has got his black mistress pregnant. Did you know that?"

A few seconds later, in a gentler tone, he said, "It appears that you did not. Stop that crying, now. I didn't raise my girls to be weak."

Ruth put her hands to her cheeks and found, to her surprise, that they were wet. She patted at them with a tissue from her purse.

"I take some responsibility for this," her father said. "I gave my approval to this man, despite some misgivings."

What misgivings? Ruth wondered. He had said nothing at the time.

"I apologize for that," he went on. "And I want you to know that I'll back you up in whatever you decide to do about this."

"What I decide to do?"

"Being the faithful, long-suffering type is well and good, but if this gets any more public, if the family name starts getting dragged through the mud, that may not be acceptable."

"Acceptable?" She was puzzled that her father would mock her fidelity after what he'd put her mother through for so many years.

"I mean you may need to divorce him, to distance yourself from him publicly."

"I would need that? Or you would?" She had never spoken that way to her father before. She was disoriented, aware of torrential emotions spinning around her, yet not able to connect to them.

"I know this is sudden," her father said. He didn't acknowledge her questions. "Take your time, do some thinking. Pray for guidance."

She looked at her shoes. "Is that all?"

"Yes, that's all for now."

She wandered out to the swings. In a crisis they drew her irresistibly with their memories of happier times. Greg knew that, so it was hardly coincidence that he came looking for her there.

"I could kill her for you, you know." He slouched against the wood frame that supported the swing set, watching her from the corners of his eyes. It was twilight. Pine pollen fogged the air; by morning the porch and the cars would be coated in a fresh layer of yellow-green dust.

"What?" Ruth asked, shocked to attention.

"Robert's whore. Something could happen to her. If you wanted."

Ruth planted her feet to stop the swing. "Don't talk like that. Don't you ever talk like that."

"She's carrying a half-breed bastard child."

"She's carrying Robert's child. Which is something I'll never be able to do. Nothing is to harm that child. Do you understand me?"

She had refused his love offering, she saw, and hurt him deeply. She thought of Cain's rejected sacrifice and wished she hadn't been so harsh.

"I understand," Greg said bitterly. "I understand, well enough." He started to walk away.

"Greg, I'm sorry," she said. "I don't like all this talk of killing. It's not right."

Greg kept walking. "You don't have to explain. You don't have to explain anything to me."

AT THE END OF MARCH, Harvey Boyette got a registered letter offering him a basketball scholarship to Duke. The next week he signed a letter of intent with his parents, new Duke Basketball Head Coach Bucky Waters, and every reporter in Johnston County present. On the TV news that night Boyette, close to tears, thanked God and his coach and his teammates. Greg walked out of the room, and Ruth's father said, "Turn it off." Ruth switched off the set and thought about going after Greg. Her goodwill, she knew, would be no match for the darkness of his despair, would only make things worse.

After another week with no letter for Greg, Ruth's father got on the phone. No, there was no mistake, they told him. Impressed as they were with Greg's ability, there were only so many places on the team. He would be welcome to enroll at Duke as a regular student and try out. He might work on his temper a bit, they suggested.

He passed all this along to Ruth, but not to Greg. From time to time Greg would look at him with a question in his eyes, the kind of look Ruth had seen on dogs who'd been sent to bed for misbehaving, waiting for some sign of forgiveness. All Ruth's father had for him was a shake of the head.

For Ruth he had considerably more.

"There's no question who the better player is," her father said. He seemed to be talking to himself. "The nigra boy got the scholarship because of his skin color. It was some more of that affirmative action like Lyndon was always talking about." Then, barely audible, he said, "I may have to undertake some affirmative action of my own."

Harvey Boyette's new Triumph TR6 crashed into a tree less than a month later. Surgeons at Duke Hospital put pins in both his knees and told him he would never play basketball again. In his sworn statement to the police, he claimed to have been run off the road by a pickup with no lights, but the open bottle of bourbon in the car raised questions. Boyette said he didn't know where the bottle came from, and friends and family agreed they'd never seen him take a drink. None of that changed the fact that Boyette was black, and newly a celebrity, and that the accident happened in Johnston County. There was no investigation.

The estrangement that Ruth first felt after the King murder became complete. If acts of equal or greater violence had taken place in her childhood, her father had taken care to shield her from them. She no longer believed in angels; until Harvey Boyette, however, her father had at least allowed her to look the other way.

She began to spend more weekends apart from her father, alone in the house in Durham. Having failed as a wife and as a daughter, she would never have the opportunity to fail as a mother. She had to ask herself, as a matter of simple logic, what the point might be in going on. Robert had a box of heavy duty plastic bags that he used for leaves and lawn cuttings. She could put one of them over her head and suffocate herself, like she had heard of people doing. Robert would find her that way, in their bed, one more bag of trash that he had thrown away.

She prayed for a sign and went outside for a walk.

It was a Saturday morning in early June, and the world was green and damp and fertile. Birds sang with no apology. How little it would take to be happy, she thought. To have the things that others around her had—Robert with his mistress, her father with his cause.

A horn honked beside her. She turned and saw Cindy Berkshire, a crooked grin on her face, leaning out the driver's side window of a new Cadillac. "Hey, Ruth," she said. "I haven't seen you in a dog's age."

It had been more than a year, and Ruth saw that liquor and cigarettes and loose living had taken their toll. Cindy looked ten hard, withering years older than her actual age.

"Cindy, how are you? How's Bill?"

"We're all just right as rain. How's that handsome devil of a husband of yours?"

"He could stand to be a little less busy, I suppose. When business is booming you can't complain."

"No, I suppose not." Cindy had a way of making the most ordinary words sound like she was looking down her nose at them. "You tell him I said hey."

"I surely will," Ruth said.

As Cindy drove away, Ruth thought, how small she is. How easy it was to outlast her, though it seemed difficult then. This must be the lesson, she thought. Time is on my side. If I wait, my time will come.

IN LATE JULY, Greg celebrated his 18th birthday. Ruth went to the farm for the party, only her second trip that month. Her father had not commented on her absences, though he had surely noticed.

It was a solemn birthday. Ruth's father had arranged to get Greg into Duke, though he would be on academic probation the first year. The possibility existed that he could try out for the basketball team and make it, though no one brought it up, least of all Greg. Ruth's father told her the boy had not touched a basketball since Harvey Boyette's scholarship offer.

Ruth had once again bought him a Shepherd puppy. The first Shepherd she'd given him, Duke, was now 11 years old, blind in one eye, and badly arthritic. Though he'd adopted various strays over the years and even taught them tricks, Duke was his great love. Ruth was afraid that when Duke died Greg would lose his last anchor.

The gift rekindled their original bond. Greg was reluctant at first to take pleasure in the dog, but it would have taken a far more bitter boy than Greg to resist for long. The puppy got under everyone's feet, ears at perpetual alert, barking and leaping and licking every face and hand he could get close to.

After the party, Greg put the puppy in a training collar for the first time and brought Ruth along for a walk to the river. Though it was difficult, Ruth refrained from making small talk and let the silence last as long as Greg wanted. The air was thick and hot, and Ruth smelled the spice of wild grasses on the riverbank. Cicadas shrilled and a thin sheet of water hissed over the dam.

Greg let the puppy off the leash. The dog tried to walk across the tops of the rocks below the dam, promptly falling in. Greg fetched him out, putting a calming hand on his head and not flinching as he shook off a shower of creek water.

Walking back to the house, he said, "What do you do when you only wanted one thing in your entire life and can't have it?"

At first Ruth didn't realize he was talking about himself. "You never give up," she said. "You just keep holding on."

He looked at her then, in a way that told her he understood. Maybe there was even a new respect for her there. Then he looked away and shook his head. "Sometimes you got to admit something's hopeless. Ain't no good in lying to yourself, telling yourself there's a chance when there ain't."

"There are other schools," Ruth said.

"Third rate Podunk colleges that have never even made the NIT. Every day would be a reminder that I'm not good enough to play for a real team."

"What about your friends? Your girlfriend? What do they think about all this?"

"There are the guys I used to play ball with. They're not my friends. They're all Harvey's friends now. As for ... the other thing..."

"Girlfriend?" Ruth said.

"No," he said. "There isn't one."

"Why not? You'd be a real catch. Handsome, athletic, sweet."

"Because it ain't right. It ain't right to do those things before you're married."

He couldn't look at her, and he was sweating more than the heat justified. Could he not know, Ruth wondered, how often the man he idolized did "those things," and with how many different women?

As if hearing her thoughts, he said, "The worst is your daddy."

"What?"

"Your daddy. I can't stand the way he looks at me now. Pity instead of pride. I feel like a horse with a broken leg, waiting for him to take me out behind the shed and shoot me."

"That's not the way he feels at all," she said. "He thinks you were robbed."

"That ain't the way he acts."

She reached up to touch his hair and he jerked away.

"Poor Greg," she said. "You've got to ease up on yourself. If you don't, you're going to explode."

SHE FOUND HERSELF thinking more and more about Robert's baby. It should have been hers. She was the one who had suffered in silence for all these years. Where was her reward?

She only cooked two nights a week now, big meals that she carefully divided and froze, her own homemade TV dinners. She had just brought her tray into the living room one night when the phone rang. The man on the other end asked for Robert and she told him, as was her habit, that Robert was out at the moment.

"This is Bill Morris in Dallas."

"Mr. Morris, how are you?" This was the man Robert's friend Arthur worked for.

"I wanted to call him personally and apologize for all the delays."

"Delays?"

"With the job. I know y'all were hoping to be down here in the next month or two, and I'd hoped for the same thing. I wanted him to know that I'm not trying to give him the runaround."

"I'm sure," Ruth said, "he thinks nothing of the kind."

"He's a hell of an engineer, and I'm looking forward to working him within an inch of his life, just as soon as I can get all my ducks in a row."

"I feel confident he knows that, Mr. Morris, but I will surely tell him you said it."

"Everything is looking good for November. We should be able to get the two of you down here and get Robert working by the end of November at the very latest."

"That sounds fine," Ruth said. "That gives us time to take care of all the loose ends here."

"Good, that's just fine. Sorry to interrupt, and I hope you have a great evening."

For a moment, after she hung up, Ruth allowed herself to believe that this was a surprise Robert had planned for her, to begin anew, far from all their mistakes. Her heart knew better. The reward Robert had planned for her was abandonment, while he made everything official with his harlot and bastard child. Would he try to pass the harlot off as white as well? Nothing seemed beneath him.

So she had until November. She knew Robert's weakness, knew what she would have to do to get him back. She needed only the opportunity, and if it failed to present itself, then she would have to create it.

THAT AUGUST SHE phoned Mitch Antree.

"This is not a social call," she said, when he started his routine of flattery and balderdash. "I am not calling you as Robert's wife, but as Wilmer Bynum's daughter. Do you understand me?"

After a silence he said, "Yes." The dancing was gone from his voice.

"I assume you know about my husband and his mistress." This silence went on even longer, and Ruth said, "Don't bother to cover up. I've known about it since it started, and I didn't expect you to report back to me."

"I know about her," he said.

"Do you know she's pregnant?"

"No," he said, then, involuntarily, "I'll be damned."

"I have no doubt that you will," Ruth said. "That's beside the point. The baby should be due sometime in the next month. I want to know when it's born. If Robert calls in sick, or even late to work, I want to know about it. Any deviation from his schedule, any mysterious phone calls, anything that might be a signal from her that she's about to give birth, and I find out about it. Is that clear?"

"Yes," Mitch said. The resentment was like a deep well on his end of the phone. She could almost hear the echo. "Is that all?"

"That's all. For now."

He hung up without another word.

On the first Friday in September, her mother called in the afternoon. "Were you planning on coming down this weekend?"

"I hadn't decided," Ruth said. In fact she had a bridge game, a secret she continued to keep from her mother. "Why?"

"I think you'd better come."

Her breath stopped. "Is something wrong with daddy?"

"Nothing like that. You'll see when you get here."

She threw some clothes into an overnight bag, arranged a substitute for bridge, and left immediately. Highway 70 East was already crowded, and Ruth thought about the highways that Robert was building and had yet to build. Someday I-40 would connect Durham to Raleigh and beyond, and traffic delays would be a thing of the past.

She parked in her usual spot, under the ancient oak in the lot north of the house. As soon as she opened the car door, Greg's German Shepherd puppy came bounding up to meet her. He was barely four months old, all energy and no grace. Greg had named him George, supposedly after Patton, more likely after Wallace.

The screen door to the house was unlatched, as always, and she found her mother making cornbread in the kitchen. She kissed her mother's dry cheek and said, "Tell me what's going on. Where's Greg? George is never more than five feet from him."

"Best let your father tell you that."

"Where is he?"

She pointed with her chin. "Tractor shed."

Ruth found him at his workbench, cutting slots in a 2 × 6 with a hand router, one eye squinting against the cigarette in the corner of his mouth. Ruth waited for the whine of the bit to stop and then said, "Daddy?"

He looked up and smiled. "Hello, Sugar."

"Daddy, what's happened to Greg?"

His smile faded like a dream. "Greg's on his way to California."

"California? Why? What's going on?"

"Greg decided to enlist in the Army. He thought maybe that would give him a fresh start."

Everybody, it seemed, was looking for a fresh start. "Daddy, they'll send him to Vietnam. Something's wrong. He wouldn't go without saying goodbye to me."

"He made the decision kind of sudden-like."

"There's something you're not telling me."

"Greg got himself in a bit of trouble. This was the best answer for all concerned."

"What kind of trouble? Was it that business with Harvey Boyette?"

"Greg had nothing to do with what happened to Harvey." Her father had all sorts of different denials; this one rang true.

"Is it some girl?" She hoped it was true.

"Honey, this is nothing for you to be getting your nose into. He's gone, and that's all you need to know. I expect he'll write you once he gets settled."

Dinner was like a bad church service. The three of them went through the motions, enduring it with blank faces, eager to get away. Afterwards Ruth's father turned on the TV in the den, and her mother retreated upstairs to read her Bible and mend clothes. Ruth washed the dishes, then sat silently with her father through *Hogan's Heroes*, the canned laughter as unconvincing as play money. After the first half of the CBS *Friday Night Movie*, another World· War II story, she went up to bed. Unable to sleep, she turned the pages of her high school yearbook and thought about other directions her life might have gone. Most of her friends from those days were married, some with three, even four children. When she ran into them in Smithfield, they seemed numb and exhausted by their lives. She would have traded places with any of them.

She woke in the early hours of the morning to the sound of her door opening. She was still heavy with sleep, not sure how old she was. "Daddy?" she said.

"Shhhh." The door closed and someone came to sit on the floor next to her bed. "It's Greg," he whispered. "I hope I didn't scare you."

She was fully awake now. "Daddy said you were gone to California."

"Not yet. He's got me a ride with a trucker headed out there in a couple of days. Until then I got to hide out in the basement."

"What happened?"

"I did something."

She longed to turn on the light. She couldn't tell from his whispered voice what he was feeling. "Something bad?"

"I don't know. It needed doing. Your daddy wanted it done, he asked for it to get done. But I did it on my own, without permission, and your daddy is really mad."

Your daddy too, Ruth thought. She'd never told him, and would not now; it was not her secret to reveal. "Greg, what did you do?"

"I killed him. The nigger, Barrett Howard, the big, tough Black Power nigger. I killed him with my own hands."

"Oh, Greg, no."

"Don't you start in on me, too."

"I'm not 'starting in.' I love you like a brother. I hate to see you come to this."

"I had to do something," he said. "I had to show him I was still a man."

"Barrett Howard was a man, too. You took his life."

"Don't tell me you never wanted to kill anybody. What about that woman, Mercy? You never wished her dead?"

When Ruth didn't answer, he snorted. "This is war. People get killed in wars all the time. He knew that when he declared war on the white race."

"Daddy said you're going in the Army."

"Yeah."

"They'll send you to Vietnam, you know. You always said you didn't want to go."

"I got no choice. Your daddy said it was the smart thing to do, and I got to do what he tells me just now. Give me an alibi, take me out of the picture. I think he's afraid I'd talk, but I wouldn't. I never would." His hushed voice was feverish, pumped with bravado and raw need.

"I know," Ruth said, a meaningless, soothing sound.

"He had to call Congressman Fogg, get the brothers to help clean up the mess I made."

"Are the police after you?"

"Not yet. So far don't nobody know he's dead but us. Your daddy says he'll take care of it, and maybe he will, and this whole thing will blow over. While all that happens, I'll be in Vietnam."

His knees creaked as he shifted his weight. "I got to go. I don't want your daddy to catch me up here, no telling what he'd do. I was listening at the pantry door this afternoon, when you came in the kitchen and were talking to your mama. I knew I had to see you, get a chance to say goodbye. You were always good to me, always treated me special. I wanted to thank you for that."

Tears ran down Ruth's face, across her nose and onto her left hand that held up her head. "Be careful," she said. "I hope you … I hope you find your way out of this."

She wanted him to kiss her forehead, or touch her hand; that was not Greg's way. "I'm going to sneak outside for a while, be with my dog," Greg said. "He'll be full grown before I see him again." He was standing now, moving toward the door. "You won't tell your daddy about this?"

Then he was gone.

ON SEPTEMBER 18, a Thursday, Mitch Antree called. "He just had a message come into the office saying 'Call M.R.' This may be it."

"Thank you," Ruth said.

"Don't mention it," Antree said, and put the phone down sharply.

She'd been dreading this day without knowing why it was so important to her. There was no plan in her mind, only a powerful and formless longing. Now that the day was here, she wished she hadn't known about it. The problem with the gift of knowledge was that you could never give it back.

Late that night she called Lincoln Hospital, the Negro hospital, and said she was Mercy's sister. The desk nurse was very sweet and found out for her that Mercy was still in labor.

Ruth slept fitfully and was wide awake again at 5 AM. This time when she called, the desk nurse already had the information. "Baby Malcolm was born at 1:39 this morning. Nine pounds and healthy as a horse."

Malcolm, Ruth thought. How many more insults could she possibly bear?

In the grip of an impulse she could not resist, she put on her oldest gardening clothes and tied a drab scarf over her hair. With a pair of old sunglasses, and with her shoulders slumped to minimize her figure, she barely recognized herself. The address for Lincoln Hospital was in the book, and it was easy enough to find.

She went straight past the nurse at the front desk and took the stairs down a flight. A janitor there sent her to the second-floor maternity ward. She took the stairs, moving slowly, on the alert in case Robert should appear. The building was old, the paint on the walls yellowed and peeling, the linoleum worn through in places. It didn't feel clean enough to be a hospital.

The nursery was across from the nurses station, illuminated only by a few night-lights. Fifteen or so babies lay in bassinettes, one in an incubator, another strapped to a kind of platform with an IV drip. After looking both ways, Ruth took off her dark glasses and peered through the plate glass window between cupped hands.

A nurse paused next to her, a middle-aged Negro woman. Of course they were all Negroes here. "Can I help you?" she asked.

"Do you know which one is Mercy Richards' baby?" It cost her extra effort to say the name. "Malcolm?"

"There in front. Third from the right."

Now Ruth saw the handwritten name stuck to the foot of the bassinette with masking tape. "Could I ... could I see him?" she asked. "I just got in town, and I don't want to wake Mercy up. I know she must be exhausted."

The nurse now took her own look around and nodded. "I don't see why not, hon. Come on in."

The nurse lifted Robert's baby and offered it to Ruth, who took it awkwardly in her arms. She opened the blanket to get a good look at the face, then checked out the hands and feet. Her heart filled with unbearable regret. The baby was white, as white as she was. How could God have permitted this? Why was this baby not hers?

She tried to imagine herself taking the baby, running with it down to the parking lot and spiriting it away. Wouldn't Robert be surprised to find his baby gone? To come home to Ruth and find the baby there?

"I'm sorry," the nurse said. "I need to put him back now. I get in trouble if the Head Nurse see this."

The baby had started to squirm and Ruth was afraid it was going to start crying, so she didn't argue. She handed it back, nodded a thank-you, and left.

She returned the next night, and the night after, and stood at the window as long as she dared, watching the baby sleep. By her third visit the nurses were watching her suspiciously; she knew she couldn't risk coming again. Mercy would be taking it home soon, in any case.

That third night she felt a protective presence near her. It was the archangel Michael, she thought, the warrior angel who fought for the righteous. "I would name you Michael," she whispered to the child, and to the angel as well, an offer and a promise. "If you were mine, Michael would be your name."

WHEN ROBERT CAME HOME on a Wednesday night, Ruth knew that something had happened. When he was home again the next night, she knew her prayers had been answered. Whether he had finished with his harlot or not, she had been given her opportunity, and she did not intend to waste it.

Ruth had heard stories about pregnancy, how women who normally took pleasure in marital relations lost interest during the last months, how it got even worse in the first months after the baby was born. Robert was not a difficult man to read, and she could see that he had been suffering for months.

She knew what to do, and she did it gladly. They were man and wife, after all, and it gave her pleasure, just as it had in Jamaica, to give so much pleasure to him.

Even then he tried to walk away from her; but the Lord had passed judgment on Mercy Richards, and at a single stroke, Robert and Michael were delivered unto her for good.

HER FATHER was not pleased.

"You want to raise that pickaninny as your own?"

It was Wednesday, the day after they'd found Mercy's body, and they sat in his office with the door closed. The older he got, the fewer social niceties he bothered to observe, making Ruth pull back even further.

"Daddy, it's Robert's child. And you know I can't ever have a baby myself."

His eyes narrowed. He had clearly taken the words as an accusation. "How on earth are you going to explain suddenly showing up with a child?"

"I won't have to explain it. We're moving to Texas."

"Leaving North Carolina." Now he was the one withdrawing, settling back in his chair. "Same as your sisters."

"Not like my sisters. I love you, Daddy, and I always will." As she said the words, she wondered how true they still were. "This is the best for everyone," she said, and gave him the smile he had never been able to resist. "A fresh start."

IN THE END he gave her what she wanted. He made the adoption happen without a hearing, Mercy's death fade away without an inquest, even provided a doctor to prescribe the pills that let Robert sleep at night.

Yet he did it grudgingly, with poor grace, and so he quietly unraveled the last strands of love that bound her to him.

RUTH WOULD NEVER FORGET her first sight of Dallas. The moving company had already brought all their furniture and belongings and put them in storage. The movers had also towed Robert's car behind the van, so he and Ruth could make the drive together in her Buick. They'd done it in just over two days, much of it over stretches of Interstate 40 in Tennessee and Arkansas, and then on I-30 from Little Rock into Dallas.

Ruth was at the wheel, and Robert was dozing with his car coat folded up between his head and the bitter chill outside the window. Michael was stretched out on the back seat, wrapped entirely in blankets except for his head. They'd gotten up at dawn to make this last leg, and it was still early morning, the sun low in the sky behind them.

They topped a low rise and suddenly the city was before her, stretching further than her eyes could see, fading finally at the horizon. They had just passed between the gigantic columns of an overpass, and it seemed to her that the city was a gift to Robert, tied up in ribbons of concrete.

She let the car drift gently onto the shoulder in order to savor the moment, here, alone, in the very first seconds of her new beginning, before Robert or Michael could awaken to distract her, where she could savor at last the fruits of God's goodness, and let her heart fill with the love that belonged to no one in the world but these two fragile creatures that she had taken into her care.

MICHAEL

2004

Friday, November 5

A T FIRST MICHAEL had prodded her with questions, but as they went on she needed less and less encouragement. He took her out for Mexican food that night—there was precious little authentic Tex-Mex in North Carolina—and they had finally broken off after 11.

Michael had spent the night on an inflatable mattress in his father's office. He left one window open an inch to hear water running in the creek. His father was in all his dreams these days, not saying anything, watching from the passenger seat as Michael drove around an unfamiliar city, or standing behind him as he sketched what appeared to be random assemblages of old clothes and appliances.

He talked to Denise for half an hour before bed, small talk, mostly. He hadn't wanted to get into the revelations from his mother, and Denise in turn hadn't mentioned being on the run, other than to reassure Michael that she and Rachid were safe. The conversation was comfortable, even intimate. Both of them, Michael thought, teetered on the edge of saying more.

In the kitchen the next morning Ruth was dressed and waiting for him at the breakfast table, one of his father's graph paper pads in front of her, covered in her prim longhand. "I made a few notes to help my memory," she said.

She repeated herself more than a few times, made corrections, and jumped around in time. Still, by the end, Michael was able to make a coherent whole from it.

Some questions had to wait until she was through.

"You do understand," he said carefully, "that you were pregnant when your father took you to that doctor in Smithfield."

"Don't be ridiculous. How could I have been pregnant? My periods were just irregular."

They stared at each other across the table. He was not sure what he saw in her eyes. It felt like a warning, telling him not to pursue this. He wondered if her denial could survive the words for what had happened to her—incest, molestation, rape, abortion. What certainly could not survive was the feeling he and Ruth had created in their pursuit of family history, the tenuous but nonetheless real openness it had brought them. At that moment he felt closer to her than he ever had, and he was not willing to throw it away.

There were other questions he did manage to ask. "So my father lived and died without ever knowing that Wilmer Bynum was the Grand Dragon of the Night Riders of the Confederacy?"

"What good would it have done—for anyone—if he'd known?"

"It's part of who you are. That's a huge secret to keep in a marriage."

"Michael, you've never been married. Believe me, it's smaller than you think. Honesty is not always the best policy, no matter what I told you when you were little."

"Is that why you never went to the police when you had knowledge of a murder?"

"I was not going to choose Barrett Howard over my own flesh and blood. Greg was my brother. I deeply regret that you never had a brother or sister, that you can't know how that feels."

"You know the rumors went around that Howard had run away to Mexico and betrayed his movement."

"Howard and his movement were nothing to me." She was drinking her fourth or fifth cup of coffee, and her tone was matter-of-fact. She seemed distant from her earlier life, distant from everything. "I was brought up to see Barrett Howard as slightly worse than the Devil himself. I was breaking loose from Daddy's ideas, but I was far from free of them yet."

It was after 2 and his flight left at 4. He had to change in Houston, and wouldn't get to Durham until after 10. "I have to go," he said, pushing his chair back from the table. His bag was packed and sitting by the door. "Thank you. Thank you for talking to me."

"Are you still planning to go to the papers about my father?"

"No," Michael said. "All that's over."

"And Greg?"

"Greg's another story. Greg is still dangerous."

"The poor man," she said. "He never had a chance."

"Your father gave him every chance."

"My father couldn't change the way he was inside, change the childhood he had."

Apparently Ruth's thoughts had gone the same place that Michael's had, because she said, "Was I really such a terrible mother?"

"I don't think I can do this right now," Michael said.

"Try. I think you owe me that much."

"Not terrible," Michael said. "It just never felt … right."

"I would look at you and I would see that woman," Ruth said. "I tried so hard to pretend you were mine, and sometimes I would believe it. And then..." She shook her head. "I loved him so much. He was everything to me. And now he's gone."

Michael drew her into a careful hug, and for a second she surrendered. Her arms tightened around his neck, and she pressed fully against him. Then, in the space of another second she stiffened and pulled back into herself.

He let her go.

"You look so like him, sometimes," she said.

"I'll call you," Michael said.

"Will you?"

"Yes," he said. "I promise."

WHEN HE GOT to the gate he called Detective Bishop. "It was Greg Vaughan," Michael told him. "He killed Barrett Howard and he firebombed Service Printing and the *Carolina Times*. Whatever's going to happen tomorrow, he's the one that's going to do it."

"The last time I talked to you," Bishop said, "you were sure that it was Congressman Fogg killed Howard. Before that it was your father."

"That was speculation. This is fact. I'm in Dallas, and I've been talking to my father's widow. Vaughan confessed to her."

"All right. We have Vaughan under surveillance anyway, but I'll double it. We'll be all over him tomorrow. If he makes a move toward the ATC, I'll bring him in."

Michael let out a long sigh. "Thank you."

"I'm glad to hear you're in Dallas. Staying there for a while?"

"I'm at the airport. About to catch a plane back."

"Michael. Don't do anything stupid, okay? We have this under control."

"I hope you do. I need to see Vaughan locked up. He would probably kill me if he got the chance."

"You shouldn't have left your burglar tools behind." Bishop's voice was more mocking than annoyed.

"Maybe I'm not the hero type. But I have information you need. Vaughan killed Howard in a shoe shop in Hayti, and he used a cobbler's awl to do it. It's in the living room of the Bynum house right now, in a glass case. Along with souvenirs from his torch jobs."

"Holy shit."

"You have to nail this guy."

"We'll get him. But we have to do this properly. We can't go on hearsay. If we're going to get a conviction, we have to build up the chain of evidence, one link at a time. That's going to take a while, unless we get really lucky."

"What are you saying?"

"I'm saying that he may screw up tomorrow and we'll have him. He may pull back and wait, and if that happens we have to wait too. In the meantime, you'd be better off canceling that flight and staying in Texas."

"I can't," Michael said. "My life is in Durham now."

As SOON AS the plane touched down at RDU, Michael called Denise. The flight had made good time, and it was not quite 10 PM. Michael felt drained. "I'm home," he told her.

"Home as in Durham?"

"Yeah, the airport, anyway."

"That sounds promising. When do I get to see you?"

"When do you want to see me?"

"Tonight," she said. It was a whisper and a promise.

"Why not?" he said. Hope, desire, and excitement closed his throat, and he could barely talk. "It'll be late, though. I have something to do first."

"Tomorrow's Saturday. I can stay up late." Then she hesitated. "You're not going back out to the farm."

"No, nothing like that. I have to see Harriman. It won't take long."

HIS ECHO WAS GONE, and he ended up in a red Mitsubishi Lancer. As he handed over his credit card at the rental desk, he remembered that he was out of work. His savings would not last forever, especially at the rate he was going.

Not the time to be worrying about that, he told himself.

By the time he got to Chapel Hill it was 11 o'clock. Two cars filled Harriman's driveway and Michael had to park behind the house next door.

He rang Harriman's bell and then, just before it opened, he felt a chill of premonition. The door swung back into the house and Charles was on the other side. Michael's response was physical and instantaneous. A jolt of pain went through his ribs and head, so strong it was all he could do not to raise his arms to protect himself. He was sick to his stomach, icy cold, and at least as angry as he was afraid.

"Michael," Charles said.

Michael couldn't speak. He was torn between the need to hide and the desire to hurt.

"Yo, man, Harriman told me you were here the other night. Listen..." He struggled for words. "I'm sorry, all right? I'm sorry for what happened."

"It didn't just 'happen,'" Michael managed to say.

"No. No, you're right." He reached out toward Michael's chin, where the scabs had dried hard and dark.

Michael flinched and pulled away. "Don't," he said.

Charles withdrew his hand. "Damn, this was wrong. Harriman keeps trying to school me, but I never listen. I'm a hothead, and I screw things up. I can't seem to help it. My temper comes up and it's, like, right there, you know what I'm saying?"

Michael was not ready to make peace. It was not yet an option.

"Anyway," Charles said, "C'mon, get inside, it's November out there."

Michael walked past him, trying not to let his emotions show. In the living room, Harriman was standing with three other men. Two of them Michael didn't know; they were young and dressed in nondescript middle-class casual clothes: Dockers, polo shirts, sport coats. The third, balding and heavyset in a brown pinstripe suit, Michael was sure he had seen on the local TV news, somebody high up in Durham city government. That man looked at Harriman nervously as Michael said, "Meeting of the executive committee?"

"You should have called first, Michael," Harriman said. "You'll forgive me if I don't introduce you."

"This is important," Michael said. "Can I talk about ... that business I was here about before?"

"Yes," Harriman said.

"It's Greg Vaughan after all," Michael said. "His army dates were faked. He killed Barrett Howard before he went to Vietnam, and he burned down the *Times* and Service Printing when he got home. He'll be the one tomorrow. Whatever happens, it'll involve fire."

"It's time to take that cracker out," Charles said. "I can do it tonight."

Harriman shook his head, and Michael kept going, unable to slow the torrent of words. "I already told the cops. They're on this. They're watching him now, and if he gets anywhere near ATC they'll pop him. If you move on him, you'll have cops all over you."

"We'll put our own surveillance in place as well," Harriman said.

"And if the cops screw it up," Charles said, "we move in."

Harriman, with some reluctance, said, "We'll do what we have to."

"Do you even know what he looks like?" Michael asked.

Harriman and Charles looked at each other. "He's the only one lives on that farm, right?" Charles said.

"Get me a piece of paper and a sharp pencil," Michael said, "and a place I can work."

He sat at the dining room table, drawing Vaughan as he would for a character model sheet: one full figure pose, standing with his weight on one leg, starting straight ahead, and another quick sketch of the profile.

The others talked quietly out of earshot. Michael worked quickly, finishing in ten minutes.

"Are you going to have anybody at ATC?" Michael asked as he handed the sketch to Harriman. Harriman glanced at it and passed it to Charles.

"Wow," Charles said. "This is really good."

The man in the suit looked at Harriman. "He doesn't know?"

"Know what?" Michael asked.

Harriman sighed. "The Night Riders have a parade permit for tomorrow. They're going to be demonstrating in the street outside the ATC."

"And the city is allowing this?" Michael asked the man in the suit.

"We had no choice," he said. "They're a legal organization. The paperwork was all in order."

"Paperwork," Charles said.

"Charles..." Harriman said.

The two men Michael didn't know looked alternately annoyed and uncomfortable, as if they'd heard it all before but still couldn't get used to it. One of them asked Harriman, "Are we done?"

"Not yet," Michael said. "What else is happening tomorrow?"

Harriman said, "We think the 'parade' is a distraction, to set up whatever act of violence they're planning. We're going to have an offsetting distraction of our own."

"Showdown time," Charles said.

"They've put the word out across the entire Southeast," Harriman said. "We think they could get as many as two hundred men there. We're going to put at least that many black men, women, and children in their way. Passive resistance a la Gandhi and MLK."

"Some of that resistance may be less passive than others," Charles said, to no one in particular. Then, to Michael, "King was good at working the media, but the truth is, it was the black people with guns and baseball bats and rocks got us what little we got. Without that fist behind King's glove, wouldn't have been anything at all."

Michael gave his head a small, dubious shake.

"What?" Charles said.

"I don't get it," Michael said. "I mean, we've got a real threat here, whatever it is that Vaughan is going to do. But a bunch of white guys in hoods, is that really the problem? You said they can muster maybe two hundred people from the only states where they've got a following at all. That's pretty sad. Does anybody even take them seriously anymore?"

Charles looked insulted. "What are you saying?"

Harriman waved a conciliating hand. "He's got a point. The NRC isn't our real enemy. We all know that." He looked at Michael. "But in the last four years it's become okay to hate again in this country. Bush got whatever votes he didn't steal in 2000 by giving every hatemonger in the US a place to roost. Hate queers? Hate those Mexicans coming in and taking those jobs you don't want? Hate those smart people that know how to pronounce 'nuclear'? Come on in. Klan membership is thriving, the NRC is growing again, mostly because of immigration issues. For the city to give them a permit is a disgrace. Somebody has to stand up and say this is wrong."

Then, for the first time, Harriman's façade slipped and Michael saw the pain and frustration underneath. "And ... sometimes," Harriman said, "you have to do something. Instead of sitting there and taking it."

"Amen, brother," Charles said.

The man in the suit cleared his throat. "The police will be out in force. Nothing's going to get out of hand. It's going to be like street theater or something. Making a point, but nobody gets seriously hurt." He looked to Charles and Harriman for confirmation and came up empty.

Michael saw that it was time to go. "I wish you luck," he said. "I mean that." He let himself out.

HE CALLED DENISE again as soon as he started the car. "I'm heading for the hotel."

"I'll be in the lobby when you get there."

His thoughts were mostly on Denise as he drove, even as he felt a slow unwinding inside. He still couldn't visualize the person he would be in another year or two. At least the pieces were all out where he could start to fit them together. He would have some time to do that now, with Greg Vaughan and the American Tobacco crisis out of his hands. If Bishop somehow blew it, he knew Charles would step up.

When he walked into the Holiday Inn Express and saw Denise, rising from the couch where she'd been sitting, beautiful in a plain black T-shirt and jeans, he understood that wherever he was going, she was going to be part of it.

"Don't say anything," she whispered, as he wrapped her up in his arms. "Don't talk, okay? Just hold me."

As soon as the elevator doors closed he was kissing her, and when he turned back from bolting the door of his suite she was pulling off her shirt.

"There's something about a hotel room, isn't there?" she said, with a bright nervousness that Michael found sexy and endearing. He didn't answer, just went to her and helped her with the last of her clothes.

•

THEY WERE BOTH exhausted afterwards. With Denise curled inside his right arm, Michael tried to tell her what he'd learned from Ruth, and found himself getting incoherent. Finally Denise put her fingers to his mouth. "Shhhh. You can tell me in the morning. Sleep now."

And he did.

Saturday, November 6

HIS CELL RANG at 10:13 AM. He'd had it off so long he barely recognized the sound, especially swimming up from deep sleep in the thickly draped, artificial night of the hotel.

He stumbled out of bed and found the phone where he'd plugged it in to recharge during one of his last coherent moments the night before.

"Hello?" he said. The room was cold, and he huddled naked in an over-stuffed chair, facing away from Denise so as not to wake her.

"It's Sgt. Bishop." Michael did not care for the sudden formality. "We've got a problem here."

Michael found himself violently and painfully awake. "What kind of a problem?" He went back to the nightstand to put his glasses on.

"Well, we followed what we thought was Vaughan over half of Johnston County this morning—"

"What you *thought* was Vaughan?"

"My men had a good description. The guy was wearing a baseball cap and a down jacket. He came out of Vaughan's trailer at 7 this morning and got in Vaughan's truck and proceeded to lead them on one hell of a trip."

"It wasn't Vaughan."

"No."

"So you're telling me you don't know where he is."

Bishop sighed. "Not at this exact moment. We do have twenty heavily armed men over at American Tobacco, and they're all watching out for him."

"Jesus Christ."

"I admit this situation is not ideal. There's no reason to think he knows where you are now, correct?"

"I don't know what he knows."

"Maybe this would be a good day to drive down to the coast. The skies are clear, it's supposed to be in the sixties. Make sure no one's following you, maybe get a motel room on the beach."

"I'm not real crazy about taking your advice at the moment." The sense of calm he'd been inching toward was gone. A gale of contradictory impulses pounded at him, urging him to pile furniture against the door, to run downstairs and look for Vaughan, to scream obscenities at Bishop, to demand that Harriman send an armed guard to protect him.

"Now listen, Michael, don't do anything stupid—"

"I don't think you're one to talk," Michael said, and switched off the phone.

Denise was watching from the shadows of the bed. "We have sex, and the next morning you get bad news on the cell phone. This is getting to be an ugly habit."

"The cops lost Vaughan."

"Uh oh."

"I don't think he's looking for us. I think he's got other business first."

"American Tobacco."

"Yeah. But once he's done there, I would expect we're next."

"Michael, it's freezing out there. Come to bed."

Michael got in next to her, still holding the phone. "I have to make another call."

She wrapped her small body around his, and he felt her naked, silken skin from his chest to the bottoms of his feet. "Make all this go away," she said. "I just got you back."

As his desire for her began to stir, panic pushed it away. He punched up Harriman's number, saying, "It's not going to go away. Not by itself."

Harriman answered on the first ring. "It's me," Michael said.

"We lost him," Harriman said.

"I was afraid you were going to say that."

"We followed the cops, and they went for a decoy."

"I heard," Michael said.

"There may be ten thousand people down there today. Black Star is giving away barbeque and beer, they have bands playing under the water tower, the Duke basketball team is signing autographs—"

Michael saw then what Vaughan wanted to do. "Duke, did you say?"

"I've got the schedule here in front of me. They'll be signing between three and four."

"If something happened to those players, Black Star would never recover from it."

"Vaughan's a UNC fan?"

"Funny," Michael said. "But yes, he would believe he has a score to settle with Duke."

"That helps. We still have to put our hands on him, though. The cops will be looking for him, we'll be looking for him, but he might still get in and do whatever it is he's going to do. I've made some copies of your sketch to hand out to our people, but the fact is, you're the only one who's actually seen Greg Vaughan in person."

Michael had seen this moment closing in through the entire conversation. Still his mouth went dry. "You're saying you want me down there."

"If you don't come, and Vaughan burns the ATC down, or does whatever he does, and injures or kills hundreds of people, I don't think you're going to feel very sanguine about it."

"I'll call you back," Michael said. He cut off the phone and put it on the nightstand.

"Michael?" Denise said.

Every muscle in his body was rigid. He tried to make his mind go through the motions of logic and reason, in vain. There was no real choice, and he didn't need Harriman to rub his nose in it.

"Michael, talk to me."

"I have to go," he said. His lips felt numb.

"Why?" She put her hand on his mouth before he could answer. "Think about it for a minute. In the last few days you've lost your father, your mother, and your job. If you're looking for a way to kill yourself and have it not be your fault, you need to tell me now. For my sake."

"Denise." He held her face in both his hands. She was so beautiful, he thought. "I love you. I'm not trying to kill myself. All I want is to be with you, and not be running from some cracker nutcase or having nightmares about a disaster I maybe could have stopped."

"And what am I going to feel if I let you walk out of here and you get killed or maimed?"

"I don't know," Michael said. "I guess that would really suck."

She stared at him, then laughter exploded out of her like water from a breaking dam. She buried her head in his neck and squeezed him around the chest with both arms. When she looked up again, her face was wet with tears. "I love you too, by the way," she said. "Seeing as how this is the first time we're saying it to each other and everything."

He kissed her, and she broke away a second or two later, laughing and crying and wiping her nose. "Can't breathe," she said.

He gently disentangled himself and got out of bed, gathering his clothes. "You might as well stay here," he said. "I should be back by five."

"No predictions," she said. "It's bad luck."

Michael looked at her. "My mother—my real mother—used to say that to my father all the time." He pulled on his pants and turned his T-shirt right side out.

"I've got my cell," she said. "If you could call me every so often I might not panic so badly."

"Okay."

He went to the bathroom and brushed his teeth and then called Harriman. "I'm on my way," he said.

"Good. I just arrived myself. Traffic is pretty congested already. It's going to be a mess. Do you know where the Durham Bulls ticket window is?"

"No," Michael said. "I imagine I can find it."

"It's on the west side of the ballpark, facing the ATC. We'll meet you there. If there's a problem, call."

Michael put the phone in his pocket and put a spare key card on the nightstand. "Room key," he said. "*Mi casa es tuya,* as we used to say in Texas."

"I wish we were in Texas."

He leaned over to kiss her and said, "Be careful what you wish for."

"I love you, Michael."

"I love you too."

There was nothing more to say. He let himself out.

TRAFFIC ON THE DURHAM FREEWAY had backed up past Fayetteville Road and the Hayti Heritage Center, a mile and a half from American Tobacco. Michael drove on the shoulder to the exit and hit more traffic on the access road. Impatient, he turned north into downtown and eventually found a parking place near the Courthouse.

The day, as promised, was sunny and clear, the temperature already up into the fifties. Michael's ribs hurt from the beating Tuesday night, and he hadn't slept nearly enough. He was terrified of what might happen to him, terrified of what might happen if they failed to find Vaughan. Still there was a primitive pleasure in the warmth of the sunshine on his face and the memory of Denise's touch.

He crossed the railroad tracks running east and west, the tracks that had once separated Hayti, off to his left, from the rest of downtown. The baseball stadium lay ahead and to his right, and beyond it the high brick walls of American Tobacco.

He was in a crowd now, mostly black, mostly middle-aged, though he also saw mothers with handfuls of kids, young men in sports franchise gear, college-age white couples in thrift-store outfits. All of them were heading the same way as Michael. A little girl pointed at the sky, and Michael looked up to see a hundred black balloons float up and away from the complex. They seemed more ominous than festive.

He crossed over to Blackwell Street, which ran between the stadium and American Tobacco. Police sawhorses had closed it to vehicular traffic. The Blackwell side of the complex was three blocks long, broken every few hundred feet by new steel and glass double doors. The walls came out to the edge of the crowded sidewalk where Michael stood, with windows that opened into retail spaces, some still in the early stages of remodeling, with exposed joists and piles of rotten lumber.

Michael found himself staring at every white man's face he saw. Logic told him Vaughan would not be wearing the clothes Michael had last seen him in, still his attention snagged on every baseball cap and every flannel shirt over faded jeans in the periphery of his vision. Ahead, a few yards from the access road for the Durham Freeway, he saw the Durham Bulls ticket plaza. Like the rest of the park, which was not yet ten years old, it tried to evoke nostalgia for a dying sport, a sport that could no longer compete with the ritualized violence of football or basketball or hockey.

Harriman and Charles waited by the entrance gate to the ballpark. Harriman looked like he'd dressed for a faculty mixer: purple V-necked sweater, checked sport shirt, and gray slacks. Charles wore a gray hooded sweatshirt and loose jeans, the very profile of a man with something to hide. Harriman gripped Michael's shoulder. Michael was not immune to the flattery of his approval.

Charles shifted his weight uncomfortably. "I meant what I said last night. I'm sorry for what happened ... for what I did. I can't make it go away, but I can try to make up for it." He offered his hand, soul-style. "Give me a chance, all right?"

Michael, reluctantly, took the hand.

"Thank you for coming," Harriman said.

"You guys both know I've been seeing Denise," Michael said. Charles shrugged and looked the other way. Harriman gave a guarded nod. "If anything happens to me today she is going to blame the two of you personally."

"You'll make out," Charles said. "I won't vouch for some other folks, but you stick with me, I'll see to it you come out okay."

"This way," Harriman said.

They crossed the street and kept walking west, to where the narrow U shape of the complex opened to the street. The pocket universe inside was designed to make an impact, and Michael could not help but respond. The immediate focus was the bright white, freshly painted Lucky Strike logo water tower, looming over the entire complex from long, spindly legs planted in concrete in the center of the courtyard. Behind it, less conspicuous, also newly refurbished, rose the landmark brick chimney with LUCKY STRIKE spelled vertically. A water sculpture divided the foreground into upper and lower levels, and, above them, an enclosed walkway joined the two arms of the U. Freshly laid grass looked surrealistically green in the November sunshine. There were small white lights everywhere.

For all the opulence and elegance, for all the worship of consumption that the place enshrined, Michael could not forget that Lucky Strikes had killed his father. His thoughts were full of death.

The walkways were as crowded as Fifth Avenue at Christmas. Lines of people moved sluggishly toward bright umbrellas offering free food and drink. Michael saw no uniformed police, only a couple of men in SECURITY sweatshirts and baseball caps. Canned soft rock whispered from hidden speakers at the same time that a live band in the distance eased into Stevie Wonder's "I Wish."

Harriman cleared a path for them like an icebreaker, taking them along the east side and into a small, glass-fronted office near the water tower.

The interior was clearly transitory. A multi-line corporate style phone sat on a cheap steel-and-laminate desk next to a fluorescent desk lamp. The woman behind the desk was in her forties, with looks out of Equatorial Africa: close cut peppercorn hair, wiry figure, lustrous black skin. Someone had taped a poster with a map of the complex to the bare bricks next to her desk, and next to that, a copy of the sketch of Greg Vaughan. A few folding chairs were scattered around the refurbished hardwood floor; otherwise the long, narrow room was empty.

"What is this place?" Michael asked.

"This, gentlemen," Harriman said, "is our nerve center." To Michael he said, "We have friends in Black Star. You've got your cell phone? You might want to put this number in memory." He read out the number of the office phone and Michael obligingly punched it into his phone.

"Is there a plan?" Michael asked.

"We have fifty members stationed around the complex," Harriman said. "They've each got a specific area they're responsible for."

"Zone defense," Charles said.

"They overlap, in case anyone should have to take a break. If they sight someone that could be Vaughan, they call me here and I call you. You and Charles try and catch up to them to confirm."

"We're the free safeties," Charles said.

"I don't do sports," Michael said. "You're wasting your metaphors. What about the demonstration?"

"We're coordinating that from here, too. That's Anika's job. Anika, Michael."

"Charmed," she said, "I'm sure." Her accent was African as well.

"This isn't good enough," Michael said. "You've got fifty men looking for a needle in ... a stack of ten thousand other needles."

"I'm open to suggestions," Harriman said.

"What about your vodou? Can't you use that?"

"It's a religion. It doesn't include crystal balls."

Michael slumped in one of the folding chairs. "Okay, first things first. I haven't eaten since yesterday afternoon. I'm about to pass out."

"Come on," Charles said. "We'll find you something."

THE BAND WAS a mixed-race outfit, the lead singer a youngish black man with long dreads who also played sax and flute. They were working sixties soul classics like "Midnight Hour" and "Knock on Wood." The snare hits sounded like gunshots, the horns like EMS sirens. Michael wished, for the sake of his nerves, that they would stop.

"Lines for the free barbeque are around the block," Charles said. "There's a pizza place down by the entrance."

"Fine," Michael said.

They got an outside table, and he ate a Greek salad while he waited for the pizza, scanning the crowd, the feta and vinegar and pepperoncini making him tear up so badly he had to keep lifting his glasses to wipe his eyes with his sleeve.

"You all right?" Charles asked.

"Are you kidding?"

Later, as he put what he could of the pizza into his shrunken, nervous stomach, Michael said, "Tell me something. That story you gave me about your sister and the Bloods. Was that for real?"

"Yeah, that was straight up. Tip of the iceberg, in fact." While Michael ate, Charles talked about growing up in the shadow of gang warfare in Durham—constantly checking right shoes for red shoelaces, left for blue, watching hands for signaled letters, reading graffiti like newspapers. It was completely alien to Michael's experience, the sort of life he imagined people lived in Beirut or Baghdad.

When Michael finished it was twelve-thirty. "Show me where the Duke players are going to sign," he said.

"Washington Building, far end," Charles said. That turned out to be the west side of the complex, north of the water tower. It took them ten minutes to get there through the crowds, long enough to hear Nnenna Freelon, the jazz vocalist, sing "God Bless the Child" and "Superstition."

The space was two stories high, with exposed support columns and a broad staircase leading to a balcony across the north wall, all of it empty except for a few chairs folded against one wall.

An old white guy in a different security uniform of white shirt and flat police cap stopped them at the entrance. "Doors open at two," he said.

"Do you know what part of the room they're going to be signing in?" Michael asked.

"Upstairs, is what I heard. Going to run the line down the stairs and all the way around the inside if they got to."

They moved off a few yards and looked in through plate glass windows. "Pretty exposed in there," Charles said.

"It won't be a direct assault. Let's see what's next door."

There was only one more office to the north. It was locked up tight, and a sign in the window promised an investment broker coming soon.

Michael called Bishop's cell phone. When Bishop answered, Michael heard crowd noise in the background. "It's Michael. Are you at American Tobacco?"

"Yes. Where are you?"

"I'm standing at the north end of the Washington building."

"Michael, goddamn it—"

"Listen. There's an empty storefront next to the place where the Duke basketball players are going to be signing in a couple of hours. If you were smart, you'd get in there and make sure Greg hasn't set up a surprise for them. And then I'd have a couple of officers watching everybody who comes near those players."

"Message received. Now will you please get out of there, before you hurt yourself?"

Michael hung up and called Denise. She answered before the end of the first ring. "Michael?"

"It's me."

"Are you okay?"

"So far, so good. Are you still in the room?"

"Yes. Watching TV with the sound off, waiting for a new bulletin to come on and tell me about the disaster in downtown Durham. I'd forgotten how bad Saturday morning TV is."

"No disaster yet. No sign of Vaughan. I just wanted to check in."

"Thank you. I don't suppose you're coming home to me?"

"Not yet," he said. "Got to go. I love you."

"I love you too."

He was putting the phone in his pocket when Charles' cell went off. Charles flipped it open and said, "Yeah?"

He looked to his right. "Yeah. When?" He beckoned to Michael to follow and started toward the water tower at something between a fast walk and a jog, drawing some annoyed looks. "We're on it," he said into the phone.

Michael bumped into a fat man, who turned angrily and said, "Watch it!"

"Police!" Charles yelled over his shoulder. "Be cool." The lie changed the man's attitude instantly. He nodded and backed away.

"Vaughan?" Michael asked Charles as they ran.

"Maybe," Charles said, and white noise filled Michael's brain. Oh man, he thought, over and over. Oh man.

Charles was still on the phone, taking directions. Smaller buildings cluttered the north end of the complex, earmarked for hotels and condos, including the one that supported the Lucky Strike smokestack. Once past that the grass opened up again, and there was more of a feeling of being in a hidden valley, protected by commercial spaces rather than hills.

A black man in a red sweatshirt, cell phone in hand, stepped off the walkway 50 yards ahead and pointed toward a set of doors that led into the long building on the southeast side.

"Tan baseball cap," Charles called out to him. "Gray windbreaker. You see him?"

Michael saw him, disappearing through the doors. It might have been Vaughan. "I don't know," he yelled back.

Charles upped the pace, nearly knocking down a middle-aged woman. "Sorry," Michael called as he dashed past. They dodged the metal legs of the water tower and ran up a short flight of stairs into the building.

Two dozen people filled the inside corridor. The walls were hung with huge, sepia-toned photos of Hayti. As Michael watched, the man in the tan cap climbed another set of steps to take him up to the level of Blackwell Street, exited the doors there, and turned left.

Once on Blackwell Street, the crowds eased enough for Charles to break into a run. Though Michael tried to keep up, his ribs screamed with pain. With his last breath he yelled, "Hey!" and then slumped to a stop, cool air wheezing into his lungs.

The man in the tan cap turned around.

Michael's legs had turned to concrete. He pictured a gun in Vaughan's hand, pictured him turning, raising it, opening fire—

It wasn't Vaughan.

Charles, who had stopped short of tackling the man, looked at Michael, and Michael shook his head. "No," he said.

"Sorry," Charles said to the man in the tan cap. The man was about Vaughan's size, except older and puffier in the face. "Thought you were somebody else."

"You boys need to calm yourselves down," the man said. "Before y'all hurt somebody."

Michael staggered into the building and leaned against one wall, staring up at a photo of Pettigrew Street in its heyday. He'd seen it before; the few surviving Hayti photos had been endlessly recycled. This one showed the Biltmore Hotel, Regal Theater, and the Donut Shop, with a pair of 1930s cars parked in the foreground by the railroad tracks. It seemed a bad omen, a harbinger of doom and destruction.

Charles came through the doors and stopped in front of Michael. He was breathing heavily too.

"This is no good," Michael said. "I can't chase after every skinny white man in a cap."

"You got a better idea, I'm listening."

"We have to outthink him. How hard can that be?"

MICHAEL PACED BACK and forth in front of the poster-sized map. It was ten minutes before 2.

"The Duke space goes all the way through the building, right?" Michael said. "What's on the other side? Any kind of schoolbook depository where somebody could shoot through the windows?"

"Trees and a parking lot," Harriman said. "And sniping is not his MO."

"Could he drive a truck up to the rear of the building, like in Oklahoma City?"

"Doubtful," Harriman said. "We can put a couple of people on it."

"Or phone an anonymous tip to the cops about it," Michael suggested. "Let them do the work."

"Good idea," Harriman said. "Anika, can you take care of that?"

"This is not getting us anywhere," Charles said. "The Night Riders are coming. I'm going to go watch."

The doors would open to the Duke space at two as well, Michael thought. Watching those doors was something the cops could do. He had to find a better use for his time.

He tried to fight down feelings of panic and helplessness. "I'll come with you," he said to Charles.

"My man," Charles said.

By the time they got out onto Blackwell Street, the police had set up barricades at both ends and roped off the sidewalk on both sides. There were squad cars every hundred feet and two paddy wagons to cart away troublemakers. As well as 20 regular patrol officers, Michael counted a dozen men with Kevlar body armor and pump shotguns, members of Sgt. Bishop's former unit, the Selective Enforcement Team. Their uniforms were flat black, and their helmets completely hid their faces. They were the stuff of third-world military dictatorships or science fiction movies, and Michael hated the thought of them on the streets of the US. He tried to tell himself the cops were the good guys in this one, here to protect him from the bad guys in white. It was a tough sell.

A radio crackled from somewhere nearby. "Here they come," it said.

•

CHARLES LED THE WAY around the south end barricades to stand on the ballpark side of the street. The noise from inside American Tobacco seemed weirdly loud as the police went rigid with anticipation and the silent crowd looked north.

"There," a voice said, and then Michael saw it too, a moving wall of white like the glaciers Michael had seen in nature films, sliding unstoppably out of the valley of downtown Durham and crumbling into individual robed figures. Like glaciers, the Klan and its spinoff groups were something he'd only seen in movies and TV. Between the cops in their Darth Vader suits and the Night Riders in their sheets, Michael felt like he was trapped in a Halloween nightmare.

"God Almighty," Charles said.

The robed figures kept coming and coming. As the police moved the barricades aside at the north end of the complex and the first Night Riders entered the cordoned-off street, more appeared from downtown. They were widely spaced, Michael saw, to maximize the effect, and the effect was chilling, unforgettable. They carried no signs or visible weapons, they were not marching in rhythm, they made no sound beyond the impact of boots on pavement, multiplied hundreds of times.

Harriman was right, Michael thought. This cannot be tolerated. The demonstration stood for everything that was killing America in the twenty-first century, everything that was wrong with the human race: greed, intolerance, fanaticism, terrorism.

Someone jostled Michael, and in a matter of seconds the counter-demonstrators took the field. They streamed out of American Tobacco and from the ballpark side as well, ducking under the ropes and moving out into the street. Instead of hidden faces and perfect white uniforms, these were women, men, and children in jeans, sweats, and coveralls, with skin colors from purplish black to dark brown to golden tan and everything in between.

A crew on the sidelines unfurled a huge banner that read: 400 YEARS— WHEN WILL IT END? In the margins, in smaller letters, were the words, "Slavery," "Jim Crow," "Urban Renewal," "Racial Profiling," "Night Riders of the Confederacy," "KKK," "White Flight," and "Homeland Security."

The police moved in on the first black demonstrators that got into the street and tried to push them back onto the sidelines. The demonstrators were well trained, going limp as soon as they were touched. Apparently the police were under orders not to arrest them. Instead two cops carried each of the protesters to the sidewalk, where they would get up and duck under the ropes again. In less than a minute the police were overwhelmed.

It was flawlessly staged, and now Michael saw ringleaders in the crowd, talking on cell phones, making hand signals, and waving more and more people into the arena. The police must have seen them too, and Michael felt their mounting frustration. He wondered if the man in the suit at Harriman's house had been the one to give the cops their orders, knowing the chaos they would cause.

At the same time the Night Riders continued to march inexorably forward. Michael felt his own nerves jumping, unable to imagine a happy outcome.

The SET cops linked arms and tried to herd the black protesters to the southern end of the street. Again the protesters went limp and sprawled across the pavement. A regular uniformed cop, caught in front of the wall of Kevlar, surrounded by passive protesters, frustrated beyond endurance, kicked a prone woman in the ribs. Suddenly there were cameras out and clicking, and one of the SET stormtroopers pulled the cop aside and sent him to the sidelines.

As the line of police moved forward, more protesters moved in behind them, standing empty-handed and blank-faced, like prisoners waiting to be executed.

Then, like a slow-motion car wreck, the first of the Night Riders collided with the first of the black protesters, a teenaged boy with ebony skin and short natural hair. He looked enough like Rachid to make Michael look twice, blinded for an instant by panic. As soon as the hooded man made contact, the boy went down. He wasn't pushed, Michael saw, but dove gently under his own power and did a judo roll, cushioned by a heavy sweatshirt.

The Riders that he blocked stayed where they were, and the others flowed around, careful not to step on the boy. As they in turn met resistance, they stopped, until the Riders filled most of the street, with gaps where black bodies lay at their feet.

"Well, that didn't work out so great," Charles muttered.

The Riders, Michael saw now, were not endless after all. They didn't come close to filling the roped-off area. Michael guessed there were between 200 and 300 of them, more than Harriman had predicted, an imposing, terrifying number, but not infinite.

They stood in silent menace for an endless time and then, startlingly, they began to sing:

> *Joshua fit the battle of Jericho*
> *Jericho, Jericho*
> *Joshua fit the battle of Jericho*
> *And the walls came tumbling down.*

The combined power of their voices was like a jet engine in the narrow, high-walled corridor of the street. Michael imagined glass rattling in the windows.

He looked at Charles to say something and stopped himself. Charles was apoplectic. "Those motherfuckers," he said, or at least that's what Michael thought he said. The singing was too loud to be sure.

> Good morning sister Mary
> Good morning brother John
> Well I want to stop and talk with you
> Want to tell you I come along.

They started into the chorus again and Charles went berserk. He jumped up onto the hood of the nearest squad car and began to scream. "You motherfuckers!" he shouted, shaking his fist. "That's our song, you sons of bitches!"

> I know you've heard about Joshua
> He was the son of Nun
> He never stopped his work until
> Until the work was done.

As far as Michael could tell—it happened so quickly he wasn't sure of his own eyes—a hooded figure reached out and swung his outstretched arm into the back of Charles' knees, then vanished into the crowd. Charles collapsed backward and fell hard into the windshield of the squad car. Before he could recover, the police were on him.

> You may talk about your king of Gideon
> You may talk about your man of Saul
> But there's none like good old Joshua
> At the battle of Jericho.

Two patrol officers dragged him down onto the sidewalk, and one of them punched him hard in the gut. Charles went down, doubled up. Michael, without thinking, ducked in and knelt by Charles' head. "I've got him," he told the cops. "I've got him."

They hesitated, and it was long enough to break the mood. "Get him out of here," one of the cops snarled.

"Okay," Michael said. "I will."

The cops slowly backed away, batons in hand, jumpy, scared, and angry.

"Come on," Michael said to Charles. "We have to get moving."

Now the Lord commanded Joshua
"I command you and obey you must
You just march straight to those city walls
And the walls will turn to dust."

"Let me go," Charles said.

He wasn't the only one upset by the song. People in the crowd were boo-ing and shouting, barely audible under the massed voices of the Night Riders. Bottles and cans and other trash had started to fly from the sidewalks into the mass of hooded figures.

"You stay here, we could both get killed," Michael said.

Charles dragged himself to a squatting position, slow rage winning out over his pain. "I been waiting for this my whole life. Somebody to answer to me. All this here?" Michael assumed he meant the protesters. "All this was my idea, to be here for this. Face to face."

Straight up to the walls of Jericho
He marched with spear in hand
"Go blow that ram's horn," Joshua cried,
"For the battle is in my hand."

It was like watching kids play with fireworks in a dried-out field. It could go up any minute, taking the entire neighborhood with it. Charles was beyond logic, and Michael understood that he would have to leave him behind. He turned toward the barricades at the south end of the street.

The lamb ram sheep horns began to blow
And the trumpets began to sound
And Joshua commanded, "Now children, shout!"
And the walls came tumbling down.

Michael looked up as they sang the last line, and there in front of him was the brick chimney, 200 feet high, looming over the complex.

He remembered the sight of it from the room where the Duke signing was at that moment underway.

If the base of the chimney exploded, the entire tonnage of smokestack— brick, concrete, and steel reinforcement—would come pounding down on the Washington building, smashing everything inside it to ruins.

Joshua fit the battle of Jericho
Jericho, Jericho
Joshua fit the battle of Jericho
And the walls came tumbling down.

He fought his way to Charles, standing at the ropes, about to wade into the sea of white hoods.

"Charles!"

"What?"

"The smokestack! They're going to blow up the smokestack!"

"That ain't my concern right now. You find Harriman and tell him."

"Charles—"

"Go on, get out of here!"

No use, he thought. No use.

IT WAS 2:15. The bomb, he thought, would be set for three or thereabouts, as the autographing started, to create maximum havoc. Not much time.

He dug out his cell phone and called Bishop. After four rings, a voice said, "This is Sgt. Frank Bishop of the Durham Police department. If this is an emergency, hang up and dial 911. Otherwise leave a message after the tone."

"This is Michael," he shouted into the phone. He didn't know if Bishop would be able to hear him over the background noise; the Riders were singing the song again from the beginning, and the boos and catcalls were getting louder. "I think Vaughan is putting a bomb in the smokestack. Call me!"

Harriman's number was busy.

Michael fought his way back toward American Tobacco. It was like trying to swim through wet cement, that nightmare feeling of trying to run with limbs barely moving, paralyzed in sleep.

He made it to the office in five minutes. Anika was there alone, on the edge of hysteria. All six lines on her phone console were lit, five of them blinking. "I'll tell him, but you'll have to wait. *Wait!*" She put that line on hold, punched another. "Walter, one of the Riders just punched a little girl. Get a reporter there. North end of the Reed Building." She stabbed the hold button and looked angrily at Michael. "*What?*"

"I need to talk to Harriman."

"He's not here. What do you want?"

"Tell him it's the smokestack. The Lucky Strike smokestack."

"He's supposed to know what that means?"

"That's where Greg Vaughan is. I think."

"You *think?*"

"Just tell him, will you?"

"If he checks in. I'm a little busy." She held up her thumb and forefinger, nearly touching. "We're that far from a race riot out there."

Michael ran outside. The place was empty of police as far as he could see. All on Blackwell Street, he thought.

He started toward the smokestack. A long line of people stood against the wall of the Washington building, shuffling slowly forward, the line eventually disappearing through the door where the signing would start in less than half an hour.

He pushed his way through to the security guard. "I need you to call the police," Michael said.

"Slow down, son, and tell me what this is all about," the old man said.

"I'm working with Sgt. Bishop of Homicide. I ... I'm an informant, okay? You need to get him a message that I think it's the smokestack."

"You think it's the smokestack?"

Michael pointed to the red brick tower halfway across the courtyard. "The Lucky Strike chimney."

"That's the old powerhouse there. They used to burn coal in that thing, make their own electricity. What about it?"

"Tell him that's where it's going to happen. He'll know what I mean."

"Your name?"

"Michael. He'll know."

"I'll be sure to tell him." The old man waved another ten people through the doors.

"Could you do it now?"

"I beg your pardon?"

"Could you call him right now? This is an emergency."

"Be patient, son. I got a job to do here."

Michael was out of patience. He ran to the end of the covered walkway, vaulted the handrail, and sprinted across the grass toward the two-story building at the base of the smokestack.

That, at least, got the guard's attention. He was standing at the rail now and shouting, "Hey! Hey! Where do you think you're going?"

"Call the cops!" Michael shouted back.

The smokestack itself was freestanding, rising up from a concrete pad where a corner had been cut out of the surrounding powerhouse building. There would have been space enough to squeeze between the building and the smokestack, had Black Star not closed it off with heavy-duty chain link fencing. If there was a way to get inside the chimney, it lay on the other side of the fence. Peering through, Michael saw an open doorway leading from the inside

of the powerhouse to the chimney. That meant all he had to do was find a way
into the building.

He turned back and circled the outside. The place was partway through
renovation, with new floor-to-ceiling windows set into the outside walls. The
inside, when Michael looked through the glass, had been cleared out, if not
substantially changed. The floor was concrete, with standing water and piles of
rusting machinery. The top half of the building was a maze of rails and girders.

He found a doorway in front, facing the water tower, boarded up with
plywood. Maybe, he thought, Vaughan had not been able to get in, and he'd
worked himself up over nothing. Michael pushed against the plywood, felt it
give, and saw that he'd been wrong again.

ALL HE MEANT to do, really, was see if it was possible. If Vaughan could indeed get into the smokestack, then Michael would have to get help somehow.
It was just that time was running out, and help seemed very far away.

There were two sheets of plywood over the doorway, one loose where it
joined the other. Michael pushed the first one back until he could squeeze past.

The dim interior smelled of damp and rust. It was a single open space,
a hundred feet on a side and forty feet high. What should have been the
second floor was crisscrossed with catwalks and ladders. A set of steel tracks
led to a hatch high up in the face of the chimney, where they must have
brought the coal in on carts and dumped it into the fire. It felt like the kind
of place you might find giant rats and used hypodermics and the occasional
dead body.

Michael eased the plywood back in place after a long debate with himself. On the one hand he wanted the attention of the police. On the other
he didn't want to have to argue if there was a bomb about to go off where
they stood.

Noise filtered in from outside: the bass guitar from the band, voices of people passing nearby, faint crowd noises from Blackwell Street, chaotic and angry.
Michael was operating in a mode of utter fear. Each step forward was harder
than the last, each new smell and sound was like a physical blow, making his
breath come more shallowly, his stomach knot itself more tightly.

He pushed the stem on his watch face to light up the dial. Ten minutes until
three. Move, he told himself, or this is all going to be in vain.

He crossed the floor, climbed three steps, and came out into daylight. The
smokestack was directly in front of him, 15 feet in diameter at the base and
narrowing as it went up. There was an iron door at waist level, a larger version
of the door on the outside of the fireplace at the house on Wildflower Drive
in Dallas, where Michael had shoveled out ashes as a kid.

The door was big enough for a person to crawl through and Michael was suddenly sure that Greg Vaughan was on the other side. The craziness of what he was doing fully dawned on him. This was a job for armed cops; if Vaughan were in the smokestack, it would be suicide for Michael to catch him in the act.

But there was no time for bomb squads and evacuations. If Vaughan had already left, and there was a bomb inside, and he could somehow defuse it...

No, he thought, this is crazy. He was reaching for his cell phone to call 911 when he heard a clank and saw the metal hatch begin to open.

HE TURNED AND RAN. He was running for his life and he knew it, and he put everything he had into it. He didn't look back and didn't need to. He heard Vaughan's heavy footfalls behind him. His lungs had caught on fire the instant he began, and it left him unable to cry out. It was all that he could do simply to run.

Now he saw that he should not have closed up the plywood. It was twenty feet away from him, and he bent forward as he ran, putting his right shoulder out to slam into the loosely anchored wood.

He didn't make it. Something caught him by the left arm and spun him around. A long metal flashlight, the beam arcing wildly around the empty building, rose and came hurtling down toward the side of his head.

Then he was lying on the floor. His hands were behind him, jerking spasmodically. Then he felt his legs move, first one, then the other, then both together. There was a spider web only inches from his nose, and that finally made him try to squirm away.

With the pain that flashed through his head then, he filled in the missing pieces. He'd blocked most of the first blow from the flashlight with his right arm. A second one had taken him down. Then the light had shone full in his face and Vaughan's voice had said, "Cousin Michael. Fancy meeting you here."

Staring at the spider web, Michael tried to move again. His wrists and forearms were stuck together behind his back. His legs and ankles wouldn't move either. "That ought to hold you," Vaughan's voice said.

He rolled Michael onto his back with one booted foot, then grabbed the front of his jacket and stood him up against the wall, none too gently. Michael, unable to use his arms or legs for balance, felt himself about to topple. Before it happened, Vaughan ducked and took him over one shoulder in a fireman's carry.

"You could stand to lose some weight, cousin," Vaughan said.

Michael didn't answer; most of his higher brain functions had yet to return. He saw the floor moving under the two of them. He saw Vaughan's navy blue coveralls, the standard uniform for maintenance workers, the kind of clothes that made you invisible.

Then they were in daylight, and then Michael was in motion again, being propped up against the foot of the chimney. Vaughan climbed over him, through the hatch, then reached down to drag Michael in after him, head first. It was a bumpy ride, and bursts of white light went off in his head with every stop and start.

At last he found himself flat on his back, staring at a translucent panel that fit inside the tube of the chimney like a lens, 50 feet above his head. He could make out the blue of the sky through the weathered plastic. It was the most beautiful thing he'd ever seen.

The inside of the chimney was 12 feet in diameter, the bricks discolored but not blackened. The floor was a soft, concave bed of ash, aged to a dusty brown, finer than beach sand, finer than the ashes of his father that he had dumped on Mercy's grave. Mixed with it were chunks of brick and broken bottles, which dug into his back and legs.

Directly across from the entrance hatch, now closed again, a set of rebar rungs were set into the brickwork. Between the rungs and the hatch, Vaughan knelt with his back to Michael.

"Don't do this," Michael said.

"I had some hope for you, the way you were with Henry and all," Vaughan said. "And then you betrayed my trust. Henry's trust, too. Breaking into Mr. Bynum's house, and now this. Even if you're not blood kin, I expected more of you."

Vaughan extended one hand to flex the fingers. He was wearing blue latex painter's gloves.

"The funny thing is," Michael said, "we *are* related. You're my uncle."

"I know who your mother is, boy," Vaughan said. "I expect you got the taste for dark meat from your daddy."

"My grandfather had it too."

"Your grandfather?"

"Wilmer Bynum. He was Mercy's father."

Vaughan was on him instantly, crouching, left hand grabbing the rebar ladder for support, the heel of the right hand coming around and smashing into Michael's cheek below the left eye, knocking his glasses half off his face. Michael's lip split, and blood trickled down his throat from the back of his nose.

"You lie," Vaughan whispered.

"He was Mercy's father," Michael said thickly, "and he was your father, too. Mercy was your half-sister, like Ruth was."

Vaughan slapped him again, this time with the back of the hand, the knuckles catching him in the mouth. Michael turned his head and spat blood. He ran his tongue along the inside of his teeth. One of the incisors felt loose.

"Who told you those lies?" Vaughan said.

Michael spat again, carefully, and swallowed. "Ruth," he said. "Ask her yourself. She'll tell you."

Vaughan pulled himself to his feet. "I heard stories, when I was a kid. I heard Mr. Bynum was my daddy, heard I had half-brothers and sisters all over Johnston County." The longing in his voice was not obvious, but Michael recognized it. "He never once said it to me, never gave me any reason to believe it, so I figured it was a lie, like the rest of it, like all those lies about him having colored harlots."

Michael thought his nose might be broken. He couldn't breathe through it. He raised his head to keep from swallowing blood, and his glasses slid back into place, letting him see the silver duct tape wrapped around his legs. It would be the same thing with his wrists, he supposed.

And now that Vaughan had stepped away from it, Michael could see the thing he'd been working on. It was the thing Michael had feared, worse than he'd imagined because of the ugly detail that made it physical and real.

Vaughan had duct-taped 20 sticks of dynamite to the brick walls, two rows of ten each, staggered so the lower row overlapped the first. The rows were perfectly even, the blasting caps like short, silver pencils jammed at perfect right angles into the tops of the sticks, the wires running neatly to the floor. The cylinders of dynamite were not red like in cartoons, but yellow-brown, waxy, and damp-looking. The wire ends came together at a battery alarm clock, sitting on a scrap of plastic that might have come from a shower curtain or a dropcloth.

Vaughan saw where Michael was looking, and it brought him back to his work. He knelt in front of the clock, this time not obscuring Michael's view. He attached alligator clips to the wires that led to the dynamite. Another set of wires ran from the clock to a big, oblong, six-volt battery.

"You can stop this," Michael said. "You don't have to go through with it."

"I want to go through with it," Vaughan said. "The brothers are out there counting on me. I ain't going to let them down."

"How many people are going to die because of this? How many innocent bystanders are you going to murder? There are kids in that line, all they want is to get autographs. Basketball fans, just like you were at that age."

Vaughan turned to look at him. He was smiling. Michael saw that this was the high point of Vaughan's life. "Hope they're black," Vaughan said.

Michael opened his mouth to try again, knowing it was futile, and Vaughan said, "Got my hands full just now. Don't make me come over there and tape your mouth shut. We got to finish up here and be on our way."

The "we" brought a moment of irrational hope. Was Vaughan planning to take Michael with him? At least out of range of the explosion?

Vaughan hooked up the last of the alligator clips and began to set the clock. "You got the time?" he said. "No, never mind, I guess you can't get to your watch at the moment." Vaughan seemed like the jovial host of a successful lawn party. "The time at the tone is two fifty-nine. Ding!" Red digits flickered on the clock face and resolved to 2:59. "Let's have our little surprise at, oh, say, 3:13." He punched in the alarm time, then twisted the function dial to ALARM.

He set the clock down gently, facing outward, then turned to Michael and grabbed him under the armpits. Michael was childishly, absurdly grateful. He no longer cared about Duke basketball, he didn't care about the Black Star Corporation. The only thing he wanted, fiercely and overwhelmingly, was to get back to the hotel room where Denise was waiting.

But Vaughan only moved him a few feet, sitting him up with his back against the bottom rung of rebar, then went for the roll of duct tape. "No..." Michael said.

Vaughan took two turns around Michael's body with the tape, passing it inside the steel rod so that he was immobilized. "And in case you should, by some miracle, happen to get loose," Vaughan said, "you better run like all hell. If you so much as touch that timer, the whole thing goes off."

He tore off one more strip of tape and brought it toward Michael's face.

"I think you broke my nose," Michael said. "If you cover my mouth, I can't breathe."

Vaughan smiled and shook his head. "You think you'll be breathing after that alarm clock goes off?"

Michael sucked in the deepest breath he could before Vaughan pasted the tape across his mouth.

"Take it easy, cousin," Vaughan said. He turned away, taking the light with him, and Michael watched him clamber out the hatch in a flash of impossibly white daylight, then close and latch the door.

In that instant, as Michael knew beyond question that he was dead, something changed. He closed his eyes and his panic went away. In the absence of hope, it was possible to act. He found the muscles that flared his nostrils and forced them to open. He discovered that he could breathe, barely, as long as he did it slowly. The air came through flavored with blood.

He tried in vain to pull free of the rebar. The effort made his nasal passages shut down, and he had to calm himself and find his breath all over again.

He had a range of two or three inches in each direction that he was able to move his hands. He moved them slowly, all the way to the left, then all the way to the right, fingering the loose ashes, finding only crumbs of brick. He tried again, and something eased, allowing him another fraction of an inch. He went back and forth, back and forth, slowly, breathing carefully, gaining a little each time.

Something jabbed the side of his right hand.

He twisted his body to the left as far as it would go, straining his fingers to touch the hard, slick surface. The ends of his fingers were wet, whether with sweat or blood he couldn't say. Nonetheless he got hold of the shard of glass between the ring finger and the little finger of his right hand and dragged it toward the center of his back, where he could pick the whole thing up and turn the point toward the duct tape, feeling his way, wiggling the glass until it caught the edge of the tape and tore it.

He kept his eyes closed and did not look at the clock. His lungs hurt. He told them they would be okay and fed them a small trickle of air.

He flexed his wrists, and the fabric of the tape ripped some more and then stopped at a second layer of tape. He shifted the piece of glass in his hand and cut the second layer. It was easier now, his hands were loosening. Seconds passed, and then the second layer gave, and then there was a third.

All the while his mind was working. Everything was remarkably clear. If he got free, there was probably not time to get clear of the building. There was simply too much dynamite, the explosion would be too big. There was also the issue of all the others who would die when the bomb went off.

Vaughan said the bomb was booby-trapped. Michael knew nothing about bombs, but he knew someone who did. If he could get to his cell phone.

The last piece of tape ripped loose from his wrists, pulling hair and skin. He brought his right hand around and attacked the tape that held him to the ladder. It took only a few seconds to cut through, and then he finally reached up and pulled the tape from his mouth. It hurt too much when he went slowly. He gave up and yanked it free, screaming with pain as it tore the skin from his lips. Then he sat for a few seconds, guzzling air and blowing it out again, half drunk with the simple joy of it.

He didn't bother with his legs until he had the cell phone out and had punched up the number. He began to work the last of the tape off as he listened to the phone ring on the other end.

He still had not looked at the clock, because it did not matter yet.

The phone rang once, twice, three times. The voice mail system would cut in after the fourth ring. Surely he was there, Michael thought, he was always there...

"Hullo?"

"Roger, it's Michael."

"Michael. I rather didn't expect to hear—"

"This is life or death. I am sitting in front of a bomb. There's a timer and twenty sticks of dynamite."

"Twenty sticks? Lord God. This is not hypothetical?"

"No."

"Describe the timer."

"It's a travel alarm clock. There's one of those big, old-fashioned six-volt batteries."

"How much time left?"

Michael looked. His panic returned. The clock read 3:11.

"Two minutes," Michael said, and as he watched, the numbers changed to 3:12. "Oh, Christ," Michael said. "One minute."

"The dynamite has fuses, yeah? That go down from the caps to the clock?"

"Yes."

"Then what?"

"Little copper alligator clips." Michael was working from memory. He dragged himself across the ashes like a beached merman, his legs still not free from the duct tape. His instincts screamed to get farther away from the bomb, not closer. He held his glowing cell phone over the clock long enough to get a look. "Except they're kind of bulbous and have wiry things at the end—"

"Model rocket igniters. This is straight out of the *Anarchist's Cookbook*. Pull the fuses out of the dynamite."

"I can't. It's booby-trapped."

"How do you know?"

"The guy who set it told me."

"He's lying."

"What?"

"Why would he have told you that if it were true? He doesn't care if you set the fucking bomb off. He meant to keep you from doing the obvious. Pull the fuses—"

The connection dropped.

"Roger?" Michael said into the vast silence. "Roger?"

Michael reached for the array of dynamite. He could see his hand shaking in the half-light from above. This is wrong, he thought, this is wrong...

As he watched, the clock ticked over to 3:13.

Michael flinched, and for a half second he thought Vaughan had made a mistake, had set the alarm for a different time. Then there was a whoosh, like the burner on a gas oven catching fire. A tiny cloud of blue smoke rose from the back of the alarm clock and twenty fuses began to hiss and sputter.

He understood then what Roger had been trying to tell him. The dynamite was hooked up to conventional fuses, and all the alarm had done was ignite them. Hysterical, Michael tore the first fuse loose, then a second, then he was ripping at them with both hands, hurling them across the room, and when he was done he threw the travel alarm and the battery as well, and collapsed in the center of the ashes, shaking and crying.

ABRUPTLY, HE SOBERED UP. Any minute now Vaughan would know that something was wrong. Would he come back? Run for it? If he'd brought his hood and sheets, he could fade into the crowd of Night Riders outside, and no one would ever find him.

He ripped the last of the tape off his legs and got shakily to his feet.

The metal door latched with a notched lever, like a garden gate. Michael pushed open the hatch and stepped into daylight. He felt the heat of the sun and the cool fresh air on his skin. It was intense, emotional.

He was not in good shape. His ribs burned where Vaughan had thrown him over his shoulder. Between Vaughan's blows and the duct tape, his face was a wreck. Blood from glass cuts covered his hands.

He heard a noise in the powerhouse. He looked around for something to use as a weapon; he would kill Vaughan, he thought, before he would let himself be taken captive again. He couldn't find anything, not so much as a loose brick.

"Michael?"

The voice was not Vaughan's.

"Harriman?" Michael said.

Harriman and Charles emerged from the shadows at the foot of the steps. "What happened?" Harriman asked.

"There was a bomb," Michael said. "I stopped it."

"Are you shitting me?" Charles asked.

"We have to find Vaughan," Michael said. "He left here ten minutes ago."

"He'll be halfway to Argentina already," Harriman said. "Or wherever it is that Nazis run to now."

"I think it's the US they run to now," Charles said.

"He's here," Michael said. "He's going to want to see it happen, and he's not going to give up right away if it doesn't go off on time." He thought again of Vaughan's face as he lit the burner in his trailer.

"Come on, then," Charles said. "Let's find the motherfucker."

As they made their way to the boarded-up entrance, Michael said, "What's happening on the street?"

"They got Mayor Bell out there," Charles said, "tried to get everybody to cool out. I remembered what you said about the smokestack, went to find Donald."

"I wish you'd gotten here ten minutes earlier."

"Yeah, sorry."

They pushed their way into the courtyard. Michael winced as he squeezed past the plywood, and Harriman finally noticed his condition.

"Good lord," Harriman said. "What did he do to you?"

"I'm okay," Michael said.

"You look like you need an ambulance," Charles said. "We should get you some help."

"After we find him," Michael said.

Logic told him that Vaughan would need to be far enough from the blast zone that he wouldn't get hurt, somewhere on the east side, to be clear of the falling chimney, and high enough up to get a clear view.

Michael pointed to the first building past the water tower. "Up there," he said to Harriman. "Second or third floor. That's where he has to be. He's in a navy blue jumpsuit, no hat."

Harriman got on his cell phone and ordered every available body to the Strickland building.

"You're sure that bomb is disarmed?" Harriman said.

"Yes," Michael said.

Harriman waved his arm and a big man in jeans and a sweater jogged over. "Cut through the powerhouse and watch the chimney," Harriman said.

Charles added, "If Vaughan shows up, take him out. Then call for help."

The man grinned and went inside.

"He saw us," Michael said suddenly, the words coming out as fast as the thought hit. "He saw us come out of there. He knows it's all over. He's running for it."

Michael started toward the water tower just as Harriman's cell phone rang.

"Wait!" Harriman said. He flipped open the phone and said, "Harriman." He listened, nodded, and looked at Michael. "They're on him."

"Where?"

"You called it. Strickland building, heading down from the second floor."

"Where?" Michael said.

"Follow me," Charles said.

THEY TOOK OFF at a run, Michael fueled purely by brain chemicals, defying the agony of his body. So many things hurt that each new pain only helped distract from the others.

They cut across the grass, through the crowds around the water tower, where the bands were between sets, and into one of the buildings in the east side complex. Halfway down the gleaming hallway a massive black man in a Carolina Hurricanes jersey motioned them on, breaking into a run ahead of them. "He got past us," the man shouted over his shoulder. "He's on the street."

"Shit!" Charles said.

The hallway emptied into a lobby area with another giant photo of Hayti. Another massive black man stood at the top of the stairs to Blackwell Street, wearing cargo pants and a black turtleneck with zippers. Either he or the man in the jersey might have been in the parking lot the night Michael was assaulted. The thought moved through Michael's mind and was gone again. "This way," the man said, and plunged into the crowd.

Michael's insides felt like he'd swallowed broken glass. He forced himself up the stairs and out onto the sidewalk, and then he couldn't go any farther. He sank to his knees to catch his breath.

The scene on the street had wound down, and boredom had thinned the crowd. Riders milled aimlessly, waiting for an explosion that hadn't come. The police had pulled back to the sidelines, and the more militant of Harriman's people had moved inside to help search for Vaughan.

A hundred feet away, Vaughan now stood in the center of the street, already protected by a hooded circle of Night Riders. Harriman's two men had waded into the crowd, and the Riders had instantly surrounded them as well, locking them in place.

Michael watched the crowd's chaotic mood begin to focus. Heads turned toward Vaughan. Charles stayed on the sidewalk, making his way north, staying even with Vaughan as the Riders eased him slowly toward downtown. Charles had his phone out, and as Michael looked around he saw a few of Harriman's other people on their phones, mostly women and teenagers.

Harriman arrived at Michael's side, also with his phone out. "Where is he?"

Michael raised his arm to point, and at that moment everything came apart.

It started with the man in the Hurricanes jersey, pinned by the Riders and frustrated beyond endurance. He reached out, grabbed the nearest hood, and yanked it off. He threw it in front of him and appeared to be grinding it under his feet.

The man under the hood was about 50, with thinning gray hair and wire-rimmed glasses. He blinked in confusion for a long second, then lashed out with his fists. The black man responded with a left jab that split the white man's lip and knocked his glasses askew.

It was as if the crowd smelled the blood. Emotions that had cooked through the long afternoon boiled over. Blacks on both sides of the street plunged into the crowd, grabbing hoods and hitting whatever they found underneath. The Riders fought back, first with their fists, then ax handles and baseball bats began to emerge from under the robes.

Instantly the police began to blow whistles and yell at the crowd through bullhorns. "Disperse," said the flat, mechanical voices. "Disperse immediately. We are deploying teargas. Disperse immediately."

At the same moment, a wedge of young black men charged from the ballpark side of the street into the knot of Riders protecting Vaughan. Something flashed in the late afternoon light, and one of the Riders jerked backward, red stains opening like a time-lapse flower on his white robe.

Vaughan panicked. He surged toward American Tobacco as Charles paced him on the sidewalk.

Michael heard muffled explosions, like the sound of a bass drum in a marching band. White contrails arced over the crowd, and Harriman leaned toward Michael and said, "Let's go. Move."

Michael made it to his feet, Harriman first pulling him up and then shoving him forward, and then both of them were chasing Charles and Vaughan north along Blackwell Street. Some of the Riders, locked in brutal combat, held their ground. Most of them backed away, some running. Harriman's two men, the ones who'd originally spotted Vaughan, had worked free and were sprinting just ahead of Michael.

Then the whole crowd caught the urgency, and suddenly everyone was on the run, most of them headed north, carrying Michael with them. At that moment white clouds of teargas billowed up from the ground, carrying a bitter, sour, sooty smell. Michael's eyes stung, then began to water, on fire as if he'd wiped them with the juice of an onion.

Harriman was on the phone again, the words coming out between ragged breaths as he struggled to keep up. "We're right behind you," he said. "Don't lose him."

There was a break between buildings, and Harriman plunged into the mass of people clogging the narrow opening. Michael fought to stay close to him as the crowd closed in, packed shoulder to shoulder and being thrust forward by pressure from behind.

Then they all burst into the inner courtyard and fanned out. Though the teargas hadn't penetrated this far, it still clung to Michael's exposed skin, burning. As he ran, he took off his glasses and mopped at his face with a handkerchief. When he put the glasses on again he saw, blurrily, that they had emerged near the back of the powerhouse. They were only yards from the chimney where Vaughan's dynamite was still taped to the inner walls.

Michael somehow kept running. He was only a few steps behind Harriman, who was in turn close behind Charles and the others. He heard a man on the PA system where the bands were set up saying, "Y'all be cool, now. We're trying to get word as to what's happening outside, so for now please stay where you are...."

The man in the Hurricanes jersey was nearly on top of Vaughan as they rounded the west side of the powerhouse, and then, in full view of hundreds of people, he caught Vaughan from behind and wrapped one arm around his windpipe.

They both went down. In another second Charles, Harriman, the man in the turtleneck, and Michael had formed a tight circle around the two of them. Charles faced outward and unabashedly used his lie again: "Police. Stay clear." A fat white man in shorts stared, open-mouthed, a fork full of barbeque poised in midair. "Everything's under control," Charles said.

Michael was not so sure. When he looked down, the man in the Hurricanes shirt had a gun. It was a dull gray automatic like he'd seen in police holsters, and it was grinding into the lower part of Vaughan's spine. His left hand was on the collar of Vaughan's jumpsuit. "We going to stand up now," the man said. "And you going to walk with us and not say anything. If you make a noise, and you live, you will never walk again and you will shit in a plastic bag for the rest of your sorry-ass life, do you understand me?"

Vaughan didn't answer. The man stood up, pulling Vaughan with him, and they all walked together in a tight group past the back of the band's amplifiers and the staring crowd and into the rented office.

Harriman turned a key in the lock and lowered mini-blinds over the window and door. The two men Michael didn't know pushed Vaughan toward the rear of the room. "Take this," the man in the Hurricanes jersey said, and handed the pistol to Charles.

Michael hung back, close to Anika's desk, and Harriman hovered nearby. Anika put the receiver in its cradle and turned to watch. "Is that him?" she asked Michael.

"Yeah," Michael said. "That's him."

"Anika?" Harriman said. "You should probably go now."

"What the hell's going on outside?" Anika said. "I lost everybody, and all I could hear was yelling."

"Had us a race riot out there," Charles said. "Cops let off some teargas. It's over now."

"What happens to him?" She hooked a thumb toward Vaughan.

Charles said, "You don't want to know."

Anika stared hard at Harriman. "I thought we were together on this. No violence."

Charles made a face and stuck the gun in the front of his pants. Harriman said, very quietly, "I don't think I can stop this."

"So you're not even going to try?"

Harriman didn't answer.

Anika stood up and said, "It's principles going to win this, if it can be won. Not more killing."

"*Can* it be won?" Harriman said.

"Donald," she said, "you disappoint me." She didn't look back as she walked away. She let herself out and locked the door.

Charles took the pistol out again and pointed it at Vaughan's head. "Hurt him," he said.

The man in the Hurricanes jersey stepped behind Vaughan and suddenly jerked him backward, off balance. The other man, with calm deliberation, slammed his boot into Vaughan's kneecap. The noise was as loud as a splintering branch in a snow-covered forest. Michael had never seen a leg bend that way, and the sight of it, on top of the tear gas and the long chase, made him physically ill. He swallowed hard.

Vaughan looked at the broken L-shape of his own leg and began to scream.

"Shut him up," Charles said, "for God's sake."

The man holding Vaughan took out a nasty-looking handkerchief and stuffed it into Vaughan's mouth. The man in the turtleneck looked around and then stopped at Michael. "Do you mind?" he said, walking across the room to peel a loose strip of duct tape from Michael's jacket. "I mean, I ain't fucking with your fashion statement or anything, right?"

Michael shook his head numbly, and the man walked back to put the duct tape over Vaughan's mouth, the way Vaughan had gagged Michael an hour before. It serves him right, Michael tried to tell himself. In fact it wasn't looking at Vaughan that bothered him as much as the sight of the men who were torturing him.

The man in the turtleneck buried a fist in Vaughan's stomach, and Vaughan's eyes bulged like those of a terrified animal. He tried desperately to suck air in through his nose, and then blew a long stream of snot down his face and the front of his coveralls.

"Stop it!" Michael said. "You're killing him."

Charles turned on him. "What the fuck you think we brought him here for? A game of Twister?"

"If anybody should want him dead it's me," Michael said. "But I don't want this."

"Look," Charles said, "all due respect and shit, I mean, you're a hero and saved Duke basketball and everything, but I've been thirty-two years taking shit off cracker terrorists like this one here. When we throw his body to those peckerheads in the white sheets, they going to see we mean business."

"Then what happens? They torture and kill a couple of you to get even."

"Let them come," Charles said. "Bring it on."

"If you throw him to the cops instead," Michael said, "it'll make C N N . Especially with the riot. The trial will get national coverage. Everybody who thought the Klan went out of business in the 1930s will have to wake up and see what's really going on."

"He'll end up walking. They always do."

"Then kill him when he does," Michael said. "Be waiting for him on the courthouse steps."

"He's right," Harriman said, stepping up next to Michael. "And so was Anika. The media is the way to win this. We may never get an opportunity like this again."

"Bullshit," Charles said. "Don't hand me all that Movement shit. All that televised marches and King tears and Gandhi quotations didn't end us up with shit. I ain't asking for no more handouts. You saw what it was like out there. That shit's been waiting to happen forever. It's wartime. I'm taking what I want, starting with this piece of shit here."

Harriman settled into the floor, solid, immovable. It happened slowly, and after a long time he said, "I can't let you do that."

"What do you mean?" Charles said. "You taking me on, old man?"

Harriman didn't respond. Michael remembered the ceremony his father had watched in the woods east of Durham. He thought of grainy black and white footage he'd seen from Haiti where dancers were mounted by the *lwa*. This was different because Harriman was still clearly himself, and yet it was the same because Michael suddenly felt another presence in the room. It was like some kind of blanket had fallen over them, muffling the violence of their emotions.

Charles felt it too. He took a step backward. "Donald, this is bullshit, man. Do not pull this shit on me." He looked to the two men holding Vaughan. They had stopped, waiting for instructions. Vaughan hung limp between them, chest heaving, moaning through his nose.

Harriman still didn't say anything. His eyelids drooped; except for the tension in his body, he looked like he was falling asleep.

"This is what happens," Charles said. "The time comes to act, and everything falls apart in ideological bullshit. You let that happen now, and we're finished, you understand what I'm saying? All of this will have been for nothing."

When Harriman still didn't react, Charles' anger began to burn off. Resignation was what remained. He looked at the pistol still in his hand, and his thoughts were not hard to guess: He could shoot Vaughan, or he could shoot Harriman, or both, and then where would he be?

Charles clicked the safety on with his thumb. He bent over and slid the gun across the floor toward Harriman. "All right. Fuck it, then. Fuck you."

Michael went over to Vaughan and pulled the duct tape off his mouth and dug out the handkerchief. Vaughan coughed and spat. The men holding him let go, and Vaughan fell to the floor, catching himself on his arms and then curling up into a fetal position.

When Michael looked back Charles was at the door. His dramatic exit was spoiled when he had to stop and unlock it; then, when he tried to slam it shut behind him, it bounced out of the frame and swung open again.

"Michael," Harriman said, "call the police."

Two lines were still blinking. Michael punched a third and dialed 911.

As he waited, Harriman nodded to the other two men. "Take the gun and go on home. Don't get caught up in anything on the way out, just disappear for a while."

"What about him?" the man in the jersey said, jutting his chin at Vaughan.

"He's not going anywhere," Harriman said. Then, reluctantly, "Good work today."

The man in the turtleneck gave the smallest possible nod. "Maybe. We see what happens next."

The dispatcher came on and Michael asked for the police and then, his legs giving way, said, "Better send EMS too."

Harriman said to the men, "Go now, before the cops come. You can leave the door open."

The woman on the phone asked for details.

"You have the address?" Michael asked. The woman rattled off a number on Blackwell Street that sounded right and Michael said, "Inside American Tobacco, near the water tower. Get them here now. It's an emergency."

He hung up the phone. "Is there a bathroom?" he asked Harriman. Harriman pointed to a door on the far wall.

Michael didn't recognize himself in the mirror. One eye was turning black, and his nose was swollen and leaking blood. His lower lip puffed out, and both lips were scabbed and torn from the duct tape. One cheek was as plump as a fat man's. Tear-streaked dirt covered the rest of his face. His hands and wrists were cut and smeared with dried blood. Ashes caked his clothes, and strips of duct tape still hung off everywhere.

He washed his glasses and then his face as best he could—the pain wouldn't let him near his nose—and rinsed his mouth repeatedly. Then he went out and said to Harriman, "You should go now, too."

"You think you'll be all right with our friend, here?"

"I don't think he's a threat anymore."

"I'll be close by, just in case."

Harriman went out.

Michael sat down at the desk and called Denise. "I'm okay," he told her. "You don't have to worry anymore."

She was close to panic. "Where are you? There was a bulletin on TV saying there was a riot, at least two people dead."

"It's over now. I can't really talk yet. I'm going to be a while longer. The police are coming for Vaughan."

"You found him?"

"Yeah."

"Was there a bomb?"

"Yeah. It didn't go off."

"Thank God."

"Don't worry, okay? I'll call you when I can."

He put the phone down. Recorded music still played from a speaker outside the door, blandly cheerful country pop.

He suddenly realized Vaughan was talking. "Is it true?" Vaughan said.

"What?" Michael asked, confused.

"What you said about Mr. Bynum being my father?" Vaughan hadn't moved, and the voice sounded like it came from somewhere else. Mars, perhaps.

Michael had already given Vaughan more than he deserved, and he resented being able to offer this additional comfort. Yet Wilmer Bynum and this emotionally crippled man deserved each other if anyone did.

"Yes," Michael said. "It's true."

Vaughan was quiet for a minute or two, long enough for Michael to begin to drift off. Then he said, almost with regret, "You're a dead man, you know. The brothers will see to that."

Michael did not know how to answer that.

A minute or so later two uniformed police, guns drawn and pointed upward, arrived at the open door. One was blond and beefy with a squared-off mustache, the other black and very young. "You call 911?" the blond said.

Michael pointed to Vaughan. "That guy just tried to blow up the smokestack. You need to get a bomb squad over there and finish cleaning up."

Both cops looked at Vaughan, and then at Michael again. "Mister," the young one said, "it looks like you've got some explaining to do."

"Call Sgt. Bishop from Homicide. He's been looking for this guy." He reeled off Bishop's cell phone number. "Get him in here, because I don't want to have to tell this story over and over. And I'm serious about the bomb squad. There's twenty sticks of dynamite taped to the inside wall of the chimney."

The blond got on his radio while the young one took a look at Vaughan. "This one's bad hurt," he said. "Sir, can you talk?"

"Fuck you," Vaughan said.

EMS was next. One tech started on Vaughan, the other on Michael. "It's not broken," the tech said, looking up Michael's nose with a flashlight. "Bet it hurts like a bastard, though." He began packing it with gauze to stop the bleeding.

Bishop arrived, wearing khakis, a polo shirt and a dark windbreaker. He had his shield in hand as he came through the door.

"You know this man, Sergeant?" the blond asked him.

Bishop looked at Michael. "Yes, I know him. Michael, what have you done?"

THE RIOT HAD FORCED the EMS truck to park by the south entrance to the complex. They all came out together, Michael under his own power, Vaughan on a stretcher, both headed for Duke Hospital. Michael had been through the story once, omitting Harriman and Charles, claiming two strangers had helped him capture Vaughan and had then disappeared. Which was, in fact, what had happened.

"Do you expect me to believe that?" Bishop had asked.

"Sure," Michael said. "Why not?"

Bishop's cell phone rang as they walked to his car, and Bishop passed along the news. The bomb squad had removed the dynamite. They'd left everything else for the crime scene unit, already on the job.

The light was starting to fade. Later that night there were supposed to be speeches, more bands, fireworks. Michael wondered if they'd be canceled. Probably not, not if there was money on the line.

The air still smelled of teargas as they passed Blackwell Street. Handcuffed bodies, black and white, lay by the curbs like trash waiting for collection, next to squad cars with flashing lights. The injured sat or lay waiting for EMS workers to get to them, while police, reporters, and a few determined gawkers milled around.

"Listen up," Bishop said, once they were in his gray Crown Victoria, "because I'm only going to say this once, and I'm not going to say it in front of anybody else. You saved a lot of lives today. If you'd left it up to us, we would have blown it. Which is not to say that what you did wasn't stupid, or that you're not lucky."

Michael didn't feel particularly lucky at that moment.

"What all that means," Bishop said, "is that I'm going to do what I can to keep you from having to answer a lot of questions that I know you don't want to answer. Like why you and Vaughan were in an office that New Rising Sun has been using. Like how Vaughan's knee got broken."

"New Rising Sun?"

"It's a militant black activist group. A UNC professor named Donald Harriman runs it."

"This is the first time I've ever heard the name," Michael said.

"Whatever. The other thing I'm going to do is promise you, on my honor as a cop, which I happen to take seriously, that Vaughan is not going to walk away from this."

"Vaughan can't walk at all," Michael said, looking out the window. They pulled onto the westbound Durham Freeway, and Michael watched the Lucky Strike smokestack disappear as they crested the hill.

"I'm serious," Bishop said. "Whatever it takes, he is going on trial for Howard's death, for the firebombings in Hayti, and for what happened here today. And I'm going to get convictions for all of them."

"Okay," Michael said.

"Next question. I can tell the media that you singlehandedly saved the American Tobacco Historical District, which is the truth, and get you some kind of special citation and maybe a parade. Or I can do what I can to keep your name out of it."

"Leave me out," Michael said.

"Okay," Bishop said.

"Vaughan told me I'm a dead man."

"Well," Bishop said, "it might be better if—"

"I'm not leaving," Michael said.

"I was going to say, it might be better if you let us keep an eye on you for a while. I don't think you're in a lot of physical danger. The Night Riders are about terror, not murder. They'd rather have you live the rest of your life in fear than have you dead."

"Not much of a choice."

"Only if you give them what they want, which is for you to be afraid."

"It's easy to talk about not being afraid."

"I know that. But try to think of it as a choice." Michael glanced at Bishop, who was staring straight in front of him at his own demons. "Sometimes," Bishop said, "that can help."

MICHAEL CALLED DENISE from the hospital and assured her once again that he was okay. She said she was on her way, but they took him back for treatment before she arrived. They numbed his nose with Xylocaine, cleaning the cuts on his wrists and hands and then sealing them with an aerosol spray and butterfly bandages. After that they treated his hair and skin with neutralizing agents to get rid of the last of the teargas residue. They checked the responses of his pupils and X-rayed the swellings where Vaughan had hit him with the flashlight and ruled out fracture or concussion. They recommended he stay off his feet for a day or so.

"No kidding," he said.

When they were done he walked gingerly into the waiting room.

Denise looked up from the magazine in her lap and said, "Oh my God!" She ran to him, started to put her arms around him, and then hesitated. "Can I—"

"Yes," he said, "please. Just be gentle."

He started the story in the car and then interrupted himself to say, "Can we get something to eat? I'm starving."

"I can't take you anywhere looking like that," Denise said. "People will think I did that to you."

"It's my new policy," Michael said. "I've got to learn to stop being afraid of things."

She heard something in his voice. "What does that mean?"

He told her about Vaughan's threat, and Bishop's response.

"Oh, Jesus."

"You may want to get some distance from me. I could be dangerous to be around for a while."

"Don't be stupid. Rachid will hate leaving his friends, but he's had things pretty easy compared to other kids I know. He can survive a move to Texas."

"I'm not leaving," Michael said. He'd thought about it while they worked on him in the hospital. "People don't want to make hard choices anymore. That's how we ended up with a few hundred rich people running all our lives. I'm not going to live like that anymore."

"Michael, if Bishop's wrong and they kill you—"

"It's not like I want to be a hero full time now. I'm just mad. If you believe in violence and I don't, does that mean you get to do whatever you want? How is that fair?"

She took one hand off the wheel to ruffle his hair. "All right. Let's consider your future heroism open for discussion, and in the meantime you can tell me about being a hero today."

"If you exit here," he said, "we can eat at Torero's."

Over dinner he finished the story. As much as it hurt to talk, he needed to put it into words, to make a narrative of it, as Roger would have said, so that he could begin to live with it. When he was done, Denise reached across the table and took both his hands. "Thank you for getting out of there alive."

"It seemed important for some reason."

"I think I would have let them kill Vaughan," Denise said.

"No, you wouldn't."

"No," she said, a moment later, "I suppose not." She pushed aside her plate and finished her tea. "So," she said, "when do you suppose you might be able to have sex again?"

Michael smiled, his first in longer than he could remember. It was remarkably painful. "Any day now," he said.

THEY GOT TO THE HOTEL at 10 PM. Michael insisted on showering, and climbed into bed at 10:30. He was asleep in seconds.

He slept for twelve hours, and when he woke up, Denise had the Sunday *News and Observer* spread across the king-size bed. The headline read, BOMB THREAT FOILED, 2 DEAD IN RIOTS. True to his word, Bishop had protected Michael's identity. The story said the bomb "failed to go off" and was "later dismantled by specialists from the Durham Police." Michael felt strange reading it, as if what he'd gone through had not quite been real. History had detoured around him.

One of the fatalities was a Night Rider who had been stabbed by an "unknown assailant." I saw that, Michael thought. I saw a man killed in front of my eyes. The thought lacked the emotional impact it should have had.

The other victim was an 11-year-old girl, trampled when the police fired the teargas. She smiled from a school photo as if she didn't care. Dozens, perhaps hundreds of others, had been injured in the fighting.

Michael spent a long time working the balance sheet in his head. Was there an outcome where the bomb got defused and Vaughan got caught, but without the rest of it: the riot, the stabbing, the teargas, the trampling? It had not, that Michael could see, been in his power.

A spokesperson for the Black Star Corporation expressed "deep regret" over the "unfortunate occurrences," as if it had all simply been a matter of bad luck. He hoped that one day soon the American Tobacco Historical District would be seen as "a symbol of justice finally done for the memory of Hayti."

A suspect was in custody for the attempted bombing, possibly linked to the Night Riders of the Confederacy.

"So the police get the credit," Denise said.

"I'm already famous," Michael said. "I don't need to be famous again."

"They could have said, 'Unknown hero saves the day.'"

"And the newspapers and the TV stations would never have rested until they found out who I was."

Denise moved the papers and lay with her head on his chest. "How are you feeling?"

"Scared," Michael said. "I'm scared."

"What are you afraid of?"

"Everything."

"It's okay," she said. "I'm here."

Later that afternoon Michael went through the messages on his cell phone from the previous afternoon. He hadn't felt the phone vibrating in the chaos of the riot. Three were from Harriman, two from Bishop. He cleared them out, and then stopped. "Roger never called back," he said.

"You're kidding."

"For all he knows, the phone went dead because the bomb went off."

"Well, I don't know Roger as well as you do, but if the bomb went off, wouldn't that have meant he was wrong about what he told you to do?"

"Yeah."

"And since that's not possible, then obviously you must be okay."

He was not, in fact, okay. Beyond the exhaustion and the physical pain, his emotions bounced from elation to despair, love to restlessness, relief to fear, all within the same quarter hour. Finally, around dusk, Denise said, "If we're not giving in to fear, does that mean I can go back to my apartment now?"

"It has to be your call," Michael said. "It could be dangerous." He assumed she needed some time alone with Rachid. The thought of being without her brought him low, but he was too proud to ask her to stay.

"Then let's go," she said. "Are you strong enough to pack?"

THAT NIGHT MICHAEL had his first nightmare. He was struggling with someone he couldn't see. His footing gave way, and suddenly he was plummeting through the air. He woke thrashing, with a strangled yell in his throat. Denise, only half-awake, held him and stroked his hair. She fell back to sleep before he did.

Tuesday, November 9

ON THE LOCAL NEWS Monday night the District Attorney for Durham County had announced charges against Gregory Allen Vaughan for a long list of crimes, including the murder of activist Barrett Howard in the fall of 1970, the arson of Service Printing and the *Carolina Times,* and attempted homicide in connection with the bomb in the American Tobacco smokestack.

Sgt. Bishop had airtime as well, showing a cobbler's awl in a baggie, and then talking behind file footage of Barrett's body coming out of the overpass in its concrete casing. The hate crimes division was investigating a link between Vaughan and the Night Riders of the Confederacy that he hoped would result in a City Council ban on NRC activities within city limits.

Late Tuesday morning, Harriman called. After the expected inquiries about Michael's health, he asked if Michael might be up for taking a ride. "The destination would be a surprise. We'd be gone all afternoon."

Denise had left for work, after making Michael promise to call if he needed her. "Okay," he said. "Assuming you're driving."

He gave Harriman directions, then called Denise to tell her. "Don't overdo," she said. "Take your phone."

When Harriman arrived at the door, he seemed cheerful, mischievous. It was cool and partly cloudy, and Michael wore a flannel shirt under a sport coat. He'd been unable to find a way to get into a sweater without pain. The soreness had peaked the day before and was still intense enough to leave him feeling frail and vulnerable.

"A beautiful day for a drive in the country," Harriman said.

They walked down to his maroon BMW and Michael settled into the passenger seat. "You're still not telling me where we're going?" Michael asked as they got on the Durham Freeway.

"Correct," Harriman said.

There was a CD playing softly, music Michael had never heard before. It had overtones of reggae, only more linear, with electric guitar and driving hand percussion. "What is this?" he asked.

"Boukman Eksperyans. They're from Haiti. You like it?"

"I don't know yet," Michael said. "Have you heard anything from Charles?"

"No, and I don't expect I will. He was never happy with the direction I wanted to follow."

"What's New Rising Sun?"

"I think it's the name of a Jimi Hendrix song. Why?"

"I think it's also the name of your group. The one that you told me didn't have a name?"

"It's one of the names we use for legal purposes. It's not *the* name in the sense you're suggesting. Names give others power over you."

"Well, the Durham Police know that name, and they know you're in charge."

"Not surprising. Every activist group in the country is full of informants and FBI plants. It was the same way in the sixties. I still think it was federal agents who pushed Barrett into becoming more and more radical, trying to lure him into something spectacular they could arrest him for."

"The little girl who died in the riots Saturday. She was one of yours?"

That, finally, dampened Harriman's mood, though Michael didn't know why he was so determined to do so. "Yes." Harriman sighed. "We took a chance. She was a volunteer, and she believed in what she was doing. As much as you can understand at that age, though they're fighting and dying younger than that every day in the Middle East." He looked at Michael. "None of that excuses it. Ultimately it was my responsibility, and I have to live with it."

A not uncomfortable silence fell and stayed with them as they followed I-40 through Raleigh and east into Johnston County. It was the way to the

Bynum farm, and Michael had to silently repeat his new mantra: We are not afraid.

When Boukman Eksperyans finished, Harriman put on a CD of African pop by two men named Pape and Cheikh. Then he began to talk about African-American visual artists, and Michael was quickly caught up in the conversation, so much so that he barely registered it when they passed the exits for Smithfield. Only after they finally turned off and Michael saw the first signs for Bentonville did he make the connection. "This is where Mercy's mother lived." He looked at Harriman. "Did you lie to me? Is she still alive?"

"No. She's been dead fifteen years now."

They passed through the decaying center of Bentonville and out the other side. As in so many small towns, time had stopped in the 1970s, the last era when there had been enough loose cash around to find its way out of the cities.

Back in the countryside, the bare oaks and dead grasses muted the perpetual green of the pines. Michael recognized the route from his father's descriptions, and a felt a mixture of hope, dread, and longing rise through him.

So he was not surprised when they pulled up in front of a decaying shingled house, alone at the side of the road. "You're expected," Harriman said. "Knock and go on in."

As he walked up the gravel path, Michael's body felt like an uncomfortable suit of clothes. He hardly knew how to move it around. He knocked twice on the thick plank of the door and pushed it open.

"Is that you?" a woman's voice said.

"Yes, Mother," Michael said. "It's me."

SHE WAS STILL BEAUTIFUL. She looked ten years younger than her actual mid-sixties, her hair falling in curls past her shoulders and only lightly streaked with gray, her breasts riding not much lower than a young woman's, her waist trim and hips gently curved. She wore faded blue jeans and a white cabled sweater. Her eyes were dark and well-worn, showing him caution and reserve. He could not picture them laughing, the way he'd seen them when his father described them.

He had to walk around the couch to get to her. He opened his arms and she stepped into them, resting her head on his chest. He closed his eyes and held on tight.

"You look so much like him," she said. "So very much like him."

He'd dreamed of this moment. The thing he'd most vividly imagined was a sense of rightness, of recognition on a cellular level, that he'd never felt with Ruth. It didn't happen. The woman in his arms was a stranger, though strangely familiar.

Eventually she stepped away and held him by his upper arms. "Donald tells me you're a hero."

Michael shrugged. He wanted to be happy in this moment, but happiness was eluding him. "Is that why you finally wanted to see me?"

"You know that's not the reason."

"How could I know that? I don't know you at all."

"No, no, of course you don't." She perched on the edge of the low shelves behind her, looking down. "Let me start again. I'm sorry for hiding from you. I'm sorry I left you to grow up without me. You have no idea how sorry I am. I guess once you make a decision, even if it's the wrong one, it's hard to turn around and go back the other way. It gets harder every year. You get this momentum…"

"My father died believing you killed yourself. He died less than two weeks ago, less than two hours from here. I put his ashes on your empty grave."

"His ashes?"

"On your grave in Beechwood Cemetery."

"Oh my God," she said.

"He was eaten up with guilt and regrets. He described you to me, lying in a bathtub full of blood."

She took a long, audible breath. "Yes. Yes, I made that for him to see."

"He said you were cold, with no pulse. He said the ambulance crew pronounced you dead at the scene."

"Come over here, sit with me."

She walked around the room, turning on lights. Michael saw the place was nothing like the one his father had described. The floors were salvaged and refinished, still showing the scars and history of the wood. The walls had been sheetrocked and painted a tasteful cream, the ceilings textured. She'd squeezed in bookshelves everywhere they would fit, the books neatly shelved in categorical order. A massive antique desk held a laptop with a port replicator, keyboard, and flat screen monitor.

Mercy sat Michael next to her on an elegant natural fiber couch. He found himself unable to fully grasp the miracle of her presence because of his own feelings of bitterness and betrayal. And, he realized, a vague sense of disappointment.

"My mama was what they used to call a root worker," Mercy said, "and she schooled me in it from the time I was a little girl. I still had powder left from my trip to Haiti, the zombie powder, tetrodotoxin made from blowfish. Use it right, you can make somebody seem stone dead for seventy-two hours."

The blood, she told him, was from a chicken she'd killed as part of the ritual. One of Barrett's friends worked at the morgue and arranged to get her out before there could be an autopsy.

From there she hid out with her mother for several months, then ended up in New Orleans and got on a boat to Haiti. She stayed there and worked through the death of Papa Doc and the coming of Baby Doc, until

she ended up on a *tontons macoutes* death list and had to escape again, this
time to Cuba.

She arrived at the end of the golden age of black revolutionary exiles. Rob
Williams and Eldridge Cleaver had already moved on. Mercy caught Fidel's
attention and persuaded him to send her to medical school. After she got her
MD, she worked in the countryside around Matanzas for more than ten years,
practicing a mixture of modern medicine, Santeria, and vodou.

The Soviet Union collapsed in 1992, taking the Cuban economy with it.
Mercy flew to the Yucatan, where Donald had arranged for her to pick up
a complete new identity. From Mexico she crossed the border into California, where she taught briefly in the UC Berkeley folklore program under the
name Mary Santos. Her fears of being recognized drove her into the safety of
the emerging Internet. She published a few papers in medical journals in her
Santos identity, then parlayed that into a career designing research programs in
folk medicine and pharmacology.

The more she talked, the more distant Michael felt. She was like a celebrity on PBS telling of danger and exotic locales and humanitarian service that
didn't touch Michael's life at all.

"If you were so afraid of being recognized, why did you come back here?"
he asked.

"This is different. I got people here watching out for me. Once Wilmer
Bynum was dead, wasn't anybody left that really cared. Donald said you know
about him. That he was my father, I mean."

"Yes. Did you always know?"

She shook her head. "My mother and I wrote long letters while I was
in Cuba. There was like a whole underground railroad thing to get letters
back and forth to the States. When she got sick and knew she was dying she
changed her mind and told me. Some of the people she did cures for kept the
place up after she died, kept it for me in case I ever came home."

Michael couldn't sit. He walked around the bookshelves, looking at titles
and not seeing them.

"Where are my manners," Mercy said. "Can I fix you something to drink?
Or eat?"

"I don't think so," Michael said.

"You want to know why," she said. "Why I did it."

"You left my father to a woman he didn't love, you left me without a real
mother, you gave up the future you would have had in Dallas, and for what?"

"I was suicidal," she said. "It was winter. The black freedom struggle, everything we fought so hard for, was over before it had hardly started. Your father
couldn't seem to leave Ruth, I was physically miserable and had been for

months, I was terrified of being a white man's wife in Texas, terrified I wasn't fit to be a mother. Then, on top of everything else, I got this letter."

Michael watched as she got up and took an envelope out of the desk drawer. "After I asked Donald to bring you out here, I went through all my old boxes and found it. I wasn't sure until now that I wanted to show it to you. I've never let anybody see it before, not even Donald." She held it in both hands, close to her chest. "Maybe it's time."

Michael walked over and took the envelope. The address read, "Miss Mercedes Richards, 109 Beamon Street, City." Michael recognized Ruth's handwriting. There was no return address.

"I sent Robert home on a Wednesday," Mercy said. "On Sunday this came by messenger."

The top of the envelope was cut. Michael took out a single sheet of his father's blue-lined graph paper.

Dear Miss Richárd, or Richards, or whatever your name really is:

My husband will not be returning to you. We have resumed our marriage, and with considerable warmth, if I may be permitted the indiscretion. He has begged me to forgive him, and I have done so, not because he deserves it, but because of the pure, strong and abiding love I bear him.

When he does not arrive tomorrow, you may take that as confirmation that what I've said is true. As to what you choose to do with the remainder of your life, that is no concern of mine, as long as you make no attempt to contact my husband again.

Sincerely,
Ruth Cooper

"Wow," Michael said. He sat on the couch and read the letter again. Then he put it in the envelope and handed it to Mercy.

The thing that surprised him most was not the letter itself. The thing that surprised him was that after all the feelings that the letter gave him, the strongest was a sad and grudging amazement at Ruth's determination. She truly did, Michael thought, love my father.

"I didn't want to believe it," Mercy said. "But things had been hard between your father and me for months by that time. When he didn't show up on Monday, or call, and the sun went down and it got later and later, I despaired. I couldn't call him at his house, couldn't go over there to talk to him. It showed me what my position was. I didn't truly believe he had told Ruth that he was finished with me. On the other hand, if he couldn't make up his mind to choose me over her, then I was going to make his mind up for him."

"And what about me?" Michael tried to say. His chest was constricted and the words didn't make it out.

"What?"

He cleared his throat. "Did you even think about me?"

She knelt on the floor in front of him. "I never thought Ruth would take you. I mean, because of your heritage, if nothing else. I assumed they would put you up for adoption, and I had people ready to get you out of the foster care system and smuggle you back to me. I couldn't believe it when Ruth took you and kept you.

"I went to a lawyer I thought I could trust, and told him I was ready to come out of hiding and go to court to get you back. He said there was no way they would let me have you after what I'd done. I even followed you to Dallas. For a while I would watch your house.

"Then one Sunday I saw the three of you out in the yard. It was January and it had snowed. You were all wrapped up in blankets, sitting in a stroller, and your father was making a little city out of snow for you, and you were laughing, and Ruth was laughing, and I saw that you lived in that city now, and I had no power to take you away from it. And that was when I went to Haiti."

Michael understood then, in the space after her words, that he had been hoping for an absolute. A blood tie so powerful and unconditional that forgiveness was not a decision but a given. And with that he realized that a bond like that would never exist for him. Maybe it had never existed for anyone. He saw that forgiveness was a choice, and unless it was a choice it meant nothing at all.

Slowly, not without physical pain of his own, he got down off the couch and knelt beside her. He saw hurt, resignation, hope, fear, and love in her eyes. He put his arms around her and rested his battered head on her shoulder and said, "You have me now."

Thursday, November 25

THE WEEK BEFORE THANKSGIVING, he and Denise and Rachid flew one-way to Austin and began to pack his house. His friends came to help and made a considerable fuss over Denise. It took them two days to load the U-Haul, followed by a two-day drive to Durham on the southern route: I-10 to Slidell, I-59 north to Birmingham, then across to Atlanta to pick up I-85. Rachid alternated between Denise in Michael's Honda Civic and Michael in the truck.

Michael had rented a two-bedroom apartment three doors down from Denise. It gave her breathing space yet let them be together every night. The light was good enough in the smaller bedroom for Michael to use it as a studio. He had other plans for the second one.

Mercy didn't have a phone or car, but she responded to email. He marshaled his strongest arguments and convinced her to stay in his apartment over Thanksgiving, and into the New Year if she'd be willing.

He and Denise drove to Bentonville on Thanksgiving Day to pick her up. She had one suitcase, her laptop, and a small box of books.

"I was hoping you would stay for a while," Michael said.

"I travel light."

Once in the car she said, "I still have my doubts about this. All my life, I've carried my own weight."

Michael pulled onto the highway. "Don't worry. I expect you to earn your keep."

"I don't do windows," she said, and then, almost as an afterthought, "as the submarine captain said." Michael looked in the rearview mirror. She was half-smiling at herself, and for the first time Michael saw clearly the woman his father had loved.

"That's not what I had in mind," he said. "I want you to sit for a portrait."

MERCY WAS THE FIRST, and Camilla Prentiss, her former neighbor on Beamon Street, was the second. He took a handful of reference photos of her, and lit the painting as a night scene, with Hayti's Donut Shop in faded greens and blues behind her.

He'd chosen to paint in oils rather than acrylics. He loved the smell of the paint and the linseed oil and the ongoing struggle to control the texture of the surface.

To cover the rent he was drawing a fill-in issue of *Detective Comics* by a Seattle writer named Ed Brubaker. The idea made Michael nervous at first, but the script was first-rate, the editor was excited to have him, and based on his first eight pages they'd promised him all the work he wanted.

Best of all, it left half his days free to paint.

Sunday, November 28

THE SUNDAY MORNING after Thanksgiving, Michael went to his car for a run to Harris Teeter. Someone came toward him as he put his keys in the car door and he spun around, adrenalin pumping.

It was Charles.

"Hey," Charles said. "Didn't mean to scare you."

"It's okay," Michael said. He stuffed his hands in his pockets to hide their shaking. Part of it was the lingering threat of the NRC, part of it something deeper that had gone into the heart of him.

"I was sitting here," Charles said, "trying to decide if I should come up and bother you. Donald let on that you were living with Denise now."

"I didn't think you two were talking." Charles looked thinner, but otherwise in good shape. He wore loose jeans, a pale blue UNC sweatshirt, and a Yankees baseball cap.

"I've been saying my goodbyes, and he was on the list."

"What do you mean?"

"I'm heading up to Philly for a while. Some of the brothers up there got a group going that's more my style."

"I'm sorry it fell out that way. I wish I'd had a chance to know you better."

"Yeah, me too. Life during wartime, you know?"

Michael offered his hand. "Good luck with it."

Charles drew him into a hug. "Yeah, man. You be reading about us in the paper. We going to make some noise."

"Make some for me."

"And you?" Charles said. "You heal up all right?"

"More or less," Michael said.

"I got to run," Charles said. "You can tell Donald I'm gone." He took a few steps and turned back. "We faced those motherfuckers down. That was a day, little brother. Never forget it."

Michael held up one hand as Charles got into a battered Toyota pickup and drove away.

Tuesday, December 21

WITH MERCY THERE, Donald Harriman became a frequent visitor. Two or three nights a week they would all have dinner together, and then afterward, when Rachid retired to do his homework, they would sit in Michael's living room and talk.

The American Tobacco riot still made headlines. Greg Vaughan's high-dollar defense lawyer had bombarded the court with motions that claimed everything from police brutality to lack of evidence to crime scene tampering to entrapment. Bishop had kept his word and continued to push for a ban on the NRC, both locally and nationally. It looked to be a long, bitter fight.

On a Tuesday in mid-December the *Durham Herald-Sun* "reluctantly" came out in favor of the NRC, calling it a "First Amendment issue."

"I can't stand reading this," Michael said to Harriman and the others that night. "What are you supposed to do? Where do you start?" He was thinking of Charles, tirelessly moving from one battle to the next, nothing ever changing.

"I went to an academic conference a while ago and Howard Fuller was there," Harriman said. "He's up in Wisconsin now, teaching at Marquette. Somebody in the audience said essentially the same thing you just did, and Fuller, God bless him, asked if he were talking about reform or revolution. And then he said, 'Reform is just learning how to accommodate repression.' When I talked to him afterward, though, he admitted that the Revolution is not going to happen, not in this country, not in our lifetimes."

"Then what's the point?" Michael said. "New Rising Sun, the tattoos, the demonstrations—why bother?"

"It's a question I ask myself every day," Harriman said. "The only answer I have is that you have to take sides and you have to show the world that you mean it. You do whatever you can, not because of what you hope to accomplish, but because to do anything else is ultimately ... not acceptable."

Harriman got up to leave shortly after that, and while they were all standing at the door, Denise said, "I've got an early day tomorrow."

Michael kissed her and said, "I'll be along in a minute."

He sat on the couch next to Mercy and she said, "You know when you've been to the dentist, and the anesthetic starts to wear off? Your face is tingling, and there's this hollow feeling, like any minute the real pain could come flooding in?"

Michael nodded, and she went on, "I feel like I'm thawing out now, and I'm scared what it's going to feel like when it's done. I've been a long time gone, and there's a lot of chickens going to be coming home to roost." She picked up her wineglass and took a sip, seeming to drift away.

"Don't stop," Michael said. "Keep talking."

She thought for a second and said, "When you try to put words to it, what I did was, I faked my own death. But it didn't feel all that fake to me. It was like I died for real, and when I came back, I wasn't the same person anymore."

"When the timer went off on that bomb," Michael said, "I knew absolutely that I was dead. It's like my life is in two parts, before and after."

"I used to be a very physical person," Mercy said. "Hugging and touching and all of that. Afterward, I wasn't anymore." Slowly, tentatively, she reached for his hand. "I guess I'm trying to say, I hope you're not too disappointed in me."

"Disappointed how?"

"Because I never called you, never called Robert, never took back that awful thing I did. Now you've brought me into your home, with Denise and Rachid, who are so wonderful, and I ... I've barely been here. And now that that's starting to change, I don't know if I'm going to be able to handle it."

"I'm not disappointed," Michael said. "I'm still angry and hurt and maybe I won't ever get entirely over that. But I'm grateful you're alive and you're here. I'll take what I can get. And a lot of the time, I'm not completely here myself."

"Still not sleeping?"

"One reason I'm sitting here talking to you is I'm afraid to go back there and lie down and close my eyes. I'm still having the headaches. And I feel like I'm getting another cold. Like you predicted."

"It's classic post-traumatic stress. You can go get a bunch of tests on your thyroid and cortisol and epinephrine if you want it in writing, and the shrinks can give you some pills with worse side effects than what you're trying to cure."

"Have you got something that'll cure it? Eye of newt or blowfish or something?"

"Baby, I don't think there is a cure," Mercy said. "Barrett used to talk about that tattoo of his. You know the one?"

"Yeah, I know it."

"For him it meant transformation. Rebirth. That's you and me both, both reborn. And I'm thinking what hurts so bad is that neither one of us has finished the process yet."

Friday, December 24

HE CALLED RUTH on Christmas Eve, after lunch. She was surprised to hear from him and, he thought, grateful. They made small talk for 20 minutes, and Michael promised he would call again. He didn't mention Mercy or Vaughan or his father. Eventually he would have to deal with those questions. For now, one thing at a time was enough.

Friday, December 31

HE'D PICKED THE PLACE out of the phone book by the sound of its name: Dogstar Tattoos. They were close by, across from Duke's East Campus. He'd made an appointment the day before, giving himself time to change his mind. As he'd lain awake thinking about it, a succession of images had come to him: Ruth at the funeral home, staring at Denise's black skin in incomprehension;

the blossom of red on a white-hooded robe as police in black armor looked on; Mercy in a white porcelain bathtub full of blood. He knew then that he would go through with it.

He was not alone at the crossroads. Mercy was meeting with Duke Medical Center about starting a research program of her own. And Denise had come home the Tuesday after Christmas and surprised him with a final divorce decree. "Not a hint for you to propose," she said, "just something I should have taken care of long ago."

He understood that it was now, on this last day of the year, his turn.

The place had a sleek look: chrome, mirrors, glass bricks. He hesitated outside the door, but only for a second.

"My name's Cooper," he told a woman standing near the door. She had pink hair and seven rings in one ear. "I had an appointment for 3 o'clock."

"Sure. What can we help you with?"

He unfolded a piece of paper with a drawing of the Sign of the Four Moments of the Sun. "I want to get this on my left wrist. I want it to look like the old-fashioned tattoos, just the lines, nothing fancy."

"Sure," she said. "Jason can help you." She pointed to a pale man with long, unnaturally black hair, straightening up his tools on a metal tray. He stood next to an antique barber's chair.

"Are you Jason?" he asked, walking over.

"That's me."

"Hi," he said, taking a breath, and then saying the words for the first time, "I'm Malcolm."

A U T H O R ' S   N O T E

I WAS JUST A KID, and I was sitting in the car with my Uncle Bob and various other relatives, driving across the flat plains of Kansas on one of the first superhighways in America. Uncle Bob was a highway engineer, and I will always remember him pointing to a concrete embankment as we roared by.

"You wouldn't believe," he said, "how many bodies are buried in those things."

WHEN I DECIDED to try to tell the story of Hayti as a novel, I knew I was making a tradeoff. I would knowingly be playing fast and loose with some of the facts in the hope of getting at a higher truth. I didn't go lightly into the bargain, and one of the conditions I made myself was that I would try to untangle the facts and fiction in an afterword.

Hayti, of course, was real, as was the urban renewal program of the 1960s. The only business I invented for this novel is the Hamilton Nursery. Descriptions of the rest of the Hayti landmarks are as accurate as I could make them.

The firebombings of the *Carolina Times* and Service Printing are unfortunately true. They remain unsolved, and likely to stay that way.

The East-West Expressway, now known as the Durham Freeway and NC 147, was actually built by a number of contractors; the first stretch, described in this novel, was built by the William Muirhead Construction Company; consulting engineers were Rummel Klepper and Kahl, LLP. No resemblance exists between these companies and my fictional firm of Mason and Antree.

I drew on press releases and press coverage of the first IBM location in RTP, but used my own construction experience when describing the details of the IBM job site and the events there.

There is no Black Star Corporation in Durham. The American Tobacco Campus is as I described it, but Capital Broadcasting of Raleigh operates it. To my knowledge they have made no connection between its restoration and the fate of Hayti.

The Night Riders of the Confederacy are my invention, but the hate groups I modeled them on, sadly, are not. The Ku Klux Klan is only one of many white supremacist groups active in the southern US.

On that note, let me point out that I used the term "rebel flag" throughout this book advisedly. There were many Confederate flags; the one southern racists most often fly today descends from two historical flags, combining the proportions of the Naval Jack (which had a sky-blue cross) and the colors of the Battle Flag (which was actually square).

Barrett Howard is a fictional character inspired by two heroes of the North Carolina Civil Rights movement, Robert F. Williams and Howard Fuller. Timothy B. Tyson's *Radio Free Dixie* is a superb biography of Williams; Fuller's has yet to be written, though he gets extensive coverage in *Our Separate Ways: Women and the Black Freedom Movement in Durham, North Carolina,* by Christina Greene. Barrett Howard's involvement with vodou and commitment to armed insurrection are entirely his own. Both Williams and Fuller survived the sixties, though for Williams it was a near thing and he had to leave the US to do it.

Denise Franklin is fictional, but her predecessor at the Hayti Heritage Center, the late Dorothy Phelps-Jones, was not. Ms. Jones was a great help to me in the early stages of this book—frank, thoughtful, and generous. Her spirit will not be forgotten.

MANY OTHER PEOPLE gave selflessly of their time, expertise, and resources to help me get as much right as possible. Errors of fact and judgment that remain are entirely my own.

My profound thanks to: Dr. Howard Fuller, still angry, still funny, and still fighting; Dr. John D. Butts, Chief Medical Examiner of the State of North Carolina, for his experience, kindness, and good humor; Sgt. Brett P. Hallan, then head of the Homicide Division of the Durham Police Department; Terence Hamill of GeoSearches, Inc., geophysicist and GPR professional; Phil Watts of the North Carolina Department of Transportation; Nancy Buttry Sparrow, Funeral Director at Hall-Wynne Funeral Home; Christy Sandy, senior staffer at the US House of Representatives; Jack Wolf, MD; Cory Annis, MD; and most especially Claire Dees, MD, who made time to share her oncology expertise amid the chaos of a new baby.

Thanks to my swing dance teachers: Richard Badu, Wesley Boz, Debbie Ramsey, and Jason Sager.

At the American Tobacco Campus, I owe big thanks to Valerie Ward, Gerry Boyle, Brooks Ladd, and Reyna Upchurch. At the Durham VA Medical Center, Hal Hummell helped enormously. Thanks also to George Robinson at the Brookwood Inn and Leslie Klingner at the Biltmore Estate.

IN ADDITION TO those mentioned above, the most important of the dozens of books I studied were: *Durham's Hayti,* by Andre D. Vann and Beverly Washington Jones; *Durham County,* by Jean Bradley Anderson; *Blood Done Sign My Name,* by Timothy B. Tyson; *A Generosity of Spirit* and *From Seed to*

Harvest, a two volume history of RTP by Albert N. Link; *The Fiery Cross: The Ku Klux Klan in America,* by Wyn Craig Wade; *The Durham Architectural and Historic Inventory,* by Claudia P. Roberts, Diane E. Lea, and Robert M. Leary; and *Johnston County: Its History Since 1746,* by Thomas J. Lassiter and T. Wingate Lassiter. The Durham County Library's microfilm collection of the *Carolina Times, Durham Herald,* and *Durham Sun* were invaluable.

I used Zora Neale Hurston's *Tell My Horse: Voodoo and Life in Haiti and Jamaica,* and Milo Rigaud's *Secrets of Voodoo,* among other sources, for the vodou ritual I describe. Robert Farris Thompson's *Flash of the Spirit* was also essential.

BIG THANKS TO Willard Spiegelman at *Southwest Review* and Steve Erickson at *Black Clock,* who published excerpts and provided crucial and timely momentum. Extra-special thanks to Bill Schafer, who first bought an excerpt for his *Subterranean* magazine, then went on to publish the entire book. Gail Cross, his designer, gave freely of her time and expertise in helping me through my first book design job. My dear friend Lesley Gasper first provided an insightful critique of the manuscript, then went on to be my copy editor.

Friends and loved ones carried the biggest load. First and foremost, thanks to Orla Swift, my partner in dancing and in life, and to Marshall Terry, teacher and friend, who has given me years of love, faith, and wonderful examples of what the best writing can do.

Many friends read the manuscript in various stages and gave excellent advice, most of which I had the sense to accept. Thanks to Arch Altman, Jim Blaylock, Richard Butner, Howard Craft, Margaret Downs-Gamble, Ralph Earle, Mariana Fiorentino, Karen Fowler, Barbara Gilly, Art Hoffman, John Kessel, Eduardo Lazarowski, Alicia Rico-Lazarowski, Tom Serafini, Carol Stevens, and Dave Stevens. Thanks also to Mike Autrey, Tom Clark, Jeff Downey, Sylvia Pfeiffenberger, Barry Shelton, and all the many others who urged me on.